Stupid Prizes

ALICE DUKE

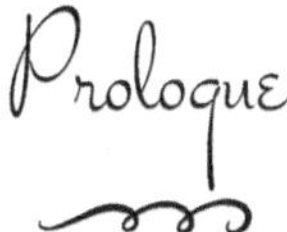

Prologue

TWO WEEKS FROM NOW

GRACIE

I still think we could have done this at City Hall. Or Vegas. Or anywhere with less fuss, but since I picked the date and the dress, I let him pick the venue, the minister, and the photography. It was the decent thing to do. But now I'm feeling flustered along with all the other emotions and I don't like flustered. Flustered sounds like someone's parakeet, not a bride about to get married.

I still have no idea who Jasper chose to play the part of minister in our fake wedding. I should have double-checked this part instead of leaving it to him. What if he picked someone who can't keep his mouth shut? But also, could you stop being so flustered, Gracie? Please? It's going to show in the pictures.

The minister standing here looks as young as we do, but he's holding a Bible that looks as old as sin. Can you say that about a Bible? That it looks old as sin? Or have I cursed us on our wedding day? The minister's sober looking like he's taking his role very seriously. And I do mean role. This is a fake wedding.

You wouldn't know it, though, from the look of the little white chapel — it's literally picture perfect. Which is good, because the pictures need to fool my father. Is there another word for flustered? Maybe I should have brought a thesaurus with me so I wouldn't keep repeating it in my head.

Speaking of pictures, you wouldn't know this was all a ruse from the photographer's expression. No. It's not. Okay, yes, it is him and now I definitely need a new word for how I feel. Unsettled? Is that it? Agitated?

He's peeking out from behind the camera like he's a rare bird photographer witnessing a hatching. He's misty-eyed, heavily bearded, and smiling like he's seeing in color for the first time. I swallow and try a wavering smile.

When I promised Jasper — my groom-to-be — that he could pick the photographer, I never once guessed he'd pick his dad. His dad! At our fake wedding. How is that a good idea? He's going to see through it. Or get too attached to the idea and it will break his heart when we "split up" later.

Seeing him here is making me more nervous than ever. It makes it feel a shade too real. Like I might actually hurt someone with this whole plan. I twist my hands in my skirt. I don't know what else to do with them. I guess that's why brides carry flowers but I don't like killing plants. Not even for my wedding.

My little lace cocktail dress doesn't feel formal enough. Not if his dad is going to be here. Maybe I should have gone out and bought something white instead of wearing blush pink. I should have texted pictures to Melissa and made her pick for me. She's great at fashion or anything artsy. But that would have meant confessing this harebrained plan before I did it and what if she'd talked me out of it? Or what if she'd decided I should go out and find a real wedding dress somewhere? Even the actor playing the minister found a real suit.

He had better be an actor. If we're lying to a real minister I'm not going to be able to sleep at night.

He's set up on the steps of the chapel, standing in front of the closed door with bible in hand and collar neatly starched. He's not jittery or sweating like I am. Maybe he plays roles in commercials so he's used to being on camera. That would explain why he's so cool right now. He actually looks like he's enjoying himself. A-plus performance.

I'm taking in all the details, trying to remember them for when my dad questions me — which he will.

Someone took the time to put an old tin pail full of wildflowers and creosote on the step to one side. And they're in earth, not cut. I feel a tug of relief at that. Someone knew me well enough to care about what I care about. That's … touching.

Okay. The wedding is picturesque. It's perfect. It's going to be just right. It's everything a little Gracie ever dreamed of for a wedding, except for the low attendance. There's just the minister, the photographer — and yeah, I'm still wondering why Jasper picked his dad — and an older buttoned-up woman who I think must be the church secretary here to monitor exactly what we do to her church steps (fair enough) and me.

Which means I'm missing one fake groom.

I smooth my skirts worriedly.

He owes me this.

And he promised.

But he stood me up once before. And that time was so much more important than this. He's not going to do it again, right? Not with his dad here?

But he let his dad down then, too. So, there's no reason to think he won't abandon us when things get hard. He did five years ago.

My mouth feels dry at the thought and my hands feel clammy like they made a bad trade with each other and now both of them are miserable. This is worse than flustered. This is ... rattled. There you go. I'm rattled.

Maybe it's a sign that we'll be miserable, too.

Maybe it's punishment from God for fooling a minister on like, holy ground, or something. That has to be a thing.

Maybe I shouldn't be doing this. I mean, there are so many better things I could be doing. My apartment is packed with projects I should be doing for my friends and neighbors. I could be at work going along with what my dad wants instead of trying to throw this wrench into things.

And just when I'm about to panic, he's there, stepping out from around the sycamore tree at the corner of the chapel with that soft smile that still melts me even after everything that's gone on between us. He smiles at me in a way that shows his dimple just like he always does when we share something just between the two of us. And his hazel eyes twinkle at me like he knows something amazing and he just hasn't gotten around to sharing it yet.

He's really put in an effort with his appearance. Is that for me, or for the pictures, or for both? Just wondering that speeds my heart rate up a bit. Of course it isn't for me. But that doesn't mean a girl can't dream, right?

His dark hair is neat and freshly cut. Did he see a barber yesterday? When did he find the time for that? The stubble on his face is trimmed down to a mere shadow and he's dressed in a crisp white shirt under a grey vest and slacks. He left his leather motorcycle boots on and tucked the cuffs of his slacks over them, though. And I can't help but smile at that.

He's wiping his hands on his pants like he made the same bad deal I did. Sweaty palm club members unite!

He crosses to where I stand on the step and hesitates for just a heartbeat before mounting it and finding his place opposite me. He's biting his lip and he isn't looking at me and I'm sure he's going to call this off and I'll be completely out of luck, because seriously who even does this?

I try to catch his eye but he avoids my gaze too well and it leaves a sinking feeling in my belly. He's going to say, "Sorry Gracie, I just can't." I know he is.

And then, to my complete surprise, he takes my hand in his. His are warm, and calloused, and brown — just exactly the way I like them — and I want to melt at their touch. If this were real, I would melt. If this were real, I'd be so giddy I wouldn't be able to breathe. But, of course, it isn't real.

It's not real when he releases the bite on his lip so it looks more normal framed by his day-old scruff.

It's not real when he finally meets my eye with an expression that I'd call naked longing if I didn't know this is fake. It is, right? He's hamming it up for the camera, right?

It's not real when he lifts my hand as if on impulse and presses his lips reverently to the back of it. His eyes go darker and then shut for just a moment longer than a natural blink would take and my breath is caught somewhere in my throat.

Not real when his dad snaps a photo of that with an honest-to-God, old-timey flash.

Not real when the minister clears his throat and we jump.

Not real when we speak our vows and his sound for all the world like he's making actual promises.

Not real when we sign the papers.

Not real when we're pronounced man and wife.

And I have to keep reminding myself that none of this is real or I might start to wish it was.

Chapter One

PRESENT DAY

GRACIE

"Play stupid games. Win stupid prizes."

That's my dad's favorite expression. But he doesn't say it judgementally. He says it with pride as he lines up his ridiculous trucks. There's the '79 Ford with the thirty-seven-inch tires, and the ten-inch lift, and the custom bumpers with "BOOM" plasma cut right into them. And beside it is the custom Raptor in a candy apple red and flat black camo pattern — what is the point of red and black camo? To blend in with dragons, maybe? It's as likely as the idea that any of the twenty trucks in this line-up will ever have any practical utility.

It doesn't matter, though. They've been practical to him because his little online channel went from ten views on a video, to a couple of thousand, to this year where if we get less than seven million views on a video everyone gets a bit frantic.

His stupid games fund all our lives. And his stupid prizes make everyone love him.

Which is why I'm standing here out of breath in the hot Utah sun, trying to look like I love wearing a "Big Daddy BOOM" T-shirt instead of the flowy white linen tank I'd chosen this morning, and smiling as hard as I can while the camera operator chooses the perfect shot.

This is not what I hoped for my life. I wanted to travel and see things. To run marketing for one of the kinds of companies I love — sustainable clothing, fair trade spices, micro-loan initiatives for women entrepreneurs in disadvantaged situations. But family guilt is real, folks. And that's why I work for my dad in the world of fossil-fuel-powered insanity.

"This one has to be perfect," Dad says sincerely and he strokes his beard and anxiously adjusts his branded trucker hat for the hundredth time. You'd think he was in a fancy-pants suit rather than dusty jeans and cowboy boots. "We start filming the minute the sun comes up. I want long shadows and bright sun rays. This has to signal new beginnings."

"New beginnings?" I ask, even more nervous than I was when he showed up at my door at three in the morning telling me he had an awesome idea and he needed me — as head of his marketing team — to get in the truck full of the gremlin men who work for him so we could drive two hours into the desert to film his brainwave. I just hope it isn't another move to try to get me to take over part of the company. I feel trapped in his vision already. I don't want to commit to doing it forever.

At least there were things for me to do beyond just coming along for the ride. I'd made granola bars the night before so I had something to offer his guys. I hate seeing people go hungry. And then one of them had a hole in his shoe, but that wasn't a problem either because I had a needle and fishing line in my purse, and while I was fixing it, the time just flew by.

This isn't the first time my dad has had a "genius" idea at

three in the morning and it won't be the last. What makes it worse is that they really are genius most of the time. This one is almost certain to increase our Q2 revenue just like his brain wave a few months ago shot us back into the black even with all his new hires and losing that deal with with the online streaming service. My dad's ideas are always extraordinary.

I just wish he had someone to share them with other than me — especially at three in the morning. But when mom died the summer I was seventeen, I became the go-to person for middle-of-the-night brainstorming sessions.

I never say no. Especially not over the past two months since I noticed that Dad hasn't been looking so well. He's paler than normal, and I've noticed him coughing when he thinks I'm not looking. I might not want to commit to a forever at his company but I know I'm needed here with him right now.

And I'm worried about him. I've asked if he's sick and if everything is okay, but he just keeps brushing off the questions. I can't help remembering how Robbie's dad was just like that and then one morning he didn't wake up and their family doctor broke the news — he'd been sick for months and keeping it quiet. I just keep thinking that my dad — my huge, strong, rock of a dad — might be trying to do the same thing.

"You're gonna love this one, Gracie," he says, barely restraining his excitement. "I promise! Once you hear it, the marketing campaign is going to write itself. You'll be so glad that you came back to work for your old dad!"

"I'm already happy, Dad," I say, stifling a yawn and trying my best to plaster a smile on my face. I hope this stunt isn't too expensive. Or too dangerous. Or too embarrassing because, yeah, that's a thing, too.

It's way too early for smiling, but Dad has been trying so hard to make sure I know he appreciates that I came back to work with him instead of accepting a different job offer. He needs all the reassurance I can spare that yes, I'm committed to our family, and yes, I'm committed to his business empire, and yes, that means I'm committed to all his ideas, even when those involve shooting handguns at Tannerite in the back of a Carolina squatted truck, or sinking his $500,000 boat as a publicity stunt. (He swears it was an accident, but his online views suggest it was no accident, just pure marketing genius.)

I reach over to smooth a wrinkle out of his branded T-shirt for him. He's cut the sleeves off again. Sleeves on my dad's shirts are never safe.

"Don't worry about the shirt, honey. Come over here," Dad says, leading me to a spot a little further out from the crew. "Can you start with a shot of her, Jasper? Maybe one with the wind blowing in her face? Make her look … I don't know, visionary?"

I startle at Jasper's name, a burst of something both hot and cold flooding through me so suddenly that my vision goes dark for a heartbeat.

It's not … it can't be the same Jasper, can it?

My heart is racing like it thinks its one of my dad's dune buggies, speeding and leaping all over the place.

Jasper isn't that common of a name. What are the odds that it's him?

We took two trucks up here. If he's here with the crew, then I could have come all the way without realizing he was with us. I didn't even see who was in the other truck. Yeah, it's possible it's him.

I haven't seen Jasper since he left for Canada the summer before my senior year of high school. He doesn't visit. I'm not even sure he calls his dad. There's no way he's here now.

"Sure, Adam," Jasper drawls out and his voice is both familiar and foreign. Is that *his* baritone voice? I haven't even seen him yet but if it is him, then the man I grew up with sounds like a stranger.

I peek over my shoulder, trying to be subtle about it, but I still can't catch a glimpse of him. He has the hood of his hoodie up over his ball cap and he's looking through a camera with a huge lens — Jasper always did like vintage cameras. I'm pretty sure it's him, but I don't want to react before I know for sure or it's going to be hard to explain why I passed out and had to be rushed to the hospital.

Staring really hard does not seem to be activating my x-ray vision. All those comic books I read in my teens are letting me down.

And then he whips his hood off and leans into the camera more.

It's him.

His dark hair is cut short at the sides of his head and a bit longer on top, his face has a light scruff like he didn't get a chance to shave when he'd been rustled out of bed in the middle of the night — hardly surprising — and his jeans and Hot Rod Magazine T-shirt cling to a startlingly muscular body which he definitely *did not have* when he was a gangly eighteen-year-old and still wearing his pants slung low so you could see the brand name on his underwear.

I can feel my face growing hot and I hate that I'm blushing. He can't see it, can he? Gosh, I hope not.

I'm pretty sure hearts aren't supposed to race like this. But mine can't seem to stop. It has no brake pressure. It's going to be one of those terrible crashes.

How is Jasper suddenly working for my dad? When did that start?

The other guys are clustered around him, out of the shot, doing the things they do as they rig up lighting shades and set up the drone for the landscape shots. But all I can see is him.

Tanner nudges him and murmurs something that has them all laughing and then he pulls back from the camera and looks up at Tanner and I want to scream. *"Look at me!"*

He knows I'm here and he hasn't said hi. What does that mean? That he doesn't want to speak to me?

The only thing that hasn't changed about this stranger who used to be my friend is the twinkle in his eye and the dimple set deep in his left cheek. He flashes Tanner both, totally ignoring me, like he doesn't realize that they have the power to stop female hearts even when they're aimed at someone else.

Or maybe like he doesn't dare look at me. Not when the last time we talked was him calling from Canada a month after he jumped out my bedroom window. Him breaking my heart over a fuzzy landline.

I swallow down a sudden lump in my throat. Someone should make him register that twinkle. It is clearly not legal in any of the lower forty-eight states. It probably isn't even legal in Canada and they legalize practically everything there.

"Gracie?" My dad is trying to get my attention, but I can't seem to drag it away.

And then Jasper finally looks up and those bright hazel eyes meet mine and I feel like I'm in the attic and the floors have all dropped out of the building and my stomach is falling first.

And he quirks a gentle half-smile at me — that old one he used to keep just between us. But hey, what do I know, maybe he gives it out like candy to everyone now.

Can your blood actually boil? Asking for a friend.

But before I can even smile back my dad repeats, "Gracie, honey?"

I whip my gaze to where he's waiting patiently for my attention, glad it's still mostly dark, and hoping beyond hope that no one has seen the flush creeping up my cheeks.

"We'll do the drone stuff afterward, guys," my dad says, like my world hasn't just been his by asteroid Jasper. "Let's set this shot up right now. I want to do this live on camera and stream it right into the social media channels, and then we'll do a longer, fuller version for the vlog with the drone and some more in-depth explanations and that promo clip we filmed on Wednesday, okay?"

"Sure, Big Daddy," Tanner says.

I realize I'm listening way too intently when I pick up Jasper's "Mmmhmm" and it lights up my cheeks all over again.

What is my problem? This is Jasper. We played together as kids. He liked to cheat at thumb wars. But that was before his dimple became a more dangerous weapon than anything Putin is flashing around in Russia.

"Gracie, let's have a quick word," my dad says. He rests his meaty palm on my shoulder really gently and tucks his head in close to mine.

I drag my attention from Jasper and back to my dad.

Dad has always had that capability of making people feel like they're the most important people in the world. I don't even think he realizes he's doing it. He just lives in this world that seems to be entirely made up of his dreams and ambitions, and he sees everything through his own perspective — never anyone else's — but instead of that making him seem like a narcissist, it makes him feel like he's a creator. You feel like you're entering this amazing fantasy world with him, where he is King and Fairy Godmother all wrapped into one. It's why he has thirty employees who adore him. It's why people line up to get selfies with him and hang around to do crazy stunts with him. It's why two trucks of guys in hoodies are yawning behind us but not voicing a single complaint on this chilly desert morning.

When he focuses all that attention on you, you feel special. And I can't help it, I feel special right now, too.

"You know family is everything, right Gracie," Dad says, leaning in so it feels confidential.

I nod along. That's what he's been telling me since mom died when I was seventeen. "Family is everything. We are stronger together." I'm worried that he's bringing it up right now. Maybe he's even sicker than I thought. He's skipped out on our shared dinners twice this month. Is he privately going to medical appointments?

"Sure, Dad," I agree, smiling at him.

His smile grows, eager now, like he's a boy instead of a grown man with a beefy body-builder's mass.

"And I've talked to you before about taking over the Big Daddy Boom brand."

I lift a hand to forestall him. "I'm happy to work for you, Dad, but running the brand — it's not my thing. I don't have your vision. I'm just here to help take care of what's important to you."

And if he's sick I'll really have to step up to help with everything. I won't mind. I'll be happy to babysit his darling company while he gets well.

He nods along, like he finally realizes this after weeks of cajoling me to surrender. "I hear you, Gracie, I do. I've been listening. That's why you're gonna love what I've come up with to settle this."

"Settle what?" I feel deeply uneasy by how he's put this. Sure, I don't want to take over his brand, but he's young — just fifty-five, and he's nowhere near retiring, unless he's so sick he thinks he has to give it up entirely. But he looks energetic and young still.

And so did Robbie's dad.

"You'll see," he says with a wink, his grin growing bigger and then he squeezes my shoulder and says, "Family is everything. Don't forget."

And before I can do more than frown in worry, he's drawing away, looking behind him to make sure he's framed properly with the rolling landscape, the buttes and valleys, the rays of sunshine all where God put them and where Big Daddy Boom can reign over them.

I swallow and he crosses his arms, puffs out his chest, and gives a slight nod over to me to remind the cameramen to start their shot with me.

I force my best proud smile on my face — the image of the

perfect daughter, maybe a bit rumpled and bleary-eyed, but the kind of tanned, blonde girl who puts her family first.

They're rolling.

And the sweat starting between my shoulder blades can't be caught on camera, so we should be just fine with this shot.

Chapter Two

JASPER

She looks so good over there — yawning in the golden dawn — that I have to consciously shut my mouth twice when she glances at me. I swear, if I'm not careful, the other guys are going to notice and then I'll never live this down. It will be impossible to get a chance to talk to her if they're teasing me the entire time. It will tip my hand in the worst possible way. And that's what I'm here for — to talk. Even if I'm five years too late. Even if I have sixty months of apologies to make up for.

The moment I saw the job posting come up, I knew I had to be here. I wrapped up my projects, packed my camera and laptop, left the best job I'd ever had, and flew out on the first plane headed back home. I did it before I'd even talked to Adam — sorry, Big Daddy Boom, as everyone is calling him now — or texted my dad.

Not that it would have mattered if I'd texted dad first. He still would have shut the door in my face when he heard I was going to go work for his old business partner. Still would have stormed all the way to the back door and nearly managed to shut *it* in my face, too. But my dad doesn't move that quickly anymore and I can still hurdle the fence to the backyard.

"Don't do it, Jas," he said thickly and he was about as close to tears as he always is. Five years isn't enough to get over losing the love of your life — or at least it isn't for my dad. It's not enough time to get over losing your mom, but I don't tell him that.

"Don't go work for Adam," he said, cracking a beer even though it was nine a.m. and sitting heavily in the old, orange-rose-print, crushed velvet sofa that my mom inherited from her grandma who bought it in the 1980s. "He's nothing but ambi-tion. He'll chew you up and spit you out. Or worse. He'll do something stupid and you'll get hurt in one of his stunts."

Even after five years it's weird to hear my dad talk like that. I have clear memories of him standing on the roof of a truck, balancing like a surfer, while Adam spun donuts in the parking lot outside the BOOM garage. They raced snowmobiles over a cliff once, hooting like a pair of owls. I think the grainy shot I have of that was my first picture of a moving object. And Dad used to be the worst daredevil of the pair of them. And he used to be the head of all their marketing. He loved it.

"You'll never guess what we're giving away this week!" he used to tell my mom and she would just shake her head and smile as he spent all of dinner telling me about the sketch he'd come up with to push their new sponsor, or the crazy stunt they were going to do while pulling a name out of a hat to win this month's build from BOOM Enterprises.

Those were the good old days. The days when I thought my dad was all the fun and my mom made all the rules. Before she died and I realized there wasn't any fun without her rules, just a lot of empty fridge, laundry piling up, beer at nine in the morn-ing, and no one visiting, no one calling, no one caring as my dad lived miserably off the fortune he made while he was young and happy.

"I have to do this," I'd told him but I didn't tell him why.

Because I said goodbye to her over the phone from a different country and acted like I wasn't breaking her heart even though we both knew we were in love, wasn't something I could say out loud. Neither was, *because I've realized I can't keep living days with her so far away.* Or, *because after they died we could hardly even look at each other anymore.* Or, worst of all, *because since then I've never been able to look at another girl and want her like I want Gracie.*

"Stay here at least," my dad, and there was a kind of sympathy in his rueful expression like he'd actually heard all the things I couldn't say. "Cook for me at night."

"Wow. Asking a lot," I'd joked, nudging him with a shoulder. "Are you going to ask me to do the laundry, too?"

"I don't hate anyone enough to ask them to do my laundry," he laughed, sinking back into his seat and closing his eyes. Unspoken was the memory of a time when we both had someone we definitely didn't hate doing that for us. "And maybe you can go through some of your mom's stuff. I put most of it in the garage. I can't even go in there, now. I needed a pair of wire cutters last week."

"And?" I pushed.

"I ended up buying new ones."

We sat in a heavy silence after that. Me, thinking about loving someone so much that you can't look at their stuff five years after they're dead. Him, thinking something that makes him sniffle. I didn't ask what it was. It hurt too much just listening to the silence.

I was crazy to be back here again. Crazy to choose this hell when I could have been in California snapping shots for *Hot Rod Magazine.*

"Just don't get mad when every meal is pasta," I said, trying to make light of it. "It's still the only thing I cook."

And now here I am in the dawn light, remembering that Utah is the prettiest place on earth — or at least that it is to me.

I can't even bring myself to say hello to the woman I took this job to speak to. One glance that meets her gaze sears me to the core, snatches away whatever breath I thought I had in my lungs and sears them like I've sucked in hot smoke. I end up muttering like a fool.

"Make sure you get his good side or he'll make you grow a beard just like his," Tanner whispers and we all laugh. It's not much of a joke, but we're all tired and I've known Tanner for ages. He used to be my dad and Adam's only employee. I think he's the one who taught me to use the reciprocating saw. Now, he runs the drone shots and they have two other camera operators for the raw footage.

I laugh at his joke half-heartedly, but I barely choke the laugh out, because I'm so distracted by the girl in my lens. Her eyes are sadder than I remember and the way she's looking at the dawn makes me feel like I might crumble apart.

I snap some stills on a whim, almost like I'm compelled to do it. I don't ignore the muse when it calls. Ignore her once and she'll stay away awhile. Ignore her again and you might lose her forever. I've already lost one girl that way.

"Alright, let's roll," Big Daddy Boom says with a confident smile. His chest is puffed out. He looks exactly like he has all my life. Like even death can't touch him. He's the only one of us who looks the same today as he did before the accident.

I nod to Pretty Boy — don't ask me his real name, that's what the guys call him — who nods to Buckstop — seriously, no idea on the legal name here, either— who makes the signal that we're rolling. Everyone shuts up and I start to film, getting the long slow shot that Big Daddy wants of his daughter, trying not to let my heart gallop too fast as I take in her serene smile while she looks out across the desert. The purples and blush pinks of dawn give her a soft flush. She wears the desert like a favorite pair of jeans — both of them making each other look good. I don't even think she realizes that she does it.

She inhales and I wonder if she's smelling creosote like I am, or if she's steadying herself with that breath.

And then my shot pans over to Big Daddy and my heart is still beating quickly, but now for a different reason. He gave me this job without even asking why I wanted it. He just clapped me on the shoulder and said, "Family is important, son." As if nothing happened. As if I were my dad come back to run his ads and giveaways. And he wasn't faking it. Adam never fakes anything. Will he still feel the same way if he discovers why I'm here?

And then he's speaking and all my worries blow away like a wisp of dying campfire smoke. I have bigger worries, it seems.

"Some of you all have been asking what the next step is for the Big Daddy BOOM Empire," Big Daddy says, the wind blowing in his beard. "With my daughter back home now, running our marketing and social media, there's been a lot of chatter asking me, 'Is Gracie taking over the company?' 'Is she going to inherit it from you?' 'Will it feel different if it's not really her passion?' And you guys need to calm down. I love the BOOM Empire and I'm not going to let anything happen to it." He pauses, dramatically. "But, at the same time, family is everything to me. Everything."

Here he starts tearing up and I feel a familiar jagged edge in my chest like someone shoved a rock inside and it's cutting me on its rough edges every time I breathe. I know what he's going to say and I want to block my ears so I don't have to be here for it.

"When the accident happened, it felt like half my world was snatched away."

I peek at Gracie and she's flinching like she has the same rock in her chest. I hate seeing that. I want to gather her up in my arms and just hold her until the pain of the moment passes, but I gave up that right when I went away, didn't I? I missed the chance to be that person for her.

"More than half."

Adam's words startle me and I realize he's looking right at me and maybe I'm going to be sick because I know he's talking about Dad and how they can't bear to speak anymore.

I suck in a deep breath and let it out slowly, four beats in, four beats out, just like I've practiced a thousand times and thank goodness he's moving on so I don't have to strangle him.

"But it just showed me so completely that it has to be family. They're all you have. They're all you can trust and hold onto. And that's why I have a plan for the BOOM Empire that's all about family. Now, Gracie," he says, reaching out and pulling her into a powerful side hug. "Gracie tells me that she isn't interested in running the company. She loves the behind the scenes stuff, but she doesn't want to be the face of the business."

Seeing as she's shooting him a look of frantic irritation, I'd say that's an accurate depiction. I think the whole world can probably tell that she has no idea what's coming next. I'm wincing for her. This video is live and streaming on all the BOOM Empire channels and her reaction is going out there live, too. Does Big Daddy really not realize that this is painful for her?

"But while I completely respect Gracie's wishes, I could never raise up a successor to this enterprise who wasn't family," Big Daddy says and he's radiating certainty.

I chance a tiny glance to the side to where Tanner stands stiff as a board with a blank face. He wanted this, I realize. And another quick glance to the other side tells me that at least three of the other guys thought they might have had a shot at it, too. They know better now. Ouch.

"But I also need someone who loves this world of big trucks, big fun, big adventures, and big ..." he pauses waiting for it, knowing the audience is filling it in at home, then he grins. "BOOM!" he says triumphantly, playing to the camera.

Gracie looks aghast, like she's watching a train come toward her but she can't move to run. She must realize something the rest of us don't. I'm frowning, confused. So is Tanner. So are the guys. If it's not her, but it's still family, then who can he possibly mean? Unless ... does he have kids we don't know about? I could see that shaking Gracie up a bit. She's always been a daddy's girl. And then Big Daddy's grin swells and he hugs Gracie tighter to him, just glowing with excitement.

"And that is why I'm going to name as successor to the BOOM Empire whoever marries my Gracie, and we're going to determine that right here on this channel over the course of the next month. So." Here he points dead at the camera. "Like, subscribe, stay tuned for the announcement of how this is going to play out, and make sure to tune in every day for the very best in off-road BOOM!"

We're all too stunned to move. Not even when a few seconds pass and Big Daddy gives me the eye. He has to do it twice before I remember we're rolling live. I shut down the feed. I'm sweating like I've just run up hill with an alternator in each hand.

And for the second time in five years, my eyes meet Gracie's in shared horror.

She's going to get married?

And she's letting her dad choose her husband?

She shakes her head and that's all the confirmation I need that she had no idea this was happening today. Or at all. And I'm equally sure that she has no idea what to do now.

But what I realize right along with it is that I'll murder anyone who tries to marry Gracie. Especially if they're chosen by her dad and not her. Gracie's the most precious human. And no one is worthy of her. And if anyone is, it could only ever be someone *she* decided was worth her time and attention.

I feel my fists clenching and my throat going tight.

Yeah, I'll definitely kill anyone who thinks otherwise.

Which won't be good, since I have no idea where I'd hide a body.

Chapter Three

I can't catch my breath. Or close my mouth, for that matter, and thank goodness there aren't flies here or I'd be catching them all.

Did Dad just say what I thought he did? He thinks he can marry me off like this is old England and he's a knight offering up his daughter to the winner of the joust? Actually, that might be preferable. Knights are hot and muscled and they ride horses that could take me far away from here.

I look up and to my surprise the only person looking at me is Jasper. His eyes carry the same alarm as mine. For just a heart-beat, I'm back to the moment we shared five years ago. The shared horror. The pain staining both our lives in shades of misery. And I can't hold his gaze. I feel sick with the emotions ripping through me. That sick look on his face — paled with sorrow when he broke the news to me. The days after — like some kind of nightmare of loss.

Keep it together, Gracie, I coach myself. *This is now, not then. You aren't dealing with a major life tragedy. You're a big girl and it's the twenty-first century. You don't have to marry against your will. And you definitely don't have to marry someone your dad picks for you to cement his online empire.*

But I'm not sure I believe it. Dad always gets his way.

Here's the thing, it's not that he'll force me to do what he wants or cut me off from family funding. First of all, I earn every cent he pays me and I could earn it somewhere else if I left this job. I work for him because I'm worried about him and I love seeing him succeed, not because I'm a charity case. And yeah, he throws in little gifts. Okay, fine. Big gifts. Like my new Ford Bronco which he fitted with a BOOM custom bumper set and a full stereo upgrade and lift kit. And yes, like the guest house he built so I could live in my own place but still be on his acreage. He likes it when I come over to eat dinner with him almost every night. They're big gifts. But I could live somewhere else. I could drive something else. I don't have to have them. So it's not like I'm stuck in this mess. I could walk away.

But if I walked away I'd break his heart. And he knows that, which is why he's confident he can announce a stunt like this. He knows I won't ever hurt him because we've both been through too much already.

And what if he really is sick? What if he's running out of time and he's just trying to preserve his legacy and also get to be there for his daughter's wedding. Can I really let "no" be the last thing I ever say to him?

He's over there beaming at me, discussing with Tanner how to set up the drone shots and telling Pretty Boy how he wants him to drive one of the trucks out in the desert at just the right angle to showcase the new custom BOOM wheels we're selling these days.

He doesn't even see the forlorn look in Tanner's eye. Tanner, who has been with Dad through everything and knows this company in and out. I remember when he was their only camera operator back when I was still worried about whether I could get away with wearing lipstick at school if I wiped it off before I came home.

He had to think he would be considered to run the business — even though I know why Dad would never want that. He's a doer, Tanner, but he's no visionary. You can set him to work on something and he does a good enough job and he's loyal as hell, but he can't see new paths. If he ran the company it would peter out slowly until it died a long painful death. Dad can see that, and so can I, but Dad can't see the disappointment. He can't see how it hurts his oldest employee not to even be considered. And he's not being considered because Tanner and I both know he can't marry me. He's single, but he's like an uncle. It's not even an option.

Jasper walks by Tanner and his hand lands on the other man's shoulder for just a moment as he passes and something like a thrill of recognition jars through me because he must be thinking the same thing I am. He's never been a physical kind of guy. A touch like that is like a bear hug to him. And he's offering it to the person on this hilltop who is reeling the most right now — other than me, obviously — and it melts me to see it.

And I can't afford to be melted by the boy who left when I needed him the most. Especially not right now.

And the thought of that jars me back to reality. What is my dad thinking? Is he going to limit this at all, or is it going to just be a free for all? Why am I wondering about the details? This can't happen. Won't happen. It's so ridiculous that I feel like changing my name and moving out of the country so no one ever has to know I'm that pathetic girl with the crazy dad who was going to marry her off for entertainment.

Wait. Everyone is going to know. All my college friends. The woman who checks my groceries. Everyone. I put my hand over my face and try to catch my breath. I'm going to have to tell Melissa. As soon as possible. If I don't then she'll find out online and that's not right.

And then another thought occurs to me. How much time does dad have if he's so sick he wants someone to inherit his life's work this quickly? Months? Weeks? I shake my head as I look down at my phone.

It's blowing up. The notifications are filing my screen so fast that I can't read one before it's replaced by another. I feel light-headed. Do people still faint or is that only Regency heroines? And — oh no — did I bring this on myself by reading all those arranged marriage regency books? I did, didn't I? Did any of those heroines get out of it? I could only think of one and she ruined herself by kissing a man in public. I don't think that's going to work here.

I steal a glance at Jasper as if my brain hasn't quite caught up and thinks a kiss with an unsuspecting stranger could fix this mess.

I open a text bubble to Melissa before I remember that she's scheduled for an MRI at seven and I shouldn't be distracting her. Her health mystery is more important than my drama. I shove my phone in my pocket.

There's a sour taste in my mouth, like my nerves are combining with the toothpaste from this morning. I fumble in my bag for gum. This isn't happening. It can't be.

"Big Daddy!" Pretty Boy calls and my dad just lights up. They call him Pretty Boy because he got a manicure once for his brother's wedding and the idea of a man with a manicure blew their minds. I still laugh over that every time I file my nails.

"Online comments already?" Dad asks like it's a surprise. But he's like that — always pleasantly surprised by good fortune. Even though most of his life has been good fortune.

"More than comments! You're already getting a response from Monkey Wrench Garage in Wisconsin."

"Monkey Wrench?" Dad looks personally offended. "Aren't they all married? And old?"

"Here," Pretty Boy says, angling his tablet so Dad can watch their live feed.

I look over his shoulder. It's like watching those videos of trucks loaded with five hundred bags of rice. They start to tip so slowly and you're wincing long before the inevitable. I can't stop watching even though I know it can't end well.

The tablet flares to life and the homey accent of our friend Mac in Wisconsin fills the air. He's dressed in branded *Monkey Wrench* coveralls and his hat is more grease stain than hat. He takes it off, flashes his down-home charming grin as he runs a hand over his receding hairline, and then replaces the cap as he leans against his latest project.

"Well folks," he says, drawling out the "folks" part. *"We're a bit too old over here at Monkey Wrench Garage to take Big Daddy BOOM up on his offer of marryin' his daughter and a grand old time learnin' his company, but if any of us were single, well, we might just jump on a chance to show the world and the BOOM Empire our wrenching skills and our ability to get up under the hood of just about anything and get that engine hot, if you know what I mean."*

He winks at the camera and I want to die.

"So, Gracie — I hope you're ready for some real engine-rumbling thunder in your life because, boy oh boy, are the boys gonna bring it this time! And we'll see you and your dad and everyone else at the Wheels of Hell Burn-Out Challenge in San Bernardino on Mother's Day weekend. Maybe by then, we'll get to meet your lucky fee-ahn-say and you two can go riding in the Monsterino!"

Here he gestures at a grotesque six-door El Camino on massive monster truck tires that he and his garage have been building over the past six weeks. It's supposed to go head to head with our BOOM Silverado on the Off-Road Hill Climb Challenge this summer and I've been working up a campaign centered around the pairing for the past week.

"Good luck to you, Gracie! And to everyone else, Don't Put a Wrench In It!"

And with his call sign said, he ends the live feed and I look up to see everyone watching me. And everyone includes Jasper. The look on his face is murderous. Is that ... does he blame me for this? Does he think I put Dad up to this? Do they all think that?

Yeah, I'm going to be ill.

"Dad," I say brightly. "Can we have a little chat?"

"Sure, Gracie." He's glowing still. He probably thinks he's a genius to kill two birds with one stone like this. Never mind that I'm one of the birds lying here stunned from the hit. "What's on your mind?"

"In private," I say and it comes out as a squeak.

"Get ready to go again, Jasper," Dad orders as he paces over to me. "I'm going to lay out the rules to entry and then we'll call it a wrap for this morning. We have that skidder recovery this afternoon, and we need to be ready to film that in," he glances at his watch, "two hours and counting."

I pull him to the side, but everyone is still staring, so I grab his arm and tug him behind the bulk of the truck. At least the windows are tinted. It's the most privacy I'll be getting all day so I'd better take advantage of it.

"Dad," I hiss. "You can't just marry me off!"

"Oh, Gracie, honey," he says, melting like he does for me while looking at me with his puppy dog eyes — the ones I can't bear to say no to. "Did you change your mind? Do you want the Empire? Because you still get half of it in this arrangement, signed over to you totally legally, but with none of the hassle of running the business. I have a prenup all ready to go and it includes full creative control for you on the marketing side as well as protecting your share of the assets against mismanagement."

"That's ... generous," I say but my stomach is sinking. This is not just a spur-of-the-moment thing. He's thought this out. And seen a lawyer. And announced it live where if he goes back on his word it will affect his reputation. Yep, the gum isn't helping. I'm definitely going to be sick. "But Dad, what if I don't want to marry a truck guy?"

He laughs like I've just auditioned for a stand-up special with Netlfix.

"What's great about this, Gracie, is you'll get the very best. Because I'll really make them work for it so you'll know you're getting a man with ambition," he starts counting off on his fingers like he's presenting this to an online audience and I put my hand over my face so he doesn't see me start to lose it. "Strong work ethic, courage, loyalty, genius, and business sense. You can't go wrong with that."

"Dad, it's the twenty-first century. You can't give your daughter's hand away in marriage!"

"Well, I'm not forcing you to get married."

I peek up through my fingers. "You aren't?"

"Of course not!" he says, his tone reassuring even though I'm not reassured at all. "I'll just have the competition and choose the best possible man — and of course your opinion on the matter will be a huge deciding factor! — and then if you still don't want to marry him you don't have to. I'll give you forty percent of the company and he'll have the other sixty willed to him for when I'm gone and I'll train him up as my successor."

"Oh," I say, feeling foolish. But why do I feel foolish when he definitely said he was giving me away in marriage? And then proceeded to publicly humiliate me before the world on the internet where anything you post stays forever? "And that's okay with you?"

"Well, I'll be disappointed," he says. There it is. He sounds wistful now, maudlin even. "Very disappointed. Heartbroken, even. But children always break your heart in the end. They don't know yet that family is everything. But you'll get older, and eventually, when you've been around the man I pick for you, you'll probably pick him anyway. Especially when you see how much it means to me."

I can feel my expression souring but then he coughs — a terrible racking cough that shakes him to the core so that he has to steady himself with his hands on his knees. A spike of fear shoots through me.

"Dad?" I ask him when the coughing subsides. "Are you sure you aren't sick?"

But he doesn't answer that question.

"You know how much I loved your mother," he says instead, tears clouding his voice. "She was my world and we lost her so soon. The idea that I could be part of helping you find happiness — of seeing you married," he's crying now. "Of seeing your children and showing them how to work on trucks and taking them on adventures, you, me, and their dad all together." He's full-on weeping now and I can't even look. "Gracie, look at me."

I look up. Oh no. I'm going to agree. I just know it. The guilt is too much. If he's dying, I'm not sure I can say no to this.

"Gracie, it would mean the world to me."

I try to say something but literally nothing is coming out. I'm feeling very under-dressed for this situation. Shouldn't I have curls at either temple, a corset, and an a-line dress? Or at least one of those double-horned medieval hats with scarves flowing from the points?

He chokes over his next words. "Just say you'll keep an open mind. Please." He pauses. "For me?"

This is him confirming he's sick, right? That he's dying and this is his last request.

"Okay," I choke out and it literally feels like I'm choking — like there isn't enough fresh air in the freaking outdoors to handle this.

"Thanks, honey," he says, pulling me into a huge hug and shaking with his contained sobs of relief.

I'm glad I said yes, despite the sinking feeling in my stomach. Because how do you say no to your last living parent when it sounds like they might be leaving you, too?

He lets me go and wipes his eyes before offering a tremulous smile. "You know this means the world to me."

And then he's leaving, striding off as he wipes his eyes again and as he moves aside I see Jasper there holding his camera, looking like he wishes the earth would swallow him.

"I'm just looking for the other tripod," he says and it's the first words he's spoken to me in five years. Five years. And he opens with "I'm just?"

I'm so disappointed by how weak they are for the situation, so furious at my dad for putting me in this upcoming mess, and so horribly guilty because I could marry a hundred men and still never make up for the fact that my choice cost my dad his whole life, that I feel my lower lip tremble, and I have to turn away and stride into the desert so that Jasper doesn't see me cry because I've already been too vulnerable with him in the past and I'm never gonna let him put me in that kind of situation again.

Chapter Four

JASPER

Damn.

Clearly, I've put my foot in it, but there's nothing I can do about that now, I need to get this tripod set up and get ready to shoot again. Taking this job as cover won't work if I don't do the actual job.

I risk a glance over my shoulder at Gracie, looking out into the desert, scrubbing furiously at her face and my heart sinks.

Great work, Jasper. You came to talk and you've managed to ruin things before you even got a word out. I thought casual was the way to approach things. Like nothing had happened. No pressure. Apparently, I was wrong.

"Jas, you got the tripod?" Pretty Boy asks, he's practically jumping up and down so I hurry over and start setting up.

I'll say this for Big Daddy Boom, he does not skimp on the equipment. Everything here is the best of the best. We're talking top-of-the-line cameras and microphones, boosters for cell reception for live media, and on-site video and photo editing. If this was just a job, I'd be in heaven right now.

"Okay, so for this one, I'm going to roll in with the truck, kick up a cloud of dust," Adam is saying, "And then we're going to do a walking shot. Buckstop," he says to the guy who swaps between cameras — a massive silent man who seems the calmest of everyone here. "You'll be patching this together so pay attention and try to think of an energetic soundtrack. Something that amplifies my message so it conveys that this is important and life-changing. Pretty Boy, you've got the initial shot of the truck. Tanner, a drone shot to compliment it would be nice, something sweeping that comes in from the east, maybe." Tanner nods. "And Jasper, you're taking the walking shot, so I'm going to be walking, looking vital and energetic to convey to the audience that this is for an action-focused candidate, and you're going to be filming from in front of me so the shot moves with me. I'll be focusing everything I'm saying straight at you, so don't get tripped up by that. You're my mental stand-in for the audience in this shot. This isn't your high-end car shoots with sheiks and their Lambos, this is quick and dirty redneck photography. Clear?"

I nod sharply. I can see what he means and he's not wrong. This kind of shot will set expectations perfectly. I hand the tripod to Pretty Boy and arrange my camera on the stick pole instead, taking care with the wind muff around the microphone.

Everyone's still setting up and Adam is hopping into the Ford Raptor and hurrying back down the road to be ready to drive in for this segment. I feel eyes on the back of my neck.

I know it's Gracie.

I could look. I could try offering her a playful wink. Yeah, and then what? She'd write me off forever. Casual did not work. At all.

I don't know why she's going along with this charade of her dad's. It's not the seventeen hundreds. Adam can't just marry her off. But families are complicated. I, of all people, know that. I pull out my phone and text my dad.

Pasta tonight?

Maybe I can make it less complicated.

I'll pick up garlic bread, he texts back and I feel a little relief at that. If he reaches back every time I reach out, we might find our way back to something that looks like family.

Someone clears her sweet throat behind me in a register that can only be Gracie. But I don't dare look back. There's no time to apologize properly for being in the wrong place at the wrong time and trying to play it cool, not with Adam's truck already racing toward us and Pretty Boy rolling. There's definitely no time to apologize for what I actually came here to beg pardon for. If I try a silent nod or look — well, it just won't be enough, and then she'll be even madder, so I keep my eyes forward.

I try not to think about how good she looks storming off when I catch her in my peripheral vision. It makes my mouth dry, but I don't have to acknowledge that.

I try not to think about how her figure has filled out since I saw her last, into something more feminine and more insanely hot than I thought was possible. That would be a terrible distraction that I don't need right now. I'm not here to get her into my bed. I'm here to talk.

And I'm really trying not to think about how this video I'm about to film is going to set who even knows how many guys gunning for her attention and if I don't figure out how to talk to her soon, then I might lose my chance entirely.

I'm not thinking about any of that.

The truck comes screaming in, aggressive tire treads kicking up clouds of dust tinted with the soft light of morning and I begin to film as Adam leaps out of the driver's side, the very picture of energy.

"Today on Big Daddy BOOM, we're going to talk competition. We're going to talk manly rivalry. We're going to talk about what it means to be a son!" Adam seems almost drunk on excitement. The gleam in his eye is just a little too glassy and his swagger just a little too obvious. He's pitching them now on how he's going to leave his empire to someone, talking about lawyers and prenups. And then his eyes zero in on me and even though I know this is really the pitch, I feel like he's really talking to me. Like he thinks *I* am going to be his son and he wants to set things straight.

"I know you," he says and I swallow. Adam has known me since I was born. "You're ambitious. You're clever. You know what you want in life."

My throat feels dry. If I'm the stand-in for his audience, he's pegged me perfectly.

"Which is why the first portion of this is the competition. I want you to pitch yourself to me. Put a video of yourself up online. Tag me in it. Use hashtag BOOM Empire. Your pitch should tell me three things: who you are, what you build, and why you should marry my daughter. I'm going to go through the entries and next week on the show we'll pick ten vloggers to fly out here for round two. Impress me. I want to hear from the best. This will be no cakewalk."

In the background, an engine starts up and I startle, but Adam just keeps talking.

"We're going to choose from the best and then —" his words cut off as a truck goes peeling out behind him, racing across the desert sand and hopping the ditch to the road. No one needs to tell me it's Gracie. I've been watching her drive quads since we were kids and she has her own distinctive style. She kicks up a rooster tail of dust and her father laughs, gesturing to the show, " — you'll have your chase cut out for you!"

He's moving on to other business — giveaways, adventures, shoutouts to subscribers. I follow his movements, but my mind isn't on what he's saying. My mind is on the girl who used to race here in the desert five years ago. My mind is on her at twelve flashing past me on a side-by-side across the sand dunes with that same rooster tail flying up behind her. My mind is on her at eight beating me racing down the driveway of the home I'll be going back to tonight — my dad never did see the sense in living large. And my heart hurts in my chest watching her dust cloud rise up over the desert.

I've disappointed her again. I seem to be a pro at that.

"That's a wrap!" Adam declares. They're going to stitch this in with the footage from before and drone shots for the weekly video. "Great work, Jas!" He claps me on the shoulder and his excited eyes meet mine. "What do you think? Great idea, right?"

I hedge. "The walking shot is perfect for your energy."

"Nah, that's not what I'm talking about," he laughs, wrapping his meaty arm around my neck in a light headlock and pulling down so I have to bend with it. This is ... humiliating, like I'm sixteen instead of twenty-four. I wince and hope no one is filming this part, before gently removing his arm from my neck. "The deal, Jas! The deal. Who wouldn't want to take a run at it? We'll be filtering submissions all week. Be glad you aren't on the marketing team or you'd have to like and comment."

Why am I the only one who feels shocked at this whole thing? The rest of the crew is just packing gear like it's no big deal.

"You mean, Gracie is going to be replying to these?"

He's laughing. "Didn't she make a great splash with that exit?"

"I think she was angry," I say, but I don't sound as certain as I wish I did.

"She's amazing," he says. "Just like her old dad, she knows the perfect timing! Maybe you'll even submit something, hey Jas?"

I gape and suddenly every eye is on me.

"I'm good," I manage.

He whacks me lightly in the chest with an open hand.

"Exactly! Exactly. You're great. I can't wait to see your submission."

I hope my wry smile is an acceptable response to my new employer because it's the best I can manage.

I'm still standing there like a chump when he's moving away, barking orders. Pretty Boy shoves the tripod into my open hand.

"Don't even think about it, Jasper," he says and he looks dead serious.

"He'll rip you to shreds," Tanner agrees with a laugh as he passes. He seems to be over his dashed hopes about succession.

"And if he doesn't, we will," Cowboy Roger agrees and they all pause to give me the kind of warning looks you give a man when he makes a move on your sister and I throw my full hands up defensively.

"I'm not planning on doing anything," I say.

"If we even see you sniffing around her," Tanner says, letting the words just hang there.

"Seriously, I did not come here for any competition," I say, trying to make light of it. "I don't have a channel, and if I did, what would I put on it? Photography? Studies in light?"

"I've seen your Jeep with the LS," Tanner says, and it sounds like a threat. "You know your way around a vehicle."

"Because I drive one to work?" Now I'm getting annoyed.

"Because you built that yourself. Don't deny it. Go near her at all when it's not part of your job, and we'll make sure you regret it. It will be bad enough having other channels here we don't need one of the crew wrapped up in this."

This is going to make apologizing to her a lot more difficult.

"Don't think we won't notice," Pretty Boy adds. "We notice *everything.*"

"Guys!" It's a plea and a protest all at once, but they aren't listening. They're busy trying to pack six guys and all the sensitive gear in a truck that comfortably seats four.

In the end, I ride in the box to babysit the gear — or so they say — and I eat dust and bugs the whole way back to the shop. It's meant to put me in my place — whatever that is. And I don't even care about that. The thing that's grinding my gears is that now I have one more thing to apologize for and even less opportunity to do it.

Chapter Five

GRACIE

"Gracie, have you checked over the new sponsorship copy? I need it approved before we can run with it!"

Chase has been waiting to ambush me. I can tell. No one hangs out next to the fire extinguisher by the back door of the BOOM shop unless they're waiting for someone.

"What do you think, Chase?" I ask and I can't help the snip in my voice. I've been trying to keep it at bay but here I am, Miss Snippety Snip despite all my efforts.

It's been three days since my dad made his crazy announcement and then informed me it was *my* job to look through the video submissions and choose the best ones. My job. As if being sold off to the highest vlog bidder wasn't enough, I have to filter through every submission and comment on them. And make it clever. And on-brand. And do it in public.

And I can't act like I'm irritated about it with *him* because he'd told me he was too overwhelmed to look through them himself and he doesn't get overwhelmed and then he disappeared for an entire evening and I'm terrified that it's his illness dragging down his energy.

I'm already swamped in hundreds of submissions I haven't viewed, plus hundreds of tags for the contest that aren't submissions that I have to reply to in a cheerful and professional manner, and meanwhile, my online ad management has slipped away from me, and approvals for ad copy, sponsorship promotions, and graphic designs have all backed up.

I could leave it to Chase, but if I do that it will be an even bigger mess. Chase is a perfect BOOM hire because this place is his whole life and he's committed to the vision. But he's not a natural at marketing and it takes all the energy I have some days to help him focus on what we're doing or *unfocus* from whatever has captured his attention that day. His ADHD has been tougher than normal and I know that, and I'm supposed to be sympathetic and kind not Miss Snippety, so I'd better pull myself together.

I juggle my notebook and coffee as I try to squeeze past the early birds already hard at work. Usually, I adore the energy of this place, but it's all getting to be a bit much.

I shuffle sideways behind Tanner who is bending brake lines for whatever that is up on the lift. He gives me a sharp nod, but the moment of distraction costs me as I almost plow into Cowboy Roger and Davis who are gapping doors on another project while Pretty Boy captures it all on camera.

"Watch it, Gracie," Pretty Boy whispers as I squeeze out of the way and around the bumper of a Ford Galaxy 500 — what are they planning with that? The rear quarter panel is nothing but rust and rats' nests — and almost slam into Chase who has appeared in front of me like a genie popping out of a bottle. I startle, clinging to the notebook but nearly dumping the coffee all over my front.

"Can you put a pause on the submissions to check it?" Chase asks, looking frantic. "Big Daddy says we need to film the sponsorship at nine this morning and I don't have approved copy."

Chase's looking pale under his neck and face tattoos. He's younger than he looks — just nineteen and skittish as a stray cat. Usually, I love working with him. He's a total softie and he brings me chocolate, and when he focuses his work is phenomenal, but today I'm mad at the world.

"I wish I could pause them, Chase," I say and I hate that when I'm frustrated I sound more desperate than angry. Angry would make me feel powerful. This just makes it sound like I'm going to cry. "I'm drowning in them. Drowning. They're towing me under. I can't catch a breath."

"Can you stop drowning for five minutes to read this copy?" he asks, waving it in front of my face.

I suck in a deep breath. Steady, Gracie. No snipping. No snapping. It's not his fault your life has fallen into the garbage disposal.

"Everything okay over here?" my dad asks, popping out from under the Galaxy on a creeper. I hadn't even seen him under there. He coughs as he emerges and I hold back a flinch.

"We're fine," I say with a false smile. No need to worry him more than necessary.

"It sounded like you were drowning in submissions and needed help," he says with a smile. "Which sounds to me like I'm a total genius because we've never had such a successful marketing campaign as this. It's trending on Twitter, you know."

"I'm aware," I say and I try to keep my tone fond instead of irritated or close to tears. "But how do you expect me to keep up with our most successful marketing campaign ever and also all my other work."

"Easy," he says, jumping to his feet. He cups his hands around his mouth, "Jas!"

I feel myself stiffening as I realize Jasper has been there the whole time on the other side of the Galaxy, quietly filming Tanner's brake line work. He looks out of place, like a panther in a pack of golden retrievers. He's dressed in a fitted black T-shirt with a motor sketched on it like an engineering design and a pair of jeans that hugs him like a kid glove and I swear I'm not staring but did he look this good last time I saw him? It's not that he's model gorgeous, I'm objective enough to know he isn't. But he's precisely to my taste like I ordered him custom from the BOOM shop.

Maybe that can be our next marketing campaign. Custom heartbreakers: a man built precisely to your taste to crush your heart and stomp all over it. People would watch that. Getting sponsors might be tricky, though. Maybe a work boot company.

"Pretty Boy can finish filming that project," my dad calls out. I jump at the sudden noise and this time my coffee does splash over my wrist. I bite back muttered despair. "You're assigned to Gracie for the rest of the day. Help her comb through submissions and pick the best one."

Jasper's mouth drops open and mine does, too. Could anything be more awkward than combing through online videos from men who want to *marry* me with the guy I once thought I was in love with?

"Sure, Adam," Jasper says calmly, handing the camera over to Pretty Boy.

I can't interpret Pretty Boy's expression as he suddenly finds himself holding two cameras, but it looks like aggression. That's more than just annoyance at suddenly having two jobs at once to do. Does he have some kind of stake in this? Please tell me he doesn't have a cousin or an old college roomie applying to be my chosen husband. I frown at that thought and it's while I have that disgusted look on my face that Jasper's eyes meet mine and I try to wipe my expression, but he catches it and his eyes shutter, and his face goes blank.

Yeah. This won't be awkward at all. Maybe a jackhammer company would sponsor the heartbreaker series.

"I hope you've had your coffee," I tell him dully. "We're going to be at it for a while."

"At it," Chase snickers.

I ignore him. When you work with nineteen-year-old boys you learn to ignore these things.

"I'm good," Jasper says easily, as if he combs through marriage resumes on a regular basis.

Who knows, maybe he does. I haven't seen him in five years. Maybe between exclusive car shoots and running around filming Diesel Week or this year's Baja 500 he's working as a matchmaker on the side, preparing CVs of prospective mates, searching their star charts for issues, and presenting the top five to the families of those involved. I almost choke on the mental image of distant, aloof Jasper sitting down with the concerned mother of a thirty-year-old divorcee who wants her daughter's marriage arranged this time around.

"Can you handle this kind of challenge?" she'd ask him and he'd look at her with all that sincerity in his hazel eyes and say "I'm good" just like he did a moment ago.

I snort a laugh as we go climb the stairs to the upper level and Jasper murmurs, "Something funny, Grace?"

I look back. He's right behind me. So close that I can feel his warmth through our T-shirts. He smells like pine trees and citrus and I want to inhale but I don't want to be caught at it. I still love how he has the tiniest barely-there dip in his chin. For just a moment, the wry expression on his face makes me think of old times and my heart does a double flip that's kind of a mix of heady excitement and pain and I have to swallow hard to handle it.

The moment is broken when Chase shoves past him to shove himself right in my face.

"So you'll look at this copy first, right? And the filming for the *Green Attack* juicing ad? If you can just do that, I can be out of your hair for the rest of the day and you and you can go pick the most bone-able guy online."

"That's a hundred percent *not* what I'm doing, Chase," I protest and I can feel my face grow hot as he shoves past me, leaving me face to face on the stairs with Jasper.

That one stair of difference leaves us level in height and when his breath gusts out in an inadvertent laugh at my circumstances I feel it on my cheek. My heart kicks up another notch. Of all the people to score front row seats to my humiliation, of course, it had to be Jasper. Maybe a car-crusher sponsor would work for the Custom Heartbreak videos.

"Do you think this is funny?" I ask a little breathily, shooting lightning at him with my eyes — or trying to. I think it might come off as more thundercloud-about-to-break-into-drizzly-tears. And at least I've silenced him. He just stands there staring stupidly at my lips for a beat and I get the joy of spinning in place — hard enough that my curls *have* to hit him in the face — and storming up the rest of the steps. Well, I try to storm. I don't do petulant or angry very well, so I have a bad feeling it looked more like I was fleeing the scene of a crime.

But even if my angry looks weak and weepy rather than thundering and dangerous, that doesn't mean I'm not furious.

I'm not a punchline. I'm a professional woman who is excellent at her job and I'm about to prove it by getting through these tasks I need to get done and then buckling down on this online sifting challenge like a pro. I'll pretend it's someone else being humiliated this way — some poor girl on reality tv, maybe, and not me — and I'll do the job and make Dad happy and then I'll tell him that I'm not ready to marry any of these clowns and I'll let him down easy and it will all be over.

The BOOM offices look out over the shop. One wall is floor-to-ceiling windows. There are leather couches and chairs around a low table you can put laptops on and then a few desks with plush leather office chairs. Jasper's dad set up this lounge office years ago and it's weird to think his son is back here sitting on one of the leather chairs he had monogrammed with the BOOM logo.

By the time I'm done going through Chase's work — with Jasper lounging in a chair nearby looking like he's laughing at me the whole time, damn him — I'm starting to realize it's not going to be so easy.

The commercial for the vitamin drink centers around a wedding. The groomsmen give it to the groom to offer him "natural stamina."

Chase's still pitching it when I look up in horror at Jasper and see him put a Jegs catalog in front of his face to hide how hard his whole body is shaking while he laughs.

The next ad is just as bad. It's for a tow rope. Which should be simple, right? Only this rope yanks a reluctant groom up to the altar as he tries to gun it away in a car that's not quite up to the challenge.

I feel my stomach sinking.

Can this get any worse?

Oh, it can.

This week, our sponsor is Bed in a Box. And that's the feature we're filming this morning. It's supposed to feature Chase laying on the bed on his side with his cowboy boots and America shorts on and all those tats hidden by the edge of sleeping bag while he says, "Bed in a Box. For when you need a quick-order bed to go with your quick-order groom."

I'm going to die. I really am.

I have to drag my hands off my face before I can take the script from his hand and slowly march out of the office to the deck outside the door that looks over the shop. I fling the script dramatically to the floor of the shop — or I try to. The papers mostly scatter and flutter. Nice statement, Gracie.

"Listen up," I try to bark but it comes out all trembly. "I am *not* a joke."

Chase runs by me, taking the stairs down two at a time in an attempt to gather up his sheets before they're hit by the open flame of torches or ripped up by someone's grinder.

"There's no use throwing them, Gracie. I have e-copies of everything," he wails between curses.

But the laughter from the guys below tells me everything I need to know. This is only going to get worse and worse the longer I let it spool out and I have no idea how I'm going to stop it. I feel like I'm one of those silent movie heroines strapped to the train tracks, coiled in ropes (tow ropes, probably for a product feature) as the train pulls its horn in warning and sparks fly off the tracks. And while I look fantastic in black and white and a sweetheart neckline, there's no hero anywhere in sight to snatch me off the tracks and save the day.

I storm back into the office, though my storming comes off as more petulant, throw myself into a chair — yes, it's dramatic. I think I've earned that — and fire up my computer. Let's see how much worse it can get.

$$\mathcal{T}hen$$

GRACIE

I'm sitting on the gravel carving it miserably with a stick. I got in trouble for trying to drive Dad's old three-wheeler myself, even though he and Mikey let Jasper drive it, and Jasper's only nine. I don't see how one year makes him any better at driving than me. It's not fair.

It's probably because I'm a girl. There are never enough girls around here. Just Dad and Mikey and all the men who come to talk about parts and trucks. They smell like cigarettes and they go on and on about old pieces of metal garbage. You'd think they'd be excited that I want to drive an old piece of garbage, too.

Mom laughed when I told her.

"Those things are too dangerous," she said.

But no one said they were too dangerous for Jasper.

I stick out my bottom lip and try to perfect my pout.

"Gracie?" I startle at the voice behind me and turn to see Jasper looking awkward. His dark hair is all messed up under his ball cap and he has a smear of grease over his cheek. But his smile is his same half-shy, half-crooked Jasper smile that makes it hard not to smile back.

He holds out a matchbox car. It's his favorite one. The Jeep with the army star on it.

"Girls can drive off-road, too," he says shyly. His pants are too short again. He keeps growing so I can never catch up.

"I know," I say, feeling petulant. "But maybe I don't want to."

"Oh." His eyes dim a little and his hand starts to pull back, but I reach out and take the matchbox car and the look in his eye is so perfect that I move the car to my other hand so that I can hold his hand in mine.

"You don't have to drive trucks to be special, you know," he says looking off into the distance. "You're already special."

"I don't do anything special," I say miserably.

"Well," he pauses, his forehead wrinkling as he thinks, but then it smooths and his shy smile is back. "You're special to me."

<h1 style="text-align:center">Chapter Six</h1>

JASPER

I manage to make my expression neutral when we sit down at our computers, and I answer everything she says with careful monosyllables.

Don't laugh, Jasper, don't laugh, don't laugh.

But her frustration with these ads is beyond funny. And Chase did not see her warning signs. When she covered her face he should have run for it, but he just kept going. And when she got that little twitch in the corner of her mouth, that was the exact twitch she used to get when we were kids and I was allowed to do things she wasn't. You don't mess with that twitch.

He messed with the twitch.

Don't laugh, Jasper, or she'll throw you out with those papers.

She signs me into the BOOM account.

"Just put the headphones on and answer any comments in a positive way and then flag any videos you think have potential for me to look at. We'll go up from the least recent to the most recent and just respond as we go, okay?" She's tense as a driver about to make a drag pass. And she isn't even acknowledging that we haven't seen each other in years. Or that the last time we did it was under intimate circumstances. She doesn't look in my eyes at all.

I nod easily. I don't try a smile. I do try for some eye contact — some acknowledgment that we have a deep history. She avoids my gaze easily.

None of this is going to help my apology when I finally get to it, but maybe if I work hard for her, she'll give me a chance. I put my head down and get to it.

I'm breezing along through the comments when she taps me on the shoulder and I have to pull my headphones off to hear her.

"What is this?" she asks, pointing at my most recent comment. I can barely look at her she's so heart-breakingly pretty today. And she's meeting my eyes for the first time since I said that stupid thing about the tripod. My heart kicks up into second at the touch of her gaze. "You replied 'okay.'"

I nod again.

"That's not a positive comment."

"Sure it is," I say and have to clear my throat because it comes out a bit burred. I can't help it. Her hand is still on my shoulder. "I said 'okay' not 'you idiot' or 'don't comment unless you can say something intelligent.' It's very positive."

She huffs a sigh of frustration and I bite my lip, worried now but also wondering if there's anything I can say that will keep her here talking with me.

Here's the thing. Social media is not my forte. I post pictures on Instagram, sure. And my website. I don't leave captions beyond what's necessary: make, model, year, location, date. I don't reply to comments. I don't "like" things because I find all of that ridiculous. I'm really not the person to do this job. I could film *her* doing the job. That would be right up my alley. I'd adjust the lighting, obviously, to bring out that light flush to her cheeks and the sprinkle of her freckles. And we'd try a slow pan and then a close-up from the left — that's her good side.

"I think we'd better recalibrate," she says in a tight voice and though she's looking at me, she's avoiding my eyes again, her gaze on everything but mine. "What if I reply to comments and tags and you watch the pitches and choose the best ones?"

I'm already nodding. This is definitely the better idea. I can't read the emotion in her eyes as her gaze lingers on my face, catching on the lip I'm still biting. Maybe she doesn't think I'm up to the task. But also, maybe if I do a great job at it, I can convince her to talk to me about something other than work for a moment. Something kind of like an apology.

"Okay," she says, drawing in a shuddering breath that makes her look vulnerable and squeezes something in my chest. "This should work."

She has to be upset about this stunt of her dad's but she's taking it in stride. If she works this hard at something she hates, imagine what she's like with something she loves. I'd like to see that Gracie in action. I missed out on the part of her life where she became a career woman with a passion for her own thing.

She lets go of my shoulder and for a moment it feels cold, like it's suddenly located in Anchorage while the rest of me is here. She's stolen the warmth right out of the room. It's back, though, when she settles in her seat and her arm brushes mine. Back even harder when she leans in to get a better look and her knee brushes mine, too. These office chairs are cheap and too small and I wouldn't have them any other way.

I steal a glance at her out of the corner of my eye. What would it take to make her my friend again? To convince her to tell me all the secrets she has tied up tight inside?

She clears her throat. Oops. I've taken too long looking at her. I'd better at least pretend to be doing this job.

I turn back to the screen and focus on the videos. Most of them are terrible. The cars these guys are building are junk. One of them is this thing called a Sera that this guy put scoops into. I shake my head and don't even listen to his pitch. If he has no taste in cars, he won't suit Adam. This next guy has a decent truck, but he makes a rough comment about Grace and I'd mostly like to just punch him. Instead, I cross his video off the list. Easy Peasy.

It's probably an hour of sifting through pitches and I'm through about twenty of them when I find one I don't mind.

The kid looks a bit rough like maybe he grew up poor, and he's young, but he makes me laugh right off the bat with a stoic face that is most certainly disguising a dry sense of humor and more intelligence than he pretends to have.

"Yeah, so I don't even know why I'm submitting this video," he says, deadpanning the camera. His name is Travis, which is appropriately country. "It's not like we have that big of a channel or anything." I snort without meaning to. This submission video is thirteen hours old and already has ten point three million views and forty-three thousand likes. "We just like to wreck stuff. And honestly, I've never thought about marriage. I feel like if a girl was lucky enough to marry me that would be like winning the lottery and that's a lot of power for a girl to have. I should probably be careful with who I give it to. So maybe watch this video and you decide. It's going to be the most impressive one, but I'm really not promising to get married by doing it. I just think you guys should probably see how this is done when it's done right."

He then proceeds to build and completely destroy an S10. And it annoys me that he destroys it, but I can't fault his skills — he definitely has them, or his camerawork — great shots of everything, or his entertainment skills because that deadpan look is working for him and I'm glued to the screen.

I take off my headphones and lay a hand on Grace's arm and for a moment it feels like a trespass and like I'm going to be arrested or something the minute she catches me, but she just takes her headphones off and when I have her attention I take my hand off her arm and I have to swallow before I can speak.

"Found one," I say.

She takes my headphones and watches the video. I'm not watching it. I'm watching her. The headphones press her hair in around their headband and it leaves little curls out of place around her ears. They wisp in a rumpled way that makes her utterly adorable and not for the first time I'm pretty sure I was an idiot to peel out of this town and this life when I could have had everything. Including wispy golden curls. Or at least, I'm pretty sure I could have had them. She might have never forgiven me for that night even if I'd stayed. I'm not sure I've forgiven myself.

She takes off the headphones and looks at me, her lips making an amused moue that's more tempting than anything. "You think this is the perfect candidate?"

"He pushed the S10 off a cliff and then retrieved it from the lake with his excavator," I remind her of the obvious appeal.

She looks like she might laugh. At least she's keeping her sense of humor about this.

"He says he doesn't want to get married. Don't you think that disqualifies him?" she asks.

"Do you want to get married?" I ask and then feel my mouth go dry. It's not really my business to ask that, is it?

"Not to Xdeath Diesel," she says reading the name off his online channel. She waits a long moment as if she wants me to say something, but I have no idea what it is. Is there where I'm supposed to apologize? It feels wrong. Like bad timing or something. She lifts a brow after a moment and with a resigned expression on her face, she challenges me, "See if you can find one more by lunch."

I do find one more. It's a near thing but I do. This guy is high-end. He's attaching gadgets to an LS engine with some very slick red valve covers branded with his shop logo. I don't even know what half these things do. They have that lovely aluminum look of performance racing gear and I know precisely what angle I'd want to shoot them, but as to their purpose ... well, he and his shop know and I suppose that's enough. The guy helping him is a Brad Paisley look-alike, but older, slightly fatter, and with an honest-to-goodness mullet with racing stripes razored into the side of it.

Our entrant, Hollis Montieth of Montieth Eagle Racing is a tall, smooth, charismatic blond man.

"I don't really need a second empire," he says with a smile that I bet works on the ladies. "But I can't quite see a challenge and pass it up. Especially when it comes to racing or motor-sports. And you all know I'm single." He winks at the camera. "I think family is the most important thing in the world. And why not find a lovely lady who values that and values going fast?" That had better not be a euphemism. "Let's check out this beauty my shop just finished."

The LS is apparently in a Chevy Blazer and he puts the vehicle through her paces, doing crazy burnouts and getting great speeds. The entire production is high-budget, professional, and really top notch.

I turn to Grace but she's already looking at me, headphones off, and when I pull mine off she says, "Montieth?"

I nod.

She sighs and leans her head on her folded arms on the desk.

And it's killing me that we have this big thing between us so I can't just talk to her about why she shouldn't let her dad pull these stunts with her life. It's killing me that we can't joke about this like we would have then.

This probably isn't the time. But there's no one around and while she isn't looking at me, she's also sitting down where she can't just run away, so I think this might be the best chance I'm going to get.

"Grace," I say really softly.

"Mmm?" she asks from her ersatz pillow, sounding miserable.

"I'm sorry." There. I said it. Wow.

"It's not your fault. You had to pick someone." Her voice is muffled by her arms.

"Not for that," I say, rubbing the back of my neck with my hand. This isn't how I expected things to go. For starters, I thought she'd know what I was apologizing for.

"You didn't ask to get assigned to me. That was all my dad. The other guys are probably relieved it wasn't them." She sounds like she's slowly dissolving into misery.

I clear my throat awkwardly and look at the ceiling. "Look, so, maybe it wasn't the smartest thing to skip town during the funeral. Okay? I can see that there could have been other ways to handle that."

I'm doing really well. That was hard to spit out but it made total sense. Maybe I'm better at apologies than I thought.

"What?" Or maybe not. She sounds confused.

"I could probably have said goodbye in person." It's a concession. After all, it wouldn't have made a difference. Goodbye is goodbye. "And I know that what I did ... the night before ... was pretty unforgivable."

"You want to do this *now?*" she asks, and I might be wrong but it sounds like maybe she doesn't want to do this right now.

"Well, you know. Clear the air. That kind of thing." I sound like an idiot. "I felt really bad about your mom. And mine. Obviously."

Wow. I can't talk. I'm not even sure I'm making any sense.

"That's what you said," she says biting off every word. I've never heard her like this. Mad Gracie is usually tearful like she was with Chase, but this Gracie is cold. "When you called me. On the phone. From Canada. A whole month after you took off during the funeral for both of our mothers."

I look down from the ceiling and right into her eyes and it

sends a jolt of something in me that's some kind of terrible brew of guilt and fear and attraction and I hate how I can't look away. I hate how I can't find better words. The right words. The ones that will say that I've been trying not to think about this for years and then agonizing about it for months, and when I finally couldn't take it anymore I came here to her like a lion with a thorn in its paw and I don't know how to fix it or fix our friendship or any of it.

"That's what I'm sorry for," I say softly.

And her expression is something that looks like disbelief. Maybe? I don't know. I thought I was good at emotion. I find it in everything. It's what makes my photos really connect with the viewer, but right now I'm second-guessing that completely.

"Really," I say, trying to dispel her disbelief.

She shakes her head and then takes in a long breath like she's trying to get a hold of her temper and now her lower lip *is* trembling like it does when she's upset. "You know what, fine. That's fine Jasper. You come home and you don't come to see me, you just get a job with my dad. And when you finally talk to me, it's about a tripod. So I try to stay professional. I figure we're going to ignore the past. Fine. But then you bring it up while we're working together at the most awkward moment possible. And you say ... 'I could have done that differently.' So, fine. Great. You realize you had options you didn't take."

Her chin is trembling with her lip and I feel like the chair I'm sitting on is sinking into the ground.

"I'm trying to apologize," I growl.

I didn't mean to growl at her. It just slipped out and now I can't take it back. This is terrible. It's like getting stuck in a mud hole on your own and the rear diff blows and your winch battery is dead.

"Next time," she says, standing up and wow her eyes are blazing so much that watching them hurts right down to my guts. She's making eye contact now. It's not the kind I was hoping for. My belly does a complete flip like I've been stabbed and I barely hold onto a grunt as she finishes what she's going to say. "Next time, try harder."

"Could we," I manage to grit out, "maybe talk about it?"

"Sure," she says and her cheeks are bright with bottled emotion and her eyes are glassy. "I'll call you about it in a month."

And then she's gone, the door closing behind her and I feel like I've been gutted like a trophy bass and laid out on the slab to be filleted.

That did not go the way I expected. At all.

Chapter Seven

GRACIE

This is the photograph that guts me every time I see it. Dad has three of them framed in the house and one is poster-sized and hanging on his bedroom wall. I know that because sometimes when his housekeeper is on vacation or ill, I clean for him. He doesn't ask me to. He wouldn't. He'd think that was sexist, which is surprising coming from a man who wants to offer me up as a bride to a prospective heir of his empire, but he really would never ask me to do something just because it's 'women's work.'"

He needs taking care of, though, and I try to be a good daughter, even though I'm terrible at it. It's what Mom would have wanted if she were still here. Melissa says it's both my best and worst quality. Best because it's generous. Worst because it's nosy, interfering, and keeps me from dealing with all my issues because I'm so busy solving other people's problems. But Melissa is like that.

I met her in college and was surprised to find out she only

lived a twenty-minute drive from where I grew up. And while I've had friends come and go over the past few years, Melissa is the one person I can text anything to. And I do. Constantly. But I can't text her about Jasper because right now her problems are so much bigger than an ex-boyfriend who is suddenly apologizing like he's never heard one before and doesn't know how to get the words out.

I draw in a long breath, try not to worry about Melissa, and look at the photo again. There are photos of Mom on every wall of this massive timber frame mansion Dad had custom built, but I can see why he has three of this one.

Mom's sitting in the driver's seat of her old Jeep, hands at ten and two, with Alicia — Jasper's mom —waving madly beside her. They both have their hair tied back with little kerchiefs,. They're wearing cut-off jeans with crisp button-up short-sleeve shirts and their grins match. The Jeep is up on three wheels, halfway through a rock crawl, and Mom looks proud as punch.

I remember those days.

If I let myself think about them, all I remember are happy times. BBQs. River-rafting adventures. Off-road wheeling. Camping in tents. Sportfishing. My mom made it look easy to pack up the family and rough it for days on end. There was always amazing food to eat, something to do, and always a neat, tidy space to rest — whether that be a tent, or the back seat of a vehicle, or just under her umbrella. And she and Alicia just exuded love, motherly tender care, and laughter.

People think my dad has the big personality — and yeah, he for sure does — but in those days he was quiet a lot while mom joked and told stories and laughed and laughed and laughed. She had the most adorable laugh that ended in a snort from her nose, and she and Alicia would sit close together speaking with their foreheads almost touching, and then the two of them would start laughing so hard that one of them would fall over and get all dusty.

When I was a kid, I thought that was what friendship was. I thought that was what family was.

I didn't know then what I know now — that it was only like that because they worked hard all day every day to make it like that.

I wish I still had Alicia.

I wish I had Mom back.

But I do the best I can.

I wipe my eyes. Yeah, I'm a huge softy and this stupid photograph still makes me misty-eyed.

Maybe someday Melissa and I will take a photo like that. When she isn't dealing with mystery heart problems and I'm not neck deep in my dad's schemes.

I'm cooking dinner for Dad tonight. I try to do it at least twice a week. And I water the plants while I'm there, and run his laundry through the washer and dryer. He could pay someone to do all of it. He has the money. And he definitely did pay someone when I was away at college, but I like doing these things for him. I'm not Mom, but it's my best.

I have steaks grilled and salad made when he arrives home with a huge grin on his face and a "Gracie! You didn't need to cook for me, honey!"

Which is what he says every time I do, like it's a constant delightful surprise that I want to take care of him.

But tonight I'm going to have to break it to him. I can't marry some crazy stranger off the internet. Not even one who loves cars. Not even one who jumps through whatever hoops he has planned. Not even if Dad is as sick as I'm afraid he is. I have to be firm and honest about this.

"I took the list Jasper submitted and went through it, Gracie," he says when I'm clearing up and he's eased back in his chair sipping his favorite iced tea.

Jasper must have worked hard to have enough videos for a list, especially after I stormed out on him. I feel a bit guilty for that, but not guilty enough to want to change it. What was he thinking apologizing that way? He broke me all those years ago and a half-hearted mumbled apology doesn't put back those shattered pieces.

"Great work, honey! You've got an eye!" Dad says. "These contestants are the perfect choices.

Should I tell him it was all Jasper? Probably not. He's way too happy. Unless maybe that's a way to segue into how I don't want to go through with this ...

"I couldn't have chosen better myself," he's still saying, "and it's gratifying to see you picked all the online bloggers I thought might have potential for this, and even a few I'd never seen. I narrowed down the twelve you and Jasper submitted to a nice easy six. We'll fly them here for round two. I've already got Tanner on it."

"Round two?" My voice comes out as a squeak. This is all happening way too fast. It's like a bad dream where I'm watching my own life on tv and I can't control what tv me is doing. She's definitely not brave enough. I'd give her two-stars maximum and that's being generous.

"Yep. Tanner was already contacting them and purchasing plane tickets before I even left the shop. We'll have just enough time to settle on the events and start working up the sponsored products for each one. I'll get you a list tomorrow so you and Chase can work your magic."

"Thanks," I say, but I feel like someone has knocked my breath out. How do I say no now? People have been contacted. Tickets have been bought. I won't just be disappointing them all, I'll be making my dad look like a fool.

"It's going to be great. We'll have a huge party here the night they arrive and you can meet everyone and start getting used to the idea. Should I have the party planner consult with you? Is this a marketing opportunity?" He looks a little concerned like he's stepped on my toes or something.

"Probably," I say weakly.

"I'm so happy that you're doing this for me, honey. It means a lot."

His eyes mist up again in that happy proud look and I see them dart over to mom's Jeep picture for a heartbeat and then back to my eyes.

"It was hard when your mom passed, honey. And I think a lot about how much I don't want you to have to be alone."

So, he's dying then. For real. I feel like I can hardly speak as the news crashes over me. But one thing I know for sure: I can't break his heart after all.

He lives in this huge yawning house that used to be full of my mom and all her love and industry and now it's cold and empty and the only family he has is me and if he's sick he'll need me to be here with him for every step of the process.

I'm going to have to marry someone. I'm going to have to give my dad the heir to the family he wants and the magical last days of his life he's dreaming of. It's that or live with the guilt of breaking his heart a second time. And this time won't be an acci-dent. It will be by my own choice.

"I have to take tomorrow off," I say thickly. I don't want to lie, so I don't make up a fake reason, but I can't face this right away. I need time.

"Sure honey," he says brightly.

I finish the dishes and kiss him on the cheek and wish him goodnight as I leave. I feel like I'm a zombie. I'm just going through the motions in a daze. I walk to my guesthouse apart-ment by memory. My eyes aren't even registering where I'm walking.

Dying.

One parent lost to me is bad enough. I'll feel so adrift when it's two. How am I supposed to live without the hurricane that is my father?

Usually, I feel happy walking into my place. It's bright and airy and full of projects I'm working on for people. Right now, I have Tanner's taxes spread out across my coffee table. Beside that is a folder of printouts I have for Chase on the best tattoo removal places in the area. He's already regretting that neck tattoo.

I keep plants wherever I can fit them, so the air is always slightly humid from them, and the scent of earth and something vaguely floral pervades the house.

Between them are a fishing rod that just needs a little super glue to attach a broken eye, Melissa's favorite dog leash that is frayed around the hand loop and I'm sure I can repair that with embroidery thread, a project I'm working on for dad's maid — she told me she doesn't know how to put her photos online so her family in New Zealand can see them, and about a dozen other small things I'm working on when I have the time.

My sofa has bright floral cushions, and my bedroom has a white quilt, but underneath are bright floral sheets, and my shower curtain is yet another bright floral. I like things bright and colorful. It makes me smile to be surrounded by nature. I even keep fresh fruit in a bowl on my table all the time. Not cut flowers. I don't like killing flowers. I don't like killing anything. Not even ants. And I get ants.

When I get home, I usually eat a piece of fruit and listen to bright, happy music in front of my massive picture windows that overlook the garden I keep outside, while I work on one of the many projects I do to help my friends.

Not today. Today, none of that brightens anything for me. Today, it all looks grey and drab.

I pull out my phone, meaning to text Melissa, and remember all over again that she's at Mayo Clinic. She's needed to see the doctors there for a long time. She can't afford any kind of stress or distraction. I would have gone with her, but Melissa has a huge family and between her mom, an aunt, and three cousins who all flew there with her, I think she's in good hands. They're staying with another aunt part of the time, so it's going to be busy for her.

I fire off a simple text, "*How's it going? Hope everything is great!*"

I hit a few random animal emojis because that always makes her laugh and then sigh. I wish she were here. She'd know what to do.

I sit heavily on my couch, grab a pillow, press it to my face and then hit my forehead into it a few times. It does nothing but get a bit of my bronzer on the lighter parts of the fabric. It certainly doesn't give me any idea on how to wiggle out of this mess.

If only I were already married.

If only I'd met some sweet boy in college and we'd fallen in love and had a baby on the way. Maybe he'd be an architectural major and we'd have to live far away from Utah and ... then Dad would be so lonely in his big empty house. It's built to perfect scale if humans were actually grizzly bears so that only he can ever reach anything and the counters go almost up to my underwire. But he wouldn't need to enact elaborate schemes to get what he needed at the end of his life.

I let out a long sigh.

What would Mom do?

Go out off-roading with Alicia and laugh. Or be at Alicia's little brick house which was normal-people sized and they'd drink lemonade in the back yard while me and Jasper ran through the sprinkler or biked up and down the street.

For the first time since we lost them both, I have a wave of homesickness for Alicia's house. Not just mine before Mom died, but hers. For a two-bedroom brick bungalow she'd never wanted to upgrade even when they were pulling in big money.

For BBQs with the neighborhood. For Alicia's boxes piled everywhere because she never threw anything away. For homemade popsicles made of juice in molds in the freezer and cut up carrot and celery sticks.

And I don't even know what I'm doing when my eyes blur over and I get into my brand new still-shiny Ford Bronco and start driving. It's Area 51 blue and I'm both proud of the pretty color and of the color's fabulous name but I can't see any colors at all as I peer out over the hood. It's a twenty-minute drive into the suburbs to Glacier Lake — the name of Alicia's subdivision. It's a dry lake the houses are built around and though it gets a skim of water after a huge rain or in the spring, it's just a big empty grey expanse right now. I don't care. I just need to see that brick house again.

And then I'm there and I don't know why I'm stumbling out of the Bronco, but I am. My mascara is probably running and I still don't care. I haven't felt like this in so long — so out of control like I'm surfing on the wave of my own emotions.

I get as far as halfway to the front door and then I collapse like someone has cut my strings and I'm just sitting on what was once Jasper's front lawn sobbing my eyes out silently like a crazy person.

I hear footsteps but I don't look up. This house probably doesn't even belong to Jasper and his dad anymore. It probably belongs to normal people now. People who don't drive to other people's houses and sit in their yards where the neighbors can watch them bawl like babies.

Someone sinks down beside me and my eyes go big as I see who it is.

It's Jasper.

Of course it is.

And he's holding a big plate of spaghetti with a fork stuck in it. He chews as he looks at me, a bit of bright red sauce on his lips makes them look redder than usual, and that only draws attention to the stubble on his unshaven face. When he speaks, it's with spaghetti still in his mouth.

"If this is a delayed reaction to my apology," he says, "then fair enough. It was pretty bad. I could try again and we could get the neighbors to vote on how I do, but one of them is Russian, and I hear they're notoriously hard judges to please."

"As in, 'the Russian judge gives it an eight-point-five' tough?" I ask, hiccuping a little.

"Or you could come inside and eat spaghetti with me and my dad." He's so calm. Like I'm not making a mess of things right here. And he *does* owe me for that terrible apology.

"Your dad still lives here?" I ask.

He takes another bite of spaghetti and nods. No explanation. Just a nod. But he doesn't need to explain, I guess. Because if I didn't completely understand, I wouldn't be here sobbing on the piece of desert other states would think of as the "front lawn."

"I just missed Alicia," I say in a tiny voice.

He looks like I've hit him in the gut by speaking his mom's name out loud. His eyes go red-rimmed and he looks away.

"I'm sorry. I'm so sorry," I say, guilt filling me.

But he makes a brushing away motion and meets my gaze with his watering eyes. He swallows his spaghetti.

"What good is a world where everyone doesn't miss her? Right?" And the look in his eyes is jagged and soft all at once.

I glance covertly at the house. It hasn't changed one bit. I half expect Alicia's bright laughter and the offer of a popsicle to emerge from the door.

What would it be like to live here in this house?

"My parents bought this house when they got married," Jasper says, following my gaze as he clears his throat. He laughs awkwardly and looks off into the distance. "I don't think my dad can leave it without feeling like he's leaving her. He couldn't really afford it when he bought it for her. But he said marrying her made him feel strong. Like he could do anything."

What would it be like to feel strong like that? To feel like you could do anything. Defy anyone. And still be there for your family.

And then my mouth falls open as I realize that I don't need to ask Alicia what to do. I already had *the* genius idea. This just confirms it. What I need to be is married. Married already so I don't have to be married to someone else, and married in a way that makes me appear strong and capable and able to make my own family-centered decisions. Married to someone who can help support my dad in his last days and be the heir to the company that he always wanted. Who better to do that with than someone who practically *is* family?

"Your apology was really awful, you know," I say but I keep my tone gentle, and when he looks back at me his head ducks a little and he looks up at me through an impossible fringe of eyelashes in a way that makes my heart stutter.

"Is that so, Boomhower?"

For some reason, his use of my last name makes my heart jump. Most people don't even know my last name anymore. They think it's the "Boom" that Dad shortens his to for the online world. Apparently "Big Daddy Boom" is a more appealing moniker than "Adam Boomhower."

"You know it's true," I say bumping his shoulder with mine almost like it's old times. Only this bump is hesitant and unsure. It wouldn't have been hesitant before.

He takes another bite of his dinner. It looks terrible like it's just noodles and cheap red sauce.

"I can make it up to you," he says after he finishes the bite. His words are so heartfelt that I almost feel bad to ask this. Almost. But not quite. Because it really was a terrible way to apologize for breaking my heart five years ago. And he *does* owe me for that.

He catches his lower lip in his teeth nervously and because it's slightly stained by the sauce he looks more boyish than ever. He plays with the remaining strands of spaghetti.

"Anything," he says, upping his offer. He looks so hopeful.

I take a breath and hope Alicia's ghost won't judge me when I tell her son, "Good. Because I know exactly how you can do that."

Chapter Eight

JASPER

I'm going to get a chance to make up to her after all. I set my plate of spaghetti aside. This is the best news I could hope for in this miserable day.

I hate being back here in this place where all my memories of my mother are still alive. Where I turn a corner and remember her smile. Where I open a cupboard and her laugh tinkles out. It's like being ambushed constantly and it sets me on edge. I woke this morning thinking she was calling me and had a very bad five minutes when it all came crashing back.

I hate being stuck in one place, too, even if it's only been two weeks so far. It's just knowing that I can't pick up and go on a whim that makes me feel trapped. It's going to the same place at the same time every day and knowing people expect me there. It makes my throat feel tight all the time. I'm itching to be out on the road again. To get to talk to people who aren't a bunch of cult-follower truck guys who are ride-or-die with the BOOM Empire or my dad who has detailed plans to be miserable forever.

Maybe if I can finish apologizing to Grace, I could leave

again. My conscience would be clear. I'd be at peace. I could put all my guilt behind me.

That's what I tell myself. But when she looks up at me with those big caramel eyes, I'm pretty sure I won't be able to go so easily. When I see them full of unshed tears I have this terrible instinct to just draw her into my arms and hold her tight against my chest where no one can hurt her again and I'd lean down and kiss every one of her tears away. Even if there were a hundred. Even if it took the rest of our lives.

And she has no idea I'm thinking this.

She wouldn't be happy if she knew. I can still hear the echoes of what she said to me on the phone when I called her from Canada.

"If you don't come back right now, don't expect me to welcome you when you do."

I hadn't come back then and I didn't expect a welcome now.

But having her here right now feels like a welcome. She has no idea how smoking hot she is right here in my parent's front yard wearing red high heels, a BOOM shop T-shirt, and jeans that kiss her curvy ass in all the places that I'd like to kiss her.

Whoa, son. You went there?

Of course I went there.

There's something about having her right here with me on my home turf that's doing crazy things to me. But I need to get a grip on myself. This isn't what she needs right now. And I shouldn't be such a sucker that I get hooked by her all over again just when I'm finally getting a chance to ease the last hook out.

I clench my fists against my own emotion and force an easy smile.

Nothing to see here, just me sitting in the dirt with my dinner and the girl I thought was my best friend and first everything right before my mother died and shattered my heart.

But all this — coming here, working this humiliating job, all of this has always been about making things right with her because I broke them back then.

It's not about how having her here makes me hyper-aware that there are a dozen videos that I sent Adam today filled with guys who think they're going to win their way into her heart.

It's not about how I've been dying to kiss her since the moment I left and sometimes I think that if I'd just turned around and done it back then, it would have made all the rest of this come out right instead of all awkward and wrong.

It isn't about how every sex dream I've ever had was about her. Even when I was halfway around the world and you'd think my mind and body would have registered one of the thousands of other women I'd seen on my way there. Nope, my unconscious mind points due Grace.

This isn't about any of that.

It's about making things right. And I thought I'd lost the chance at that this morning. I can't believe I have it back. I'd better not blow it this time.

She seems hesitant, like maybe this favor is a big ask, and she's not sure I'll go through with it. Without seeming to realize what she's doing, she reaches over and tucks the tag back into my shirt. Grace is like that. Always trying to mend people. Always trying to fix all the broken things.

"Anything, you want, Daff," I say, trying out her old nickname to see if it helps anything. Maybe if she's comfortable, she'll be able to tell me what she needs from me. Maybe if she remembers old times she'll forgive me.

Her wan smile isn't very encouraging and I suppose it's not the most endearing thing to hear a nickname from when you were six years old. It's still cute, though. Her hair had been so yellow that she'd insisted she was a daffodil, too, and tried to get me to plant her. In the end, we were both in trouble and both head-to-toe covered in mud. On Easter morning. Before the big gathering our parents were hosting together.

"Can I tell you in the house?" she asks, looking around nervously like we're going to be overheard by the neighbors. I mean, we're probably the most drama they've seen in years, but I don't care what people think. Their thoughts aren't my problem.

"Sure," I say and it comes out a bit like a purr. I can't help it. Just having her this near does things to me. I stand first, taking my plate with me, and then reach down for her hand. When she takes mine so I can help her up, a warmth spreads through me, starting in my hand. I can smell her scent — a feminine musk mixed with lavender. Every one of my senses is standing to attention at that, waiting for the chance to be used. And not just my senses.

Awkwardly, I force thoughts like that aside, rubbing the back of my neck and looking away. What's with me? I'm not like this at all. I'm usually so focused on my work that I hardly notice people unless they want to chat about lighting or shutter speeds. Of course, I find women attractive. I'm a man. But I'm not a teenager and normally it takes more than a distracted thought to override my systems like that. It's like she has my nuclear codes or something.

I guide her to our front door, opening it for her and allowing her inside before I follow.

"Nothing has changed." The words come out of her in a whoosh. That's when it hits me that she hasn't been to my house in all this time. And I haven't been to hers.

The world feels like a foreign place when you just say it out loud like that. Like maybe there are a million probable universes where things could have gone differently and somehow I ended up in the wrong one.

I don't know what to say to that, so I don't say anything.

Instead, I lead her through the living room where my dad is leaning back in his recliner, spaghetti plate on his belly and mouth wide open as he snores. I'd been worried he was watching us from the window. Turns out I should have been more worried he might choke to death.

I'm in the kitchen running water for dishes with my head bent down when she joins me. It's humiliating having her here. The place is a wreck. I didn't even see it before, but I do now that I'm conscious of her eyes on all of it. It needs a declutter and a cleaning. It needs to not smell like beer and pizza. It needs someone to do these dishes. Anxiously, I start, but when she hands me a used plate I look up confused.

"I think he's done with it, don't you?" she asks gently and I look over my shoulder to see that she took the plate from my dad and put an afghan over him instead.

It's such a nice thing to do. The kind of thing no one does for the pair of us anymore, and I just don't know what to do with that, so I take the plate silently and put it in the water. And I swallow down a weird lump in my throat.

The dishes are very dirty. Which is good. I need the chance to scrub them so I can clear my thoughts.

I felt like I had a handle on things out there, but the second I'm in here, it all spirals away from me again and I'm a broken teenager with his mom dead, along with her best friend, and I can't tell anyone how I feel because I don't fucking know how I feel, and I can't do anything to fix it because there's nothing to do, and the only thing that makes any sense is to go as far away from it all as I can.

Only to find it never leaves you.

Only to find it just sits there in the pit of your stomach making it ache all the time with all the shit you got wrong.

We don't dry dishes around here. We just stick them in the rack.

And I've been so absorbed in my thoughts that I haven't even noticed that Grace hasn't left them alone. She's dried every one and put them away. Because she knows where they go. Because she knows how things around here are supposed to be.

And wow, I'm the biggest dick in the world for thinking about her pretty ass in those jeans instead of the golden soul inside. The soul that asked me for something.

I drain the sink, turn my back to it and lean back against the counter with both hands for support. They're still kind of sudsy. I must look like a mess.

I try to run a hand through my hair and then realize I've probably left suds up there, too.

"You said I could make it up to you," I tell her and I still haven't looked up into her eyes but I do now. She's standing across the room by the old fridge, arms crossed protectively over her waist. She bites her lip and watches me.

"All of it?" I ask and it feels like I'm begging for clemency.

"I guess," she says, uncertain.

"All —" I gesture like maybe a motion can replace the words I can't find.

"I'll forgive you for being an idiot in the shop today," she says meeting my eyes with a kind of vulnerability that draws me forward a step before I realize it's happened. I end up standing in the middle of the kitchen like I don't know how to be a human. It feels like she's a religious figure telling me how to absolve my soul. "And I'll forgive you for ending seventeen years of friendship by running away when I needed you the most, and not even calling to tell me what had happened for a month."

I swallow.

"Anything," my whisper is mostly a gasp. And I really will give anything. A kidney? Sure. My heart? Oh, Grace, you have a big chunk of that already.

"And you do owe me," she says, looking up with her chin tilted down like she's too shy to meet my eyes but is meeting them anyway.

I nod, fervently, a religious worshipper. Maybe I'll raise my hands and sway. Wear a choir robe.

Abruptly she cuts off and lifts a plant from the counter and goes to the sink to water it. I don't even know where it came from. I think they were giving them away free at the grocery store. She busies herself with it for a few minutes and those minutes are complete torture. Her back is to me and I can see the delicate little curls on her neck and watch her graceful hands work through the leaves. I can see her heart racing through her T-shirt.

What's she going to ask me?

Are we going to rob a bank? Kill someone? Stop a cult? I pause. *Start* a cult?

By the time she turns around, I can hardly breathe.

"Jasper," she says, and wow her lips are full and they stay parted for a full moment before she spits out the rest, and I can't help it. I think about fitting mine into the shape of them. I want to feel them all over my skin. I bet they're amazing. I bet —

"Jasper, will you marry me?"

Dear God, yes. "I —"

She cuts me off. "Not for real, of course," her laugh is almost manic. "Because that would be crazy. Just for pretend. But at a real church and with all the stuff there like it's real, and we'll take pictures and tell my dad it's real, and then he won't marry me off to these other guys and ..."

She's rambling. This time it's me who cuts her off.

"Yes." I say it way too quickly. But now that she's put the idea in my head I can't get it out. Me and her married. Her in my arms as my bride. Her on my lap as I kiss her lovely throat. Her in my bed as I kiss —

"Really?" she interrupts my thoughts.

"Yes," I manage again. It might be the only word I'll be able to say from now on. There don't seem to be any other ones.

"You'll have to fool him with me. All the way. We can't do it halfway," she sounds stern now like these details are going to change my mind, like I won't like being married to her. Or rather pretending to be married to her. But is there a difference? "We have to be convincing."

I can be convincing. So convincing that she'll believe it herself.

"Nobody can think it's pretend. You'll have to look like you're in love with me."

Done.

"You'll have to kiss me … probably in public."

"Is that a threat or a promise?" I ask and I feel like someone should give me a medal for managing to speak in a sentence.

She rolls her eyes but she actually smiles a little relieved smile. "You'll do it?"

I feel like I've said yes too many times and it's not getting through to her.

"Just promise you won't hate me," I say, as I take one of her hands.

She looks over her shoulder guiltily at my sleeping dad. "Why would I hate you?"

"You've had reasons before," I say, swallowing down a lump of shame. "And sometimes when people lie together, they don't like the results."

She quirks an eyebrow but I really didn't mean that as a double entendre.

"I promise not to hate you," she agrees.

And for someone who hasn't heard "I love you" in five years, this is the closest thing to it and I have to force my face to neutrality so I don't betray how hard that made my heart lurch.

Chapter Nine

GRACIE

I can't believe I just did that. I'm crazy, right? Full on certifiable. What kind of person proposes a fake marriage to a friend who owes her one? A mercenary, conniving person, I guess.

And apparently, I'm more willing to wear that moniker than "bad daughter" or "the girl who ruined her dad's career and left two dozen people out of jobs" or worst of all, "the girl who wouldn't grant her dad his dying wish."

I'm a terrible person. I know it. And a little part of old Gracie who saw boy-Jasper as her best friend is deep inside me screaming right now and beating her fists against my ribs. "It's Jasper!" She's screaming, like I don't know or something. "Jasper! You love him." But she's wrong about that. I buried the love I had for him in the same grave as my mother.

Anyways, back to the plan.

If I fake-elope, then I can just present it as a whirlwind love affair that my dad couldn't have predicted. He can still run his events and come out looking great to his audience and I will just have to lie to ten million subscribers and all my friends and family for a while. No biggie, right? It's not like I have another boyfriend who might get jealous. It's hard to meet guys when your dad is always there giving everyone side-eye and showing up places in his young-man-intimidating vehicles.

This way, Dad can mentor Jasper in his enterprising ways and get that out of his system and Jasper and I will both be there for him for whatever weeks or days he has left. Not the end of the world, right?

So why can't I slow my breathing?

Jasper is still looking at me with something dark and deep going on in those unreadable hazel eyes. Since I came here to his old house he feels less like a stranger and more like a version of the boy I used to know, but I've still lost the ability to read his nuances. It doesn't help that he's like the manliest man I've ever met even though he's only in his early twenties. It's hard to explain. It's not that he's more muscular or more aggressive or more capable than the other men I know. It's just that any time I so much as glimpse at him I'm reminded very strongly that he's a man. It's in all his movements and expressions in a way I've never noticed in anyone else. It's like I can smell it in the air when he's around. It makes me suddenly conscious of myself. Will that get worse when he's thirty? Forty? Will it age like simmering herbs in a sauce? I shouldn't be wondering. I won't be around to see it.

What does it mean that he tucks one hand in his pocket and scrubs at the scruff on his face with the other? What does it mean that he's still looking at me? His eyelashes are so delicate. That's weird, right? He's all hard lines and masculine energy and then those eyelashes are just there edging those blazing eyes, like no one gave them the message that this is a hard manly man who doesn't need frills.

What will it mean to pretend to be his wife? To kiss him in public? My mouth feels dry at the thought. Me five years ago would be dancing around singing at the top of her lungs. Me right now doesn't know if I trust myself with him. He hurt me before. He could hurt me again and despite all this "don't hate me" stuff he could blow this whole thing up in my face. I think that having my heart broken by man-Jasper would be worse than having it broken by boy-Jasper was.

I have to make myself a promise. No enjoying it. No getting swept up. No blurring the lines between deceit and reality. This is simply a pragmatic arrangement.

But what if I can't do it? I was in love with him before. I didn't realize it until he left but by the time he called me on that terrible, cold line with his monosyllable answers and his indifferent voice that didn't even sound like my friend Jasper, by then I knew it. I knew it because I'd been living through a month of heartbreak and once something has been killed and is rotting in your front yard you have to admit it is there. Yeah, I'd been in love with him. And that old Gracie could slip back. She's frustratingly hopeful. She's an optimist. She waters plants that are brown and dry with leaves that crumble when you touch them. She feeds chicks with broken legs through a pipet. That bitch cannot be trusted.

So, I won't trust her. I'll keep an eye on her.

There's an old saying that goes, "who watches the watchman?" only it's in Latin which I don't speak and don't remember. But I know the answer. It's going to be me.

Which is why we need to do this right away and establish some ground rules.

"I want to do this right away," I stammer, picking up a shirt of his dad's that's been thrown across the back of a chair. It has a massive rip in it. I can fix that and bring it back. It won't be any trouble at all.

"Yes," he says and I have no idea why he's agreeing to this so easily. He must have felt really guilty about that call — and he should because it was awful — but all this compliance is making me nervous.

"Tomorrow," I say, like it's not the most ridiculous thing to say. I set his dad's shirt down. I can't remember why I picked it up.

"I know a guy," he says and that dangerous dimple appears and winks at me. That dimple is going to be an issue.

"At City Hall?" I ask, twisting the edge of my T-shirt between nervous hands.

He's there before I realize it, gently, oh so gently, removing my hands from the edge of my T-shirt and taking them into his. His gaze is on those hands.

"No," he says and it's the first no he's said. "That won't look very nice in the pictures. There's this little chapel on Horizon Road."

I know the one. It's tiny and white and made of rough-hewn boards like it came straight out of the old west. I doubt it could hold more than a dozen people at most.

"Won't that be a lot of trouble?" I ask as his calloused palms meet mine and he weaves his fingers into my own.

He looks up and my breath hitches when his gaze meets mine because it looks sincere. Too sincere for two people planning a faux marriage.

Maybe I haven't entirely thought this through. I've worried about humiliating my father. I've worried about losing sight of the deception myself, but should I be worried about him? What if he's taking this too seriously?

"It will look better for the pictures," he says and then his mouth quirks into a half smile, and his eyebrows lift hopefully. "If we're going to have a fake wedding, can't I at least have real pictures? I have to humor my muse or she might leave me forever."

I can't tell if he's joking. "You can't take the pictures if you're in the wedding."

"But I can set up the shots," he says and I think he means it. "My artistic integrity won't accept less."

He does mean it. Wow. I did not think the clincher here

would be the pictures. But we'll need them to convince my dad it's real. And he'll want pictures because he'll be mad he wasn't there for the wedding. I can't have him there. If he's there, he'll smell that this is fake. He has a nose for that kind of thing and if he looks at me and asks me what's happening, I'll break under his gaze. But good pictures? Yeah, they'll convince him. And they can be a memento for him, too. He can use them to sell our story to his fans.

"Okay," I say. "I can get Tanner to come take pictures. Or Chase."

How pathetic is it that I'm offering guys from my dad's empire? I could text my friend Amy and ask her to help, but somehow the thought bothers me. I don't want to lie to my friends about this — or at least not all the way. A little lying might be inevitable, but if I don't see them for the next few weeks, then I won't have to lie outright. And I won't lie to Melissa. That's a total deal-breaker. She'll know everything once it's a good time to tell her.

"I have someone for that, too," he says and his breath gusts over me in a way that makes all the hairs on my body stand up, and for just a heartbeat my brain tries to play me a movie where we're getting married for real and he wants me. Shut up, brain, I tell it. You're being silly.

"Okay," I say again and he bends just a little and for a wild moment I think he might try to kiss me, but no, he just leans in a little more so he can get a good look at my face.

"Are you sure this is what you want?" he asks.

"I have tomorrow off," I say, even though it isn't an answer.

He laughs. "I don't. How do you feel about an early wedding? There's some great light at golden hour right after dawn."

I laugh without meaning to. Of course. I'm worried about fooling people. He's worried about the light.

I should be grateful. If we were both bundles of nerves this couldn't happen.

"How can I say no to something called 'golden hour?'" I ask coyly and pick up his dad's shirt again. Oh yeah, I was going to mend it. "Listen, we'll need some ground rules."

"Like vows?" he asks and his eyebrow lifts teasingly.

"No," I said, my face growing hot. I guess there will be vows. Fake vows for a fake wedding. "Like rules. Like, you still live here and I live at my place."

"Won't people notice that and talk?" he asks.

"Oh. Yes. Okay, like maybe no sex— "

He cuts me off with a finger to my lips. "Why lay out rules? Why not just go with it and use our best judgment? We don't know what issues might crop up so it makes more sense to deal with the specifics when they do."

That's irritatingly logical. I wanted the security of rules, not the responsibility of "best judgment." But he's the one making all the concessions. Maybe I can give him this and convince him to make rules with me later.

"I should go," I say instead. "I need to get ready."

He nods like this is the most natural thing in the world. I pause for a moment to take him in. I just proposed marriage to this man. To this perfect, sexy, knee-weakening piece of man. Gracie, you crazy girl. You're braver than I thought.

"Okay," I squeak. Fine, maybe not that brave. "I'll see you tomorrow."

"Can I text you once I talk to the minister?" he asks, and I laugh a little too loudly.

Oh yeah. He has to pull together the fake trappings of a wedding. I'd almost forgotten. And I'll need a dress. Who would have thought I'd pick my wedding dress with less than twenty-four hours to do it in?

I offer him my phone and he inputs his number and texts himself a single word.

Grace.

This is all feeling very real. I need to get out of here. I let go of his hands and the scrape of his rough callouses as I let go sends little shivers up my spine. When I glance at him he has his eyes shut like he's savoring that single touch, too. That can't be right. I'm imagining things. The fake romance is getting to me.

"I should go," I say again. "Tell your dad I'm going to mend his shirt."

I pick it up and hold it in front of me like acquitting evidence. He nods gravely.

"I'll walk you to your truck," he says, but I'm already shaking my head.

Wow. Why am I so feverish? Am I getting sick? I feel like I can hardly breathe.

"Wait, how are you going to get there tomorrow?" I ask.

He smiles almost like he's laughing at me. "My Jeep."

"I didn't see it parked outside," I say, stupidly.

"I parked it around back. Brakes need work."

"Oh." Why am I stalling? This is insane. "Umm okay goodnight," I say way too quickly and then I'm out the door and I accidentally slam it behind me — that wind is stronger than it seemed — and I'm in the Bronco and speeding away with sweat pouring out of every skin pore.

What have I done?

What have I done?

And what am I going to wear?

Chapter Ten

JASPER

I'm a simple man. Or at least, that's what I've always told myself. I don't need a lot of worldly goods, though I'd be pretty upset if I had to go without my Jeep and my cameras. Just give me a camera — even a cheap one, or the one in my phone, which frankly is not that bad — and some freedom to move around and I'm happy for hours. I don't drag a lot of stuff around with me. I don't think a lot about emotions or nuances. I don't say things I don't mean. I don't speak if I don't have something to say. And I don't try to manipulate people.

So I don't know how I got here.

I'm behind the Horizon Chapel, leaning against my Jeep and sweating bullets. A casual observer might think it's because a minister and a bride are waiting for me on the other side of the chapel. They'd be wrong. It's the papers in my hand that have me nervous. The papers and the ring.

I'm staring at them both second guessing myself.

My dad steps out around the corner of the chapel just enough to catch my eye and I feel again the moment of guilty-kid that I felt when Grace left our house last night and he sat bolt upright in his recliner and said, "I'm the photographer for your wedding. Don't say no."

He'd held up a single threatening finger and I'd watched him warily.

"Should I assume you were never asleep?" I had asked him casually. I find the easiest way to keep people out of my business is to pretend that I don't care if they are or not.

"She sure hasn't changed," he'd said, avoiding the question. "I bet I'll get that shirt back and I'll hardly know it was mended." He'd crossed his arms over his thick chest. "But if you think I'm not going to be there for your wedding, think again. I'll be the photographer."

"Fake wedding," I'd corrected, scratching the back of my neck.

He'd laughed.

"There's no such thing as a fake wedding, son. Either that or else they're all fake. The papers don't matter. The other people don't matter. I guess the vows matter, but not really the saying of them. It's the keeping of them that matters. There are folks who make a big show and say all kinds of lovey-dovey things and then forget those vows before they've even taken off their wedding outfits. And there are those who keep unspoken vows for years who are more married than people with a paper. That's why this won't be a fake wedding. Because I know you. You'll keep your vows. Spoken or unspoken. So, at least do me the favor of not excluding me from my only son's wedding."

I half wanted to tell him that I didn't have to be his only son. That he was forty-eight and he could still marry again and father a whole second family of kids. But I bit those words back. Instead, I just nodded.

"But you'll take the photos with my Nikon," I said and he grinned.

"Deal."

He'd held his hand out then, and when I took it he'd pulled me into an unexpected hug. I was so startled that I just froze, not even hugging him back. My dad didn't hug … anymore.

And then he'd ended the hug awkwardly to go dig through his closet and see if he had anything nice to wear for the wedding.

I chewed my bottom lip. I still had time to *not* do this. I could just leave this fake marriage certificate I'd printed off the internet and this ring right here and go out there and tell them all that this was crazy and of course, we weren't going to do it.

But I just couldn't do that. Grace wanted this and I couldn't say no to Gracie.

But whether it was real to Grace or not, I was going to keep my vows, so it was going to be real to me and that made it feel terribly solemn.

I slammed a fist against my forehead.

I was crazy to go along with this. I should go out there and tell her to go home. That this idea was a bad one. That if she didn't want to get married to someone else she should just tell her dad that, or get in her car and drive, or start sending out resumes. That fake marrying her old friend was only something crazy people did.

Yeah, that's what I was going to do.

I swallowed. Was it normal to have such a dry mouth?

My dad signaled again. My bride was here. No more delays.

I drew in a long, nervous breath and launched myself forward. I'd been lucky. I had this nice vest and trousers set from some of the fancier shoots I'd been part of. No fancy shoes, though. I drew the line at pretentious shoes. Hopefully, she wouldn't mind. Especially since we wouldn't be getting married — even fake married — once I broke the news to her.

At least it would just be dad and Grace — I'd heard her Bronco purr up to the chapel — and Scotty and his aunt. That wasn't too many people to disappoint.

I knew Scotty from high school. He hadn't changed much. In school he was always hanging out with the kids no one else wanted to hang out with, listening to their woes and incidentally playing a lot of Dungeons & Dragons. As an adult, he still hung out with the people no one wanted to be around, but now he listened to their woes while trying to help them with their opioid addictions, preaching sermons at this very chapel, and taking the time to text old friends once a week with inspirational quotes and well wishes. Even I — Jasper, the man with the heart of ice — wasn't mean enough to ignore Scotty more than three out of four times. That's how we'd stayed friends, and why he was presiding at my wedding today. Or would have been, if I went through with this. But I wasn't going to.

Because I'd do a lot of crazy things for Gracie, like move back here and work for her dad, but this wasn't just crazy because getting fake-married was a silly hoax to try to pull. It was crazy because too much of me wanted it to be real and I didn't actually know this girl anymore. I hadn't been around her in years. Sure, I knew all her little tells. I knew her history. I knew that she loved the smell of vanilla anything and hated seafood. But I didn't know what she was hoping for in life. I didn't know what relationships she'd had these past five years or if they mattered to her. Maybe she had a boyfriend she was keeping hidden from her dad. I'd do that if I were her. Maybe she had changed who she was inside. How would I know? So that made it stupid and crazy to want to get married to her. The girl I wanted to marry was nothing more than a memory of happy times in a world before I was motherless.

Scotty would be disappointed. I was still a little in awe of how he hadn't batted an eye when I called him up last night to ask a favor.

"I love weddings," he'd said. "Can I prepare a brief homily?"

"Umm ... brief," I'd allowed.

"Are you writing your own vows or do you prefer traditional?"

"Traditional," I'd been definite about that. This was crazy enough. I was already risking some kind of divine punishment for faking a wedding ceremony. I didn't want to make it worse by bringing home brew vows into the equation.

"I'll ask my aunt to be the witness," he'd said. "She'll be at the chapel anyway doing the bookkeeping. She's an early riser. Oh, and Jas? I think it's special that you asked me. And special that you're marrying Gracie. I always thought you two were sweet together. I'm lucky to get to be there."

Scotty was a good friend.

And now I was stepping nervously around the corner of the church and running a hand over my hair. How was I going to break this to Gracie? The aunt slid the papers from my distracted hand, which was fine. We won't be using them, even if Auntie Mary is grinning like *she's* the bride. I catch a thumbs up from my dad who's hidden behind my Nikon 850 and it makes my stomach twist. He's going to say I'm an idiot. And I am, of course.

And then I turn and I see her there on a white-washed step below Scotty. I haven't seen Scotty in years, but he barely even registers as there. He could be here in Hawaiian shorts and a scholar's cap and I wouldn't notice because all I can see is her.

She's so beautiful it feels like a knife driving into me and then hooking my breath in my chest and snatching it away from me. I can't seem to remember how to get it back.

It's not her anxiously lovely face or the way her curls are a little tangled from the breeze, or how her sweet little dress clings so innocently to her seductive feminine curves. It's that feeling I get every time I see Grace, like I've found something I've lost. Like I don't have to look over my shoulder for trouble. Like it's okay to let down my guard and open my heart. Like I'd take any curse to keep her well, any madness to keep her sane, any poverty to keep her flush, any loss to keep her whole.

It hits me this way every time. And it's hitting me doubly hard now because she's offering herself to me as a wife. Or at least, that's how my brain is interpreting this since it doesn't seem to get the message that this is a hoax.

She looks so nervous, and she doesn't have to be. I give her a reassuring smile and a tiny wink. We don't have to do this. She can just go home and sip her favorite mint tea and call it a day. And I'll tell her dad for her that she doesn't want this contest.

But when I step up to tell her that it's too crazy, I end up taking her hands instead. And when I open my mouth to tell her that I've been a fool, I bring them up to press a soft kiss against them instead. And I'm swept up in a memory of a long time ago and with it comes all the longing of years of nights where I sat on a beach or a hotel bed or the edge of a parking lot and thought about holding her hands again and how I'd do everything differently if I ever had the chance. It's too much. I can hardly breathe.

I still think I would have gone through with calling it off, but when I finally meet her eyes, there's something in them so precious and so vulnerable that I find I can't break it. It's hope. And she's looking at me like she's putting it all in my hands. She's looking at me *exactly* the way she did the morning of the funeral when she asked me if it was going to be okay and I hugged her.

And I don't care that what we're about to do is ridiculous. And I don't care that I'm irrationally invested in it.

This time, I just can't turn around and walk away.

I guess I'm doing this.

Scotty surprises me by launching into his ceremony while my head is still spinning, and when he gets to the vows, my heart is racing like one of her dad's cars, because the words I'm speaking are real vows to me. I mean them with everything inside of me.

I think most men would be smart enough to guard their hearts. They wouldn't let this be real for them because they'd be wise enough to know it's going to end up hurting. But I'm not most men and I speak these vows and I mean them, even though they sear like a cattle brand, and make their mark just as permanently as that fiery brand as I repeat things about loving, honoring, and cherishing in sickness and in health and for richer and for poorer and until death parts us.

And when she says them back to me it's like something is burning in my chest. It chokes me up, makes my eyes water just a little bit, like a salve spread over the harsh pain.

I almost forget the ring, and then I huff a low laugh when Scotty reminds me. I'm just a touch proud of this part. It's an alexandrite shield-style ring. I saw it in a pawn shop in L.A. when I was killing time in between shoots. The second I saw it, it made me think of her and I'd bought it on the spot, thinking even then that I was a fool to buy a ring for a girl I might never see again.

But now here I am slipping it on her finger and sharing in her surprise that it fits and we're still looking at each other with laughter in our eyes when Scotty surprises me with his declaration, "You may now kiss the bride!"

And my eyes are wide, I think. My lips have fallen open. I'd forgotten about this part of wedding ceremonies. And suddenly, I'm overwhelmed with emotion and I can't move. I can hardly breathe.

She pushes up on the toes of her dainty pointed shoes and my eyes close involuntarily with the touch of her feather-light kiss. It's like being caressed by the sun — ethereal, barely there, and yet it consumes you. It's entirely too intimate for an audience, and yet so brief that I wonder if I've imagined it. I feel like I've been touched somewhere deeper than my lips.

I'm still blinking in awe when Aunt Mary is hurrying us over to a little bench and table and she has Grace sign the paper,, and then she signs, and I'm sweating all over again as Scotty and my dad sign and the pen is pushed into my hand. I sign the paper without really looking at it. My dad is snapping shot after shot, immortalizing the signing.

"Let's get a shot with your hands laid over the license," my dad says, and we put our hands down on it and I look down at them there, her delicate hand on top of my rough one.

I'm about to smile at that pretty image and how old-fashioned my dad is to want this shot, but the smile falls from my face as I realize something. This isn't the fake marriage license I gave Mary a few minutes ago. Someone has switched it out.

This is a real marriage license. And it's signed and witnessed by both of us.

We're legally man and wife in the eyes of the government and God. This isn't a fake wedding after all.

I feel suddenly light-headed.

Fuck.

She's going to think I set her up.

There's a roaring in my ears that's so loud I can't hear as my dad directs us into another pose for his camera and my heart is racing so fast that I can't think. What have I done?

For a fake wedding, it's actually pretty nice. When I'm done signing the fake paper — how did they come up with one that looks so very real? — Jasper takes my hand to examine the fit of the ring and his dad snaps a few more shots while the preacher speaks to us about the sacredness of holy matrimony like he's a real preacher. He's going to look phenomenal in the pictures.

I bite my lip and look up at Jasper through my lashes. I'd kissed him. In front of his father. Not exactly the way I expected our first kiss in five years to be, but I have to remember it wasn't a first kiss. Not really. Because none of this is real.

Jasper's aggravatingly sexy in that trouser and vest outfit with his white shirt sleeves rolled up, and for just a second I get an ache in my chest realizing that someday some other girl will get to see him dressed like this and they'll be getting married for real. And he'll be taking her off to Hawaii or Alaska — didn't he say that was his favorite place? — or Brazil or somewhere amazing for their honeymoon. He'll slip that calloused hand around her waist and whisper sweet things in her ear and draw her into his embrace, and into his bed, and then he'll start slipping her wedding dress off and —

I cut off my own thoughts abruptly, remembering first, that I'm in public and second, that I'm not married to him and so none of that is going to be me, and wow am I uncomfortable now. I'm all spooled up to where the light touch of his palm against mine is making me crazy hot. It's the way our fingers are woven together so that our hands kind of slide apart and then fall back together with every movement. All I can think about is sliding of skin on skin.

I shake my head. And look down to see his scuffed leather boots.

Will he wear those biker boots to his real wedding? That thought has an appropriate cold-water-over-the-head effect and I'm already calming down when Jasper's phone rings midway through the preacher's chat about bearing the sorrows of one another and mending the tears. It's kind of a sweet talk. I wonder if he found it online.

"I have to answer," Jasper says, looking at the preacher and the man nods kindly.

Jasper's still holding my hand when he answers, his thumb rubbing little circles unconsciously as he speaks.

"Jasper," he says. He drops my hand like it's hot. "Yeah, sure. Where is that? Mmmhmm. Yeah, I'm on my way." He shoots me a guilty look and his cheeks are a little flushed under his stubble before he turns back to his phone. "Sure, Adam."

He's talking with my dad. My stomach feels like it's going to fall through my knees.

He kills the call and smiles awkwardly around the gathered group. "I, umm, gotta go. Late for work."

And just like that, our wedding is over and the lady clutching our fake marriage license is hugging me, and then the preacher is, and then when he's done snapping my photo, Jasper's dad hugs me, too.

He whispers in my ear, "Alicia would be so proud."

And my lip trembles, and my hands fall from his shoulders, and I feel a stab of something like guilt because we've fooled his dad. It's wrong. I know it's wrong to use Jasper like this. I know it's wrong to deceive my dad. But it's even more wrong to deceive Mr. Hunt because he never did anything wrong to me, and he lost his boy at his wife's funeral just like I did. Everyone in town knows that he spends his days driving alone in the desert or drinking in his house. What will this lie do to him?

Maybe I should have thought of that.

I'm trembling a bit when he pulls back and I see Jasper striding away toward where he parked his car behind the church. And it feels so weird — like I'm being abandoned by him — that I can't quite tear my eyes away from him even when my phone starts ringing.

It's my dad. My mouth feels dry as I accept the call.

"Dad."

"Hi honey, you're out early!"

"Yeah, watching the sun rise," I say and it's not a complete lie. The sun is still rising, golden beams spilling over the hills and across the land like happiness spills over families.

Over by the Jeep, Jasper is unbuttoning his vest and I can't tear my eyes off him as my dad speaks in my ear.

"That's great. Listen, Tanner made a mistake when he was booking those flights for the guys flying in."

"He did?" I'm hardly listening. There's something absolutely riveting about watching Jasper unbutton his vest, looking down at himself as he does. I glance around to make sure no one is watching me watch him, but the other three are huddled around Mikey Hunt's camera reviewing the pictures. They can't see Jasper from where they are. I risk a look back at him and the vest is already off and now he's working the buttons of his shirt. I swallow hard. I could watch this all day.

"Yeah," my dad's voice jars me back to reality and I swallow again, feeling my cheeks flame scarlet like he caught me watching Jasper undress. "He accidentally clicked the wrong buttons. You know how he can be. I've been scrambling all morning calling them. The tickets are for today. They all fly in at six tonight and I have nowhere to host them except my house."

"Your house?" I ask, my blood pressure spiking because his house is right in front of the guest house where I live and that means all the contestants in his little contest will be *right there.* He has room for them. His rambling mansion has twelve bedrooms. Twelve. "For people, you know," he'd said when he was building it. "There are always people who need a place to stay."

"It's just for the first night. We'll get hotel rooms after that. Marcia is cleaning and putting out fresh sheets, and of course Daniel is on deck for food, and the party planner can be there in an hour," my dad rattles off all the details, but in my stunned state I've looked up again and I feel like my eyes might melt at what I'm seeing.

I swallow down something hot and rough in my throat and I can't quite breathe.

Jasper has stripped right down to black boxer briefs while I was talking. The church hides him from the road and our guests. And there's no traffic anyway. But I can see everything. He looks ... really, really good.

He's shucking on a pair of jeans and Oh. My. God. (And yeah, it's not blasphemy if you're praising him right? And who wouldn't be freaking praising God for making something that looks like this). He does *not* look like he did at eighteen.

He's not a tall man or a big man. He's that kind of rangy lean figure that ages really well if you don't hit the drink too hard *cough* Mikey Hunt *cough* but every muscle he has seems to have toned and hardened into pure manliness rather than the half-grown boyishness I'd seen the last time we'd been swimming together five years ago.

I think my jaw has dropped as I watch him zip his fly up. Certainly my blood has rushed to all kinds of places that are suddenly tingling in anticipation. Who zips up so slowly? And can I just say I could watch this all day? Oh. My. G—

"Gracie?" I blink hard and it takes a minute to come back to my senses. My dad is on the phone. My dad. While I'm watching ... this.

"Dad," I manage and I sound strangled even to me.

"Did you get all that? I need you to go over there and supervise, okay?"

"Yes," I agree. "Yes, I *need* to go."

Before I spontaneously combust.

"Okay, love you honey."

"Love you, too," I say and if I'm distracted can you blame me? Jasper's slipping on a black T-shirt and it just flows over his lean body like it's used motor oil being poured over him, and how in the hell is that a sexy metaphor? But it totally is. And oh no. I'm going to have to live with him and pretend to be married to him and how am I going to do that if I can't stop blushing.

Or worse, if I can't stop replaying that zip-up in my mind. Because I totally am.

He looks up suddenly and catches me watching and I think my face might be on fire. Like actual, literal fire, but all he does is smirk very faintly, pull his phone from his pocket and tap something into it.

My phone buzzes and I look down.

See you tonight?

It's a text from him.

Tonight.

At my place. My stomach twirls like a ballerina trying to prove something.

My place? I type with the winky face emoji, trying to pretend that I'm totally cool and not at all drooling over my new fake husband. Not at all remembering exactly how close those jeans hug him.

It's that or pasta with my dad.

I look up to catch a glimpse of him watching me and there's something deep and dark in his eyes that I can't read. It looks a bit like guilt, but it also looks exactly like what I think my eyes must have looked like when I watched him getting dressed and something hot and fiery speeds in my pulse.

I'll make up the couch. I text in a desperate bid to remind us both that this is fake, fake, fake.

It had better be amazing, he texts as he slips into the driver's side of his Jeep and starts the engine. *I've slept on couches all over the world.*

Unnngh. The idea of him sleeping on a couch in those ass-hugging boxer briefs is killing me.

Couch.

Think about a couch that you won't be sleeping on, Grace. Think about putting your old camping sleeping bag on it. And you won't go near it while he's living in your house. Okay.

Who watches the watchman? That's supposed to be you.

Joke's on you. My couch was rated best in Utah, I text.

We'll see about that. I'm taking pictures and submitting them to Couches of the West Magazine.

His Jeep peels out, shooting up gravel. He's in a hurry.

It can't have much of a readership. I've never heard of it.

But he's not in too much of a hurry for a parting shot. *It's very exclusive. Fake husbands only.*

Chapter Twelve

JASPER

Fuck. Fuck. Fuck.

That was all I could think as soon as I stopped texting Gracie. With my Jeep whipping down the road, I called my dad frantically from my cell.

"Dad," I gasped the second he picked up.

"Hey, son," he said easily. "You'll like my shots. I used the settings you picked."

"That's great," I say but I'm so panicked I don't care if he left the lens cap on and the whole thing was nothing but black. "Dad, I need your help."

"Sure thing. Gracie gave me back my shirt. It looks amazing. You should get her to do one of yours."

Shirts. At a time like this. I try to quell him with my tone.

"Dad, when you took the license picture, I realized it wasn't the one I brought. It was a real marriage license. I need you to talk to Scotty and tell him not to file it. Do you understand?"

"Sure."

"I'm counting on you, okay? This is supposed to be a fake wedding. But we signed a real license."

"I told you, son, there are no fake marriages."

"Yeah. But will you talk to him? Right now? Please?"

"Sure."

After that scare, relief was my primary emotion for the rest of the day.

The shoot was great — and even better with relief flowing through me.

We were filming the guys rescuing a four-wheel-steer truck that had tumbled down a mountain last week. Everyone in the truck was fine because Big Daddy BOOM overbuilds his roll cages to an extreme level. By sheer luck, only a few body panels ended up dinged, and the steering was messed up, but that was nothing for the BOOM shop to fix.

The driver — an extreme online stunt artist — did flips and tricks all through the rescue and I was able to line up amazing shots with him flying through the air in slow motion like a squirrel jumping tree to tree, arms and legs splayed out as if the sky were welcoming him with a full-body hug.

It was bright and sunny and perfectly gorgeous outside and by noon everyone was grinning like crazy. The crew had forgiven me for helping Grace with the video selection and apparently, I was one of them again.

"Great picks for the contest," Tanner had said, clapping me hard against the back while chewing on one of our sponsor's energy bars that they'd named for the show. The label read "BOOM Body Build Protein Bar" and at the rate Tanner was downing them, he'd have built himself a skyscraper by the time the day was through."We went over them last night after I bought the plane tickets for everyone and even Jimmy thinks they're a solid selection."

Jimmy winked at me. He perpetually looks like he's about a minute away from robbing a convenience store and then getting his girlfriend to pierce his tongue in the back seat of a Ford Focus - which apparently he did in high school. And he's a shit talker. I'm pretty sure it's his entire role on the BOOM show.

BOOM stands for "Best Of Off-Road Motoring" and is not just a reference to how much Adam's guys like to blow stuff up, or a play on his name, but Jimmy's not very vehicle-savvy. He mostly pokes at the other guys while they work. It makes for great entertainment. I sometimes wonder how guys like that wrangle something that isn't even a skill into a profitable career, but if I'm being honest, that was kind of my dad's deal before his very early retirement. Adam was the genius and the hard worker. My dad just joked around and made him look good. Sometimes I miss those days. I miss how light-hearted it was. How there was a joke around every corner.

"Hey Jas," Jimmy said when we were finally loading the recovered truck up on the trailer. I was filming them drive it over the fenders which was going to be a problem since this trailer didn't have drive-overs and I could see the metal giving at the weight. "Got some pretty fancy duds in the back of the Jeep there. What were you up to this morning?"

"Went to church," I said, zooming in on the bending metal.

"Oh crap," Tanner said, inevitably, and because I saw it coming, I caught his reaction perfectly with the camera and that's pure gold.

"Getting religion?" Jimmy pushed.

"After being with you boys, it's basically an insurance policy," I'd said and then he'd moved on to hassling Tanner for screwing up while they hammered the fenders back up so they didn't rub the tires.

I was relieved to have escaped notice so easily. But now that it's all over and I'm driving over to Grace's house with my gear, I'm feeling a bit sad. They'll find out we're married tomorrow and all the good camaraderie we built today will fade away.

I'm also worried because when I texted Grace for the address of her place, it had looked awfully familiar.

155B Pleasant Drive

And now that I'm driving to it, I'm getting more worried because this is the way to the Boomhower mansion — that huge timber frame home that Adam built in the middle of a desert that hadn't produced timber that size since the last time the climate changed.

There it is. Looming.

I start to sweat a bit.

She didn't tell me she lives with her dad. I wasn't ready quite yet for this confrontation.

A text comes in.

I live in the guest house. Park in the back.

It's a relief, but not much of one. I take the second driveway that loops around the massive house, the detached four-bay garage, and the carefully manicured gardens that look like a spread from a magazine and far, far too green for the desert. The water bill for this place must be off the charts.

My dad's well off. The BOOM Empire was doing well even five years ago when he cashed out. But this place, this garden, this garage, all serve to remind me that Adam Boomhower is off-the-charts wealthy. I drive by a hangar and remember belatedly that I'd heard he bought a helicopter last year. And he'd taken lessons so he can fly it himself. Adam never does anything halfway.

The guest house is tucked away on the other side of the garden and I see Grace's Bronco parked neatly to the side. It's small. The kind of place you'd build for a mother-in-law who you expected to do little more than sleep and have her old lady friends there for tea, and who would live most of her life in your big house. I swallow my nervousness at the proximity to her dad's home.

I'd hoped for a little space. I didn't expect a real married life with Grace, but I'd hoped there would be some room for the two of us to talk and figure out how this is going to work.

But there are windows everywhere. We'll basically be in a fishbowl. One with an amazing view and an in-ground pool between it and the main house. But a fish bowl all the same.

And in the middle of this, I'm going to …what? Convince her to make me her friend again? Convince her to absolve me of the past? Admit that I've probably been in love with her for the past five years and that watching her say vows to me today threw that into overdrive and now I'm not sure I can ever just walk away without at least trying to persuade her to love me, too?

I wonder if Grace swims. Does she have a little yellow polka dot bikini? No. It's not the time to think about that, Jasper. You can't afford to be distracted. Things just got a lot harder.

I ease my Jeep in beside the Bronco, turn off my engine, and take a bracing gasp of air. It's my first night married. Maybe I can manage to not embarrass myself entirely. That's the only goal here. That, and to keep from making her hate me.

I get out and grab my duffel and my camera cases and stride up to the door. Someone has filled the courtyard with a jumble of potted plants and only half of them look like they're going to make it through the rest of the afternoon. It's the only really Gracie thing here, and when I see them I start to smile. I'd bet almost anything she rescued these today and she's trying to nurse them back to health.

I go to knock on the door but it opens before I can.

"Thank goodness you're here!" Grace says with a squeak, pulling me inside and closing the door behind me. "Put your bags there and go get the rest. We need to get you moved in before he gets back."

"Back?" I say stupidly, but I'm staring at her.

She looks amazing. Gone is the demure lace dress, and in its place, she's donned an orange filmy shirt that flows whenever a breeze hits her and a pair of tiny white shorts so short that all I see are tanned legs. I'm so fixated on them that I don't even realize that though her place is cluttered with plants and paperwork and mysterious broken objects, it's been absolutely stripped of furniture. When I do, I frown.

This place is tiny. I can see the kitchen and the small breakfast nook, and the only two doors in the place are wide open. There's a small three-piece bath in one, and a wide bed with a white coverlet in the other, and that's it. No couch.

"My dad will get home any minute now and I don't want him to catch us in the act."

My face flames at that. I know perfectly well there will be no "act" for him to catch us in, but my blood doesn't know that, apparently.

"The act?"

"Of moving you in. You're particularly slow today," she scolds.

"These are all my bags," I say distractedly.

Her apartment is adorable and a complete disaster. It looks like there's a year's worth of receipts organized in piles in one corner of the living room. Beside that are sliding stacks of physical photos — all of a family of people who burn red in the sun. They certainly aren't Gracie or her dad. There's a pillow with the stuffing pulled out, and a few racks of potted seedlings in the window. And the plants are everywhere — big and small, flowering or leafy. It's like she tried to transport a tiny corner of the Amazon rainforest into her house. There's even a plant on her stove in between the burners. It's a succulent.

I can't help the tiny laugh that escapes my lips. If I had tried to picture the kind of home Gracie would live in, it would be exactly this. If I were a betting man, I'd bet you everything in here, including at least half the plants, are things she's fixing for everyone she knows, and for a strange moment, I wonder if I'm one of those things. Maybe I'm arriving here broken and messy so that she can work on me for a couple of weeks and then push me back out into the world, mended and ready for another beating like that fishing pole with the dangling eyes.

"These are all your bags?" she sounds disbelieving.

"Four cameras and gear, a laptop and chargers," I say holding up one arm with the metal case that I carry equipment in. Then I lower it and hold up the duffel. "Clothes and stuff."

She shakes her head like my very clear explanation is some kind of mystery.

"Well," she says, and now she wraps her arms around herself. "You'd better put them all in the bedroom."

I raise an eyebrow. This is unexpected.

She laughs a little uneasily. "You might have to wait to shoot your article for *Couches Monthly* because we're officially down one couch and both chairs. They needed them for the big house and they took them before I could object. And I couldn't exactly tell them that I needed a couch for my fake husband, so you're going to have to sleep in the bed with me."

The words "sleep in the bed with me" ring so loudly in my head that I think I might have brain damage.

"It doesn't have to be sexual," she says, her face going bright pink. "People sleep together ... I mean in the same bed ... I mean totally platonically, all the time. In some countries, your whole family sleeps with you."

I make a show of peeking at her bed. "I don't think you have room for that. Besides, my dad snores."

Her laugh bursts out before I think she even realizes it's there.

"So I'll just put my bags in here then?" I say as I put them in her room. "In our totally non-sexual bedroom beside our non-sexual marriage bed?"

"You said we could just use our best judgment," she reminds me smiling in a way that brings out her dimples. I'm melting.

I pull a very sober face and turn to her trying my best to look serious as I say, "I judge this as best, if that helps."

And I've won because she's laughing again.

"I can sleep on the floor," I offer. Although I'll have to fight a half-woven basket and what I think might be a knitting project for a place on it. There's barely room for my bags.

She's still laughing. "Don't be silly. We used to sleep in the pup tent together when we were kids. I'm sure we can handle this."

I don't think it will be that simple, but keeping my inner thoughts pure as the driven snow will be the least of my worries. I sure hope that my dad spoke to Scotty. Speaking of which, I should tell her about the mix-up before someone else lets it slip. We can laugh about it together or something.

I take a step toward her, sharing her smile, and say, "I need to tell you something, though, before things get crazy."

"Okay," she agrees, taking my hand in both hers and wow, those are such small, soft hands.

They do things to me. They make me think of all the ways she could use them to caress me and ease away every trouble I could possibly have, and I think she's wrong about that bed. I can manage to keep my hands off of her, but there will never be a time that we are side by side and it won't be absolutely alluring to me. Even if she sleeps in old sweats or a T-shirt with her dad's face on it. Although I'm hoping she doesn't wear that. I'm hoping she wears something small and lacy like an itty bitty slightly transparent version of what she wore this morning.

Yeah, Jasper, that will definitely help you not to touch her.

"This morning," I start to say, blushing at both the thoughts I'm having and the confession that's coming.

"You were amazing," she interrupts, biting her lip in a way that makes it hard to focus.

"So were you. And gorgeous, which could not have been said of me."

Surprisingly, there's a denial in her eyes. Does that mean she finds me attractive? Hope pops up like a bad habit and I shove it back down. Unlikely. She's known me since I thought it was fun to write my name with my own urine. I push on. I need to get this out there.

"But there's more I need to tell you," I say. "I —"

My words are cut off when the door to her home is opened suddenly and her father's voice booms into the room. "Gracie, honey? Are you here?"

"Dad?" she's out of the bedroom like a jackrabbit jumping from a bush and streaking out toward the horizon and the moment is gone and I'm left with the empty guilt that I still haven't told her everything.

Chapter Thirteen

GRACIE

My dad is here and I have a boy in my room. My heart thunders as I repeat that to myself. Wow. What am I? Sixteen?

But actually, this has never happened and it makes me feel like I *am* sixteen and about to get in huge trouble.

It's not like I've been a nun all my life. Okay, maybe it has been a bit. The thing is, I was a pretty happy kid in a happy family and we were busy all the time so I didn't think much about boys. I didn't really have any teenage crushes other than Jasper, and I was busy trying to keep that a secret because I didn't want my parents watching my every move when I was around him. Or his parents watching. Or the whole world watching.

And then my mom died and it was me and my dad and honestly, when you're struggling with a loss like that, having crushes or going on dates feels so stupid and shallow — or at least it did for me. I bet other people are better at it. I bet they cope in other ways. But I coped by taking care of people. And I coped by making my bond with my dad stronger and it just didn't feel like something I needed to bother with.

I guess I could have dated in more college, but the thing is, my dad hooked me up with a shared apartment with three other girls my age who were the daughters of his friends, and they were just the best but college was hard for them. They were homesick and their credit cards had super high limits, and the combination got them into a lot of messes. Messes I was always helping to fix. I was the designated driver every time. I was the girl you text a picture of your date and the place you're going to and when to expect you home. I was the girl you called when you had a flat tire or a fashion emergency or a pregnancy scare and you know what? I was really good at it.

I liked being there for people. I imagined it was what mom would have been like in college and it made me proud. So sure, I could have gone out on more dates then.

I mean, I was with Carter for six months. He was hot and we ... well, we did a lot of the things you do with your first college boyfriend. I thought maybe we'd get married and have kids and a future before he ghosted me. He didn't even bother to break up properly. And it turned out I wasn't as heartbroken by that as maybe I should have been.

There were a few others, but they were just casual. A sporting event here, a coffee hang out there. Some group things. But no one made me want to go out with them again. Except for Steve, but that was just because I felt bad that he was failing Biology. Once I'd helped him get his grades up, he didn't really need me anymore, and besides, I was busy, and I was happy being busy.

And honestly, have you met the guys in college? Would you date them? Because all I ever saw when I looked at them were boys who were going to run off at the first sign of real trouble and I'd be left at the funeral all over again — abandoned and alone.

Okay. That's a lot of baggage. That might be another reason why it's been a pretty dry spell over here.

So that's why I've never been in this position before.

I think my face is on fire. Again. It's Gracie Humiliation Month and everyone is tuning in.

"Hey honey," my dad says. "I just got back. Everything looks great. You're killing it!" He's so excited that he's doing his bouncing on his toes thing. "Come and give your old man a hug!"

I give him his hug and feel him freeze in my arms.

"Jasper?" he says and there's a weird note to his surprised tone. Almost like he half expected this and isn't quite surprised enough. Which is weird. Am I really so pathetic that he guessed I'd fall right into the arms of the boy who abandoned me the minute he grew up and came back to town?

"Adam," Jasper says quietly and I extract myself from my dad's hug.

Okay. I guess it's cards on the table time. Sort of.

"Dad," I say brightly. "I'm so happy you're here. I have something to tell you."

My dad's face has gone blank. He's looking from Jasper to me and back again and he looks so pale that I feel my familiar spike of fear that he really is sick and this really might be what he needs from me.

I'm ready to deliver.

"We got married," I say with a huge smile and show him the ring — I'm still surprised by how gorgeous it is. I have to ask Jasper about that. How did he find it on such short notice?

"No," my dad says. Just that one word. His eyes are still locked on Jasper's.

I glance over my shoulder at Jasper who is standing in the doorway to my bedroom.

My bedroom.

Jasper.

I have to slap my inner romance heroine before she swoons at that. But he's not even trying to look bubbly and bright with me. He's just standing there with his shoulders back and his chin thrust out in defiance like he's one half of two bulls squaring off to fight.

Ummm no. This is not how this goes.

"Well, we did," I say brightly. "This morning."

"Jasper was working this morning," my dad says, as if that settles it.

"Early morning. At dawn."

"No."

I fumble for my phone and get it out. Jasper's dad sent me copies of all the pictures which was terribly sweet of him, and it turns out also one hundred percent necessary.

"Look," I say, thrusting my phone out like a talisman to ward off punishment.

The first picture is of Jasper and I standing on the steps of the chapel with the minister behind us and the cute little church behind him. Golden sunlight haloes our heads and makes us seem to almost glow and whatever lens Mr. Hunt used caught the little dust motes in the sunbeam and they look like sparkles. Like literal fairy dust.

It's basically the most romantic thing I've ever seen.

My dad takes my camera with a grunt and flicks through the pictures, his expression morphing from denial, to surprise, to hurt.

"You got married and you didn't invite me?" he asks, still flipping through the pictures.

"I was afraid you'd try to stop us," I said. "I was afraid you'd be upset because you have this whole thing planned."

"Jasper's dad was there," he says, holding up the phone.

Oh yeah. I'd forgotten that the minister took a picture of my fake father-in-law with his arm around me after Jasper peeled out in such a hurry. It had been his dad's idea, and I didn't have the heart to say no.

"He was our photographer," I say pathetically.

"I can take pictures," my dad says and his mouth twists with hurt.

And this is exactly what I didn't want to happen. It's why I got married in the first place.

"Why?" he asks but he's not looking at me, his look of betrayal is directed right at Jasper.

I suck in a gasp of worry. I haven't talked to Jasper about this yet. We don't have a plan or a script to work from. Is he even going to know what to say?

He hesitates for a moment, and I grimace, feeling this opportunity slipping away. I begin to open my mouth to speak for him, but he shifts position and uncrosses his arms as if in surrender.

"I never stopped loving her." He's not looking at either of us. He's looking at the wall where a picture of my mom holding me when I was a toddler is framed. "It just took me five years to realize it."

Oh.

Oh, that's good.

It sounds so real in his voice that I almost believe it myself.

My dad looks back at me. "No."

And for just a moment, I think he really doesn't believe us, that even with the photographs as proof he thinks it's staged. Which would be accurate. After all, we staged all of this for him.

"You get your heir," I plead and in my peripheral vision, I see Jasper jerk in surprise. Had he not taken that part into account? "You get your happy family. You get everything you wanted. It's real. Look. One of the pictures shows our marriage license with our rings and everything."

He flicks through my photos, peers at them for a moment, and then shakes his head. "It looks real, sure. But you've been married what? A day? And he's been working for me all that time. Which means nothing has been settled. You can just drive on back to the church and annul it."

And now I straighten. "Don't I get to pick my own husband? Didn't you say I could? Well, I did. That doesn't mean you still can't have your competition. If you want to pick your heir that way, you can. It doesn't have to be my husband. But marriage to me is off the table. No one will blame you for that. You can tell them it was a whirlwind romance with my old friend who turned up again unexpectedly."

He grunts, still staring at the picture of the license.

I shoot a desperate look at Jasper. He looks a bit pale but he isn't jumping in here. Great. How do I convince him I'm married? Should I start making out with Jasper right here in front of him? The thought makes me horribly embarrassed for myself.

"No," he says and looks up finally, glancing from one of us to the other. "You haven't fooled me. Not even with a real marriage license as a prop. Not even with him moving in here. I think you're tricking me and you aren't married at all."

I open my mouth but he holds up a hand.

"No, Gracie. No more lies. I'll tell you what you can do. Convince me that you're really married. Convince me you aren't just going to get a divorce the moment I send those gentlemen home."

I'm nodding. That's reasonable. I can be very convincing.

"And while you're convincing me, your new husband will be one of the competitors, taking part in every event and being scored just like they are."

Jasper opens his mouth and I see his cheeks flushing, but I shoot him a pleading look — is this really so bad? He's good with cars. And it's just for a couple of weeks — and he shakes his head.

"Fine," he says, with no emotional weight to the word.

"Fine," my dad says like he just won a lawsuit. "Starting tonight. And if I don't think your marriage is real, you'll marry the winner of the competition, Grace. Deal?"

He coughs suddenly, a terrible wracking cough that shakes him right down to the core and he has to grab the wall to stabilize himself. When he's done my worried voice is small.

"Deal," I say.

"We have supper with the guys in twenty minutes on the patio. Tanner's already driving everyone in from the airport. Be there on time and remember, I'm going to need to be convinced."

And then he leaves, slamming the door on the way out and my eyes flick over to Jasper. He looks like he wants to bolt out that door, get in his Jeep and drive even farther than he did the first time. He hates me now, right? What guy wouldn't hate a girl for putting him in this mess?

"I'm sorry," I say, looking down. I can't even look at him. "I understand if you want to leave."

"I took vows," he says in a tone I can't read. But he hasn't moved and I can't look at him. I feel too awful.

"Fake vows," I remind him. "For a fake marriage. You don't have to stay and pretend it's real."

"What if I want to?" he asks and his voice is husky in a way that sends warmth all through me, pooling low in my abdomen.

"Want to what?" I ask hesitantly.

"Want to pretend," he says, and he steps toward me and his hands find my waist and for just a heartbeat, I'm looking up into those dark eyes and watching his Adam's apple bob and thinking he might just kiss me and that I would seriously enjoy that right now, but just when I think he's going to do it, he folds me into a hug instead and lets his chin fall on the top of my head. It's so sweet and I feel so safe that I almost don't regret that he didn't kiss me.

Almost.

Then

JASPER

I'm miserable and it's too hot. This popsicle isn't making it any less hot, and if my mom tells me one more time that I have to stay still and let my collarbone heal then I'm going to scream. I was sick of tv, so she told me to sit on the wicker porch chair and watch the road. The road in our suburban neighborhood has seen a grand total of three moms driving by in minivans and a cable repair guy. Everything hurts and the heat makes it worse. Why did I have to break my collarbone right in the middle of summer vacation?

"People get hurt all the time riding dirt bikes, Jasper," Mom told me. "Next time, don't show off. Wheelies get you broken collarbones, right?"

I don't like being told I was an idiot. I don't like our stupid street or this stupid brick house. I don't like living in the stupid desert. When I grow up I'm never gonna live in a house, I'm just going to go wherever I feel like whenever I want, and if it gets too hot I'll go to the arctic with the penguins. People do that, you know. And if I'm too cold I won't go to the desert. I'll find some kind of nice beach with water and palm trees and those colorful drinks you see on tv. I bet they taste way better than kool-aid.

It's while I'm dreaming about that that Gracie arrives on her bike. A pedal bike, not a dirk bike, so she probably won't break *her* collarbone and have to sit here on the stupid porch while everyone else is having fun.

"Jas," she says, giving me her huge sunny grin. She gives those away like they don't cost anything.

"Daff," I say and I look away because something about her looking at me always makes me uncomfortable. She's in grown-up shorts and a grown-up shirt instead of kids' stuff and it feels weird because just last year she was a kid like me and now it feels like maybe she isn't really a kid anymore, but how can that be true when I still am and I'm a year older than her?

She flips her curls over her shoulder and that feels weird, too, because why would I even notice? And then she's taking off her backpack and reaching inside and offering me an orange pop and a deck of cards.

"I thought we could play a card game," she says. "Dad's been teaching me poker."

"Like gambling?"

"We can bet M&M's." Her grin is twice as big as she pulls out a family-sized bag of M&Ms. "That's my favorite part so far. That and eating my winnings."

"I guess," I say. Secretly, I'm thrilled not to keep sitting here alone, but I can't admit that.

"Oh, and I brought that watch I fixed for you."

She holds out my old Timex. I got water in it and I thought it was ruined, but here it is, patiently counting down in digital numerals. She's even stitched up the worn edge of the watch-band. I don't know how to say thank you. I never do, but she also never stops doing this kind of stuff for me. Even when I'm being stupid to her.

"Thanks," I say and it feels weak. "I can't really pay you back, but maybe I can take you with me when I travel the world."

"I'd like that," her smile has turned shy and she looks up at me as she deals the cards. "We could play real poker in Vegas."

"Or that place in James Bond, what's that called?" I ask.

"Montenegro," she laughs. We watched all the Bond movies together last week. There was a binge week on tv, and I couldn't do much else but sit still. I think she secretly wants to wear the pretty dresses the Bond girls all get to parade around in. They look impractical to me. You can't fix anything in those.

"Yeah, we can play poker there," I say, picking up my cards. "Or wherever else you want."

"Deal," she agrees, and thinking about her coming with me makes me want to travel the world even more. It would probably be more fun with someone. We could play poker together. Or do whatever grown-ups do when they're on vacation. Drink those colored drinks, maybe.

And I have this weird feeling like it's already happened even though this is the first time I've ever thought about it.

Chapter Fourteen

JASPER

"Are you ... are you okay with this?" she breathes into my chest.

Let's see ... woman I'm crazy about in my arms? Check. I get to spend the next two weeks with her? Check. Soft and perfectly curved? Check. I'd say I'm pretty okay with that. In fact, I'm maybe a little too okay with it. I need to breathe carefully and remind myself this is all fake. It doesn't mean anything to her the way it does to me.

I'm *not* okay with competing in her dad's online games. I could do without that. But I owe her five years' worth of apologies, so I guess I can stomach a few weeks of awkwardness being uploaded for the world to consume. At least I know vehicles, so I won't look like a complete chump. Maybe if I keep my mouth shut and wrench, I can still get other jobs someday.

"I made you a promise," I say. "I think I can manage to see it through." I give her a slight smile as she pulls away so she can look up at my face. "I might even win. I'm not that bad with engines."

She laughs. "I don't think that part matters so much, but

Jasper, if I'm going to convince my dad that we're really married, we're going to have to do a lot of things together."

A lot of things. The thought gives me a swimming feeling in my belly — the good kind like you get at the top of a zipline just before you kick off and you're flying down the rope. Husband and wife things? Parts of my body start to stir like sleeping lions awakening.

Shh. Go back to sleep. It's not time yet.

She looks so worried that I almost laugh. As if she's thinking she's the evil villain from the silent films kidnapping the innocent heroine and forcing himself on her. Yeah, I'm not so innocent and she's not taking an unwilling victim.

"A true hardship," I say dryly.

"I might have to touch you," she says and I clench my jaw super hard to keep from shivering. I need to look away or that sleeping lion is going to wake up with a roar. "Kiss you. Be affectionate."

"Well, then I'm definitely out," I say in my best teasing tone.

"Do you need a safe word?" she presses, "Something you can say to get out if things are getting to be too much?"

I keep my tone dry as the desert — or at least the part of it that doesn't have the water bill footed by Adam Boomhower. "Yes, I'll say, 'I'm leaving. This is too much.'"

She laughs. "I'm serious. I don't want you to feel uncomfortable and I don't want to take advantage of you."

I blink and an image forms in my mind of Grace taking advantage of me, of her pressing me down on a bed and covering me all over with kisses and I have no words because yeah, I wouldn't mind that at all. I swallow and I have to swallow again, and my shorts are feeling a bit tighter than I'd like, so I take a careful step back. I need that prowling lion to calm the hell back down again.

Keep it light, Jas. Keep it easy.

"When it comes to me and you, Daff, you're always going to have the advantage."

She frowns. "I don't like that nickname."

The frown — for some reason — is all the libido crusher I need. Instantly, the savannah is safe again. I feel this hollowness in my heart. Like I lost something precious. Intimacy, I realize. I lost the sense that we know each other right down to the bones. We used to have that and there's just this big yawning emptiness where it used to be.

"You don't? You always said it was cute."

She looks tense. "There are a lot of things that have changed between us and about us since then. Which reminds me. I need to change my clothes really quick and then we can go."

I nod, taking a seat on a stool beside her kitchen counter. Why doesn't she like that nickname? It was our thing.

"Hey, Jas?" she asks as she shuts the bedroom door most of the way. She's left a crack so she can talk to me as she changes and the ease of that feels ... right. Maybe we can patch over that hole a bit at a time. "Where did this ring come from?"

"I saw it and thought of you," I say. No need to explain that it was a year ago. That I'd sat on the sand of Santa Monica after and stared at the stupid thing while sand got in my boots and totally ignored Sally Sharp, who was trying to kiss my neck and tell me that we could totally hook up if I wanted to.

"That's so sweet! I didn't even think you could get something like this around here, but you've always had an eye for pretty things."

Do I ever. There's a pretty thing just past that door.

"Will you be okay sharing this place with me?" she asks. I can hear her making an effort to keep her voice light. She's as upset about the Daff screw-up as I am. Wow. She must really hate that name. I'm an idiot.

I hear the sound of cloth sliding over skin. She must be fighting her skin-tight jeans to get them on. The visual lingers in my mind. I swallow and swallow again. Will I be okay? I don't know. At this rate, I might not be able to think straight, and I'll have to rely on her to do all my thinking for me. Which would be pretty inconvenient. I like this brain. It's been good to me.

"Just like old times," I manage but I have an idea. "I think I know one way to seem more like we're married."

I take a banana from the fruit bowl and spin it around my hand. I'm still playing with it when she comes out of her room in white skinny jeans and high heels. Very few women look better in skinny jeans than my fake wife. Can I say that out loud?

"What's your idea?" She asks, fussing with the clasp of her necklace. I love how the tip of her tongue sticks out like that when she's concentrating.

"Questions," I say awkwardly. "Why don't we text each other questions and answer them to get to know each other better."

She looks up at me with a suspiciously playful smile. "What kind of questions?"

"What have you got?" I hedge.

She shoots me a look that is more of a dare than a glance and takes out her phone.

Nicknames? She texts.

I think you mean aliases, I text back and wink at her.

I have neither, she texts with a shrug emoji.

Noted. Food allergies?

That's a boring question, she texts, her eyes meeting mine in a challenge.

But a useful one unless you want to swell up and die.

She shakes her head and texts. *Fine. None.* Her eyebrow raises and she gives me a naughty look, catching her lip between her teeth in a way that has me holding my breath. *Sexual history?*

Yep. It's history alright. You?

Way to avoid the question. But yes, there was a guy in college.

I didn't expect her to be so forthright and I'm surprised in a good way, but I don't like how my stomach clenches at the thought of her with someone else. Someone else in her bed. Someone else with his hands on her.

Just one? I text her. Keep it light, Jasper.

One was enough.

Tell me more.

We were together for six months.

So he was in heaven for six months? That must have been nice for him. How did he screw it up?

It takes her a long time to text back and I almost want to convince her to speak out loud, but she's frowning over her phone with her forehead all wrinkled in concentration.

He was playing on his phone after ... after you know ... while we were cuddling and he followed a rabbit trail down the internet and found one of dad's videos with me in it and I guess he freaked out. He leapt out of bed, making all these accusations that I tricked him. And he just never texted again. Or took my calls. I saw him a few times, but he'd just turn around and go the other way.

Replying in a text to that feels too insensitive even for an ice king like me. I meet her gaze, lift my hand and make a little motion telling her to come to me, and to my surprise she actually does.

I take her hand and roughly pull her close. Not so close that it might be taken as a play, but more possessively than a friend would. She needs me to be a bit rough so that she pays attention.

"People who don't realize what they have, shouldn't be missed when they get what's coming," I growl. Because wow, what an idiot that dude was. His loss.

"I think it was realizing what he had that freaked him out," she says, meeting my eyes with a steel I don't usually see in them. "It happens to me a lot."

She steps back, dismissing my attempt to strengthen her. She doesn't want that from me, I realize, and I'm surprised when the air between us cools.

"Let's go eat," she says, leading the way out of the house.

I follow, but I'm distracted. What did I do wrong? I need to turn this around fast. I text, my thumbs flying over the screen.

If you had to choose between eating a dead snake — uncooked — or watching all your dad's videos in a marathon, which would you pick?

It's a gamble. Her dad might be a sore spot, especially with that painful story in the background. Or ... she might like having someone understand what it's like to be the progeny of an online celebrity.

She lifts her phone, still walking, and then pauses to read my text and laughs but she doesn't stop walking.

Snake. She types back. *Would you rather be famous for being filmed skinny dipping or for being a celebrity's significant other?*

She looks very good from behind in those butt-hugging jeans and I have the best view from here, but I am not going to be happy until she lets me back into her friendship.

Depends on the celebrity, I text back. *I'm very into Tom Selleck.*

This time when she laughs, she stops and waits for me to catch up.

"Ready to go pretend to be married?" she asks me.

"You can tell them all that I picked you over Tom. It's something to be proud of," I say gravely, and I know I've won because she slips her hand into mine to lead me the rest of the way to dinner.

GRACIE

I like this playful side of Jasper. It makes me think of old times and even better, it makes me think this won't be a disaster, that we could pull it off, that it could even be fun. I'd like to linger with it, dancing between teasing and revealing — but I can't.

It's show time.

Literally.

The cameras are already rolling when we arrive at Dad's pool patio. Pretty Boy is filming with food in one hand and his camera in the other and Chase is madly working his phone to keep our social media on point. Our timing is perfect. The vloggers have just arrived and are clasping hands with my dad and giving him those shoulder-bump hugs that men do.

They're a rowdy bunch and I'm immediately greeted by someone booming out "Graaaaaccce!"

Before I can catch my breath, I'm swept away from Jasper and into a group of laughing men. One of them nurses a bottle of beer, watching as Travis and Hollis lift me on their shoulders to a round of cheers from the others. My dad is laughing as he helps himself to the Texas BBQ his chef has whipped up and we do a full lap around the pool deck with the guys beneath me whooping, before I'm finally put back on the ground again. I feel more like a human trophy than a woman.

"Here's yours, Gracie," my dad says, putting a basket of BBQ in my hands. "Dig in, fellas!"

I try to look for Jasper, but before I can, Paul intercepts me. His shop builds rat rods, I think. He's a bit shy but kind of a good-old-boy.

"Gracie, I hope you aren't made too uncomfortable by all this," he says in his slightly southern drawl and aims a shy smile at me. "You know that it's all in good fun, right? Of course none of us is fool enough to think you're really gonna go to the altar with him."

He laughs like that's the funniest joke, and he figures I'm in on it and I laugh nervously, glad that at least one of them gets how silly this is.

"Honestly, I'm just here to meet your dad and build some cool cars and drive 'em around, so don't you worry none about me."

He tips his truckers cap to me and then he's gone and I breathe a sigh of relief at how human that was.

My relief is short lived. Before I can blink, Travis is there, giving me that intense stare he usually reserves for the camera.

"Kids?" he asks, his eyes glaring into me and I don't know if he's serious or playing to the camera that Pretty Boy practically has shoved in my face. I can see the sauce in the corner of Pretty Boy's mouth. I give him a glare.

"There aren't any around here," I say, taking a bite of BBQ. Where has Jasper gone?

"How many do you want?" Travis says, still doing that mock serious thing he does that I'm pretty sure is a facade. "Kids, I mean. I want to know what I'd be getting into."

My phone buzzes. I pull it out to see Jasper's text.

Question: How many parakeets do you want to have? I need to know what I'm getting into.

I choke on my food and Travis smacks me so hard on the back that my sunglasses go flying off my head and hit the pool deck. They break on impact. They were more a fashion statement than a high-impact clothing item. But I liked them. I got them on sale.

"I've got you," Travis says, taking his own Oakley's off and arranging them on my head. The arms are sticky. As these are car guys, that could be anything from Gorilla Glue to motor oil. I'm praying for motor oil. I don't want to live the rest of my life with Travis's cherry-red Oakley's stuck to my temples.

"Thanks?" I say, feeling stunned, which I suspect is the usual reaction to Travis. But he's gone before I can say more than that, off to scrounge up his own plate of Texas Beef Brisket.

"Oh, Gracie," Mark — another contestant — says when I bump into him. He's bearded. I'm not a fan of beards, and his seems to own his face and possibly significant portions of chest real estate. It looks aggressive, maybe it will do a hostile take over of his back. "I brought you a shirt."

"Thanks," I say lamely, looking at the shop shirt he offers me, complete with his logo on the back, a sewn on patch with my name embroidered on the front, and high-vis stripes that go horizonatally around the chest. "It's so nice."

It's an XXL.

My phone buzzes. *I vote we go camping for our honeymoon. You already have the tent.*

If I could see Jasper, I'd glare at him, but every time I try to scan the area to find him, someone else is there. Randy gives me a branded T-shirt - medium this time, so they're getting closer — and Hollis tells me I have the right kind of attitude to drive a stick shift, which I think is a compliment, but it's hard to tell.

My phone buzzes. *Married women don't drive other men's sticks.*

I roll my eyes. Wow. I should text with Jasper all the time. For a man of very few words, he sure is gregarious when his thumbs are captaining the ship.

I've barely eaten my dinner when my dad stands up and steps onto a nearby decorative tree stump. It was intentionally put there by the landscapers for moments like this.

"Gentlemen!" He announces, grinning like a kid, which is how I know this is going to be bad. "I'm excited to welcome you to what I'm calling the Heir Games!"

There's a cheer that's half real and mostly just the guys egging him on but it only makes him grin even more. I wish the ground could open and I could disappear into it like entering a fallout shelter from the fifties.

"You guys think this is all fun and games." He's clearly playing to the cameras. People are going to watch this. My friends. People I went to college with. People who hate me and always wanted to prove I was a joke. "But I am going to put you through your paces." He turns directly to the camera. "And you guys at home will never have seen anything like this. We're talking junkyard builds, dry lakes races, hill climbs, and off-roading adventures. It starts tomorrow and it's all happening here. Paul, Randy, Hollis, Travis and Mark you know well. Watch and subscribe to their channels. Tomorrow, their guys will be here filming, too."

Because we didn't already have enough cameras in our faces.

"Fritz from 'Fritz Goes Faster' couldn't make it. He had a family emergency last night. Everyone is going to be okay, but he won't be able to be here for the Heir Games."

Everyone makes appropriate sympathy sounds, but my dad is still talking. "We planned this event for six people, and six are going to run it, which is why I'm slotting Jasper Hunt in Fritz's place."

Now they're silent. No one saw this coming.

"As you all know, Jasper is the son of my long-time friend

and former business partner, Mikey Hunt." Dad's face is tight when he says this. He never talks about Mikey. Not even to me. They haven't spoken since the funeral. Since the yelling when no one could find Jasper and they were all on edge. "And he seems to think he'd make a good son-in-law."

There's a sparkle in my dad's eye when he says this and he waves to someone over my shoulder. I turn to see Jasper there, nursing a lemonade.

"Come over here, Jas."

Jasper strides over, looking wary and slightly unhappy. I think he prefers being behind cameras, not in front of them.

"Think you're man enough to marry my daughter?" Dad asks, tucking his head in tight beside Jasper's so the camera can zoom in close and get them both.

There's a long pause and Jasper's face is blank. When he speaks its still not very revealing.

"I guess I'm man enough for just about anything."

This is, apparently, the right answer because it makes everyone laugh.

"You heard it folks! Tune in tomorrow and every day this week. You're going to love what you see!"

I grimace. Jasper does not look happy at all. My dad's arm is still around him when he says, "Get your beauty sleep tonight boys. We start rolling at four-ahy-em!"

There's a collective groan and Jasper finally manages to disentangle himself from my dad.

I quickly tap out a text to him.

Question: Would you rather marry me for real or work for my dad the rest of your life?

He meets my eyes before he texts me back.

You're no Tom Selleck, but your hug game is way better than your father's.

Chapter Sixteen

I've been so busy teasing her that I completely forget that we're going to be sleeping together in her bed until we're standing in her cluttered apartment looking at it from the doorway.

She laughs nervously. "Good thing I bought a queen, right?"

Even if I wanted to take the floor, there's not enough space to lay out anywhere. I stretch my arms over my head, conscious of how my T-shirt tightens over the muscles. I'm achy and tired and ready for that bed. Excitement will do that to a body.

"I could sleep in my Jeep," I offer, giving her one last chance to back out. I can be a gentleman. Really.

"No one will believe we're married if you're sleeping in your Jeep."

She pushes past me with a polite little head bob and blush like she's in my way instead of the other way around, and just her hip brushing past mine ignites a fire in my belly that I have to force to calmness. I swallow.

We aren't really married and she's not really inviting me into her bed. I have to keep reminding myself of that. Well, she's inviting me there to sleep, but not to seduce her. Not to run my hands all over her and draw sweet sounds of contentment from her lips. And thinking about how I could do that won't help either of us.

"Maybe we're unhappily married," I suggest.

She pulls an eggplant-colored sleeping bag from her closet and hands it to me and her eyes are huge and a little sad.

"Are we?"

I can't tell if she's playing or if she means it. Can she tell? Can she tell how much of her life on camera all the time with her dad is real and how much is pretend? Is it as mixed up in her head as it always was in mine?

I settle on the truth. "Umm. No."

She batts her eyelashes at me and okay, I guess she was playing. "Well, then you should probably sleep here. With me."

"I don't mind," I say. Everything here smells like her. Like vanilla and musk and Gracie, and the scent alone is almost too much for me. If I dwell on it, I'm going to lose my mind.

"I'll just get ready for bed then," she says, slipping a few things from a drawer and then closing the bathroom door behind her.

I busy myself with the sleeping bag and then shuck off my boots, socks, and jeans as fast as I can so she won't catch me undressing. I'm not usually this shy, but something about being here in her bed — even if I'm divided from her by twelve mils of down filling — has me nervous as a teenager sneaking through his girlfriend's window. I've only done that once and it was a disaster. The memory is really not helping.

She comes out of the bathroom in a halo of light in the teeniest pink shorts that I've ever seen and a big faded T-shirt that once was black and had "The Eagles" on it. I know. It used to be my T-shirt.

I swallow down a pang and a memory at that and it eats at my heart in a way I can hardly handle.

I know I should look away. I know I should close my eyes. I mean, I pretend I'm looking at the crown molding, but actually, I'm watching her out of the corner of my eye and I'm memorizing every inch of exposed skin. Her curls bounce adorably, and then she flicks off the bathroom light, and the bedroom goes dark except for a little nightlight in the bathroom that barely outlines everything in a weak, aqua half-light. I sigh with relief - well, limited relief anyway. Thank goodness this sleeping bag is one of those super thick kinds and I kept the zipper to the other side of the bed from her. She won't be able to tell that I'm actually very far from relieved.

I hear her slip into bed beside me and if you want to know how to torture me for information, like say if I am a P.O.W. or something, well this would be how. Put Gracie right beside me with the strict understanding that I won't touch her. Let me breathe in her intoxicating scent and feel her warmth as she settles down beside me.

I'll talk. I'll spill state secrets. It will be so much more than name, rank, and serial number.

She flicks her hair behind her head and a strand falls across my face and I don't even move it. If her hair wants to sleep on top of me it can. I promised I wouldn't touch and I won't. Not even that.

"See?" She whispers. "Totally platonic."

And *of course* I am not going to touch her. I respect her too much to betray her trust. Actually, I wouldn't touch anyone against their will. That's not even a question. But even without touching, I'm in some kind of exquisite hell here.

I'm lying right next to the girl I've been obsessing over for … well, for always, if I'm being honest. The one I'm so infatuated with that I was willing to pretend marry her. The one I moved all the way back here to apologize to. And every single nerve of my body feels like it's on high alert. If she rolled over right now and touched me — anywhere at all, even the tip of my nose — I'd be in real danger of embarrassing myself, because she has me *hot* for her and I can barely breathe as I replay her standing in the bathroom doorway in my old shirt over and over again, while I breathe in that sweet smell of her and feel the side of my body next to her growing slowly warmer and warmer.

I want more. Make it never stop. Make it go on forever.

But it really can't, or I'm not going to get a wink of sleep. In a desperate move, I try conversation, whispering, "Are all the things out there projects?"

"Mmmhmm," she murmurs. Is her voice always so husky at night? I should keep a record of whether it is or not. For science.

"I thought I saw Tanner's taxes."

"He's terrible at them," she giggles but then she goes still.

"What's wrong?"

She shuffles and I hear the sheets move. "Nothing."

"Just tell me, I'm not good at that game where I have to guess." I'm really not. Girls love playing it and I'm pretty sure I lose no matter what I say.

Her voice is small when she speaks and the vulnerability opens my heart like a biometric lock on a safe.

"I told you an embarrassing story about my college boyfriend and how he watched my Dad's show online and then rejected me after sex, but you never gave me a straight answer about you. I feel ... embarrassed that you know that about me and I don't know anything like that about you."

"Ah, but I don't watch your Dad's show after sex. Kinda kills the vibe, I think."

She laughs despite herself. "Not that, silly, about the girls you've been with."

"You don't want to know."

"I do. It's only fair. Tell me a story."

I turn onto my side so I can face her through enough sleeping bag to keep an arctic explorer alive and I whisper, "I was kissing a girl named Jules once and I stopped midway through the kiss."

"It's not embarrassing to be distracted," she scoffs.

"I wasn't distracted," I say, laughing softly. "I just realized halfway through that she wasn't the girl I wanted to be kissing and it just felt wrong after that. Like a betrayal."

"Of Jules?"

"Maybe. Or maybe of the other girl. Or maybe of me. Or maybe of destiny or something. I don't know. Either way, when I suddenly was still and unresponsive, she thought I'd had a stroke and began to dial 911."

"You're kidding," she's rapt with horror —as she should be.

"I couldn't convince her there was nothing wrong. Not even when the paramedics got there and were furious that their time had been wasted. I was so embarrassed that I never called her again. And she didn't call me. I guess she wasn't ready to be with a stroke victim at the ripe old age of twenty."

She's laughing now. "Who were you thinking of when you were kissing Jules?"

I freeze for a moment and then try to play it off casually. "The girl from my dreams the night before. I'd been cuddling her in the dream. I think I wished it could be more."

"Jasper?" She asks in a small voice and I'm afraid she's going to ask me to clarify who that might have been. Instead, she whispers confidentially, "Would you cuddle *me*? Tonight was ..."

"A bit of a night," I agree. And my heart is beating so fast that I'm afraid it will explode.

"How do you know?" she asks as I gather her in my arms, the sleeping bag still keeping its thick guard from my chest down.

"I'm your husband," I whisper in her ear. "I know these things."

"What else do you know?" she sounds sleepy.

"I know you like pumpkin pie, and helping people, and that

you hate dancing when people are watching, and your singing voice is atrocious. Right so far?"

"My best friend is at the Mayo Clinic getting tests done for a mystery disease," she confesses in a tiny voice. "And I worry about her getting sicker. What if they can't figure out the problem."

"It will be okay," I say, knowing it's a useless thing to say. I wonder how she copes with a dead mom and a needy dad and a best friend who is ill. And I realize — again — that I could know that and I could be helping her with it. I could be the friend she needs to lean on, the one who shows up when she needs it. I suddenly don't want that to be someone other than me.

"And I think my dad's sick," she says in a small voice. Is it rough like that because she's crying?

Suddenly all thoughts of seduction are far away.

I pull her close and tuck her head into my chest and bend my face over her head so I can press a kiss into her hair. And even though her soft hips press back and against me and one of my arms is trapped under her in the curve of her waist while the other is tucked over and around and could easily "slip" and caress her breast, the time for sexual thoughts is over. It's replaced entirely by this new instinct to protect her. To keep her safe. To show her that she can just rest and be taken care of for a little while instead of always caring for others.

"It's why I agreed to do this for him," she murmurs. "It's why I married you instead of just saying no. I think he's dying. That's why he's on about all this inheritance stuff and seeing me married."

Her voice trails off and I make soothing sounds and press kisses to her hair and she shudders on a sob that seems half-trapped in her chest. I want to kiss it free. I want to tell her she's probably wrong, but as I think back, I think all the evidence is mounting. She might be right. Her dad might really be sick.

"I just can't bear to break his heart before he goes," she

confesses. One of her hot tears slides down her cheek and soaks into the shoulder of my T-shirt and I think this might be the moment where she took my heart out of my chest and put it into her own.

"It's okay Gracie, honey," I whisper in the darkness. "I'll take care of you. It will be okay."

And I keep murmuring those things and kissing her sweet hair until she's almost asleep.

"Why did you agree to it?" she asks and the words are barely distinct.

"Because you asked me," I whisper back.

I don't think she hears me, and I'm fine with that. And I don't think I'll be sleeping at all tonight. Not when I can be memorizing the feel of her in my arms, the heave and sigh of her sleeping breath, the way she snuggles in against me after she falls asleep, and the little sounds of satisfaction she makes. It's pure torture and the best pleasure I've ever experienced, all rolled into one.

If this is fake married life, then I want to be fake married forever.

Chapter Seventeen

GRACIE

I wake to the smell of Jasper — masculine with a hint of whatever his deodorant is, something citrus and pine, I think. Sunlight pours through the window. His arm is draped over me and I spend a moment enjoying the feeling of this casual closeness. With him asleep, there's no embarrassment when I let my eyes trail over the light dusting of dark hair on his arm, enjoying the way his hand is so much bigger and rougher than mine.

In sleep, his eyes are closed, thick black lashes displayed in a perfect half moon. His lips are slightly parted and fuller than usual, and his breath gusts between them. It makes me wonder what it would be like to put other things between them. My own lips, perhaps, my tongue, the tip of my finger.

I swallow down that thought as a memory floods through me. We'd been camping, both our families together. I was fifteen. I felt awkward in my own body that summer, wondering who would ever want to embrace my gangly limbs and A cups. Most people didn't notice me in the baggy car event T-shirts I always wore, so I'd tried wearing something more fitted with a lower neckline to school the day before our trip and no one had given me a second glance. Fashion, I had realized, was not the reason no one was asking me out on dates. Though I was at a loss to think of what the reason was except to think that maybe it was that I just wasn't that attractive.

Hello, fifteen-year-old-Grace, it was your Dad who even then was a loud mouth with a garage building monster off-road trucks and terrifying any teenage boy who so much as glanced at his daughter. But I didn't know that then.

I'd stumbled out of my tent to the fire ring. I could hear the low murmurs of our parents still half asleep in their tents. Jasper, however, had opted to sleep by the fire and that's where I'd found him with an arm flung over a log like it was a lover. He was cuddled right into it. I'd never really noticed Jasper *like that* before. Not like he was a guy at school or someone I might potentially date. He was just Jasper. He was just there. But sleeping there with his lips parted and a sliver of tongue visible, I'd paused. And in that pause, I'd noticed for the first time that he had a little stubble on his jaw and a light fur of hair on his arm and that his biceps and shoulders were actually pretty defined even in sleep. His sleeping bag had fallen to his waist and he wasn't wearing a shirt and his chest rose and fell when he breathed, in a way that made me want to touch it, to touch him, to run my hands through his dark hair that was shoulder-length and tangled back then.

He was beautiful. So beautiful that it made something inside me ache.

And the rest of the camping trip I'd been awkward and tongue-tied whenever he was there, so much so that my parents were worried about me.

"Is it because your dad wants to try this online thing, honey?" my mom had asked. "You don't have to be in the videos."

"Of course she wants to be in them," my dad had said. "It's

just the trip. It was too stressful driving up here. Someday, I'll have a helicopter to bring us here so we don't have to waste all that time on the road."

It wasn't the trip. It wasn't even my dad and his helicopter dreams — which, for the record, I thought were silly.

It was Jasper. It was like I couldn't even look at him, but I couldn't stop looking. And suddenly what had been an easy friendship had become complicated by carefully hidden desires. Because I knew my parents — my dad especially. If they had any hint about how things had changed for me there would be drama. Family meetings about it. Family meetings *with* the Hunts about how to handle it. Talks about sex and how to use protection and why we shouldn't even need to use it because we shouldn't ever go there.

And my weak flickering attraction would be extinguished under a flood of good intentions and plans. They'd make a bunch of decisions to "protect" us and make sure things were done "the right way" and then I'd really never be able to look at him again and I'd literally die of embarrassment while he looked on in disgust at this stupid girl who thought she could be his girlfriend just because their families were friends.

Yeah, I'd kept my mouth zipped up and let my burning attraction for him be my own private secret. It was a good secret. Something to cherish and return to again and again while in the real world no one knew about it. And I'd had two good years of enjoying it before he disappeared from my life. Two years of getting to steal glances at him while my family shared Christmases, two years of vacations and weekly dinners, and catching glimpses of him down school halls or in the shop. And I'd enjoyed every bit of my precious secret right up until he broke my heart.

But did he know he was breaking my heart? Maybe he'd thought it was a passing thing for me. Like it clearly had been for him. Maybe he thought we were just friends who got caught up in the moment.

But even if he had, it was a dick move to go off like that when a friend needed you.

All at once, my buzz at waking up beside him is muted. I have a new secret now, in the opposite direction. The secret that I'm not really married to Jasper and not really in love with him, and this secret isn't fun and tantalizing. It's potentially a nightmare.

Remember Gracie, you weren't going to let yourself feel things for him. You were going to be the watchman making sure nothing happened. Great job with that last night, by the way. Asking for cuddles isn't exactly being the frost queen, now is it?

And I never did get a proper answer to my question, did I? He won't tell me if he's been with other girls. He won't tell me if they were serious relationships. He just keeps dodging that question. What is he hiding?

With a sigh, I roll out from under his arm, let myself take one last glance at him over my shoulder, and feel again that stab of attraction that jolts right through me at the idea of my old crush asleep in my bed, and then I'm off to the bathroom, to showering and getting ready for my day. I do everything I need to do in the bathroom and I do it twice as quickly as usual. I don't want to hold him up or be a selfish roommate.

To my surprise, I'm distinctly disappointed when I open the bathroom door and see the bed empty. Wow, Grace. You've got it bad. Do you know how messy this will be if you get involved in this fantasy? I know exactly how messy. Heartbreak kind of messy. But is it so wrong to enjoy the cuddles and the kisses to my hair that he doesn't think I noticed? As long as I don't get emotionally tied up, is there anything wrong with having a little fun and indulging past Grace? I haven't had someone kiss me like that ... well, ever, if I'm being honest.

Jasper's sleeping bag is zipped and stowed, and the bed made up. He's tidy, I remember and realize both at once. Very tidy.

I can keep my emotions just as tidy.

I can.

I'm careful and strangely anxious when I walk into the open living space. Is he going to judge me for the tragic mess my home is?

Maybe not. He's sitting at my kitchen counter patiently gluing eyes back on that broken fishing rod with a look of complete concentration in his eyes and the tip of his tongue stuck through his lips. An overwhelming gut-deep urge to kiss him unaware, to kiss him deeply and possessively, and to take that tip of tongue into my mouth and caress it with my own, seizes me. And suddenly my knees are weak and things are growing entirely too hot in places that aren't going to be used any time soon.

I run a hand through my hair to try to disguise how I'm drawing a very long breath in.

Jasper looks up at me with his dimpled half-smile and asks, "Coffee?"

He's made coffee. Because other than abandoning the people he loves, he's basically perfect. He's done something to his short hair that makes it look neater and he's changed into fresh jeans and a T-shirt.

"I hope you don't mind. I put the laundry in," he says with a nod to the closet where my stacked washer and dryer are. I gape at him. He does the laundry?

"I have to be gone in about ten minutes. Umm." His smile turns charmingly awkward here. "Did you want to ride with me or drive separately?"

I am momentarily speechless as I stare at this beautiful man and his gorgeous dimple and his laundry-doing, fishing-rod-repairing hands.

"Separately," I say stupidly. "I want my freedom."

He bites his lip.

"Gracie?" he looks suddenly stricken.

He puts down the rod and picks up a matchbox car and rolls it back and forth over the counter nervously. It's the car from on top of my dresser. The one he gave me when we were kids. I feel a blush coming on. What does he think, knowing that not only did I keep it, but I have it displayed in my bedroom?

The car stops. He bites his lip and meets my eyes.

"I hope I didn't cross a line last night?"

"No," I manage. Or if he did, he can keep crossing it. I might know it's a terrible idea to let my emotions get wrapped up in this, but I'll take all the cuddles and hair kisses that I'm offered. "No, that was fine."

Great move, Gracie. He's never going to cuddle you again after all that enthusiasm. Wait. Am I really sabotaging myself and the boundaries I've put up to keep myself safe? This is crazy. I'm a mess. I clearly don't know what I want. I can't operate like a functional adult in his vicinity. I'm worse than my hot-mess apartment.

I try to shove my hands nervously into my pocket and the ring on my left hand catches on the edge. I pull them back out and look at my hand. The wedding ring is still there. His ring.

I feel hot all over, looking at it on my finger.

My watchman is pathetic. He's not watching anything.

"Do you need something for breakfast?" I ask, trying to take refuge in hospitality, and worried that I might not have anything but fruit. I'm not great at keeping my fridge stocked. Not when I can just walk over to Dad's and take any of the world-class groceries his chef stocks.

As if on cue, both of our phones buzz. I look down at mine. The text is a group text from my dad.

Crew breakfast. Shop. 8 am.

I meet Jasper's eyes. "Okay," I say nervously. "Let's go be fake married again."

He nods but his mind seems to be on something else and he glances at me a few times before setting the fishing rod aside. It's fully repaired.

"I guess I'll see you there," he says, and there's a bit of a wistful look in his eye as he picks up the camera cases he had at his feet, and leaves without another backward glance.

I can't help the sinking feeling I get watching him walk away, as if I made the wrong decision by choosing not to ride with him. I don't have too much time to dwell on it, though. My phone is buzzing again. It's Melissa.

First tests down. More today. Won't be able to talk until the afternoon. Wish me luck!

Good luck! I text back, and I really hope I can text her in the afternoon, because maybe she has the answer to whether it's okay to be totally, maybe even fatally, attracted to your fake husband.

JASPER

She might not be riding with me, but I don't think she regrets last night.

I'm in a good mood when I hop into my Jeep, fire up her smooth LS, and pull out of Gracie's driveway. I pass Adam sitting in his lifted Ford Raptor as I pull past his mega-house. His eyes narrow under the brim of his trucker hat, but he's going to have to pick a lane. Does he want to see Gracie married, or does he want to be mad that a man spent the night in her house?

He can't have both.

I'll admit, I have enough of my dad in me to enjoy tweaking Adam. He's always taken life so seriously that he's one of those people who are just too easy to tease.

I check my texts while I'm driving. I know. I shouldn't. But I have a lot of lonely road to cover and it's hard not to scroll through them as I cruise down the blacktop.

There's a chain of texts from my Dad.

9:15 - No pasta tonight, I guess.

10:50 - I'll admit, it's lonelier here without you.

That one makes me feel a bit guilty.

12:45 - I'm glad for you, son. I've always wanted a family for you. You were never meant to be alone.

I don't know how I should feel about that last one. Because I'm still alone. This fake marriage is only temporary and I'm pretty sure that when it's over and Gracie has gone on the next leg of the journey and left me at the side of the metaphorical road, that I won't be able to ride with anyone else. I'll never get the scent of her out of my nose. I'll never get the feel of her body pressed against me as she sleeps out of my mind. And I'll never get the sweet look of her brown eyes showing how she trusts me out of my heart. I'm ruined. Ruined for anyone else but her.

But I was already ruined. I've been ruined for anyone else by her all my life. I've never bothered with anyone else — not really. I can't give away a heart I no longer have.

Some things are made for just one use. Drinking straws. Wineskins. Paper napkins. And just like those things, I think I just have one use in me. Just one love to offer, one time. And after that, I'll be too stretched out, too crumpled, too ruined for anyone else.

Maybe I should be thinking about protecting that use, if I only have one. But I'm not because here's the thing — if you can only use something once, you should save it for the best. And I've already found the best.

I'm still thinking that as I drive, listening to Lee Brice on the radio, and I never really paid attention to this song before, but as the singer waxes on about kissing his girl from her head to her "toes-es", I find my fingers drumming on the steering wheel and I'm pretty damn happy for a used up paper straw.

It's in that moment of bliss that I get the text from Scotty.

Thanks again for letting me be a part of your big day. The papers all got filed at City Hall. Sending you a pdf for your records. Congrats, man. Seriously, so happy for you.

I nearly steer off the road — thank goodness there's no one

else on it as far as I can see in either direction — and have to throw my phone between my legs and get a hold of both my Jeep and my breathing before I can look at it again.

Fuck.

Fuck.

Fuck.

I pull over and reread the message three more times.

I can't breathe. This is a heart attack, probably, and I'll die right here on the road and maybe that's the best-case scenario right now.

When I can think — and honestly, this is barely thinking — I text my dad.

Did you ask Scotty not to file the papers?

Waiting for his answer is an entirely different kind of torture than last night was. Three little dots dance and tease and then the texts pops up. I'm glad I didn't eat at Gracie's place. I feel like I might be sick.

Oops, he texts back.

I've broken out in a cold sweat. A sudden burst of adrenaline has my heart racing a million miles a minute. She's going to think I set her up. She's going to think I did it on purpose. She's going to think I tried to trap her and deceive her and use her.

I pull out and start driving again. I don't even realize how fast I'm going until the State Trooper flashes his high beams at me as I pass. Shit. I take my speed down and mentally thank him for giving me a pass this time.

What am I going to do?

Obviously, I have to tell her. And, obviously, I can't be kissing hair or cuddling now. Not now when she might interpret that as taking advantage of her. *Is* it taking advantage of her? Probably.

I flex my hands uncomfortably. I can still smell her sweet scent if I let my mind wander, still feel the heat of her tempting slender body drawing me in, still see the curve of her hip when she lays on her side and I want her so badly it *hurts*. And now I don't dare so much as brush against her.

How crazy is that? It would have been honest to touch her, kiss her, even make love to her when she wasn't legally my wife, but now that she is, all that could be thought of as levels of betrayal. Or at least, it will be until I tell her what happened and give her options.

What options are there? Annulment? I don't know what's involved in that but I think the fact that we haven't had sex makes it more possible. Or at least, that's how it is in the movies. Maybe it's not even a thing in real life. Movies lie about stuff all the time, right?

Divorce? She could divorce me, no problem, and that would be totally legitimate. I wouldn't stop her. She'll probably want that once she hears what happened.

I find that I don't want it. I want to go on like this. Which just proves I'm a sucker for punishment. Who *wants* a fake relationship that has no possibility of a future with someone they're wild about?

But I like pretending to be married with her. Even with all this added ridiculousness, it just feels right to have her around. If I tell her, I know Gracie, she'll want to fix it right away. It will be like that fishing pole I mended this morning or Tanner's taxes. She won't be able to help herself. She won't rest until it's put in order again. And then all this will be over.

Maybe I could just delay a little bit and then bring it up later. Just a few days. I mean what's the hurry? We have to pretend for at least two weeks, so we can't sort this out until after that anyway. Why make her stressed out for two weeks when she doesn't have to be?

No, that's a cop-out and I know it. I run a hand over my face. I'll have to break it to her somehow and let her decide what to do next.

I pull in to park behind the BOOM Enterprises shop with

the other vehicles. I open the pdf and look at our signatures signed right there on the legal document, and my heart is in my throat, my hands are sweating, and I realize with sudden clarity that there's nothing in the world I want more than to be able to keep this — to keep her — but also that the only fair way to treat her is to give this up, willingly, quickly, and without ever suggesting that I want to keep her worse than I want to keep my own heartbeat.

The looming understanding that I'm going to have to share this with her — that all the friendship we've rebuilt, all the closeness and fun, might just disappear under this sudden new pressure — is so overwhelming that I seem to sleepwalk through the morning.

I make it inside to find Adam is revealing to the crew that Gracie and I eloped. I hardly even register the furious looks aimed at me from the guys.

The moment Gracie walks into the room, though, and our eyes meet, I feel a flash of possessiveness. That's my wife. Actually, legally mine. And something flips in my stomach and my brain. Something that makes it suddenly very important that I stand right next to her and glower at everyone while Adam breaks our news to the crew.

"Make sure to try to get some lovebird shots of the two of them through the shoot," Adam tells them. "Then, when it comes time to reveal it to the audience we'll have a believable montage of footage."

"Why do we have to make it look believable?" Tanner complains. "Either it is real or it isn't."

Which explains why he's still just one of the guys working in the shop and creating drone footage instead of stepping up to be Adam's right-hand man after my dad left.

"What's the point of all this if she's already married?" Pretty Boy asks Adam, "And to *him*?"

He gives me a sour look and I cross my arms over my chest. I want to take Gracie's hand but I'm suddenly shy about touching her. It's like someone slid a plexiglass sheet between us that keeps us from each other as long as I have this secret and she doesn't.

"Are you saying something about my choice of husband?" Gracie is asking him and he's stammering like a fool and then Adam puts his hands up to make peace.

"Look," he says, "the guys didn't come here to get married anyway. They came for the competition to win my empire and that hasn't changed. Besides, throwing her real husband in there is only going to make this all more exciting for the audience. They're going to love it. The views will be through the roof. Although, Jas, I'm going to ask you to be filming as well, okay? I love your work and I want to make sure we really get some great shots on this one. You might have to work a bit of overtime to do both. But as to the viewers, don't worry! We just have to explain it to them first — the whirlwind love story, the shock I felt in finding my daughter married. The evidence that it happened." He turns to us. "You guys have proof right? Beyond the photos? A marriage certificate?"

Gracie looks at me, pale. Okay, here's my big moment. I have to do the right thing and not run away from this. My heart is pounding in my chest and I can feel my cheeks flushing.

"Yeah," I say and feel kind of proud of myself. I've done it. I've confessed the truth right in front of them all.

To my surprise, Grace is not freaking out. Instead, she takes my hand in hers and smiles at her dad.

"We're all set," she says sweetly. "You don't have to worry about a thing, Dad."

He smiles really wide. "We'll have dinner at my place tonight. We need to celebrate as a family." I clear my throat and he pauses, going incredibly red in the face as he says, "Umm. So. Tell your dad it will be at seven."

And then he pushes past me like he's going to be ill and

needs to get out of the room fast. Maybe he really is going to be. He hasn't seen my dad in years.

"I think we're in for it now," Grace whispers to me as the crew filters out. "We really have to sell this."

"We told you not to touch her," Tanner mutters as he passes and the other guys give me similar glares. I know one thing. When these two weeks are over I won't be operating a camera for her dad anymore. Not if I want to keep all my teeth.

I look down at her nervously when they're all gone and it's just the two of us. She was so easily accepting in front of everyone. Am I going to get hammered by her now that we're alone?

"Thanks for doing this, Jasper," she says, standing up on her toes and kissing my cheek and I'm so surprised that my mouth falls open. "You're the best fake husband a girl could ask for. Don't worry, I'll make sure it's not too bad for you."

And her eyes are huge and caramel brown and the look in them is just so sweet, and I feel my heart sinking. Did she not understand my confession?

I'd very clearly said, "Yeah."

"Uh, Grace," I say feeling worried. I rub the back of my neck with one hand.

"Yes?" she says.

"So, we're actually married," I say, trying a second time.

She smirks at me and says. "And we had a wonderful wedding night, don't you think?"

I look over my shoulder and there is Pretty Boy filming. Shit. Not the time for confessions.

Her phone rings and her eyes light up, and there goes my chance.

I shuffle back into my day and start setting up my camera equipment. We're headed to a junkyard and Adam expects me to help film the vloggers as they each choose a vehicle from the junkyard for an ultimate budget off-road build. I need to choose one, too, but Pretty Boy is supposed to film "sneak" shots of me doing it while I'm also filming — so like kind of a break of the fourth wall sort of thing.

He's actually excited enough about the artistic merit of this that he seems to almost forgive me for breaking the crew's rule about going near the woman that I married. Real married, not fake married. I get a feeling like a stone in my gut every time I confess to that even in the privacy of my own head.

I'm excited about the idea, too. Not excited enough to erase the awkwardness of this whole setup or the guilt I feel about the secret I have not managed to spill to Gracie, but excited about the way we're going to shoot this. It's pretty clever and I think it's going to work.

We're deep into the junkyard and I've already been shooting Hollis for three hours before I remember to text my dad.

Hollis is actually a really great guy: super easy to get along with, treats you like an equal even though you're carrying his camera, explains everything to the audience very clearly and with a kind of down-home wit that makes you automatically want to be his friend and invite him to all your cookouts. He's explaining the merits of a smaller versus longer wheelbase for off-roading and why he's choosing an absolutely classic Chevy Blazer as his junkyard build truck.

I keep rolling but pull out my phone.

Dad, I text. *Dinner. 7. Adam's place. I don't think it will be pasta.*

He texts back, *No.*

You owe me one. I have to explain to Grace about the papers.

What's to explain? She wanted to get married. You got married. He sounds smug in his text.

She wanted it to be fake.

It was never going to be fake.

Just come to dinner, I text, and then I stop looking at the phone. He'll either come or he won't. Either way, it's going to be awkward. But either way, I get to spend it with Gracie, and I can't shake the feeling of her in my arms last night. It keeps creeping back into my mind like a suggestion that maybe if I can manage things just right I could have her like that for real.

"Hey man," Hollis says in an undertone when we finish up and start walking back to the group. "I didn't know there was a thing between you and Boom's daughter. I just want to say I'd never step on your toes."

I wave away the apology.

"No, really," he says with an easy grin. "This is fun. And great entertainment for the people at home, you know? I love building things, but for real I have a serious girlfriend at home and I was only ever here for the fun of the builds and the races. You know they're going to be epic right?"

"I'm counting on it," I say, tapping my camera.

"Just so you know, I've got your six. You don't need to watch your back."

He gives me a solid nod and I nod back. At least someone doesn't want to kill me. Not like Tanner who is giving me the evil eye from where he's filming Travis. Or Cowboy Roger who spits and narrowly misses my boots.

Yeah, it's gonna be a long day.

I get a text from Gracie as we're wrapping up.

Question: Would you rather eat dinner with both our dads or spend a week in the Amazon naked?

I text back promptly, *Naked alone or naked with you?*

The three bubbles on the screen are there teasing me for a few minutes and then her reply arrives, *Would it make a difference?*

You make all the difference, I text, and it's absolutely true.

Chapter Nineteen

GRACIE

I am a mess.

Yes, anyone could have predicted this. Anyone but me, apparently. One night in bed with him and he's all I can think about. I have questions.

First of all, how does he smell like actual heaven? I peeked into his bag and he literally has a bar of soap — generic, white soap, an electric buzzer, a toothbrush, toothpaste, and a single stick of Old Spice deodorant in there. That does not add up to smelling like something I could gladly drown in, and yet every time I turn a corner my brain is sending some kind of signal to my nose to try to smell that again and every time it fails to find it, it returns with a disappointing report.

Second of all, how are men so incredibly sexy when they sleep? I've never slept with a man before. I've had sex. But no one has ever slept beside me and just seeing him there with that defined forearm slung over his eyes, and his hand limp and relaxed, as his chest expands and contracts with his breath made something contract inside of me. It might have been my heart. It might have been *significantly* further south than my heart. No one should look that good while they're asleep. It's just asking to be kissed awake like Sleeping Beauty and isn't that considered sexual assault now?

Third, he's impossibly hard to read and it's driving me crazy. What is he thinking? Is he freaking out about all of this? Is he thinking about backing out? Does he hate me? He doesn't say much and his mild expression is so opaque that it seems impossible to guess. I would have known with the old Jasper but how do I know what this new, mature, damn sexy Jasper wants?

I'm so grateful when Melissa texts me midway through the day that I nearly cry. I text her back in a flurry of thumb-tapping in between tweaking online ads.

I've been dodging the devil-eyes Chase keeps turning on me all morning and this is a welcome relief.

"You could have said you were getting married!" he huffs as he leaves, seeing that I'm now distracted on my phone and leaving me to it. I want to run after him and fix it but if I don't spill my emotions to Melissa soon I'm going to be an even worse disaster. I desperately need someone in my court.

Tests all done. I'm exhausted. We're headed to the hotel before I go to my folks' place.

Have a good rest, I text her with a hug emoji. I shouldn't burden her with this.

Chase texted me, she replies. I never should have let Chase meet Melissa. He's obsessed with her, age gap notwithstanding, and last time she visited me at work he charmed her into giving him her number. *He asked me if I KNEW. What does he mean, KNEW?*

Her thinking face emoji has me hunching in my chair ready to spill my guts.

I don't want to worry you.

Are you kidding me? I'll be so much more worried now! What's going on.

I'm a hot mess. Like really. A mess. I can't figure myself out.
In what way? Her text comes in fast.
I got married.
YOU WHAT?

A flood of GIFs follow the words. Celebrating Wedding Crashers with champaign bottles, a cartoon cake topper with a middle-class biracial couple, then a confused-looking Jimmy Fallon.

It's fake, I hurry to clarify. *Or, at least, it's supposed to be.*
Supposed to be?!
It's Jasper.
OMG. OMG. OMG. Why?
My dad is hosting a competition for my hand in marriage like it's the freaking Middle Ages. I just wanted something safe to keep him from marrying me off.
Oof. Talk about choosing the least rational option.
Melissa!
Okay, okay, what's done is done. Tell me you're not in too deep.
I'm not.
Tell me you're not falling for him all over again.
I'm not.
He broke your heart.
I know.

I don't need her to remind me about the heartache I felt five years ago.

Sure, you're not. That's only why you've been so hung up on him for years that you don't even date.
I've dated.

Wow, even my text sounds defensive.

What you did with Carter doesn't count. That was like a rebound gone bad. It was desperation. It was "I swear I'm not in love with the guy I wasn't even dating who left me" screwing. That's what it was.
Wow, you paint me in such a positive light.

Don't take this the wrong way, Gracie, but you aren't the dating type. You're the marrying type. You're the "let me make you dinner and darn your socks" type.

I am not.

Let's try an experiment. Tell me how many actual pairs of socks you have at home waiting to be repaired.

Not fair! I like helping people. What does that have to do with dating?

It's just not who you are, Gracie. You're a one-man kind of woman. What you did with Carter sucked because in your mind it was basically cheating.

I didn't cheat with Carter. Neither of us was with someone else!

But it felt like it, didn't it?

I don't answer. It did feel like that. I'd felt guilty the whole time. I'd felt like I was going to get caught, like it was a big secret, like I didn't dare let anyone know. Which might have been why I didn't bring him home to meet my dad. Which might have been why he found my origin story so shocking, Which might have been why he ended it. Wow. Maybe I owed Carter an apology. I didn't think I even had his number anymore. Would he be on Instagram? LinkedIn? Not likely. TikTok was more his speed.

Gracie? Look, don't be mad.

I text her the sad face emoji.

Listen, just hear me out, okay?

K, I text. I don't feel okay enough for the full word.

This could be your big chance. Have you thought of that?

Big chance for what? To date?

LOL. No.

What then?

To get Jasper, silly. He's stuck pretending to be your husband. You could ... I don't know, show him what he's been missing. Show him why he should stick around and not run away like a little boy.

Harsh.

She sends me three shrugging emojis.

I guilted him into helping me with this. What if I scare him and he takes off again and leaves me here to my dad's crazy plan.

What if he doesn't?

What if he gets mad and thinks I'm taking advantage of him?

What if he doesn't?

What if he never speaks to me again?

Remind me how that's different from the last five years.

I'll think about it, okay? I text, but my heart is throbbing painfully in my chest.

Okay. Don't let me hear about it from someone else if you take this thing to the next level. I need a nap though, so maybe wait until later to convince him he's the love of your life and he never should have left.

Melissa!

She texts me three sleeping emojis and I know the conversation is done. And that leaves me sitting in my office, staring at my phone, thinking of Jasper. Thinking of how good he smelled. Thinking of how amazing it was to have him cuddled around me. I can't wait for tonight. I want to do it again.

But first I have to have dinner with my dad. And his dad. And we have to convince them both that we're married. And I have to do it all while convincing Jasper that he made a huge mistake when he ran away and left me. That break between us — it's been driving me crazy for years. The one thing I can't fix. The one thing other than death, that is.

Maybe if I fix this, maybe if we can be friends again at least, or more than that — is it okay to think about more than that? Maybe it will fix this feeling in my heart like all of this has always been my fault.

I open my phone and scroll to the picture I keep there for moments like this. It's of Alisha and mom and me. They were in that car that day because of me. Because I wanted to make a book about their adventures. Because I wanted to show that girls could be bad-ass off-road wheelers, too. And look what happened. If they hadn't agreed to pose for pictures for the how-to part of the book then they never would have been in the truck that day, driving down that narrow bit of highway. And if I hadn't convinced Jasper to drive up separately with me to take the pictures, then he wouldn't have been there, too, and they would all be okay and there wouldn't be anything to fix.

But you can't fix the past. "You can't fix the past, Gracie." That's what my dad says when he sees me crying about it and almost, *almost* I believe him.

Chapter Twenty

JASPER

I'm trying to unload the project vehicle I found at the junkyard long after everyone else has gone home. It's very resistant to leaving its new home on the back of this trailer. I'm not excited about the project like I usually am with something new. It's not that I don't think that I can do the work. It's just that I don't care. And that's not like me. I don't usually do things I don't care about. But I'm doing this.

I'm scowling as I think about it. I haven't been around Gracie in years, and all she's seen me as since I came back is a flunky — first working for her father, then slotted in as her fake groom, and now trailing the pack in an online race for her hand. If I want to impress her, then I need to show her more.

Wait. Am I trying to impress her? I pause and run a hand through my hair. I haven't really stopped to think any of this through. The drive of events has been carrying me along and now here I am, tangled all up in the wild and unbelievable life of the girl I've been obsessing about for years. And I think maybe I have a choice. I could just keep drifting along, letting fate take me, or I can decide what I want right now and try to push for it. But what exactly do I want?

Her. The answer is there before I take a second breath. I want her however I can get her. As a friend, if she'll allow that — and I think we're edging into friends-again territory already. As more than that if she decides she wants it, too. I want to push this as far as it will go.

I clench my jaw. That's a big thing to admit. It feels like almost a relief to admit it to myself. I want Gracie Boomhower to whatever level she'll let me have her.

The footage I took today isn't going to help with that. I need her to see me for who I am and respect me for it. And right now, I'm making other people look good and myself look like a backup plan.

Today, I made Hollis shine from his cleft chin to his perfectly sneakered toes. I made Travis look like the king of chaos, catching a few candid clips of him backflipping off of his choice of project and absolutely sticking the landing like he's a pro athlete and not just a country boy who wrecks vehicles and films it for the nation to watch.

But, I'd also filmed a great B reel for the projects, and I'm pretty sure they'll need most of that footage. I managed to show both the strengths and weaknesses of every build from rusted cab corners to rotten floors to a frame that had been boxed by the previous owner.

That was what I need to show Gracie. That I know what I was doing. That I'm competent, not just an accessory to her world. Plus, it wouldn't hurt to find somewhere private to talk to her. Maybe she'd want to explain why she was so calm about our legal marriage. Maybe she'd just want to enjoy herself doing something for Gracie instead of everyone else. She needs to get away for a bit and I need to go with her. Then I can see what she wants because what I want doesn't matter if it doesn't line up with her.

I should text her and see if she has free time before this dinner with our dads.

Busy? I text her and when she doesn't reply, I text, *How do you feel about sunsets?*

"Is that a pick-up line?"

I freeze. She's right behind me. So close that I imagine I can feel her breath on my neck and for a second I can't think at all as heat washes through me. I feel like I've been busted, but I don't know what my crime is.

Was it a pick-up line? I hadn't meant it like that.

Words aren't working on my tongue, so I settled for turning around and raising an eyebrow to remind her that I don't do pick-up lines. And she's *right freaking there* and my breath snatches away in a way it never does around anyone else, and I feel that familiar ache like she's a magnet drawing me toward her and any kind of resistance physically hurts.

She's looking tired and wrinkled from her day, her curls untidy and slipping out of the clip she's put them up in. She couldn't look better to me right now. I want to sneak my fingers in under that collar where the button has popped open and revealed the edge of her lacy bra. I want to see if the skin there is as silky soft as it looks. I want to taste it and brush all the softest parts of myself against her *right there.*

Uh oh. If I don't calm this down I'm going to be in trouble. My jeans are already feeling too tight. I'm going to have to start wearing old man loose fits like my dad if I don't get a handle on this.

I grab the camera and tripod I had set up to film my own unloading sequence and stow them in the bag trying to do anything I can to distract myself from Gracie and her deliciously exposed skin. My cheeks are hot and so is everything else, and my words come out thick as I heft my camera meaningfully.

Eyes up here. Please, up here.

"There's a whole lot of desert out there about to light up for the camera as the sun goes down, and I thought I'd take a few shots before dinner," I say.

"Oh. I thought maybe we'd ride together." She twists a curl around her finger, biting her lip and she looks nervous, which is crazy. Gracie has nothing to be nervous about. Unless this is where she asks for the divorce.

What do heart attacks feel like? I should have searched that after the first one this morning.

"You can have whatever you want, Grace," I say, having to cough when my voice comes out too low. I mean that. About the ride. About taking pictures. About the divorce. About me. Whatever she wants.

She nods but there isn't a lot of certainty behind it.

"I, umm, am I taking advantage of you, Jasper?" she asks in a small voice as I lead her to where I parked my Jeep. She's adorable when she's nervous. I want to leave her stewing about it just to watch her chew her bottom lip like that.

"Well, you can chip in for gas if you're worried," I say, quirking one side of my mouth in amusement. She can take advantage of me whenever she wants.

She's biting that lip again and it's lush and full and I want to bite it, too. Gently. While I kiss her. I feel like I've been zapped while trying to jump-start a vehicle. Every nerve of my body is on high alert and ready for action. And now I can't shake that image of kissing the corner of her mouth, of running my hands through those tangling curls until my fingers get stuck in them, of pressing her warm body to mine and then closing my eyes and just absorbing the feeling of her, the presence of her, like a plant takes in water.

I miss what she's saying to me. What are words when we have bodies? I've got it bad. She takes a step toward me as if she can feel it, too. As if her body knows these words mean nothing compared to what we could do if we just slid our skin against each other and forgot the world.

Some of her fumbling words make it through to me. "It's just that I basically guilted you into being married to me, and it's so much trouble for you, and so much stress, and I'm already regretting pushing you into it."

"Gracie," I say quietly as she steps back and crosses to the passenger door of the Jeep. I don't know if I'm begging her to stay or telling her she should leave. I don't know which it should be. I'm just overwhelmed with the *her* of her right here near me and legally tied to me, even if it's temporary, even if it's just for convenience. It feels real.

"It wasn't fair for me to ask," she says opening her door.

I open mine so I won't miss anything else she says. "Gracie."

It's a prayer, I think. A prayer for mercy because all my thoughts are winding me tighter and tighter and I'm not sure I can bear it. And at the same time, it's a prayer of thanks because I love this tension. It's riding the edge between pleasure and pain and I just want to keep riding it.

It's like off-roading. The best trails are the hardest ones, the ones where you can't see where your wheels are and you're an inch from falling right off a precipice and rolling the truck to rubble. And the thrill of it has me hard in its grip and I just can't stop. I can't make it stop because I love it too much.

She's still talking like she doesn't know I'm being shaken by emotion like a floormat after a desert run.

"It just seemed like a great idea at the time and now I'm realizing that I really took advantage of you and—"

"Gracie," I say again, this time with authority and she finally looks at me. Those eyes. Mercy. "You can take advantage of me any time."

She goes pink. She's heard my double meaning. But she plows on with her rambling apology, dropping her gaze so she's looking at her fingers twisting together in her lap instead of having to look at me, but the problem is that now I'm looking at them and I'm imagining them threading through my hair as I draw her into a kiss. And I wouldn't stop with a kiss to her lips. That wouldn't be fair to the rest of her. What would her neck think? Or the wing of her shoulder blade? Or her inner thigh. They'd all need a turn. And I'd give them all their due. Slowly. I'd take my sweet, sweet time over it.

"I was just so upset for so long and now I realize that you're still my old friend and I shouldn't have roped you into this mess and wow. Yeah. I'm a mess. I just ... what was I thinking?"

"Gracie," I say and I have to swallow down this longing to kiss away all her worries. That's not mine to take. Not mine. Not unless she says it is. "You can be married to me for as long as you like. It's no problem for me."

"It's not?" she looks up at me and I melt at the torn emotion in her brown eyes. At the way her lower lip wobbles. She can have anything she wants. Anything at all. It's already fucking hers.

'You are never a problem." I pause. I don't want to have this conversation here in front of her dad's empire, where I'm nothing and no one. "Will you come with me to take pictures of the desert?"

"Yes," she's smiling slightly, like she finds my insistence on this amusing.

We have a wonderful time in the desert. Gracie doesn't bring up the marriage again. Or our families. Or our past. Or the competition. She talks with me about photography instead and I tell her about my favorite shoots — the Race of Gentlemen last year — and my least favorite — hello Chad and his wedding, but I did owe that guy.

I remembered this canyon from when I was about sixteen wheeling on my own for the first time. I'd thought then that it was picture perfect. I help her over a wind-beaten fallen tree and then snap a shot of the way its whitened branches are reflected in black shadows on the orange desert ground. I show her and she grins.

"Take one for me," I say, pushing the camera in her hands, inhaling the scent of her hair when she leans in to ask about the settings on the camera.

"Sometimes I forget how stunning your work is," she says quietly as she scrolls through the pictures I've taken.

I look over her shoulder and see a candid I took of Travis today. The sun catches his eyes and it makes him look like a cherub caught dressing up like a gremlin. I'm proud of that one. I think I caught his essence in it — like if there was one picture ever that said *Travis,* it's this one. But is it the skill of the piece she admires or the man in it?

I feel a sudden burst of something that twists in my guts. This could be us, sitting side by side on a fallen tree as the sun sinks into the horizon, me snapping playful pictures of her and more serious ones of the scenery. Her, laughing as she steals the camera and takes one of me. Me, rolling my eyes at her as she cackles like this is the funniest thing ever.

Or.

Or she could divorce me and I could go back to roaming the earth, sleeping in cold hard beds, my only happiness in my work, without connection or home or friends and she'll marry someone else. Maybe not one of these jokers, but someone. Someone who isn't me. And she'll mend his clothes and he'll live in her jumble of perpetual chaos and maybe make some chaotic babies and that bastard will love his life and be the happiest man on earth and I already want to smack him hard in the jaw and tell him he doesn't deserve any of it.

But none of that is real. This is real, right now, the two of us laughing and smiling in the desert and I feel myself warming and relaxing and opening up in a way I haven't in ... years, I guess. Years and years. And it feels good, like when a tense muscle finally releases.

And I'm still smiling that goofy smile when she starts to lead me back to the Jeep.

"Don't forget, I promised to build you an online empire to rival my dad's," she says coyly.

"I don't need that," I say reflexively.

"I'll build you a website. We can put your work on it. I'll make it the best possible, and I'll add some reviews from your stuff, and then we'll get you the best photography jobs. You can work all over the world."

"Really, I'm fine," I say, but I wonder if she wants me to do this so that I won't be around embarrassing her when it's all over. Her fool of an ex-husband always hanging around the place hoping for scraps like Tanner does with Big Daddy Boom.

"A promise is a promise," she says but then she goes quiet as we drive toward her dad's house and I'm worried that I've hurt her somehow.

"You can build the site," I say as we pull into the driveway.

"It's the least I can do, Jasper," she says and when she says my name I shiver and I'm right back in fantasy land kissing her neck with my lips parted so my tongue can taste what I'm kissing. "After all, you gave me this fake marriage. It's kind of a big deal."

Wait. I've already parked. The engine is already off. She's opening her door.

"It's real, though," I say, a sudden stab of panic rushing through me. I thought she understood. I thought she realized …

"That's right, real," she says, drawing herself up with a look of concentration on her face before she comes around the Jeep and hooks her hand through my arm. "I can't slip up while we're at dinner, can I?"

Her laughter sounds a bit high and tight but not nearly as tight as the fist gripping my lungs right now.

Shit.

I couldn't have been more clear. But she still doesn't realize, and she needs to know. She needs to know right away.

I open my mouth, but I'm cut off by a voice from the opening door.

"There you two are! Don't let Jasper give you bad habits, Gracie," Adam says with a wide grin. "You should teach him *your* punctuality, not learn his relaxed view of time."

I glance at my watch. It is 7:01. Yeah, dinner's going to be a real treat.

GRACIE

This is what I imagined life could be like. This right here. Sitting on this dead tree so close together that his hip brushes mine and sends tingles up my spine and all through my abdomen like he's infected me with some kind of Jasper virus.

He's talking about his work and his hazel eyes are shining with passion.

"What did you do all these years we were apart?" I ask him in wonder and he just talks about photography after that. About nature,. About the places he's been. About really neat car builds he got to shoot. It's his whole life, I realize. Taking pictures of beautiful things in the exact perfect way that suddenly they're immortalized.

I can hardly hold in my astonishment when he reveals his pictures of Travis and Hollis. They're ... perfect.

In marketing, we're always trying to boil our brand down to fewer and fewer words. What is your brand in a five-word slogan? How about in three value-rich adjectives? How about one?

But here he's captured a whole person in a single shot. Like the most powerful marketing on the planet. If I were Hollis I'd buy this one that makes him look playful and genius and squeaky clean all at once and I'd pay a million bucks if that's what it took and plaster it on *everything* because it's perfect.

His life has been this for the past five years — obsessively perfecting his craft. And he's so, so good. But I get a hint of something else in his work, in how all his shots seem to have subjects angled away from him or looking at something else. I think he might be lonely.

"I could take you someday," he says and he seems to be in earnest, his eyes shining. "I could show you these places. We could do a shoot on the snowmobiles of Alaska and then go fishing for a week, just you and me and a backpack."

And I want that. I could *do* that.

"I could take you to Dubai to film the custom cars of the truly rich — like, richer than your dad — and then I'd show you my friend Rupa's home and you could meet her family. Her husband wanted three children and she wanted four but they compromised on eight. Or at least that's how they tell it."

I'm already laughing. I could do that, too. And I'd love it.

"Do you want children?" I ask him but he just looks into the distance looking sad, so I change the subject. "The backpack thing sounds nice. Kind of like *Alone*."

"You watch *Alone*?" he asks, staring at me.

Is there something wrong with how I look? He's staring so intently.

"Umm. Yes. I've watched every season," I admit, looking down. I shouldn't have looked down. He's so ... so damn sexy that I feel tongue-tied when I look at him. He can slouch and make it look good. Even now, hunkered down on a tree, he looks like he's about to pounce on something. He's always like that — just a breath away from action. It gives him this kind of energy that's addictive to be around, like anything could happen. Like he might take me on an impromptu photo shoot in the desert before dinner. I've missed it.

Suddenly, I want to keep him from being lonely. I want to be the friend he needs as he goes out into the world. Honestly, I could do what I love with a laptop and an internet connection. I could do it anywhere. I could do it with him.

"I've watched every season, too," he says with a shy smile. "I applied to be on the show but I didn't make the cut."

"You did not!" I exclaim. "You were ready to take ten items and go live indefinitely in the woods?"

"The cameras they send don't count towards the ten," he says like this is shocking.

"Because they film the show! There's no show without them."

"How wild is that? The one thing," he stumbles over one like maybe it's not entirely the truth, "that I'd want to bring and they just hand it to you for free."

"You're crazy," I say.

"Don't you want to be on the show? You watched every season of it!"

"Yes. While eating chips and chocolate ice cream in the comfort of my own climate-controlled home on a couch so comfy it could be declared the comfiest couch in Utah."

"I can't tell if you're lying about that, but now it seems even harsher that I won't be able to write that article for Couches Monthly," he says dryly, but he can't hold his straight face, and then we're both laughing.

And for some reason, I feel so bright and sunny just being with him that there's hardly any need to talk. I think I say something about building him a website just to try to contribute, but my mind isn't on it. My mind is off far away in a daydream about traveling with Jasper, about being the friend who keeps him company as he takes the most beautiful pictures in the world, about spending long days in the sun giggling with him, and long nights cuddled close in a single sleeping bag, and for just a moment I wish we were really married and that this wasn't fake, and didn't have to disappear at the end of these two weeks.

I'm barely even thinking straight when we reach dad's house and he reminds me to pretend to be married. As if I could forget.

"It's real," he says and I can't help the almost hysterical laugh that pops out of me because wow, I wish it were real and that he was mine to keep. I try to brush it off, but I think I make it worse, and then my dad is there ushering us into the house, nervous as a mother hen. I can tell because he's hung up on us being a minute late. A literal minute. And he obsesses when he's nervous about something else.

I should be thinking about how to fix whatever is bothering Dad, but my mind isn't focusing correctly. It's like a broken camera, all it can seem to bring to clarity is Jasper walking in front of me. Jasper with a stiff expression on his face but still so ridiculously attractive with that unshaven scruff and strong chin. I want to run a finger along his jaw to see if it really is as sharp as it looks. Jasper with those deep brooding eyes that seem to be able to see things in me that even I don't know are there. Jasper with that completely mind-blowing body. No one, and I do mean no one, should have shoulders that broad for his height. He's not a tall man, and he's lean so there's not a lot of bulk there, but those shoulders are to die for and they taper into the narrowest waist and ass, and I ...

I drag my eyes upward before I get myself in trouble and my gaze meets Jasper's dad who is sitting in one of my dad's over-sized leather chairs on the outdoor terrace where it looks like we're going to eat. The gas fireplace is lit — more for show than warmth on a night like this — and maybe the reflection of the flames is what is making his eyes dance, or maybe it's something else.

"I always wanted a daughter," he says when he stands to hug me in greeting and there's a weird twitch in my dad that looks an awful lot like bitten-off jealousy, and another twitch in Jasper that looks — I swear — just like the twitch in my dad.

Feeling awkward, I return the hug and then give my dad one for good measure, which seems to soften his moody sulk.

I pull back and I'm surprised all over again when Jasper slings his arm around my shoulders possessively. A moment ago I was mentally drooling over him. Ten minutes ago, I was building a life with him in my mind, but now? What in the world is going on? I mean, I guess he needs to sell this ruse that we're married but this feels so much like claiming his territory that something in me rebels.

I try to laugh it off, easing myself out from under his arm and I say, "Wow, once someone says you're a prize, everyone wants to put you on their wall."

It's not very subtle, but then again, neither were they. Jasper shoots me a look that's both guilty and apologetic and just that little acknowledgment is enough to calm me down a bit. They might be three idiots, but I'm still me and I'm a woman, not a prize.

My dad clears his throat, looking suitably chastened. "Let's get some dinner and then we'll talk."

It's BBQ. It's nearly always BBQ at my dad's place. He didn't pick a chef who was a finalist on *Grill Masters* as his personal chef for no reason.

We sit around his table by the pool. It's this massive oak thing with the BOOM Enterprises logo inlaid into it and the overhang that shelters the table is made of heavy timber and a faux thatch that makes it look half mountain lodge and half tiki hut. Lanterns are hung around the perimeter and they flicker like they're real flame lanterns even though I know they're LEDs. It's all *so* my dad. Over the top, dramatic.

"So," he says. "You're married. That deserves celebration. To the kids!"

He raises his glass to Jasper's dad who pauses for a heartbeat and then raises his, too.

My heart is in my throat. I haven't seen them together since the funeral, except for that one shouting match. I'm pretty sure Mikey broke his knuckles punching a tree during that. He's been so kind to me these past couple of days that I almost forgot that he and my dad aren't friends anymore.

"I've thought for a long time that Jas was dumber than a brick not to marry you ages ago," Mikey says and there's something gleaming in his eye as he looks at me. "But I'm glad he came to his senses. Family is everything."

I feel awful. I've deceived this man. I've lied to him about something important. Jasper is looking at his drink, his cheeks flushed. As ashamed as I am, he must be doubly ashamed.

"Family *is* everything," my dad says and he's practically glowing. He's at the head of the table where he loves to be, sitting in the only chair that has arms. That's intentional, I'm sure. My mom probably ordered it like that. She loved indulging him. "And I'm glad that the BOOM family is back together, drawn together — as it always should have been — by marriage and blood. And I'm just so pleased, kids. I'm sad you didn't see fit to invite me to your wedding, but I'm just so pleased."

He tears up, and at first, I think he's just emotional, but then he starts to cough and the cough goes on and on, wracking his whole body. I'm on my feet and rubbing his back before I realize what I'm doing. This. This is why I'm lying and why I'll keep on lying. My dad is really sick and he isn't telling me about it which can only mean one thing — his chances of survival must be really low. It won't hurt me to make him happy for whatever time he has left, will it?

He must be thinking the same thing because when the coughing finally releases him, he says "For whatever time we have left on this earth, we're family. And that means everything. So, I think we should celebrate. I'll throw you the biggest, grandest wedding party you've ever seen and this time, I'll be there!"

"No, Dad," I protest.

He looks confused. "I could fly you to the end of the aisle in my helicopter, Gracie. No other bride has that."

"Adam," Mikey says, stealing a little glimpse at my dad and for a moment they hold each other's gazes like they're going to fight, and then something between them melts. "I think that might be true."

If Dad was glowing before he's blazing now. "And you'll need a house. A grand house. One that you pick. You can't live in a shed in the back."

"No, Dad," I say again.

"Nothing is too good for them," Mikey agrees and he lifts his drink and my dad lifts his with a smile, and oh my word, these two. If one was having a bonfire then the other one would be throwing gasoline on it. I'd forgotten how dangerous they were when they got together. I'd forgotten how they could be like brothers pushing each other to worse and worse heights.

"We'll film the whole thing. We'll do promotional deals with contractors. We'll build two of them exactly alike and give one to Gracie and Jasper and one to a lucky fan."

"No," I whisper in horror. This is spiraling out of control. This is worse than raffling me off to a car guy with a famous online channel. This is my whole life made into a marketing tool.

"It's going to be amazing, Gracie!" My dad says, not even listening to me. "Start thinking about what color you want your kitchen."

"No," Jasper says and he says it so quietly that I would never guess that anyone but me can hear it. *I* hear it, of course. *I* get little goosebumps all over my arms at that tone. It's the kind of tone that stops a war, that restores order, that gets stranded hikers off of a mountain. "Gracie has had the wedding she wanted. And she has the home she wants right near her father, who she adores. There will be no additional weddings, or houses, or publicity. My wife gets exactly what she wants. Not what you want," he says, pointing a finger at my father and I swear to God my eyes are going to fall out of my head. He turns that finger like a loaded gun onto his dad. "And most certainly not what you want."

Everyone is silent and for a moment I think there's going to be a fight. It will be like five years ago with Jasper blasting off into his lonely life of running from everyone and everything, and my dad and Mikey duking it out until they don't speak again.

But I'm wrong. Instead, my dad breaks out into one of his huge, idiosyncratic laughs. If I lost my vision, I could find my dad in a crowd of fifty thousand just by listening for that laugh.

"Good move, son," he says clapping a palm on Jasper's shoulder. "Always take your wife's side. I did and ..." his voice drops off as we all freeze. He just stepped into a swamp of sorrow and self-loathing that everyone around this table shares.

To my surprise, Jasper glances at me, his eyes unguarded for a moment. There's fear there and hurt and something that looks lost, and I can't help myself. I put my small hand over his larger calloused one on the table. I don't even realize that everyone is watching that until my dad clears his throat.

"What I meant to say is," he pauses for another coughing fit. "Family is everything. Which is why I've done a thing. I know my Gracie would never enter into marriage lightly. She's not the fooling around kind. And I know you wouldn't disgrace her by marrying her and running, Jasper. I know that. But I'm also betting on it." His grin could put a shark to shame. "Did you know there are people who will take bets on just about anything? It's crazy, right?"

Uh oh.

"I met this guy in Las Vegas and he takes bets on social media pop culture. I guess they had word that you two love birds got married. They're taking bets on how long the marriage lasts."

No.

"So I placed a bet myself. I placed a bet on until death parts you."

No, no, no.

"Bit of a long-term bet I guess, but it felt like the right kind of dramatic. None of us will see the money multiplied by twenty — no one but your kids, I guess, but it feels like the right kind of bet to make."

"I ..." This is crazy. What has he done? "I ... Dad, what did you bet?" I ask him in a voice that sounds strangled even to me.

"Well, I bet everything, Gracie," he says, waving his hands as if to encompass the house and shop, the helicopter, and the fleet of vehicles. "Everything I own. I know. It's a crazy, totally unnecessary gesture, but I just wanted to show you both that I'm on your side, betting on this with you. I might not have been there for the wedding, but I'll be damned if I'm not committed to the marriage!"

I think I might pass out. No, really. That's the thing that happens after your vision starts crackling like an old tv, right? It's the thing that happens when you can't catch a breath.

I hear a forced laugh beside me and then I feel the warmth and surprising firmness of Jasper's arm slipping around me, drawing me into the protection of his chest and he whispers in my ear, "Breathe Gracie, just breathe."

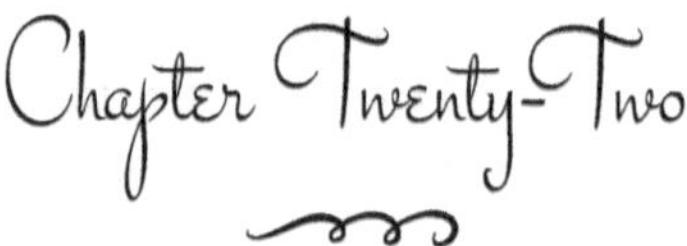

Chapter Twenty-Two

Fuck. Fuck. Fuck.

This mess is getting worse and worse. There is no fucking way that Adam Boomhower has bet his entire net worth on his daughter's marriage, but I can tell by the way that she's hyperventilating that she believes he has. And I know Gracie. Gracie, who always thinks the best of people. Gracie, who always idolizes her dad. I won't be able to convince her otherwise.

"What have we done?" She wails in a whisper into my chest as I hustle her into the door of her house.

I made hasty goodbyes for the both of us and claimed I'd heard a sound that might be a rod knock in my Jeep engine that I needed to figure out before tomorrow morning. Our fathers had nodded sagely at that. Rod knocks are serious business.

"You can use a bay in my garage here," Adam had offered generously.

And I'd kept her close to me as I hurried us out past the pool and down the winding path to her place nestled in among the sycamore trees.

The moment the door closes behind us she pulls away and I feel cold with her warmth gone. I don't like it. If I had to pick, I'd hold her to my chest for the rest of my life.

"What have *we* done?" I can barely contain my disbelief at that. "What has *he* done? Your dad is being ridiculous."

"He thinks we're married, Jasper. Married. Of course we wouldn't get a divorce if we were really married."

My heart seems to want to be a surfer these days. It's just up there riding the wave of those emotions when her next words crash me back to reality.

"But it's all fake and now he's going to lose everything."

"I really don't think he will," I say, soothingly. "He's probably messing with us. He'll post a video about the bet and make a million dollars on advertising on it and it will all be a big hoax."

"He doesn't do hoaxes, Jasper," she says and she's so wound up that there's a bite to her words. One I've never really heard from her. Surprised, I take a step back. "It's all real. The helicopter license. The deep sea rescues. The sinking boat. It wasn't staged. It's real."

"Sure," I say easily. If she wants to believe that about her dad, that's okay. I don't. I'm not that gullible.

"It is!" She huffs. I guess she can read me well enough to know I'm humoring her. "And do you know what that means?"

"What does it mean?" I find myself crossing my arms over my chest defensively. Maybe this is where she tells me that she understands our marriage is real and that she knows the trouble we're in legally, as well as with her dad.

"It means that we have to keep pretending to be married until he dies, or he'll lose everything," she sounds upset.

Wow. Does she hate spending time with me this much? I cross my arms over my chest. I knew she'd done this for her own reasons, but I didn't think it was a miserable time for her. I'd thought we'd had a moment last night. And then this evening in the desert, well, I'd felt something.

"We'll have to keep this up for months or maybe even a year. We're stuck, Jasper."

She throws herself onto her bed and I can see it from where I am in the little kitchenette. She looks so tragic there and so freaking hot. I want to ease myself onto that bed, too, and kiss away her troubles and explain to her in no uncertain terms that I absolutely will pretend to be her husband for the rest of our lives — and while we're pretending, maybe she'd like to see some of the benefits that come from being married to a man who is absolutely obsessed with pleasing her.

But just as I'm thinking about giving that a try, she moans, "We're so, so, so stuck."

And something in my chest crumples. She's really unhappy being with me.

"Look," I say, not looking at her because it will kill me to look at her now. "I don't have to stay here if you're unhappy."

"Are you kidding me?" She huffs like I've suggested we empty our bank accounts and fly to Hawaii — not a bad idea, actually. "You can't *leave*. It's more important to pretend than ever." She freezes as if something has occurred to her. "You're not going to ... You wouldn't ... My dad."

She tries all three of those starts and then she sits up, pulls her knees to her chest, and collapses her forehead to them.

"I'm sorry. I can't ask you to do this for months. Two weeks — well, that was what you owed me, you know? For what you put me through? But months and months of this? Maybe years? I don't know how sick he is. Maybe he'll hold on that long. That's too much to ask for. That's your whole life. You should be dating someone you have a future with."

She doesn't think she has a future with me?

"You should be making a family with *her* and starting a life with someone who loves you."

Oof.

I mean, I knew she didn't love me and it would be silly to think she could after all these years, but hearing it stated so baldly like that. There's a massive knot in my throat and I can't swallow it down. It kind of feels like I'm going to choke on it, which I guess explains the watering eyes.

But she's wrong about the rest of it.

I make my way quietly into the bedroom and sit down on the edge of her bed … our bed. And I lift her chin up gently with one finger and swallow to try to clear my voice enough to speak, even though it still comes out as a croak. There are tears on her cheeks and they make me feel ill because I let them happen.

"I'm here for the long haul, Gracie. For as long as you want me, I'm here."

"Even weeks?" she says, aghast.

"Even weeks."

"Even months?" She asks and her voice trembles with vulnerability and I can't help it, I lean in a little closer to her, as if just by being close enough I could protect her.

"Even months," I assure her, and I have to clear my throat because that lump is back.

"Even years?" Her voice is weak and her mouth draws down and trembles a little like she's asked for something impossible that no one could ever give. And I want to kiss her so bad that it makes my chest actually ache. I seriously should have searched heart attack symptoms while I could. But I'm done. I'm so done over this girl.

"Even years," I agree. And I realize the moment I say it that it's true. My heart kicks up into a gear I didn't know it had.

I gasp in surprise as she shoves forward and closes the gap between us. Her soft lips are against my parted ones and they fit between mine in a perfect embrace as if two halves of a whole have been nestled together again. I close my eyes on instinct, my arm wrapping gently around her upper back to cradle her close.

And the slide of her wet lips, silky and smooth against mine, does something to me. Not just physically — although seriously, if I move right now it's going to hurt I'm so instantly hard — it's something more than that. It's something that maybe starts at my groin but then bursts up into my chest and brain until I'm just live wires in every nerve, tingling with an excitement so powerful it erases thought, it writes over me like a blank computer drive and whatever I was, I'm not that anymore. I'm this. I'm *this kiss* with Gracie forever.

I kiss her back, as gently as delicately as I can. I know this is forbidden fruit. I know that when she knows about the truth she'll never kiss me like this again and somehow that just makes me want it more and I part my lips a little deeper and let my tongue touch her lips. When her sweet tongue touches mine instead, I think my eyes roll back into my head and I can't ... if I go on I will never stop. I'll lose myself in her forever.

I'd be fine with that. But maybe she wouldn't be.

I pull myself backward, the soft suction of our lips against each other sliding free in a way that makes everything from lips to groin ache with exquisite desire, and I'm on my feet before I can swallow, before I can lick the taste of her from my lips.

She's on the bed, looking up at me, her hair rumpled sweetly from our kiss, her lips pink and swollen and oh, sweet mercy, I can only imagine what else I could swell up with my kiss and no, I have to get myself in hand. I stumble back to the door.

I should say something. Words aren't coming.

I swallow.

Oh yes. The Jeep.

"Rod knock," I say thickly. And then I'm stumbling through the door and out of the house, sucking in the cool night air. I stub my toe on one of her rescue planters — awesome — and the pain clears my head enough to manage to get myself to the Jeep, start the engine, and pull it into her dad's garage.

However bad I had it before, I have it a hundred times worse now. And when I said "to death do us part" I didn't realize she'd be the death of me in a matter of days, but I'm pretty sure she's going to be, and with her kiss still on my lips I'm not even sure that I care.

Chapter Twenty-Three

GRACIE

He breaks away from me, panting, leaving me gasping with the taste of BBQ and something so incredibly Jasper laying thick on my tongue. I feel like I was finally drinking cold water after being lost in the desert only to have it snatched away from me again.

He's so ... he's so incredibly kind, to be willing to do this for my dad ... for me. Where has this kind Jasper been these past five years?

Running away.

Just like he's doing now because I kissed him. How insane is it that he's willing to promise me months of his life but he panics at a single kiss? It was a good kiss, though. A kiss like I'd never felt before. It made every kiss I'd ever given Carter feel like a mockery of the real thing. This kiss — it was souls touching. It was more intimate than sex. It lit a hunger inside me that was suddenly blazing.

And maybe I'm not the bravest girl. I haven't traveled very far because I'm worried about people using me as a drug mule, or about losing my passport and ending up stranded and then sold as a slave, or making a terrible mistake and offending the locals. Or worse — exploiting the locals. I would never in a thousand years jump out of a plane. I don't even like driving over the speed limit. And I file my taxes promptly and with enormous care because I'm terrified of the IRS. But when it comes to people, I'm brave. When it comes to people I care about, there's nothing I'm afraid to do.

So, I take a minute to calm down, and then I take a big breath, and I leap out of bed, run my hands through my hair, decide it's fine — the windswept look is in, right? Or maybe it's beachy tangles? I don't care. I'm already out the door and skipping across the yard toward the shop, hoping that my dad and Mikey don't happen to be wandering around and notice me. But no, I can hear them laughing by the pool. You can't see it from here, but the sound carries far, and in the descending night they can still compete with the livening insects.

I find him in the garage, just where he said he'd be. His Jeep is pulled into an empty bay and he's under it on a creeper. I can really only see him from the chest down. His black shirt has ridden up, exposing exactly two inches of pale flesh — paler than his brown face and arms. This part of him never sees the sun. Which means no one sees it. No one but me. And I have this insane urge to straddle him right there and kiss that band of exposed abdomen where strong muscles flex under his skin and where the lightest trail of black hair meets in the center, just below his belly button, and draws a straight line down his torso, diving under the waistband of his jeans.

I lick my lips.

I want to follow it. I want to kiss down it like following a path. I want ... I stop myself. I want him to know that I want all of this. That I'm grateful for what he's offered me. That I can give, too. That's what I want.

I find a second creeper leaning against the wall. I ease it gently to the shop floor, lie on it and draw myself under the Jeep beside him. In the shadow of the vehicle, he freezes, his eyes going wide as he sees me joining him. He's half in the shadow under his vehicle and it makes it look like I'm finding the secret parts of him. The closer I get, the more blown out his pupils are until they're pure black and his lips part and then bite his lower lip as he makes a face of concentration. It's like just the sight of me requires all his brain power to process and I love it. I

want all his attention on me. I want it on us. And I want to give him mine.

His knuckles around the wrench he's holding are sharp white. I don't care that they also have dark smears of grease and dirt on the back of them — or maybe I do care and I want those skilled hands that fix off-road vehicles and take glorious pictures to take their time with me.

I lick my lips.

"You don't really have a rod knock," I say.

"No." He's staring at me like he can't look away, his chest heaving like he's fighting something heavy into place but all he's really fighting is the intimacy of this as I roll my creeper closer.

We're on our backs, our legs out in the shop, our torsos under an oily, clay-encrusted Jeep undercarriage, but our faces are just inches apart and I've never felt more compromised than I do right now, fully clothed, with our hands kept to ourselves.

"That kiss," I say as I roll so that I'm half off my creeper and half on top of him. The length of his body is pressed against mine and his warmth radiates into my skin. "It felt like a promise. Didn't you like it?"

"I did." His words are a gasp.

"Didn't you want more?"

"I did."

I can feel his heart racing under my hand, feel his breath hitch. Feel something incredibly hard spring up under my belly and I bite my smiling lip nervously. I know exactly what I want to do with that, and he seems to know it because his lips part in a huff of something like disbelief and hope all rolled into one.

I have him pinned under me, his shoulders held down by my hands as I move over him, sliding up so that I can kiss his forehead, his cheek, the curve of his jaw, the shell of his ear, his neck, but not his trembling lips that gasp with each of my kisses. Not just yet. And I wonder if he's done this before. I wonder if it's as new for him as it feels like it is for me because I've never been bold like this before. I've never been so certain of what I wanted as I am right now.

He's breathing like he's running a marathon. He doesn't say a word, but he follows where I lead and the look in his eyes when I meet his gaze is something like surrender and despair and longing all rolled up into one. But he needn't despair. I'm not going to leave him unfulfilled.

His hands come up and gently — oh so gently — encircle my waist where my shirt has ridden up, too. He's reverent in how he touches me, like I'm coated in a half-a-million-dollar paint job and he's terrified of scratching me.

I reach up to run a hand through his short hair and this time I get to gasp because he's so, so beautiful. How can one man be so beautiful? The world must break beneath it. It can't possibly hold something so terrifyingly desirable. And all that beauty is here under a dirty car.

His fingers flex at my touch, digging just slightly into the line of my hipbone as he clutches me to him and his grunt, low and deep and so masculine, is followed by an involuntary moan that he tries to bite down on as I nip his chin.

I want to do it again. I want to leave him looking flushed and breathless for me again. But I can't let him suffer. I catch his mouth with mine, feeling that same slide and merge that I felt in the bedroom as we came together, the mingling of lips and tongues and the tangling of breath. I'm being woven into the fabric of him and he into me, and I can't quite tell where one starts and the other ends and I don't want to.

If anyone would have told me that my most romantic moment ever would be under a Jeep, I would have laughed at them outright. The undersides of vehicles drip. They're dirty and uncomfortable and they smell like coolant or gasoline or brake cleaner, and no one wants to make out under one. No one but me, it would seem.

Because here, under this Jeep, I can't get enough of him. His scent is in my nose, intoxicating me, pulling me under, even as he kisses me hungrily, his hands traveling up my waist to my mid-back and then his arms slide further around me until he's holding me with a palm spread between my shoulder blades, pressing against the ridge of my spine, his fingers splayed out possessively, and another on my lower back, holding me securely to him as if he's afraid I'll go.

"Gracie," he whispers just my name like a plea. "Gracie."

And I just want to live this moment forever. I just want to sink into his kisses and never ever emerge. My fingers slide under the edge of his T-shirt, and I press my palms to his flat belly and then slowly ride up his ribs and to the light dusting of hair on his chest and I shift my weight to get a better angle for kissing, and as I do I accidentally slide against him. He's hard as a rock, the bulging cotton of his jeans barely containing him. I lean into that hardness instinctively, letting the slide of my motion press along the length of him as I deepen our kiss and it's good. Damn, but it's good, and I just want more and more even if it's never enough.

I lean in again, pressing my hips to his, sliding my hands down his torso toward his waistband but the moment my fingers reach beneath the band of his boxers, gently sliding between the curling hairs there, there's a squeal from the wheels of his creeper as he shoves back, panting roughly. Gentle, gentle hands reach out and with the greatest care ease me back onto my own creeper, and his eyes are glassy and his breath rough, as he draws my hands away from him with the softest touch and sets them onto my own body.

He lays back for a breath, chest heaving, while I'm still stunned, and then he grits his jaw with a low "Fuck," and with a flick of his heels he's out from under the Jeep and sitting up on the creeper on the floor. I can hear the huffs of his rough breath from here. Little sounds escape him almost like protests, as he puts his face into his big, calloused hands, but he's not saying any words. And I don't know what to do. This isn't how I planned that this would happen.

I ease out slowly from under the Jeep, my face burning, body trembling with all the emotions and desires I still have only half reigned in.

"Jasper," I gasp. "I ... I'm sorry. Didn't you like it?"

"Of course I liked it," he says gently and he looks at me for just a breath, and the look in his eyes — the last time I saw that look was the last time I ever saw him before he vanished on me, and something inside my heart cracks.

I don't understand what I did wrong. I don't understand how this was bad. Should I have left him alone? I thought he was just nervous. That he just needed to know that it was okay to be with me. Should I have let him run away? And then what? Wait another five years for him to come back to me?

"I don't understand," I say heavily, and I'm trying to keep the hurt out of my voice but it sounds a bit too thick even to my own ears and I can hear the tremor in it.

"I don't do that," he says softly, almost kindly, and it's the kindness that stings so much. He's not looking at me. He stands, gathering up the creeper and shoving it back into place on the wall. I stand, too, but I leave the creeper. Who cares about tidiness at a time like this?

"Don't do what?" I ask, forcing myself to be brave. Forcing myself to meet the humiliation of his rejection head-on. "Don't make out under Jeeps in Adam Boomhower's garage? Because you did just now. With me."

"I don't do any of that," he says, turning his back to me now so that I barely hear him. His face is in his hand again and his words sound stricken. "Not without commitment." I see his Adam's apple bob as he swallows. "Not without love."

And then he's gone, and the close assist on the shop door makes it slam behind him, just like it does every time it closes, but this time it feels like a real slam, and I feel like such a fool. Worse, I feel unwanted. No, worse than that, I feel like a thief, like I took something from him that wasn't mine to take. Because he only gives himself to someone he loves and it turns out that he doesn't love me.

Wow, Gracie. Nice work. You just threw yourself at a man who doesn't want you.

But he didn't kiss me like he didn't want me. He kissed me like he wanted me too much.

I do the only thing that makes any sense at all. I sit down on that stupid creeper on the floor of my dad's garage and bawl my eyes out until my mascara leaves black drips on my shirt and I can't see quite right because my eyes are too swollen. It should make me feel better. It usually makes me feel better. But this time it doesn't, because no matter how hard I try to fix all of this I just keep making it worse and that's not me. That's not Grace Boomhower and it's not how I want it to be.

Chapter Twenty-Four

JASPER

I think about driving off into the desert, but she's in there with my Jeep, and I think I hear her crying, and I want to be sick. That quiet sob I hear is all it takes to bring me down from a state of raging excitement to frigid cold. It's more effective than an ice water bath.

I think about taking one of her dad's vehicles — he leaves the keys in them, says if someone stole one the cops would recognize it by sight, which is probably true — but driving off in a BOOM truck would just delay the inevitable.

I don't know what to do. This isn't the kind of thing I'm good at.

I run my hands through my hair and huff out a breath. I didn't know it would be like that until it was. I thought we could make out, and I could enjoy her body and give her all my affection. I didn't realize that I wouldn't be able to do *just that* without even a promise of more.

I don't kiss girls. So I have no experience with this. I've never wanted to.

Because no other girls are Gracie. And that kiss we shared in her bedroom was so intense for me that I nearly lost myself to it. I didn't know it could be like that. I didn't know that I'd lose myself like that. Didn't realize it would burn itself into my heart like a brand.

All that fantasizing and then I get my chance and ... I can't do it. Not if she doesn't love me. Not if there's no hope for more.

I shove my hands through my hair.

I'm so gone on this girl, so hopelessly tangled up in her sweet smile and twining hair. I'm like a fish caught in the net, dying already, but still thrashing deeper and deeper into its fate. And that kiss sealed it for me. I'm hers or no one's.

And I can't be half hers, either. I can't be hers for one night but not hers in the morning. And I didn't know that was true until just now.

It had taken all my willpower to wrench myself away, to remind myself that she wasn't really mine to take. That if we kept going, then in the morning, when it was all over, I would still be her old friend who had let her down, and who was holding a secret she didn't know, and she would still be the girl who gave him a thank-you roll she didn't really mean.

Wouldn't that just be like Gracie? She'd give without ever thinking about what she got out of it. And if someone gave to her, she'd always want to be sure they were getting something in return.

She saw this fake marriage as a favor to her ... so she'd do a favor for me in return. It sounds crass even in my mind, when I put it that way. But I know her. I know she'd prioritize me over her. I know she'd give herself to me out of a desire to please, out of a feeling that she was somehow in my debt, and never think once about the consequences for her. And I'm not having it. Not like that.

I huff out a breath and lean my forehead against the cool metal of the exterior shop wall.

I thought I was pretty clever using the same excuse on her that I used on her dad and hiding out here — literally holed up under a vehicle. But then she was there, and she washed over me like a wave and took me out to sea and I was drowning in her all over again, clinging to her warmth like an addict, only falling in deeper with every hit I took off her skin. Every breath inhaled her, every touch was full of her tender kisses and silky smooth skin and I would have gladly taken anything she gave me and given it back twice as fully. I would have taken her as mine under that Jeep on that hard creeper and it would have been the best moment — no, it already was the best moment — of my life. Even the way it was. Even with it having to end like it did.

But it had to be that way. Because I can admit it now, to myself at least. I'm hopelessly in love with Gracie. I can never shake her out of my system. Years apart won't do it. The affections of others won't do it. Even this terrible tangled web we're weaving can't turn me away from her.

But I want more for her than this. I want her to be with someone she loves, too. I want her to be with someone she wants to be with — not because she's being kind, not because she's Gracie and she gives — but because *she* wants it, wants *him*.

Maybe that person isn't me. Maybe that person won't *ever* be me when she hears what I have to say, so I *can't* take a piece of her that she doesn't realize she's giving away. I refuse to steal from the person who always gives.

And I want to give her everything. Every little bit of what's good or worthwhile in me. But only if that's what she wants. Sinking into her sweet body right now, taking the taste of it, the feel of it, the knowledge of it for just one night — as ridiculously fucking tempting as it is — would sabotage that.

I clench my fists and instead of running, I make my way back to her house. I water the sad plants by the door. I take a crack at fixing a kid's bike I find in the coat closet and I think I finally have the chain tight and the brakes loose again when she comes back into the house.

Her eyes meet mine and they're wide and full of hurt and I feel like dirt.

I am dirt.

To have hurt her like that. I flex and unflex my fingers, wishing I could hold her. Knowing I must not.

"I have to show you something," I say stupidly, setting the bike aside. I need to do this before I lose my nerve. I need to be so clear that there won't be more misunderstandings.

She huffs a disbelieving laugh that says I'm too much, and she looks away, crossing her arms defensively over her chest, but it's not cynicism or arrogance on her face, it's bone-deep hurt and my stomach flips all over again.

Fuck. Fuck. I've ruined something beautiful, like stomping on a blossoming rose.

I swallow down that thick lump in my throat and try again. "It's important."

I bring my phone over to where she is and open up the pdf Scotty sent me. I hand it to her.

"What is this?" Her voice is shaking as she looks, zooming in on the document.

"There was a mistake," I say. "Scotty didn't understand."

"What is this?"

This time she says it with rising horror in her voice, like she knows, but needs me to tell her. Maybe I'm not the best at reading emotions, but even I can see that the idea of being bound to me by legal marriage is unthinkable to her. My heart kicks up a gear like it wants to start racing again, but this time for different reasons. Her big eyes are so full of betrayal and worry, that I want to just tuck the evidence away and tell her it's nothing but I can't do that, can I? I owe her this truth.

"It's a Marriage License. One we signed and had witnessed."

"We're married for real?" Her voice is a ghost of its usual self.

"Yes," I say and I'm relieved that this time she understands, even as I brace myself for her fury. I don't know why I feel so vulnerable telling her this. Maybe because telling her it's true is an awful lot like admitting I want it.

"How long have you known?" Her voice is empty, robotic. It worries me more than rage would.

I have to clear the lump out of my throat so I can speak. "Since this morning."

"And you didn't say anything?"

There's a muscle jumping in her jaw and suddenly my mouth is dry. I could try to tell her about all my attempts to explain this to her, but what is the point? I just shrug uselessly.

Wow, Jasper. That's a dynamite move.

"Let me get this straight," she says carefully and now I know she's really mad, and I feel my cheeks growing hot and my eyes growing hard and cold as she speaks. "We're actually married. Legally. For real. Which means we aren't pretending and we'd need a legal divorce to end this thing between you and me."

Something inside me shrivels. Which is ridiculous. I hadn't honestly thought she'd be okay with it, had I?

I'm such a fool.

Maybe it was the kisses. They made me stupid. I can still feel them pressed on my neck and the shell of my ear, as if even the most boring parts of me are worth something to her.

She's still talking. "My dad has bet his entire net worth on our marriage, so we can't leave each other while he's alive which might be for years."

I don't bother reiterating that I think that's a lie. I'm lost in her golden brown eyes, lost and drowning.

"And what you said back there in the shop still stands?" There's a hint of a question at the end of that.

"What I said in the shop?" I'm confused — both by her question and by the tearing sensation I'm feeling inside as if my organs are all coming apart at the seams at once. Maybe the next part comes out harsher than I mean it to. I tend towards harshness when I'm in pain. "About not fucking people I don't love? What does that have to do with this?"

Her face goes very, very still and I can't read it. I don't know what she's thinking. I just know that I feel her slipping away and I want to reach for her and pull her back, but the way she's taken this news confirms all my worst fears. She feels trapped. By me. And I don't want her to be trapped. I don't want her to feel obligated.

I step back. Try to give her space. It's the wrong thing to do.

"I'm taking a shower," she says, turning away and I think I catch the edge of her face crumpling as she goes, and I don't know what to do. I don't know what to do.

I hear the shower turn on in the bathroom. I could still leave. Take the Jeep out into the desert. And then what? Keep going? Run away? Leave her legally married to a man she can't divorce, facing this ridiculous situation on her own?

I can't do it. I can't do that to her. Even if she doesn't want me here, she needs me to be here now, and I can't leave her if she needs me.

I strip the sleeping bag off of the bed, pile enough of her things to the side to make a space, and lay it out on the floor so that I can crawl inside. I won't be sleeping tonight, but I can do one thing for her. I can stay put. I can show her that I won't cut and run and leave her here alone.

I think I hear her crying in the shower and I feel like a complete ass. I sigh and look at the wall. And I don't look up when she comes back into the room and settles on the bed.

"Get off the floor," she tells me a bit thickly.

I don't answer.

"You can sleep on the bed," she says and she sounds tired. "I would never ask you to sleep on the floor."

But that's the problem, isn't it? She never asks for anything for herself. So, I stay on the floor and I leave the bed to her and I wish I could go back to last night when everything was different and I hadn't ruined it all. I can still feel the slide of her body on mine, still taste her on my lips. I'll probably never get to taste that again, and I don't really have the right to dwell on it, but I do anyway.

"You're not asking me to sleep on the floor. I am," I say roughly. "I'm not asking *you* for anything, Gracie."

She doesn't reply to that, but I hear her flop down on the bed and then turn aggressively to one side and then the other, as if it's as difficult for her to get comfortable as it is for me.

I replay every moment of the two of us moving together, fitting perfectly in all the right places, and I'm so bothered that I can't sleep. I just lose my thoughts in memories of her kisses and her hair tangling around my fingers and her lips pressing around mine. I want to dive down into these memories forever and never emerge from them again.

You're an idiot, Jasper Hunt. You've ruined your life, and you have no one to blame but yourself, I try to tell myself, but my accusations aren't sticking. Instead, I keep falling back into those memories that I have no right to possess until sleep finally sweeps me away.

Then

GRACIE

I wander out to his garage. It's after school on a Friday and mom and I just drove over. There's a crispness to the air that reminds me it's November, but I'm not really all that cold.

Jasper's working on his Ford Ranger. He bought it with money he earned from photographing a friend's wedding. A "windfall" he calls it. Four hundred bucks was all the old man wanted. The paint is matte from the sun and what used to be a shiny black is now a dusty charcoal.

He's been working on it for weeks. The engine needed a rebuild and the exhaust and brakes all needed replacing. He steadfastly refused help from his dad or mine.

"It's my truck," he kept saying. "All mine."

When I get out there, he's sweeping the floor and all the tools are away and the jugs of the various fluids vehicles consume are lined up on the shelves on the back wall. Jasper is the tidiest young man I've ever heard of. Not a neat freak, I wouldn't say, because he doesn't care if anyone else is tidy, but he always keeps everything he touches in perfect order.

The garage smells like brake cleaner and gasoline, and for a moment I'm worried, but then Jasper looks up. His crooked grin blooms across his face and he looks down shyly before meeting my eyes.

"She's all done," he says proudly. "Hop in."

I do hop in. Jasper's had his license for a year and I've driven with him before, but it's always such a thrill when it's just the two of us — no parents, no rules. Well, the rules of the road, obviously, but there's no one to say that it's not a good day to stop for slushies and red vines at the corner store, or that we're on a schedule so we can't do donuts in that empty parking lot.

I'm buzzing with excitement before he even fires the truck up.

"You did it!" I squeal when it turns over. He revs the engine, laughing, right there in the garage.

"Hold onto your butts!" he says and then he burns out of his parent's garage — he's going to be in so much trouble! — and I squeal as we spin out onto the road and zip down it.

"It's really fast!" I say, breathless with joy.

He's laughing, his cheeks pink, pride in every line of his face, his eyes half-closed in ecstasy as we turn onto the highway and let loose.

"Where are we going?" I ask him, still giggling with him as the pair of us can't believe he has a functional vehicle he built himself.

I know it should be safetied first. That it probably isn't insured. That it probably doesn't have a real plate on it, just some random one they pulled from another truck to test it with. We shouldn't be on the highway with a truck like this. But I can't help it, I don't care.

Jasper has always represented freedom and fun for me and I want all the fun in the world right now. This school year has been hard, and we've barely seen our dads now that they're online-famous, and I just want to leave all that behind and just drive.

Jasper does, too.

"Wherever we want," he says and that's exactly what we do.

We get our slushies and red vines and M&Ms. We drive down the road to a place where the locals like to off-road and then Jasper puts his Ranger through the paces and I eat too much sugar and try to keep our drinks from spilling. Sure we'll be in trouble when we get home. But we don't care. Right now it's flashing eyes and lit-up smiles and endless laughter and I want to bottle up this moment and live in it forever.

GRACIE

It's the next morning. You know, the one after my heart was broken. No big deal. I wake to an empty bed and after just one night of it being full, it feels like a crime that it's empty again. Jasper's already awake and in the shower.

When he comes out, he's barefoot, dressed in his signature hip-hugging jeans. He catches me watching him while he's drying his hair with a towel and gives me a sheepish expression.

He's not wearing a shirt which seems like an unreasonable thing for him to torture me with. That hard flat abdomen and muscled chest and arms are killing me. They aren't the muscle that comes from working out in a gym, it's the muscle of a physical man who's always working and it's totally doing it for me.

But it needs to stop doing it for me because he's off limits. He made that enormously clear last night. My cheeks are still stinging from the embarrassment of basically throwing myself at a man who says he doesn't want me.

He looks good enough that my mouth waters. Traitor mouth. Maybe my brain hasn't told it yet that this man doesn't love me. Doesn't want me. Is shackled to me with a legal document, vows I thought were a joke at the time, and the expectations of literally millions of people. And also the dreams of my dying father, but there's no reason to be dramatic or anything.

My heart is totally racing, whether that's dramatic or not. It makes it hard to think.

Jasper's my husband. Legally. Actually.

I swallow.

I can't shake that feeling in my stomach like a heavy rock is lodged there or the sweat that pops up between my shoulder blades every time I think of that. Maybe if he hadn't rejected me so thoroughly last night, I would have felt differently. Maybe I'd be … intrigued by the idea of being married to a man I find so completely attractive. Maybe I could have even embraced the idea. After all, this is what I decided to do, right? Use this opportunity to go after him? How better than with legal backup?

Instead, I feel humiliated. Sick to my stomach that I put it all out there and was shot down. I've never done that before. It's not the kind of thing I do.

And now, I just want it all to go away. And it's not going anywhere.

I hug my knees up to my chest.

He's frozen there, with his towel still in his hair, like he didn't expect to see me in my own bed, and then he licks his lips like he's about to say something but nothing comes out but my name.

"Gracie." It's like a prayer.

But I can't have *another* one of these agonizing conversations with him. I just can't.

I reach for my phone at the side of my bed instead.

Question Time, I text, playing our game. *Would you rather be legally married to me or lose the use of your legs?*

He swallows when he hears his phone buzz, looking from my phone in my hand over to his and back.

I arch an eyebrow, unsmiling, and when he hurries over to it, I slip into the bathroom and lock the door behind me. No more half-naked men tempting me in here. Genius move, Gracie.

Maybe I shouldn't be congratulating myself so quickly. This whole room smells like him. It's like breathing in a hit of Jasper with every breath. Okay, this is worse.

Growling, I turn on the shower and strip.

My phone buzzes. *They make great wheelchairs these days. Powered ones. All you do is drive.*

Screw you, Jasper. I throw my clothes in the corner with more energy than I usually use. Maybe I don't want to be married to you, either. I huff over to the shower but before I can step in, I fire off another text.

Would you rather break your "rule" or get stabbed in the heart.

There. Let him stew on that one. My hair isn't even wet when I get a response.

I've already been stabbed in the heart. I think I can manage it twice.

I'm so furious now that I run the shower cold. I can't take any more heat. But my phone buzzes again. I grab it from the counter with one hand while I'm shampooing with the other.

Would you rather sleep with me in your bed tonight or sleep in the desert with no sleeping bag?

Desert, I type and I add a purple smiling devil emoji. Take that Jasper and your ice-cold heart. I finish my shower in such a mood that I cut my leg while I'm shaving and the sting of it is welcome after the sting I've been feeling from him.

Would you rather give up chocolate or sex? I text and then a moment later I add, *Oh wait, I already know the answer. You 'don't do that.'*

Okay, maybe the sting is still there.

I get ready quickly, doing my makeup and hair in the bathroom. I don't want to face him without it, like it's a mask to cover up how much it hurts me that he didn't want what I was offering. I needn't have bothered avoiding him. He isn't in the little house when I get out. Frustrated, I slip on my own jeans and a bright blue tank top. I hope he hasn't forgotten that we left my Bronco at the BOOM shop because I rode with him last night.

Would you rather ride with me or walk? His text comes in.

I slam the door behind me, purse in one hand, phone in the other, and hurry to the bay where he'd left his Jeep last night. You know, the one I bawled my eyes out in like a love-lorn fool? I won't be making that mistake again.

He's idling outside the garage door and I leap into the vehicle and shoot him my best angry-eyed look. Take that, Jasper Hunt.

But honestly, it's not him I'm mad at, it's me. I should have known he'd blow me off. This was the same man who had disappeared at my mom's funeral. Who hadn't bothered to call for a month and then when I was so relieved and asking him to come right over because I missed him and I was dying for a hug, he admitted he was in Canada. Why did I think this would go any differently?

He has shades on, so I can't see his eyes, but he texts me again.

If you had to choose whether to publish your mom's memoir or make your dad happy, what would you pick?

The air huffs out of me at that. It's too personal. It's too … right. How dare he bring that up?

If you had to go back and choose again, would you tell me that you tricked me into being married to you, or would you keep it a secret? I text back.

"Where does this bike go?" He snaps at me, gesturing to Joshy's bike he's thrown in the back of the Jeep. Oh. I'd forgotten he'd fixed it.

"It's on the way," I say coldly. And no, it does not melt my heart that he did something kind in the middle of our fight. It does not. Not even when we drop it off at Joshy's and he's all grins and excitement. Not even when Jasper cracks a joke and Joshy gives him a goofy six-year-old smile.

If you had to pick between having kids or shooting the two-hundred-year celebration of National Geographic, which would you pick? I text.

Who cares about the damn Geographic? He texts back and my heart definitely flips at that. He does want kids, after all.

But not with me.

Because he doesn't love me.

I need to keep reminding myself of that before I forget and fall in love with him.

I'm sick of this game, he texts me.

"You shouldn't drive and text. It's illegal and irresponsible," I tell him aloud.

He ignores me, tapping away with his perfectly calloused fingers. The fingerprints are black, filled in with oil and grease residue that won't wash out. His perfect hair is ruffled by the wind, his perfect clothing hugs his perfect figure, and I want to slap that perfect chiseled jaw that's looking sharp today. He must have shaved before I woke up.

I'm not like this. I'm kind and generous. I don't think about slapping people. I definitely don't fantasize about it. Until now. Until this man.

Let's play a new one, he texts me. *I'll present you with a feeling and you give me a 1-5 rating. 1 means you barely feel that. 5 means it's killing you.*

I text back an angry face. He ignores it.

Angry, he texts.

I text a 5.

Well done. You're a quick study.

"Jasper Hunt," I say very deliberately. He has yet to look at me this whole ride. "I might hate you."

Scared? He texts. But I don't answer that. And not just because I'm getting that stone feeling in my belly again.

There's a crowd outside the BOOM Enterprises shop. A huge one. It's like half of middle America has crashed this party and I know without a doubt that this is the moment where we either turn and run or have to be a fake couple indefinitely.

But Jasper doesn't turn the Jeep. He keeps going, and without missing a beat, he stretches and puts an arm around me and despite everything that's happened, that little traitor in me melts a bit.

Chapter Twenty-Six

JASPER

I work like mad all morning trying to tune up my junkyard find.
I cut the wheel wells wide with a reciprocating saw so I can put
thirty-seven-inch tires on this rig, and then I go over the basics to
make sure that she runs and drives. I'm not going to be winning
any competitions with it, but at least I won't disgrace myself
with nothing to drive on the desert run tomorrow.

While I work, I hear the buzz and chatter. There's difficulty
getting the fans to take a step back and not crowd the shop.
Gracie had the brilliant idea of selling them all merchandise, and
now BOOM is out of T-shirts except in kids' sizes and out of
basically everything else except some BOOMerangs Adam had
made on a whim. They have his face on them.

"I'll be a hundred before we unload those things," Tanner
confides to Pretty Boy.

They're pretending that I don't exist, but they're nervous,
glancing at me from time to time. Adam did a video today
where he shared his joy in his daughter secretly falling in love
with and marrying his former partner's son. He'd strongly

implied that while this competition is still for an heir to his empire, he would want to keep "family first" and now no one knows if they hate me or want to suck up to me. It's totally isolating.

If I were a people person, I'd be dying.

Fortunately, I'm an introvert. I'm happy to work quietly on my rig for tomorrow on my own. I have a lot of acquaintances all over the world. I can crash on a couch in any city from here to Dubai. But I don't have friends. I have my camera. I have my Jeep. I've thought about getting a dog. A nice blue heeler would be my style. But that wouldn't work for international stuff.

Frustrated? I text Gracie midway through the morning.

Five, she texts back lightning fast. But my game is a poor one because now I don't know if she's frustrated by me or by this situation.

New game, I try, midway through the afternoon. I'm hastily installing a roll cage. It's not even close to pretty. It's all straight lines because I don't have time for bends and the welds are rough. But I'm running out of time. *Answer my questions as if you're me and I'll answer as if I'm you.*

Fine, she texts back, which even I know is girl code for "eat dirt and die."

How are you doing?

I'm way too into my work to realize what a jerk I am and how much I deserve to suffer for it, she texts, pretending to be me.

She's wrong about that. I'm well aware.

It's more than an hour before she texts back, *How are you doing?*

I'm furious that my husband didn't tell me about a particular legal document, I text. *But also, I feel pretty good because I delivered a kid's bike to him this morning and I've already agreed to help Pretty Boy get the perfect picture for his online dating profile, so my good deeds of the day are covered.*

I'm not that bad, she texts back.

She's not bad at all. She's sharp as a whip. Even when she hates me, she's amazing.

Stay in character, I text back. *Jasper is very bad.*

Criminal.

I, on the other hand, am the golden daughter of Big Daddy Boom and there are thousands of people literally setting up campers and tents in the desert outside my dad's shop just to catch a glimpse of me, the men vying for my dad's business, and the husband I stole.

Stole?

I stole him with my smile and my messy apartment.

My apartment isn't messy!

Good job staying in character, but Jasper doesn't have an apartment.

She stops texting after that, and I'd feel hurt except I know why. Her dad is making his presence very known in the shop. Pretty Boy is filming him examining everyone's builds as they ready their junkyard vehicles for an intense off-road run.

Two days is not long enough to get a vehicle ready for that — even a running and driving vehicle, even with all the parts we could ask for coming out of Big Daddy's extensive warehouse, or Tanner doing non-stop parts store runs.

But the builds around me are a tribute to the skills of the men who came here to do this. They look great. I can see they focused on essentials — brakes, oil pan protection, winch installation, roll cages, etc. But they put their personalities into the builds, too. Travis painted a haunting skull in spray bomb on the side of his black Suzuki and the paint drips make it look like it's leaking black blood. Hollis has sprayed rippling Stars and Stripes on his. He could be a graffiti artist with those skills. He also took the doors off the Blazer and ran some kind of netting there instead. It looks badass.

Gracie's dad works his way from one competitor to the next doing interviews, and that's when I see what has been on her mind. He is coughing. Between interviews, he stops and coughs like he can't quite clear something out of his throat and he has a look in his eye that I've seen on shoots a thousand times before like his thoughts are far away. He doesn't want to be here because he wants to be somewhere else.

Maybe she's right. Maybe he really is sick.

Gracie has been trailing him, hurrying to update his social media with shots of him in front of all the vehicles and something about a big giveaway that they're tying into this display. She looks adorable in one of the BOOM branded T-shirts that she has rolled the sleeves up on and tied in a knot at her waist. Too adorable for this place. I look around casually and see a lot of eyes on her and I want to say, "That's my wife! You can't look at her like that." But that's silly, because she doesn't really want to be my wife. She just wants to have a cardboard cut-out to put on her arm and in her apartment to keep her dad happy.

And who am I kidding? Anyone in their right mind would be staring at Gracie. Her smile is as stunning as ever. I can hear her laughing at some joke Tanner told and she immediately makes the whole place light up and dance with sparkles. She's cheering up Randy who had a rough time getting his points gapped this morning and he's offering her a shy smile. She does that — makes people feel better just by being there. And I hurt that sweet-hearted person last night when I lifted her off my body and set her aside like I wasn't dying to sink into her and lose myself forever.

I want to sigh. I want to bang my head against the winch I'm installing. I want to get out from under this rig and go put my arm around her so that every one of these staring guys sees it when they look at her, like putting your company logo in the corner of your video. And I kind of hate myself for that because I know how primitive it sounds and how presumptuous. I am owed nothing by this girl and I have no right to claim anything from her. The very best thing I can do is to protect her freedom to make her own choices right up until she doesn't need me to protect that anymore.

I swallow down a lump in my throat and try to pay attention to whatever the girl beside me is saying. I think she helps with Travis's merchandise or something and she's currently designing an event T-shirt for tomorrow to sell online.

"We need signatures from everyone," she is saying but my eyes are on Gracie. Idly, I sign the paper she hands me.

"You could be a doctor with a signature like that," she teases and I laugh hollowly.

Wait, this *is* Travis's girl, right? Maybe I should double-check that I didn't sign anything important away. I do a double take. Yeah, blank sheet of paper. My eyes snag on her tight little pink tank and the cleavage she's displaying. She winks at me. Oh. She's one of *those* car girls.

There are three types of women you find at car shows.

The first is the wives and moms. They're dressed normally or in event T-shirts and busy making sure everyone is hydrated, and wearing a hat, and not about to collapse. I've been given granola bars and drink boxes from more of these sweet women than I have any right to.

Then, there are the car girls. These ones are there for the sport. They have their own vehicles. They know how they run. They're nice to the wives and moms but they are very clear about how they aren't there to support the menfolk. They're there to participate. I respect that. When you have to fight for respect, sometimes it makes you twice as good at what you do, and frankly, it's invigorating to be around people who are just plain great at what they love.

The third kind is the kind I don't know what to do with. They're there, I think, to get publicity so that they can move on to something else. They're display models, essentially. They sell T-shirts with car art on them and wear the T-shirt sliced down to where it's barely covering their tanned cleavage. Or they take pictures with guys' cars for magazines while dressed like 50s pin-ups. Or they wander around in pin-up outfits on the arm of a guy in a white T-shirt and slicked-back hair and they talk to important people. They confuse me. I feel like they have a purpose I'm too stupid to understand, but I'm not so stupid as to think their displays are in any way for me. Around them, I generally try to keep my eyes to myself. I don't want to accidentally tumble into a game I don't know how to play.

But I've slipped and fallen into one. I can tell when the girl who took my signature tosses her hair and pops a hip. There's something going on that I don't understand.

I look over to Gracie and finally, I catch her eye. Her cheeks are flushed pink and her eyes are bright with some emotion that I can't understand. She must be worried about her dad, too. I should take her mind off of that.

I'm starving and I want to eat dinner with my husband, I text her, still playing our game.

I'd love to eat with you but I have to finish making my wreck of a vehicle ready to drive in the desert tomorrow. Also, my roll cage looks like it was welded by a third grader and I'm never going to get it fixed if I'm busy joking around with the marketers.

Ouch.

I look up at her and she has a smug expression on her face and those brown eyes are glittering under the LED shop lights like melting caramel sundae topping. At least she's taking her anger out on me for last night instead of retreating into silence. I send her one last text before getting back to work.

I'll don't have time to eat anyway, I'm too busy being admired by my online fans and considering whether I might forgive my husband.

I'm under the vehicle when my phone buzzes.

That's okay. I just made plans with someone else.

Is she still joking with me, or is she really going to dinner with someone else?

I scoot out from underneath the vehicle and scan the shop but she's already gone and I feel a weird tugging in my chest like I'm anchored to her and I can't stay here while she's moving away.

I run a hand over my face and sigh. The more I try to make things better, the worse they get. I'm starting to think that this is just like the situation with the marketer. It's a game with rules I don't understand, and everything I do just seems to make it worse.

Chapter Twenty-Seven

GRACIE

He didn't come home last night.

I lay in my lonely bed and I replayed him gently lifting me off of him over and over again and I thought back to the night before my mom's funeral and how much this reminds me of that. And still, he didn't come. I don't know if I want him or I hate him.

I ate dinner alone. I'd tried to text Dad to see if we could eat together but he said he was busy and had given his staff the night off and when I said we could get take out, he said he didn't want to "cramp my honeymoon vibe" and then ghosted me. It left me feeling more hollow and achy than ever.

Then I went home and found a nice nursing home online that would be the right fit for Vivianne's mom — she's the cashier at the grocery store I go to. And then I called Hazel from college to ask if her design company had an internship program for Marlon's boy because he's graduating next year and he doesn't have the requisite experience in his field. And she does, yay!

And then I lay in my lonely bed and didn't sleep a single wink. Not one.

I don't like fighting with Jasper. It feels kind of like losing him all over again.

And I don't like that I keep wondering if he ate dinner with Jenessa. If she's the reason he didn't come home tonight. If they just hit it off when she was collecting his signature. I've known her kind of off and on for years — seen her at events and stuff. She's a genius artist — just like him, bright and clever — again like him, totally beautiful — him!

And I wouldn't blame him for a second if he lingered over the idea of what it might be like to have a date with a girl he shares so many interests with.

I want to throw something. Something big would be best. But then I'd have to fix it.

I want to talk to someone. I'm so tangled up in his huge revelation that we're really married and I don't know what to do about that other than wait these two weeks out. Or the revelation that Jasper doesn't sleep with girls he isn't in love with — is he the last guy on the planet like that? I need to talk so bad that I'm aching with it.

I text Melissa while I make coffee. I need it. I'm a walking mess. I showered but I'm having a bad hair day. All my clothes look wrong on me. Why do I have to live this day? I just want to go back to bed.

I'm dying over here. I text and I make liberal use of the death head emoji.

Spill. But know I've had no coffee and I might not make sense.

My percolator is dripping as I text. *Remember how you told me I was the marrying kind?*

Yes?

It turns out we're married for real.

No.

Yes! There was a mix-up. I signed a real marriage license and it was filed! The only way out is divorce.

No.

Yes!

Are you freaking out?

What do you think?

I think this doesn't change anything. This is still your big chance to try to get him to fall for you. She sends a kissy emoji.

I tried that, I text back with a see-no-evil monkey emoji. *I was all over him. I was very clear about what I was offering. He practically threw me across the room.*

The bastard.

Well, okay, I'm exaggerating. He very gently set me aside.

Did he say WHY? She sends me the monocle emoji.

My coffee is done brewing. I fix it up and start to drain my mug as I type quickly to her.

He said he doesn't do that unless there's love.

Awwwwww.

Don't you dare awww me. Listen. He doesn't love me and he basically said so and now I feel like a fool.

Well, is that exactly what he said?

I don't remember the exact words.

Did he say specifically that he didn't love you?

He said he doesn't have sex with people unless there's love or unless he loves them or something, I don't remember but it was heavily implied that I was not a candidate.

Well, maybe he thinks YOU don't love HIM.

MEL. IS. SA! I text, *You are supposed to be on my side.*

I am!

Then be mad for me!

Fine. I'm totally mad. She sends me three angry gifs while I hurriedly gather my things and drain the last of my coffee. *Why don't you ask him,* she texts when she's done. *Isn't he right there? Oooh. Is he reading these over your shoulder?*

He didn't come home last night. My text looks as miserable as I am.

Her three little dots dance for so long that I'm in my Bronco and halfway down the road before her text finally arrives.

Uh oh.

I don't text back. *I* do not break the law.

It'll be okay, she texts.

Maybe he slept in his truck.

I'm almost at work before I get her last text.

Just don't do anything stupid, okay? Are you at work?

I maneuver through the busy parking lot. Already, there are trucks loaded with trailers and off-road rigs ready to go. The crowds from yesterday are back and this time with signs. One says "BOOM. You're It!" Which makes no sense. Another one reads "Team Hollis." I have to swerve around a very enthusiastic woman whose hair forms a perfect triangle and whose T-shirt reads, "I'll marry Travis if the blonde says no."

I feel bad for Travis.

It takes me ages to find a place to park — way at the back, of course — and by the time I do, I have another text from Melissa.

Don't feel bad. Guys are jerks. It will all be okay.

But I do not believe it will be okay.

My dad is filming an ad inside the BOOM shop and he segues immediately into a big banner reveal for the event, displaying Jenessa's T-shirt design — how does he already have one printed and the sleeves cut off of it to wear? — and then he's doing a walking shot down the garage showing every one of the builds that isn't already trailered.

"This is going to be a blast," he says. "We were going to do Moab but then a friend offered his private property to really test these vehicles out. And, of course, I said yes, so we're driving four hours to get there, and then we're doing a four to six-hour run on this guy's amazing property — you guys are going to love it!" He's gesturing with his hands, his beard bristling with excitement. Was he really here all night? He looks well rested and freshly showered. "Expect multiple different videos on this one, guys. There's no way we're going to get all the footage crammed into just one! Each of these vloggers is running his own camera crew, so like and follow them as well as us, so you get all the deep cuts on this one, okay? It's going to be amazing."

When the feed kills he's bouncing over to me. "Ready for the day, Gracie?"

"Sure," I say with a smile. It's not his fault that I feel like all my edges are burning up and my life is up in smoke.

He coughs and I feel bad for even feeling sorry for myself for even a moment. This is about him. This is about making his last time here as sweet as possible.

"Listen," he says confidentially to me. "I know Jasper didn't sleep at your place last night."

I freeze. Where is he going with this?

"If this marriage of yours is a ruse and you aren't happy, you don't have to go through with it. Not to make me happy. I'm just happy being your dad."

I feel like I have a brick in my stomach.

"Besides," he adds, conspiratorily, "if you look around you'll see there are a lot of really qualified young men here who would be happy to take that role. Watch them today. Maybe one will stand out."

I roll my eyes. "I'm married, Dad. Stop trying to set me up."

He backs away with his hands up and his little-boy mischief face on full display. "I'm just saying ..."

"So am I." I got married to make him happy. I won't do it twice.

"Oh," he says as he backs away, "I forgot to mention it, but we need you along for the wheeling today."

And just like that my stomach is plummeting through my knees. Brick? What brick. Everything feels like sloshing water inside. It's going to spill out any minute now.

"What?" I ask in a tiny voice.

"Hollis' cameraman ate something rotten. He needs a replacement and all my guys are tapped for other spots. I need you to run a camera. You can do it. You've done it before."

He's already two cars away from me. If I'm going to object I'll have to chase after him or shout so everyone can hear me.

"What about Chase?" I try in a last-ditch effort to get out of it.

"His mom had a thing," my dad shouts back, but he's turning now and Tanner is running up with some last-minute emergency and I'm left staring at his back with my palms sweating and my belly swimming.

I don't go off-roading. I haven't told anyone this. I've just managed to not do it for five years. There's always a good excuse. Always a reason to slip out of it. This time, when I look around at the swarm of activity around me, I realize I'm caught. I can't get out of it unless I confess to why, and I just can't do that. I can't.

I bite my lip and gather my things like I'm in a dream, and before I know it I'm being loaded into the truck towing two of the project vehicles, and I put my head between my knees before I even see who I'm riding with, and I try not to panic, but it's not working. I'm panicking hard.

I can't do this. I can't.

A hand reaches out and grabs mine and I don't even care who it is. If it's Hollis or Travis or Pretty Boy or Tanner. I don't care. I cling to it like a lifeline.

Then

JASPER

We're almost at the turn-off to the off-roading site and I'm laughing at some joke Gracie is reading to me off the back of her candy packet. It's super cheesy but she thinks it's hilarious and keeps doing this laugh-snort thing that's utterly adorable.

My camera gear is packed in the back and Gracie's gone over and over it all with me. She wants all this to be perfect for the book she's going to write about our moms and their off-roading history. We don't fit in their off-roader, which is fine. They're clearly having a complete ball riding in front of us. I see my mom gesturing wildly with her arms as her hair whips in the wind and Gracie's mom hunches over the steering wheel laughing hysterically.

We're traveling right behind them — my Ranger will be able to follow them down the trail well enough to get our camera gear in place, even if it can't take the bigger obstacles like Amy's Jeep can. Amy's blonde curls tangle up with my mom's darker hair as the wind whips up and I ease up a bit on the throttle to put more space between us and them. That's quite the wind. I wouldn't want to be following too closely if it makes them slow down or something. We're on a freeway, but it's only one lane in each direction, so there's not a lot of room if things go sideways, and I like to be cautious. I have the most precious girl in the world riding with me. I don't want to give her whiplash from braking too hard and fast.

"Don't you think so, Jasper?" Gracie is asking me and I start to turn to ask her to repeat herself when it happens.

A car coming from the other direction crosses into our lane and smokes the front driver's side of Gracie's mom's Jeep. They're spinning immediately and the car that hit them is crashing right for us. I pull hard to the left and take us across incoming traffic — barely missing an SUV — and to the shoulder on the other side, and then to the desert sand beyond that before I can slow us in a skid of sand and dust.

My breath is huffing in my chest.

None of this feels real. It's like my brain is taking photographs every few seconds instead of a running video.

I stumble out of the vehicle before I register what I'm doing. I don't even know if I've killed the engine.

Through the clouds of dust, I see cars slowing down. Coming from both directions. But I can't see the Jeep.

I choke on my own breath.

Mom.

I think my rib cage might be crumpling. Maybe I hit something and didn't realize it.

I hear Gracie's door open and then I'm right there, trying to urge her back in the vehicle.

"No, no, no," I'm saying but she keeps trying to get out.

"Mom's there," she says breathlessly. "She .. she…"

"Are you hurt?" I ask stupidly. My voice trembling.

"No." It's little more than a gust of breath.

"Then, dammit, Gracie, stay there."

I don't wait to see if she does but I sure hope she listens. I'm already sprinting across the sand to the highway, to where an eighteen-wheeler is blocking my view. I skid around it and run into a wall.

"Easy son, easy."

It's a man's chest.

"My mom. My mom's in that Jeep," I say, trying to dodge around him.

He grunts like he's hurt. I look up. Way up. He's a huge black man in a cowboy hat and boots. His wallet is stuck in the breast pocket of his mother-of-pearl button shirt. I think the eighteen-wheeler might be his rig. He has that slow patience of a man who spends hours a day watching territory pass by.

"Already called for an ambulance, son," he says but that's not good enough.

I try to pull out of his grip and get to her. She's going to need me. She's going to need to hold my hand.

"You can't help any," the man says, grappling with me and winning and moving me physically around the nose of his truck so that my view is completely blocked. "There are others waiting with her for the ambulance."

"She needs me. I'm her son." I try to explain to him but he shakes his head.

"It's a kindness they're doing for the dead, son. I've seen a few of these in my time. Trust me. You don't want to wake up in the night and remember this."

And I think I might be crying and I'm definitely not thinking straight, because somehow I'm being held against a stranger's barrel chest that smells heavily of cigarette smoke, and then I'm being eased back onto my own feet and a hand clamps onto my shoulder and steers me back toward the Ranger.

"Let's see if you've damaged your truck," he says kindly.

I'm grateful for his hand. I can't see a thing. It's all a blur. And if he lets go, I know I'll run back to the freeway because I can't leave my mom. Not like that. I can't.

"Don't even think about it," he warns, and then we're back at the Ranger, and I have other things to think about.

Gracie takes one look at me and says, "Are they ... are they ..."

I never learn the name of the trucker who spent an hour keeping two teenagers together while the police do their thing and my dad eventually arrives to claim us. I know that he spoke low and steady and sometimes when I find myself in a crisis even now, it's his voice in my mind coaching me through it. I know that the smell of his cigarette smoke lingered in my clothes long after I washed them. And that every time I see a man step out of a big rig wearing a white cowboy hat, I feel a bit shaky. Some things just don't fade.

Chapter Twenty-Eight

She hasn't even looked at me all morning. Not so much as a glance. I'm bone-tired from working all night on the build. I managed to grab a cup of some kind of battery acid Tanner was trying to pass off as coffee, but I've had no breakfast and no shower. I cleaned most of the grease and grit off under an outdoor hose in the back, and then Pretty Boy threw a BOOM T-shirt at my head with a "don't say we never give you anything" and I jumped into the truck I was assigned to and off I go.

Travis is driving. He's joking with his camera operator in the front seat, giving a mock weather report that I hope Mark never hears because it's clearly making fun of him and his obsession with starting every video he makes with a report on the weather conditions.

"It's a sunny day today," Travis is saying totally deadpan, "Let's be really clear about that. It's sunny. And hot. Hot and sunny. I can hardly believe I'm saying that here in Utah. Do you know how often they get hot sunny days? Well, not often enough, or we wouldn't have to point it out to you."

I'm glad that they're distracted. I've got Gracie's hand tucked in mine and she's hyperventilating with her head between her knees. It took me all of two seconds to imagine why. Does no one else realize that she doesn't want to go off-roading? That it's bringing her right back to that day?

I draw little circles on the back of her hand with my thumb and in my mind, there's the smell of cigarette smoke and I can still feel the ghost of a heavy hand on my shoulder.

I swallow down a lot of emotions that I can't seem to bottle up, and I just sit there with her for maybe half an hour as her breathing calms down. Just like this, we're back there again in that terrible day. Just like that day, we're the only ones who can anchor each other. And my heart is in my throat because I know that when she looks at me she's going to see all the pain and regret I've had carefully packed away for years. It will all be right there on display.

"You look grim there, man," Travis says and it takes a second for me to realize he's talking to me. "I don't blame you. You've lost before you've even started. I bet the big man makes you get divorced and give over that pretty wife of yours to the winner."

I feel Gracie freeze beside me but Travis is just being a dick.

"That's not how marriage works, Travis," I say easily.

"I was thinking of giving it a try," he says waggling his eyebrows into the rearview mirror. "Wanna get divorced so I can see how I like it?"

"It's flattering," I tell him, deadpanning just like him. "You're clearly a successful and attractive man, but you don't have Gracie's hair. I have a thing for blondes."

His cameraman — Phil — is snickering so hard they have to cut and move to something else.

"You're a character man, you should have your own channel," Travis snorts, while Phil tries to get a hold of himself. "Remember that guy in Phoenix, Phil? What was his name?"

I ignore their conversation and look over at Gracie who is

peeking through her hair at me. She tries to slip her hand away, but I hold on tight. She might not like me right now, but she needs me.

"I didn't sleep all night," she says in a small voice, as if she can explain away her panic attack that way. "I kept waiting for you to come home."

I feel a pang at that. I should have texted. But also the word "home" twists something inside me in a way that I really like. I want her to keep saying it to me.

"Come here," I say instead, and I pillow her head on my lap and rearrange things so the arm holding her hand is folded around her. "You can sleep on the way."

And I'm grateful when she doesn't object. So grateful, that when she closes her eyes I play with her tangled curls in my free hand, running my fingers through them over and over as I caress her to sleep. I could do this every day. Watch her sleep. Help her get there. I don't need to sleep at all. I'll just do it vicariously through her. It's like heaven.

Something inside me feels melty and fragile. It's not a feeling I've had before and I don't know what to do with it.

By the time we get to our destination, I know Travis a lot better. When Phil turned off the camera and went to sleep, he and I had a long chat about his home in Indiana and his first truck, and how hard it is for him to get contractors to come through for him as he's building his new shop. I tell him about some of the shoots I've done recently. He likes the foreign ones. I don't think he's traveled outside the US.

I thought this guy was an idiot. Turns out it's just his way of making money.

"Look, in a minute Phil's gonna wake up and I'll have to bust your balls again, guy," he says to me like he doesn't know my name and we didn't just have a nice two-hour conversation. "But don't take it personally. You're alright. You can come by to my place and help me wreck stuff the next time you're near Indiana."

"Thanks," I say and I realize it might be fun to blow off some steam like that.

I have to wake Gracie up when we get there and that's the worst part of my day. I could have sat like that with her forever. She gives me a kind of shy half-smile and then looks away immediately like it hurts her to look at me. That's okay. She can do what she needs to do.

I'm busy after that, helping to unload vehicles and sort out equipment while her dad does a spiel for the camera about the route and how this is the closest you could get to a completely untamed trail while still being safe. He's really hamming it up for the viewers but I do think it would have been nice to have a map or something because this private trail really isn't that well marked.

I'm just starting up the engine on my wrecker build and making sure everything is okay. It's been cutting out at funny times and I can't tell if there's a problem in the wiring or something worse. Adam appears in my open window with a huge grin on his face.

"Hey, so Jasper, we're running light on camera operators, so I asked Gracie to come along and I figured she could ride with you because if she has any camera issues you'll know what to do." He's clearly up to something because he always is, but I'm not sure what it is this time.

"Does she want to go wheeling?" I ask mildly. After her freak-out on the way up here, I'm going to guess she doesn't.

"You tell me," Adam says with a knowing look in his eye. "After all, you're her husband."

I make a sound that he can take for assent if he wants, but it's mostly annoyance. And then Gracie is there, looking miserable.

"He's all ready for you, honey," her dad says, kissing her

cheek and then leaving at a jog to go talk to the vehicle ahead of us. The way things have shaken out, we'll be the last in line.

I try to focus on what a beautiful day it is out here, how the rocks are shadowed so extremely at this time in the morning that any picture would look like it was not quite real. But it's hard to focus when Gracie is climbing in the passenger side and getting comfortable on the long bench seat. It's almost long enough that she could lay out on it. A momentary vision of Gracie relaxed and lying on this truck seat agitates me enough that I lean low over my steering wheel and wrap my fists around it to keep out of trouble.

"Gracie," I say by way of greeting.

"Jas," her voice is small.

"Rather be here going off-roading or base jump from a sixty-story building?"

"I pick the jump," she says tightly. "Even if there's no parachute."

I swallow. My throat feels thick. I steal a glance to the side to see she's working to set up her camera, but I don't care if she gets any footage.

I drum my fingers on the steering wheel. I want to ask if the reason that she's upset is because this is off-roading and her mom died on the way to do this or if she's upset because she's trapped in here with me. But I don't know how to get the words out.

She's quiet for the first while as we get rolling. I see her shooting but I'm not an on-camera kind of guy so I just drive and don't pay any attention to that. The guys in front of us are doing their thing and I hear whoops and cheers as they get warmed up on the easier obstacles. I'm not really into the ride and I can't find I care. I'd rather be filming it — but even then, I'm exhausted and miserable, and for once I don't even want to look at my camera.

"You look awful," Gracies says eventually.

"I was up all night," I agree.

She makes a huffing sound kind of like disbelief.

"Why do you think I didn't come back to your place?" I ask, annoyed now.

"I thought maybe you'd gone for dinner with someone else," she says tightly.

I look at her, frowning. What's she talking about?

"That was a game, Gracie. Can't you tell when we're playing games?"

When I meet her gaze she has her eyes leveled on me and my heart kicks up a notch. I just want to stop this stupid truck and pull her into my lap and kiss her until she can't form words. I bite the inside of my cheek and wince at it. Stay focused, Jasper.

"It's hard to tell," she says in a tight voice. "Because I think we're playing a game and then a real marriage license makes an appearance."

"I told you that you can divorce me." It comes out like a growl, even though I don't mean it that way. It's a sore spot and she poked it.

"And I will," she shoots back. "Just not yet."

I nod like it's no big deal even though it feels like a knife to my chest. As long as I've known Gracie I've wanted her. I've never gone a single day without wanting her, thinking about her, dreaming about her. She's been with me in Malaysia and Italy, in New York and Brazil. Anywhere I've been, her presence came, too. Until I couldn't breathe without the memory of her sneaking in with every inhale.

My dad was right. I meant those vows. I'm married to her in my heart even if she walks away from me when her ruse is done and never looks back. Even if she hates me or forgets me, I can't hate her and I won't forget her.

Some people talk about love. I don't talk about things that matter to me. But if love means that all your dreams whirl around one person, and all your memories are drenched in the sunlight of that person's presence, and every thought of making a home or even about sex is only ever of *her*, then who needs to talk? Who needs to talk about the air when it's all around you? Who needs to bring it up when you're drawing it in with every heave of your chest?

I sit and just let myself enjoy the agony of her being right here. She's like the sun. I need her for survival but when I get too close she burns me up and makes me blind and crazy.

I think my jaw is clenched and my body is rigid. Every jarring bump of the truck just rattles everything together more than usual and as I steal little glances at her my whole body just floods with this constant awareness of her being *right here* and this longing to draw her in close and be with her properly, to take my sweet time and taste every part I've been dreaming of for years, to show her with my hands and lips how my heart is completely hers.

Not mine, I remind myself. Not mine to touch or kiss. And she's doing her best to remind me of that and I'd better listen.

"I didn't sleep last night, either," she says and I think she's trying to be kind but the thought of her asleep all tucked up in her bed does something extremely uncomfortable to me and I have to adjust my seat to keep from making things worse.

But then she says, "I was lonely."

And there's something so true in the way that word rings out that it twists something in me. I shoot her a sidelong glance and thoughts of attraction all evaporate as an urge to protect her, to take care of her, to shelter her from every storm hits me like a wave. I'm overwhelmed by it. I'm not sure what to do about it.

I clench my fists on the wheel a bit tighter and glance over at her and melt at the sadness in her eyes. Her fingers are white-knuckled where they grip the dash of the truck. She's not enjoying off-roading at all, but maybe this conversation is at least distracting her a bit.

"Gracie," I say and it comes out like a grunt, like I've been hit in the gut. "Listen."

But I don't know how to say more. She's looking at me and there's uncertainty in her huge eyes. I have to get this out even if I don't have the right words.

"I didn't do this on purpose. I would never tie you to something or force you — ever, in any way — not physically or emotionally or ... with a commitment you didn't mean to make. You don't ... you don't have to have me around."

"Is that why you didn't come home last night?" The word home sets little butterflies fluttering all through me. It's not a thing I get to have. But if I did have a home again, I'd want it to be with her. "Because you didn't mean to commit to me?" There's an edge in her voice. Something accusatory, though I still have no idea what she's accusing me of doing. "I ... wow, I'm sorry," she says suddenly. "I've asked for so much from you and it sounds like I'm asking for faithfulness, like you're actually my husband." She huffs out a disbelieving laugh. "I'm sorry, I'm such an idiot."

I look over at her, totally confused. "You don't have to ask me for things, Gracie. Not when they're already yours."

"I don't think I understand."

Maybe we're both confused. I'm not good at this. I swallow. I think my hands are shaking and it's not just this climb up a bald rock I'm doing as I talk. I don't like talking about deep things because they hurt to talk about.

"You can have whatever you want from me, Gracie. Or not have it. Whatever you want. If it's commitment, well you can have that. If it's single-minded devotion, you don't have to ask, it can just be yours."

"It ..." her voice wobbles. "It didn't feel like I could have anything I wanted the night before last."

Well, shit.

Shit.

"I," I clear my throat but my words come out all gravelly. "If you're saying it's my body you want, then you can have that, too."

Even if it feels like some kind of deal with the devil to agree to sex without love. Like it might damn us both.

She practically chokes and then catches herself. "Jasper, every time we get close, you run."

And that's fair. Sure.

"I mean it," is all I can think to say. "Anything I have is yours."

This conversation is not helping what I'm doing. I'm totally distracted, not paying enough attention, and the other vehicles have gotten pretty far ahead of us.

"What if I want you right now?" she asks and those words send little shivers right up me but I'm sure she must be teasing me. She must know what her words do to me.

I shoot a glance at her but her face is deadpanned. She's better at that than Travis.

"Take whatever you want," I say gruffly.

She doesn't say anything and after a few minutes, I steal a glance over at her to see she's chewing on her thumb. Something she does when she's nervous about a test at school or about getting in trouble for something she's been caught at.

"What if I decide I'm going to leave all this and travel with you. And make you stay my husband?" she asks.

"What if you do?" I growl. I'm sick of hypotheticals.

She laughs nervously. "Well, can I have that?"

I glance over and catch her eye and she seems to catch her breath at the look in my gaze and I like that. I want to see her catch her breath like that as I breathe into her neck, and do slow, luxurious things to her body.

"I already told you," I growl. "You can have anything you want."

"What if I want to stay here and work for my dad and I ask you to stay with me?" she presses.

I grunt. I do not like working for her father. But for her? If it meant keeping her?

"I'm starting to think you don't understand the word 'anything'," I say.

"This isn't good," she says and it's almost a whisper. "One person shouldn't have that kind of power over another. Not unless ... unless it's love."

And I don't answer that because I'm not an idiot and I know perfectly well that if I open that door and admit that I'm overwhelmed with love for her, I can never close it again, and when she admits that she doesn't love me back, I'll be a wreck of a man and no one will ever be able to drag me home and fix me.

$$\mathscr{T}hen$$

JASPER

I'm supposed to be at home and if Dad comes looking for me and finds I'm not there he might panic. But I don't think he will. He started drinking when we got home from the funeral parlor and he hasn't stopped in hours. He just sits there on his la-z-boy with the tv on mute, drinking, and staring, and drinking more. He hasn't said a word since he came to get me from the side of the road and the cops told him Alicia was gone. He's been letting Adam do all the talking, make all the arrangements. He just nods to anything Adam says. He's always been a follower, but right now? With mom dead? Shouldn't he step up and be a father. Can't he see that I'm hurting, too?

Whatever. I'm grown. I can take care of myself. And I'm not going to go drinking. I don't see how it would help.

My chest feels like something crushed it. I can't take a full breath. I can't shut off my mind. It loops round and round and round. I didn't sleep last night. Just threw up a bunch and then lay in my bed miserable. If mom had been there, she would have noticed and been worried and there'd be ginger ale, and saltines, and a cold cloth for my forehead. It made me sob until I choked and threw up all over again to think of that.

But today isn't last night and I can't just stay like that forever. I'm not the only one who lost someone.

That's why I'm here to see Gracie. I can see her dad pacing back and forth in the living room. The light is on. I don't know what he's thinking but at least he isn't drinking himself into cirrhosis of the liver, so he's one up on *my* dad.

Gracie's house is bigger than mine and all on one floor, so it's easy enough to crunch around it on the gravel path and sneak past the bushes to tap on her window.

My heart's in my throat as she parts the curtains and opens the window enough for me to slip inside. I don't know if she blames me. I don't know if she'll talk to me. I just knew I had to be here. And then she's there, throwing herself into my arms, her eyes puffy and red from crying.

I hold her and kiss her hair as she dissolves into me.

"Jas," she breathes and that's all it takes for me to start crying, too.

I kiss the top of her head again and then gently draw her after me so that I can stumble back to her bed and put her on my lap. She's crying, and our tears mingle as I press my forehead to hers and kiss her forehead and her cheek, cupping the other cheek with my palm.

"I'm sorry," I whisper and the words barely escape around the solid lump in my throat. "I'm so, so sorry Gracie."

"Me, too." Her voice is small, as small as mine feels, like maybe her chest is crushed, too.

I swallow down shaking tears and press a tender, loose kiss to her lips. I've never done that before, but I don't have words for how I feel for her right now. I don't have words or even thoughts. And when her lips open and fit into mine and they slide into a kiss so easy and natural I can't seem to stop. This kiss is like a lifeline thrown when you're drowning. It doesn't dull the pain but it washes through it with a shiver of something else and I want more … need more … so I don't stop. I keep going, soft, gentle, whisper sweet kisses at first, while I caress her cheek, feel the tears in a gentle pinch of her chin, tangle my other hand in her curls to hold her delicately, while I turn all my attentions to her sweet mouth.

When she sighs into my lips, I release her hair, and my arms wrap around her waist so that both my forearms rest there, one over the other. I draw her into my chest. I can't get enough of her against me. I feel like I'm still drowning, but now I'm breathing her. And she's so soft and warm and dainty under my arms that it breaks some wall I've put inside. Why have I never done this before? Why have *we* never done this when times were good and hearts were whole. Why is it only now that we are broken that we hold our jagged edges together?

And then my hands are moving of their own accord, fanning out so my palm can rest over the center of her back and the other over her hip so that I can hold her to me, but hold her lightly so she could slip away if she wanted to.

I don't think she wants to. She puts her little hands on my chest and pushes me back onto her bed and straddles me and before I can do more than groan, she's on top of me, deepening our kiss, panting into it. I feel her sweet tongue slip into my mouth and I'm desperate to respond, to show how welcome she is. I open my lips for her and caress her tongue with mine and when she draws back, I follow, heavy-lidded, absorbing her like pain killers into the bloodstream, but she isn't killing the pain at all. She's intensifying it and lighting up all the edges so that danger and excitement and pleasure all dance through and highlight the agony rather than removing it. Maybe this isn't a healthy thing to do. Maybe I don't care.

I don't care as she reaches and pulls my shirt over my head but I'm gasping, lips parted when I see her face. The faint blush on her cheeks and the way she bites her lip make me instantly hard, and now I'm blushing, because I can tell she feels it. Her wobbly smile lights for me and then she's sliding her own T-shirt over her head and I gasp with a kind of broken longing at this look at her body. I've seen her in her bikini before. Her in a bra shouldn't be new territory, but that she is showing this to me specifically, to me intentionally, charges the air in a way that a breezy visit to the beach does not.

I think I might be drowning in Gracie and I don't want to come up for air. She presses herself to me and I flip her over, tucking her gently under me, like I can protect her and I'm so deep into kissing her, into pouring my whole self out into this passion, this moment, in a desperate desire not to feel any other moments, that I don't even notice that she's fumbling with my pants until she's pulling my boxers down and wrapping her hands around my length and then it hits me.

I'm at Gracie's house in her bed mostly naked. I'm pretty sure covering your calves is pretty meaningless with everything else exposed.

I'm about to have sex with her for the first time. Our first time. My first time. Maybe hers, too. I have no reason to think otherwise.

And we're going to do it the night after our moms died. While we're supposed to be crying for them. And we're always going to remember that we betrayed them like that. And will she even be able to look at me in the morning? Or ever? If I let us do this?

And I can't think past that. I just roll away and pull my pants up roughly.

I choke out, "Sorry, I'm so so sorry," to her shocked face.

And then I'm rolling out her window, hitting her gravel path with a bruising fall to my palms and knees. I've forgotten my favorite "The Eagles" shirt behind on her floor and I'm racing away from her dad's fancy house like I've robbed the place, choking over the need to start sobbing all over again.

Chapter Twenty-Nine

GRACIE

Things feel ... different ... between us. It's as if his declaration that he'd give me anything has ushered a new color into the world. It's not that I'm seeing new things, but everything I see looks a little different.

We're at the back of the pack and after a few hours, there's no sign of the others at all except the tracks they make in the occasional sandy spot, or the black of tire rubber on some of the rocks. I have to get out on the tough parts to guide Jasper — to tell him where the holes are he can't see and where his tires are grabbing or spinning. I'm not very good at it. He doesn't seem to care.

And everything that's been between us this whole time is just hanging there in this electrically-charged air.

He left me before when I needed him, when I thought we had something special together. He could leave me again. But he's here right now saying he's okay with being actually married to me and he's okay with staying married. That he'd stay or go depending on what I want, and I'm not sure how that isn't love. It sounds like love to me.

If it's not love, then it's still something that paints him in a different light entirely, and suddenly I'm seeing him not as a reluctant ally but as a hopeful friend, betting all his dignity not because he's driven entirely by guilt, but because he feels this ... intense desire to be a part of my life in every way and be close to me.

Which is exactly how I feel about him. I want him close. I don't want him even as far away as the floor of my bedroom when I'm sleeping. I want him up in the bed with me. I want him on my kitchen stool when I get up in the morning. I want him constantly in my texts telling me things and revealing little hints of secrets. I want him making me laugh at the ridiculousness of my dad and his BOOM Empire.

I want him like the old days where everything bad and good was shared, when I didn't know where Gracie ended and Jasper started. I want to sleep in all his T-shirts, not just that Eagles one he left in my bedroom. I want to be covered by his kisses and his tender hands.

And it lights up something between us that makes our silence seem full — full of all the things we aren't saying.

When he glances at me, it's electric and I know he feels it, too because his breathing gets heavier. When he praises me for helping him up an obstacle, it feels like a warm fire in winter, relaxing me, opening me up.

When we stop to admire the view and eat a quick snack up on one rocky obstacle and his arm brushes mine, I suck in a breath and I just want his arms around me. I feel cold without them. I want all his kisses, every single one of them. I want to catalog them and know them by heart. And it makes me wonder if maybe he could see this color before. If maybe it's the reason he panicked and ran.

Everything he did back then looks different now, too. Has he felt like this all along ... for years? The thought sends a delicious shiver through me.

I wasn't supposed to let myself fall for him again. I knew it was a danger. I knew I was close to slipping up, because ever since that night before our moms' funeral, when I close my eyes, it's still him there with me, kissing my hair and stroking my back with those big hands of his and holding me in his strong arms with a touch so butterfly-light that I never feel trapped, only treasured.

And I'm lost again. Lost to the beauty in his eyes when they catch mine and go darker. There are little sun-kissed lines around them from all his time outdoors and I want to press kisses to those lines. I'm lost to watching his big hands drive the truck so capably, his long legs working the pedals, his shoulder and arm muscles rippling and flexing as he looks over his shoulder and works the wheel. I'm falling so hard that I'm staring at his full lips, my heart skipping a beat when they curve into a half-smile. He's watching me constantly. It's like he's seeing this color shift with me.

It's when I'm guiding him up a huge chute of an obstacle that everything changes. I have to get out and climb up ahead of him and I'm nervous about it because I can't quite see everything he needs me to see.

"I think you're okay if you stay right," I call to him. It's late afternoon and the sun is glaring on his windshield and I'm trying to catch a shot of him doing this because I haven't remembered to film much of this ride, I've been so caught up in seeing things all new.

Something isn't working with the camera, and I glance down to see what it is. That's when I hear a strangled curse and then the sound of something squeak and then smash. I look up in time to see his vehicle slipping sideways and backward, falling down the obstacle he'd just climbed.

It's not just falling. It hits a rock at a strange angle, and flips and I gasp as it lands on the roll cage I didn't think he'd done a good enough job making.

I'm too scared to scream but I'm already running forward, trying to scramble down the rocks without breaking my leg.

It's too quiet. The only sound is one wheel spinning in the air, wobbling just enough to make a sound.

I've lost him. I've lost him right when I realized I want to keep him forever. Right when I realized he'd probably *let me* keep him. I've lost him before he was really found. My breath is sawing out of me in harsh whistles as I hurry down the rock.

This time, I'm not waiting in the truck to see what happened. This time, I'm going to have to go see for myself.

My whole world is spinning. Little flares of light pop and crackle in my vision like my brain can't handle the stress of using my eyes properly on top of everything else, and then I finally reach the truck.

It's on its side, battered and scraped. And I manage to climb up and look in through the broken window. Little bits of tempered glass are crumbled everywhere and under them, I see him slumped on the far side of the cab. He hadn't been wearing a seat belt. I wasn't even sure there *were* seatbelts for this rig.

"Jasper," I gasp. "Jasper."

He looks so still. So broken. And something terrible rolls in my chest, echoing like the grief I've been feeling for five years, calling me back down into the blackness.

And then he moves and my breath huffs out of me with a little cry. He's not dead. It's not the end.

Oh God. It's a prayer, I think. Not a curse.

I can't stop shaking. I can hardly breathe, my chest hurts so badly. I hurry to stand up on the box of the truck and I work to get the driver's door open, but it's too dented from rolling and it won't swing free. I'm gasping through a sob.

What do I do now?

How do I get to him?

He might be badly hurt.

And then he's there, pulling himself through the shattered window. I didn't even realize I was crying until he's sitting on the door with his feet still through the window and I'm leaning over him trying to check for a head wound and my tears are splashing on his cheeks. There's a little blood, but not much.

"I love you," he says and it comes out all raw and broken. One of my tears is caught in his unshaven stubble. A bit of crumbled glass is in the shell of his ear. I remove it gently.

"Are you okay? Is something broken?" My hands are all over him, checking for injuries, terrified that I'll find one. They're running down his arms and over his chest, checking his back, his ribs, his collarbone. "Your truck, oh my god, your truck."

"Gracie," he says, but I can't stop. It's just a scrape on his cheek, I think. That's the only injury I can find. Just a scrape. I dab it with the hem of my shirt and he winces, grabbing my hand in both of his and tugging it down. "I love you so much it hurts."

"You what?" This isn't making sense.

"I love you." His eyes are wide and vulnerable, lips parted.

"You love me?" The words stumble free with my disbelief. "You said you didn't. You said you wouldn't have sex with me because you didn't."

It's crazy to be talking about this right now with his truck a wreck under us, but I can't help it. It just spills out.

"What?" He sounds stunned. Maybe he does have a head wound after all. "Gracie, I ... what?"

"You said you didn't love me. But it doesn't matter. You're alive. You're ... I don't think you're badly hurt. Let me look at your eyes. I think your pupils are supposed to be big if you have a head injury."

"Gracie, I never ... I would never" he sounds mystified and a bit reverent, "... never ... say I don't love you."

"But you did," I insist.

I'm supposed to be checking for injuries. I know that. But I'm distracted by this conversation. I'm distracted by how he takes my face in his hands like a bowl he's going to drink from and I don't know what a head injury is meant to look like in a man's pupils, but I think I know desire when I see it, and he wants to drink me up.

"What I told you, *Daf*," he says my nickname, like he's giving it back to me. "Is that I would never slip into your bed and then slip out of it just because you're grateful to me for helping you out. Or because we're married by accident. Or because I want it so bad that even after a car wreck, all I can think about it is undressing you and worshiping every inch of your flesh. *That's* what I was saying to you. Because I would never take from you when all I want to do is give."

His eyes are so intense that I'm afraid they might light me on fire.

"It isn't taking if I want to give it," I say a little breathlessly.

"It is, if you don't love me. Because then I'm taking things you could be sharing with someone you do love. And it is if we aren't so tied up together we'll never part because then I'm taking all the things you could be saving for someone you *do* want to love like that. I meant *you*, Gracie. I meant that I wouldn't have sex with you if *you* didn't love me, too. There was never any question at all about whether I loved you."

"There wasn't?" I ask, creeping a little closer. The truck shifts in a way that makes him swallow, his Adam's apple bobbing. And there's nothing sensible at all about sitting up on a wrecked truck with my lips an inch from his. And I don't care, because I'm not going anywhere. Not right now.

"No," he says. "There wasn't."

And it's almost a growl. And my heart is racing so fast that I have to swallow to try to keep it calm. My eyes don't want to focus. All they'll look at are his lips and his eyes. They're black holes trying to swallow me up and I can't help it. Not when he's looking at me like that.

I lean in and I kiss him — not a gentle "thank God you're alive" kiss but a kiss of possession, a rough, stubble-brushing, lip-twisting kiss that tells him he's mine right through.

I want him like I want to breathe.

And he loves me.

He ran, but he loves me.

He abandoned me, but he loves me.

And now he's back and the idea that he loves me sets me on fire. I can hardly breathe. My breath is hot and heady in my lungs and I cling to the front of his shirt and taste his lips and taste them again like I can never get enough. Was he always this ridiculously kissable?

When we break apart, I'm panting, and so is he, his lips swollen from my kisses, his eyes glassy and open. He swallows and his Adam's apple bobs and I'm undone and I reach for him again, my hands so hungry that they can't get enough of his warm flesh through his cotton T-shirt.

My mouth is even more insistent, as if it is afraid he'll run again if I don't bind him here with all my passion.

"Stay," I beg him in the little gasps between kisses. "Stay here with me."

He can have anything — any part of me — if only he'll just *stay.*

"I don't care if it's only for a little while. I know I'm a lot."

"You're everything," his voice is raw and he's shivering as he lets the tip of his nose run down the length of mine like a caress and then softly nuzzle to the side as his mouth opens and his breath is mixing with mine again, and then he's tasting me like I'm something sweet he's been craving.

I just want as much of him as I can get. For as long as I can get it.

I let my hands find their way under the hem of his T-shirt

and run along his warm skin as I moan into his mouth. He moans with me as if we're one. Bright light shoots through my closed eyelids and I gasp, pulling away as I try to shade my eyes to see who has caught us. I feel his hands fall away from me.

Busted.

No, no, no! I wanted to keep his hands on me. Don't go, I want to beg them.

"Oh, hell yeah, brother!" It's Hollis calling down to us. Our moment is as done as this poor truck.

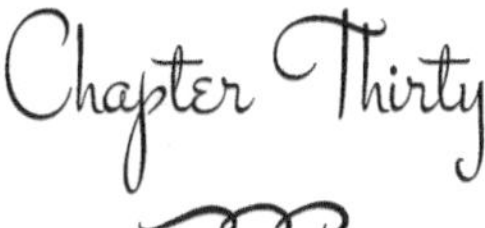

Chapter Thirty

JASPER

I feel like I've been caught with my pants down. I scramble off the truck and offer Gracie a hand and her lips part as she takes it. She's a little breathless, her hair mussed by our frantic kisses and a look in her caramel eyes that melts something inside me.

I wish I'd had time to talk to her more. I just laid my heart out in front of her pretty little feet and she can walk all over it now if she wants to. I feel as vulnerable as if I were naked out here with my hands tied behind my back. She knows everything. That our marriage is real. That I want it to be real.

But at the same time, fear shoots through me, bringing panic to the surface, bringing back all those terrible memories. Is that clouding our judgment?

And I can't help but think that if she hadn't been out of the truck to guide me, then she might have been hurt? And that would have been my fault. The feeling of that rips at my heart and makes my mouth dry.

I'm seeing little flashbacks. My dad's face when he came to the crash site to get me. The grim looks of the police. Gracie's wide eyes as I held her and then her hand torn from mine as she sprinted into her dad's arms.

I have to shake my head to dismiss the memories.

Last time, I screwed up. I went to her with no desire to do anything but love her, comfort her, and tell her it would be okay. And I'd ended up on top of her with my clothes half off, taking advantage of her when she was vulnerable. A good guy would have just hugged her and left. A good guy would have waited. I didn't do any of that. Can I even trust myself with someone as precious as Gracie?

I've got a lump in my throat when I look at her. She's dazzling. I wish I had my camera. I've never seen anything so beautiful as Gracie mussed from my kisses, her eyes all soft and deep.

"Hell yeah!" Hollis says, finally slipping down to join us. He left his truck and camera operator up top. "Way to crash proper, brother! She ain't comin' out of here tonight!"

I steal a nervous glance at Gracie and she's looking right back at me. Her is expression tight and nervous. And I'm realizing right now that as amazing as that kiss was, I told her that I loved her and she didn't say anything back. That tense look in her eyes right now could mean "Wow, I can't believe we're doing this" but could just as easily mean, "Wow, that's so surprising but actually, I'm not really serious about any of this."

I reach out and gently tuck a strand of her hair behind her ear, but my hand shakes a little.

"The guys noticed you two fell behind and I have a backseat, so I volunteered to check on ya. I sure hope you caught this on camera, Gracie, it is epic!"

I shouldn't have admitted to loving her.

Not that it isn't true. It might be the one constant thing about me. But I've put all this extra pressure on her now. What is she supposed to do with that in the middle of all this craziness with her dad and with our marriage turning out to be real? Is she thinking right now about how to let me down easy?

She gives me a sad ghost of a smile, but with Hollis here, it's like there's a barrier up and I feel like I can't cross it to get to her, like she's slipping away from this moment before I can tell her that my feelings are my own problem and they shouldn't ever tie her down.

And then she slips her hand in mine and I close my eyes for a moment. Her warm skin is against mine and it's a luxury to just feel her there for a moment.

"We'll talk later, okay?" she whispers.

She's definitely going to let me down easy. Something squeezes in my chest at the thought of it, but would I really want to burden her? Of course not. Not my Daf. Not my sunshine girl.

"Well, did you get footage?" Hollis asks Gracie, inspecting the wreck with a flashlight. "Boy, you did a number on this poor truck, Jasper. You aren't worthy of her!"

I hardly even noticed the sun setting and now it's slipped over the horizon and the world is shrouded in the half-light that's harder to see in than full night.

"You're bang-on there," I agree gruffly. But I mean Gracie, of course. There will always be other trucks.

"I didn't get footage," Gracie admits in a tiny voice she meets my eyes apologetically and I give her hand a little squeeze.

It's okay, I'm trying to say with that squeeze. *Just because I gave myself to you, doesn't mean you have to keep me.*

"Well, don't you worry!" Hollis is cheerful. "We'll film the recovery tomorrow! It will make a fantastic video. But come on now, you look cold. We can't have you shivering out here. Warm her up in the backseat, lover boy," Hollis says as we follow him up the steep rocks to where his Blazer is parked.

We take the seat he pointed out and I wrap my arms around Gracie, trying to warm her.

"Are you cold?" I whisper, as Hollis starts the engine.

"A bit," she admits and we share a stolen glance that makes me feel like I've been stripped bare right here in the Blazer and I'm breathless all over again at the memory of her lips on mine and all that bottled-up intensity she brought to our kiss. How does she do that? One glance from her and I feel like she can see me right down to the bones. She's the only one who gets to me like that and it's its own kind of pull because how can you not want to be around someone who understands you to the core?

"Let me warm you up," I breathe, tucking her gently against me and then shifting my arm so that it runs over her back and clasps her hip so I can tug her just a bit closer. I breathe into her hair as I tell her, "It's okay. We'll get you warm again, Gracie honey."

Maybe I'm stealing this moment away from her because she should be sharing it with someone else, but it's hard not to indulge in it anyway. It's like the knowledge that this might be all I ever get of her makes me want to lean into it harder.

She's shivering still, so I rub the top of her arm with my cupped hand. Her T-shirt sleeve kind of rolls up a bit and exposes more of her arm and I'm drinking in soft warm skin, almost drugged with the feeling of being able to touch so much of her. As Hollis and his camera operator run the rest of the course with us in the back, I keep murmuring sweet things to her. It's nonsense, just her name and endearments, but I can't seem to stop. I think I might be saying goodbye. Getting ready for when she tells me this is too much and she needs space and I pack up and go back to my dad's house of memories.

She's so quiet that I can't tell what she's thinking. Maybe I run away when I feel threatened, but Gracie runs, too, it seems. She runs deep down into herself where no one can ever find her or hurt her. She's running right now. I can tell.

I swallow and I try not to kick myself too hard. Eventually, it was going to come out. I follow her around like a lost puppy. I sleep on the floor by her bed, for crying out loud. She was going to notice after a while that I'm utterly in love with her. But I wish I'd waited. I wish it hadn't burst out of me so I could have had just a little more time with her.

I pull her in a little tighter, and I'm not too manly to admit that I'm the one who needs this touch, this comfort right now. I keep seeing those rocks whirl by as I plummeted backward. That could have been the end for me. Just like it was for our moms.

The ride goes by in a whirl and Gracie falls asleep cuddled against me and I'm absolutely intoxicated by the movement of her chest and shoulders as she breathes. I talk with Hollis — seriously, he's the nicest guy, and way smarter than me about milking every bit of speed from an engine.

"Think about stopping by my place in Louisiana sometime," he says generously. "I've seen your photos man, and I'd die to have you do a shoot of my shop."

I've seen photos of his shop and it's a photographer's dream. Old signs and tools in nifty little nooks and crannies all surrounding the cars they build like a shell.

"You'd better believe I will," I say, and then we're finally back with the group, and my happy bubble in the back of Hollis's Blazer is over. We exit into the chaos and questions and load into our highway truck to drive home with Hollis's Blazer on the trailer and a big empty space where my truck should be.

Tanner's there to pry the camera out of Gracie's sleepy hand.

"I'll get it to you later," I tell him as I help her get into the back of the truck and then adjust her so she can sleep on a rolled-up sweater on my lap.

Her dad pops his head in, grins devilishly when he sees Gracie curled up mostly asleep on my lap, and then whispers to me.

"I heard you made a mess of things, Jasper. We'll fix it in the morning."

And then he's up front taking the wheel and talking to Hollis out the window in a stage whisper.

"I'll take this rig back to my place and meet you in the morning," he's telling Hollis. "You can take the Raptor back to the hotel. It's crazy late. What? No, a late start. Everyone deserves a little sleep."

Yeah, I made a mess of things.

I'm pretty sure they won't be fixed in the morning.

And it's okay. It had to happen.

Everyone is watching, so I don't kiss Gracie, but when the interior lights go off, I can't help it. There's an ache in my palms that can only be dulled with her touch. My hands skim her sweet skin and I steal little kisses on her shoulder and cheek. Reverently. Worshipfully. I get to guard her for this one trip. I'm not going to waste it.

She takes one of my hands sleepily in hers and my heart kicks up a notch.

"Jas," she says in a small voice, and I'm dying. I'm so gone for this girl.

I close my eyes and just let the way I feel about her rock me, turn me inside out, gut me completely. No regrets, Jasper. It would have felt like a lie to never tell her. At least she knows now. And she can do what she needs to do and you can go nurse your broken-ass heart knowing that at least she knows your hers if she ever decides she wants you.

I'm still thinking that when the truck stops at Gracie's dad's house and I gently shake Gracie awake.

"We're home, sweetheart," I say as she stirs. And the word home sends a little shiver through me. She's my home. Forever. Even if I never get to come back to it once we have our talk.

She says a tired goodnight to her dad and she's looking around blearily when I put an arm around her shoulder and guide her to her house. She stumbles and that's too much for me. I sweep her up into my arms and let her rest her tired cheek against my chest.

"This okay, Gracie?" I murmur and her "Mmmm" is enough for me to carry her the rest of the way to her house, and into her bedroom, and to set her down on her bed, and ease her shoes off.

I'm saving up the feel of her in my arms and the sight of her cute little yawn. I can come back to them in my memories any time.

I'm about to get off her bed when she yawns again and then sits up and the look in her big eyes as she says, "Jasper, can I tell you something?" seizes my heart and squeezes.

Oh, sweetheart, you can tell me anything. You can break me into pieces right now. It's okay, little honey. You do what you need to do.

I think all of that, but all I can manage to say is, "Sure, Gracie."

Chapter Thirty-One

GRACIE

His eyes are so sad when they flick up to me and how can he be sad and yet so achingly tender? He's already carried me to our bed and gently removed my shoes like I'm a fairytale princess. He's worn out, and dirty from his crash, and he probably wants to take a shower, but he looks at me through his eyelashes with his head ducked a little like he expects me to hurt him and he's ready for the blow.

I'm so sleepy that I have trouble clearing my brain but I know this is important. I can't let us just fall asleep and not say anything after he poured out his heart like that to me. Tired as I am, I want him so much more than I want my soft bed.

He loves me. It's been like a hot burning coal in my chest ever since he said it to me.

Jasper Hunt loves me.

He rubs his neck with one hand, looking uncomfortable, and when I don't speak immediately, he busies himself collecting something from the little bathroom and then messing with his bags.

I don't know how to tell him all the tangled thoughts in my brain. I've been trying not to let them spill out during our ride back with everyone else listening and now that I'm free to talk, I don't know what to say.

Wait, he's not fiddling with his bags. He's packing them.

I go cold.

He's rolling up the sleeping bag.

He looks up at me with that kind smile of his as he reaches in his camera bag and fits a lens in place.

"Maybe I shouldn't ask, but can I have a picture first?" he asks a little wistfully. And that look in his eyes shreds me up.

I want to soothe it and fix it. I want to put salve on all his wounds.

"A picture?" I'm so confused and my heart feels like it's seized in my chest. It can't quite seem to move the blood around. He's going to run again. I'm not going to see him for months. Something has panicked him and I haven't even said a thing yet.

And he looks so beautiful crouched there over his camera bag, his fitted T-shirt riding up around his waist, and those jeans hugging his butt and thighs perfectly. He's slightly dusty from our day and his eyes are tired and glassy when he looks at me, waiting. I want nothing so much as to run my fingers through his short hair and tussle it and then taste his dusty skin until that throat bobs because he's swallowing down his desire for me. I want to feel those blunt fingers caressing my bare skin. I just want him here, in my bed tonight.

Scratch that. I don't want it just for tonight. I want it for all the nights. The way he's looking at me is making me ache inside, too. I feel like I'm losing something I never had. He's saying goodbye with his eyes and his shallow gusting breaths and I don't want goodbye.

I want to fix all his broken bits one by one and hold him against me forever. I want every sad-eyed look and sigh. I want to keep them just for me.

"Can I take a picture of you," he says eventually, and his eyes are running over me like he's trying to memorize me and he doesn't bother trying to be a gentleman. He lets his eyes run over *every* bit of me.

I'm tingling just from being looked at. Hot tension starts to build inside me, spiraling down and through, and making me wet and ready. I've never been so worked up just from a man's eyes on me.

"You can take a picture," I say, clearing my throat because the words are coming out roughly. "You can take all the pictures you want. Do you ... do you want it a certain way?"

And I feel a little thrill. Will he ask me for something sexy? A pose that turns him on? A certain look? Maybe ... maybe he'd like a picture of me with fewer clothes on? My heart is galloping at the thought and I already know that as embarrassed as I would be if he asked, I'd definitely say yes. I've seen what he does with that camera. I know he can take all my imperfections and make them beautiful.

"Just like this. Just the way you are," he says.

So I stay where I am and I smile for him, matching his sad smile with my own.

"Are you leaving?" I ask quietly.

"Yes." He snaps his picture, but he doesn't put the camera down. He stands and it's still there in front of his eyes.

"Why?" I tug my dusty socks off and draw my feet up on the bed and the camera pulls down and he looks at me like I've stabbed him in the gut. He gestures at my feet and legs.

"Can I?"

"Ummm ... I guess?"

"They're just ... every bit of you is beautiful, Gracie."

He snaps a shot and then another and when he gets in close, I pinch the sleeve of his shirt and I end up twisting it in my hands nervously.

"Why are you leaving me again, Jasper?" I ask him, gravely,

and the look he gives me is like a boot to my stomach. That is the look of a heart split open and bleeding out. It's all over his face.

He's so close that I feel his warmth as he turns his head toward me and says, "I put all that on you like you're somehow responsible for how I feel, and that's not fair, Gracie. It's not. You are already in an impossible situation. You don't need me piling more on you. I think it will be best for you if you only have one thing at a time to worry about."

"You care too much about me," I say, and his breath catches for a moment as I reach out enough to cup his unshaven cheek.

This man, this achingly beautiful sweet man, loves me. It's so overwhelming that I can barely process the thought. Maybe I haven't yet and that's why I feel so tongue-tied.

He closes his eyes, as if he's absorbing my affection like the warmth of the sun and then he draws back again, careful and gentle like he doesn't dare let himself linger. He raises the camera again, but this time, before he can take his shot, I pull my shirt over my head.

It's a crazy gamble.

He might just run.

Or he might freeze, as he has right now, staring at me as if he can't believe what I've done. His lips are parted and I want to slide my tongue between them.

He loves me. He said he did. And I believe him. Can you really walk away from someone you love when they offer themselves up to you like this?

Can you do it twice?

"Take the picture," I say a little breathlessly. My voice is husky and his eyes are dark as his strong masculine chest heaves under the uneven pressure of his breath. But his hands are sure and with a black hunger in his eyes, he raises the camera again and takes another shot.

When he lowers it, his eyes meet mine and we drink each other in, him with deep longing layered all through something that looks like goodbye, but me — I look at him with my own plea in my eyes. Don't go, my eyes are trying to tell him. Don't. You said you love me. Show me that by staying.

He blinks and his breath saws out raggedly like he can hear all of it.

"Jasper," I say and I can hear the pleading in my voice. He tilts his head to the side like he doesn't know what I'm asking, so I show him.

I shuffle out of my jeans and he makes a sound in the back of his throat like he's choking, but he hasn't moved and when I look up at him his camera is hanging from his hand like he doesn't remember what to do with it and his other fist is flexing and flexing again so that his knuckles are white.

He breathes out in a huff.

"Gracie," my name sounds choked on his lips.

"Don't go," I plead with him. "Please."

I lean back on the bed, tucking my legs up and to the side. I hope it looks like an invitation as I slide back to make room for him to join me.

I reach for my bra clasp and he manages a very hoarse, "Oh honey, you don't need to show me all your skin to keep me."

"I know," I say and I have to swallow, too. Just his gaze, so heated, so hungry, is driving me wild. These panties aren't fit to wear anymore.

I start to slip my bra off and a sound gusts from him that's like a grunt and a gasp all wrapped up into one and when I look back his mouth is open and a look of torture elongates his face.

"Oh Gracie, honey," he guts out and then his words seem to dissolve and he has to look away, but I know he isn't looking away because he's not interested. Not when his pants are announcing so loudly that he's just as excited as I am. He's thick and long inside them and my hands are itching to rip all that cotton off and see him like he's seeing me.

"What are you doing?" he asks, but it's a rhetorical question and his gaze is already back on me, like he can't make himself stop looking. He sets his camera on my dresser with a kind of intense care that always makes me shiver. It does it to me again right now.

"Keep going," I whisper. "Take another picture."

"No," he gasps and I don't think he means to, but he takes a step toward me.

"Why not?" My throat is raw. I can barely get the words out.

"Because." He has to stop to swallow and then he's another step closer and his eyes are drinking me in. They keep darting up to mine like he's waiting for me to say goodbye. Like he's waiting to be told to look away, but I don't give him that. I keep offering him what he thinks he can't have.

"This." I see his throat bob and I think that's where I'll kiss him when he gets close enough. "This is just for me."

He sits on the edge of the bed. Camera-less. His eyes are running up and down me.

I quirk a half-teasing eyebrow. "And those others weren't?"

He gusts a nervous laugh and his eyes flick back up to mine again and he bites his lip like he's in pain and sharing that with me before he manages to speak again.

"Yes." It's more of a gasp than a word. "They were, too. But even my camera doesn't get to share this with me."

But then he turns, barely sitting on the edge of the bed and he puts his face in his hands. And ... I feel my cheeks heat as I realize he's talking himself out of drawing nearer to me. He's not going to do it.

I crawl up on my knees and scoot in close. I want to put my arms around him but it feels too close when I'm naked and he's been so careful not to touch me. Have I ... is it possible that I could have misread this somehow? That he *doesn't* want to touch me?

"Jas?" I whisper and he shivers when my breath touches his neck. "Will you look at me? Please?"

He turns, his hands falling from his face but he keeps his eyes on mine as he says, "I can't say no to you, Gracie."

And he's so close now that I can reach out and take his hands and put them on my waist. His eyes close and he shudders out a shaky breath as his fingers wrap around it so, so gently like he's picking up a butterfly.

"I don't want to say goodbye," I whisper to him and he bites his lip so hard it's going white.

"I don't want to either," he admits. "You still wear my shirt."

"Almost every night," I say and I feel the press of his thickness against my hip.

"I want you to keep your hands on me," I say, taking one of his hands and drawing it up the side of my ribs. He swallows hard and under the stubble on his neck, his Adam's apple bobs again. "I want you to *stay.*"

His eyes roll back into his head and his breath is harsh.

I can tell that he's fighting for control when he grits out, "You don't have to have sex with me just because I'm in love with you, Gracie. It's ... I should have expected that someone as ridiculously generous as you would ... I ... you're just too kind ... I shouldn't have put pressure on you." And then his eyes widen and I can tell his heart is hammering because my hand is on his chest. "Not that I'm saying you were necessarily offering sex. I just ... Gracie, I'll stay. Of course, I'll stay. I'll roll the sleeping bag back out and ..."

I press a finger to his lips and his sigh is almost a sob, and this time I'm the one biting my lip as I say, "Jas can I touch you?"

"Gracie, it's still ... I still think it's best that we don't. You ... you ... deserve to be with someone you love."

He's the sweetest man on the planet. My knees are melting at this. Right now with me mostly naked, he'll still say no ... for me ... and who even does that?

"Is that all?" I ask in a small voice, wanting to be sure. "It's not that you don't want it?"

He gasps in disbelief and his eyes are still closed. He lets out a chuckle that is dark with despair. His fingers are still feather light, but they trace little circles on my skin now like he can't quite help himself.

"Gracie, there is nothing I want more than you, I swear it. But I told you ..."

I lay a finger gently on his lips and he kisses it without seeming to realize he's done it. So I lean to where my lips are right next to his ear and I feel his hand slide down along my hip, one finger tangling in the waistline of my panties, and I'm about done. If he were to tug those at all, I think I might lose my last shreds of restraint and physically pull him on top of me.

I whisper in his ear, "You said you loved me. Is it true?"

"Yes," his voice is so faint I can barely hear it, and as I press against him so only the thin cotton of his T-shirt separates my skin from his. His gasp is gratifying. I want him to do that again in my mouth.

"Jasper," I whisper, pausing to savor this moment. "I love you, too."

His eyes snap open. He pulls back from me so he can look at my face and I could just about die from the tenderness in his eyes it's all combined with disbelief and confusion and his words are just as tangled.

"I ... wait, you what? You love me?"

I try to smile but I think I'm biting my lip, nervous about what he'll say — just because he confessed he loves me doesn't mean he expected it to be reciprocated. What if it freaks him out?

"Oh fuck," he whispers like it's a prayer. "Oh, sweet fuck."

He doesn't seem to know what to do, but then the hands that had been holding me so lightly move to a firmer grip, and he slides me around him so I'm straddling him, and he pulls me in to his heaving chest.

He's whispering something in my hair and I think it's "Sweet, sweet Gracie. Oh God, Gracie."

But I'm not sure because I'm melting at his tender touch and when he smooths my hair back and kisses my neck it sounds like he's finally breathing again. There's relief in his kisses, mixed with something that almost sounds like a growl as he kisses up my neck and seizes my lips in his.

"Gracie, I love you, oh fuck I love you," he's saying as he breaks away and presses his forehead to mine. I think he realizes I'm crying at the same moment that I realize he's shaking all over like a leaf. He wipes away my tears with the pads of his thumbs and then kisses where they were. "Can you say it again, sweetheart? Can you tell me again?"

So, I tell him again, "I love you, Jasper Hunt. With all my heart, I love you."

Chapter Thirty-Two

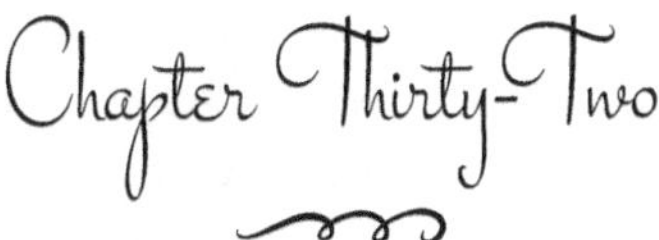

JASPER

She loves me.

It's too big a thing to make sense of, so I don't bother trying. I just let it vibrate through me while my hands trail up her waist, my thumbs skimming the skin with my fists loosely closed so that the backs of my knuckles brush her back muscles.

I can't think.

I'm so overcome by her that I can barely breathe, and I don't even notice she's lifting my shirt at first, but when I do I murmur, "Is this what you want?"

I pull it off and her gasping "Yes," makes me harder as she reaches for me, spreading the fingers of her little hands across my chest in a way that feels like possession and ownership and love and shit but that undoes me.

I lean into the sensation. I want to be owned by this woman. To be hers in literally every sense. My head falls forward and I gasp into the skin of her shoulder. It's tight and firm and smells like lavender.

Just like that, my thoughts shatter. They're only coming in

sharp shards that are all shuffled up so they don't make sense anymore.

It's just Gracie rolling over me like a tide. Gracie right now kissing my throat as it bobs with my swallow and a flashback to Gracie back then with her huge eyes turned to me.

Gracie right now gasping my name as she pulls me closer and tugs my waiting hand to her full breast and Gracie back then putting a bandage over my skinned knuckles.

She's not just the woman here right now caressing me, she's the girl from every meaningful memory of my life.

I gasp hard as my palm curves around her and I know I bite my lip and it's almost too much. I'm drowning in her.

"Slow down, honey. Slow down and let me look at you," I beg and I draw back.

Every nerve is on fire with pleasure. I'm in a daze of it. I can't slow my eyes down enough to linger as they should. They race jubilantly over every bare inch of her. I want to capture every second of her heaving chest and those glorious breasts with my camera. I want to snap shots of just the pinch of her waist and the curve of her hip, of how her belly swells sweetly with just the right amount of softness, at the line of her jaw and the way her hair falls over one shoulder, obscuring one breast just enough to set me on fire.

But I never will. I'll protect her privacy, her image, with my dying breath. This is not for stumbling eyes to find by accident. And yet somehow, this is all for me.

"You're so perfect," I gasp and I hardly know what to do when she replies, "So are you," and I realize she's been taking me in the same way. Me. I'm just a regular man. I don't spend hours at a gym. I don't look like I belong selling board shorts or cologne. I'm not in her class at all.

And yet somehow she loves me. She's looking at me like she desires me.

It unleashes a warm hunger inside me, building slowly as it burns through my veins.

I lean forward and draw her close so that I can twist her gently in my arms and turn her back to me. I let my lips trail down her neck, encouraged by her moan of delight, and then down her spine, one knob at a time, letting my hands wander slowly downward with my kisses. My fingertips skim lightly over the skin of her sides to run parallel to my kisses.

I've dreamed so many nights about what I would do with her if she were mine, of how I'd learn her every inch, of how I'd stroke and kiss and caress every huff of pleasure from her curving lips. I work my way until I can fit my thumbprints into the dimples above her rounded ass and I gasp as my last kiss is lost in the lacy waistband of her panties.

"Can I … " I have to swallow for my hoarse voice to keep going. "Can I slide these down?"

"I'm all yours, Jas," she says and when I look up she's glancing over her shoulder and down at me in a half-shy way, and something low in my abdomen pulses and then flips over at that look in her eyes.

My eyelids flutter half closed and I have to pause and swallow again to get a hold of myself as I slide that lace band down a little more and press a kiss to the very top of where her sweet cheeks meet her spine and I can't help it when my tongue slides out between my lips just a tiny hint so I can taste the apex of that little valley. Her little gasp of surprise sends flutters through my chest.

I swallow and come back up to my knees so I can look down over her shoulder and when she turns her face in toward mine, we're cheek to cheek for a moment and we both sigh together in something like surprised anticipation as I press my front to her back and revel in the feel of it. My arms reach around her to gently cup her breasts and I can feel the heat of her blush against my cheek as I let them fan wide to wash down her rip cage and inward to her belly. I pause for a beat with her gasping moan, and then spread my fingers over the flare of her hips, tuck them under that lacy band and slide them down and toward each other until it's just the very tips of my fingers touching the intimate place where she spreads gently like flower petals for my touch.

She's so slick that I make a groaning gasp into her neck and have to press my mouth against her shoulder as I fight for control. I'm suddenly very aware of my own hardness pressed against her back as pleasure washes over me and over me in dizzying waves. I fight it to hold back this overwhelm and it's just from touching her. Just that much has ruined my ability to plan, to think. I lean my pelvis in so that the length of me presses against her back, as if to remind the hungry parts of me that there is so much here still to enjoy.

"Is it ... is it alright?" Gracie asks shyly and I'm helpless against the animal sound that falls from my lips. Helpless about how I freeze and shudder, eyes closed to hold myself together. There's a whirlwind clawing at my chest from the inside. It's going to sweep me away.

"Perfect," I finally manage to whisper. "So perfect, sweet honey."

Her cheeks are hot and rosy and her smile is so timid for someone who started all this. It's a combination that unfurls me. I manage to pull myself together enough to reach up and cup one of her cheeks as she twists in my embrace. I've lost that sweet touch of her inner parts and I gasp at its loss, but suddenly she's facing me and I'm catching sight of her pretty smile, of how she catches her lower lip between her teeth right after, and I think my breath is caught. It won't gust out as it should. It's stuck, helpless in this moment, just like I am.

I reach forward enough to cup her hips with my hands — gently, so she can pull away if she wants to. And I'm trembling a little, the anticipation building until it's almost too much.

And I don't even realize what she's doing until I feel her fumbling for my pants, feel the button come loose, and the zipper go down, and feel as she slides them carefully around an erection so firm it might seriously rip the cotton. I swallow and reach to help her, shucking off my jeans and socks all in one go and there's nothing now between us but the tight cotton of boxer briefs and her tiny shreds of lace and just that much seems like too much.

I grasp her waistband and stretch it out a little, tilting my head in a shy question until she catches my gaze again and smiles her assent and I'm about to strip them off her when she runs a pink tongue around her lips and I'm stunned all over again — worse than when my truck fell back and flipped over. Worse than that time I was hit in the forehead with a softball. I'm frozen just watching that and then I'm gasping as she reaches out, bold despite her flushed cheeks and ducked head and she makes a pleased sound as she wraps her hand around my hardness and slides it upward, only the tight cotton in the way.

The shuddering breath that comes out of me deepens her smile as if she can share that jagged pleasure just by touching it.

"You're wearing too many clothes, Jasper," she teases with a little laugh and I finally gasp in a breath.

"Can you help me with that?"

"Sure," she says with a coy little look up at me and those caramel eyes. I swear, I'm only ever eating caramel from now on.

And then her small hands are tucked into my waistband, tugging, and my shorts slide off, freeing me and leaving me completely bare to her. I tighten my abs under her scrutiny which only makes other parts of me look a little more eager and when a delighted laugh falls from her lips I'm delighted, too.

Our eyes meet for just a moment and the look we share is like the togetherness of friendship but deepened by intimacy. Like we're both doing this and enjoying watching ourselves do this all at once.

And when she ducks her head shyly again, I reach out and tangle my hands in her hair and lift her face up to look at me and I can't stop this smile that's spreading across my face. I can't even tone it down so I don't scare her with how much I love this — love her — love every little laugh and blush.

"Gracie," I breathe, happy to be saying her name.

"Jasper," she says in return, a little breathlessly, leaning forward as she takes me in her hand again.

I'm pretty sure my eyelids flutter when her palm skims over me, light but bedeviling. They close, unable to process sight when my brain is barely holding on to thought. It's only when the sensation changes to something ridiculously good that my eyes pop open and I realize she's ducked down and licked me and ... wow ... I could lose myself in that. I could let her keep on doing that forever.

Let her? I'd beg her not to stop. Call her name like a prayer.

Instead, I reach down and gently pull her back up.

"You don't like it?" She bites her lip again and I accidentally thrust forward against her thigh at the sight of that.

A growl of desire ripples out from the back of my throat, entirely unbidden, but it's not enough of an answer.

"I'd give up a year of my life for more of that," I murmur, skimming my palms up her neck to cup her face again, but when she smiles a little mischievously and tries to duck down again I lean forward too, and gently lay her out on her back. "But not right now, my Gracie," I murmur as I lean over her to kiss her temple and then her cheekbone and then her sweet lips. "You're always giving to everyone. You never take anything for yourself. Let me give you something for a change."

And this time it's my turn to run my tongue lightly from the peak of her chin down her throat, along her breastbone, dipping down between her ribs, down into her belly button, and then further until I meet that lacy waistband. I strip off her underthings with one motion and discard them. They aren't needed here. And I pick back up where I left off, sliding my tongue down, down until I meet all her warmth and welcoming wetness and take a moment to taste pure Gracie.

To my surprise, she's the one to pull my head up this time.

"Fair," she gasps. "You have to be fair. If I don't get to, then you don't get to either."

I laugh at the ridiculousness of this but it's a happy laugh. "What would be fair, Gracie?"

In answer, she gently flips me over onto my back, straddles me and my eyes close. I think I hear something rip and then she's sliding a condom on me and my eyes are still closed as I groan at the thought of her tending to me like I'm precious to her, and suddenly she's sliding herself onto me and I'm sinking into all that softness.

It's so much I can barely take it. Like the best taste and sweetest sound all rolled together into one thing.

"Would you say this is fair?" she whispers in my ear as she slides down, down, down until all of me is lost within her.

"Fair," I gasp, because I don't know how to talk anymore beyond repeating her.

She begins to move over me and I resist the urge to let my eyes roll back in my head. I don't want to miss a moment of this. I meet her pretty eyes and catch her sigh in my mouth, drawing it into me just as she's drawn me into her, and I kiss her long and deep and sweet so that we're tangled up in every way possible. One of my hands is spread in her hair, the heel of my palm supporting her cheek as she leads us into a gentle rhythm, the other hand clutching her hip, my fingers sinking slightly into the softness there.

She's all softness and welcome and sweet, sweet taste, and I want her tongue tangling with mine forever. I can't shut my eyes because every time I do, I miss something, and my eyes are hungry to see it all.

They want to see how she carefully places her hands in a

splayed-out position across my chest as she braces herself. She looks at me in question when she does this and I nod my enthusiasm.

That's right, honey. Use me to hold you up. I want to be that for you.

My eyes want to see how her brow crinkles with a little line in the center, when she's focused on what she's doing.

Focus, my Gracie, focus on what feels good.

They want to see how her sweet lips fall open as sensations wash over her and her breath huffs in tiny gasps that I steal from her with thief kisses.

They want to see her skin close up when I lean in to taste her shoulder, her bicep, her sweet forearm, her luscious breasts. I take my time there, going back and forth between them as I follow the rhythm she's setting. Maybe that's unfair to all the rest of her, but it's hard to resist that level of soft warmth and it needs a lot of kisses and gentle licks — I'm pretty sure it does, at least, and I'm willing to test that theory.

And they want to see her eyes as I lean back and catch her hazy gaze again and drink in a look, long and deep right to the center of her soul, as she slides up and down the length of me — the most glorious goddess gracing me with her very self. The most perfect of all perfect women right here in bed with me, tangled in sheets and limbs and long golden hair.

If there's a heaven better than this, I can't imagine it. I'm so gone, so terribly in love that I'm worried that getting my heart's desire might tear me in half as bad as not getting it might have done. I'm living right now for her sweet sighs and breathless moans, working my body to draw them out of her, and clinging to that eye contact that makes this so terribly, intoxicatingly intimate.

And when pleasure finally crashes over her and she sways, her arms no longer supporting her, I shift so now I'm holding her, and drawing her down and into my chest where she can rest.

I run my fingers gently through her hair, threading them in, and stroking them through.

"Breathe my Gracie, breathe," I murmur. "You're so, so good. So sweet."

Maybe I say other things. I don't know. I'm so intoxicated by her, by this moment of culmination, that my thoughts are scattered and hard to find.

She draws herself up, still resting on my chest, to where she can kiss me and whisper, "Jas. I've loved you all my life."

I think that might be true. Just the possibility of it makes me tremble as I reach up to find her kiss.

And then she's moving again, this time with a smug look on her pretty face.

"You promised to play fair," she whispers as she increases her speed and intensity.

And it's just too much for me. I'm swept away, clinging to her as a man clings to a rock when he's lost at sea in a storm. I think I might buck against her as I'm shaken apart and when my head finally clears, my breath is heaving in my chest and my lips are pressed to her shoulder and I feel like I've been shredded and then stitched back together by the girl who fixes everything.

Chapter Thirty-Three

GRACIE

Tonight is not like the first night we slept together — all longing and unrealized desire. This time, it's like a victory lap. I fall asleep in his arms with one of his legs thrown over me possessively and I've never been so happy in my life.

When I blink awake to the feeling of him nuzzling my cheek with his nose in this sleep, I'm so thrilled that I feel like I'm going to burst at every seam. He's tantalizing when he's half asleep. Galvanic, because sex with him has changed me and taken me from being a single entity to being one half of a whole. I do not find the idea offensive. I revel it. So few people own me. My dad. In a way, Melissa. But no one owns me as Jasper does now.

When he blinks awake his eyelashes brush my cheek and I shiver a little at the intimacy of it and right away I'm back to last night and instantly ready to repeat what we've done. I lean toward him and press a kiss over his heart and mine feels warmed right through at his contented sigh.

I meet those hazel eyes and linger there drinking him in.

"I've been so lonely without you," I whisper, biting my lower lip. I want to drink him in. Sex with him was good, but this waking up sleepily together, this sharing the early morning moments together — this is the kind of intimacy I've been craving.

"You have friends. A whole life here." He looks confused as he tangles a lock of my hair lazily around one finger.

I nod. And I'm not quite sure how to tell him this part but I have to somehow, don't I?

"That night before the funeral," I say, risking a glance at him and then quickly looking away. He's too much. Too beautiful. I can't think when I'm looking at him. "When you came to my house and kissed me ..."

My voice trails off and his sigh of, "Gracie" brings my eyes back to his. There's an apology there.

"I shouldn't have left you," he whispers and he's not looking at me. He's looking down as if he's ashamed.

I reach out and take his cheek in my hand and I love how the rough stubble there rubs against my palm. He leans into it, but he still isn't looking at me. And I've always thought of men as rougher and tougher than women but right now as he melts into me he feels someone I should protect. Someone I should stitch back together.

"I shouldn't have let you go," I whisper back. "You took a part of me that night that belongs to you forever now. Even though you didn't mean to."

His gaze shoots up to me and it's open and hurting and I want to bind it up and stitch it together.

"That's why it felt like betrayal when I was with someone else."

"Gracie," he objects but I shake my head.

"No, listen. Part of me was still yours and it knew it. And I shouldn't have done that. I should have waited for you."

He's shaking his head. "You ... you owe me nothing. I wasn't here for you. And I shouldn't have been at your house on the night we were both mourning. I was taking advantage."

He looks miserable but if we're going to heal this, we have to push through this part. I scoot in a little closer so I can run my legs down his and tangle our toes together and I let my fingers run through his hair, combing his scalp as I talk.

"You weren't."

"I was."

"Then I was, too," I say softly, biting my lip and practically melting when his eyes catch on that. "Because I needed you and wanted you, too. And what I need now — most of all — is your forgiveness."

He looks confused. "Forgiveness? For what?"

"For not coming after you," I say, leaning in to kiss his temple and treasure the way his fine hair lies so perfectly there. I draw back so I can look him in the eye so he can hear me properly. "I have been missing you every single day for five years." His eyes go wide at that. "I've been dreaming about you." And they darken at that. "I've been fantasizing about you." His inhale shudders like this is too much and his hand shifts to cup my hip as he swallows hard enough to make his throat bob. "And I didn't ever do the brave thing. I didn't drop everything and find you and bring you home. And I should have. I fix everything for everyone else. But I didn't fix this for us. Can you forgive me for that?"

His soft lips catch mine while the words are still dropping from them and they slide in a gentle caress and then another and then another and then the kiss deepens and his arms come around me and he draws me in close to his chest and pulls his lips from mine with a gasp.

"You don't need to apologize, Daf," he says and he's so sincere he makes me melt. "But if you need me to say I forgive you, then I do. And, honestly, I need to be the one apologizing. I never should have left you. You shouldn't have had to be lonely for me. I knew the day after I left that I'd made the wrong choice."

"Then make the right one and stay with me?" I ask, drinking in his eyes.

"Always," he says and his breath gusts out with the word just before he kisses me again and I put everything I have into that kiss, all that pent-up loneliness and need. I have so much time to make up for.

When we break apart his half-smile shows off his dimple. "I badly need a shower. Join me? Maybe we can show each other what forgiveness looks like?"

I nod shyly and his hands are tangling in my hair already, drawing my naked body flush against his. I love his warmth and the way his skin slides against mine. It feels familiar even though it's new.

I open the drawer of my bedside table and pull out a condom and he nearly chokes. "Are those ... those are *not* BOOM Empire condoms."

I think his eyes are going to pop out of his head and I can't help my laugh. He must not have had a good look at the one from last night.

"My dad ordered a whole case of one thousand for the online store. They have his logo on them."

"They're hot pink," he says taking it from me with his mouth falling open.

I'm smiling now, barely able to hold back my giggles. "They were supposed to be bright orange, 'like traffic cones,' he said, and when they accidentally got the order wrong, he nearly had a fit."

"Does he know you have these," he says looking at the nine hundred and ninety eight hot pink condoms still in my bedside drawer.

I shake my head, not able to contain my laugh anymore. "He thinks I donated them. To charity."

"To charity?" His dimple is showing as he repeats me and his eyes dance with laughter.

"Yes." It comes out with a snort.

"Which charity?"

"I told him," I say, stopping to snicker. "I told him I gave them to 'Our Sisters of Charity.'"

"You did not!"

But now we're both laughing as he flicks the condom at me. Two can play at that game. I grab an entire handful and throw them at him and is there anything more adorable than Jasper naked in my bed with the sheets pooled around him and hot pink condoms raining down like confetti?

"If you think I'm going to be able to use all those while we shower you have way too high an opinion of me," he says, leaning in to steal a kiss. "Let's try three and see how far we get."

"Three?" I hoot. "Now who has the high opinion?"

He scoops me up suddenly in a bridal carry and I'm so excited to see him on his knees, on my bed that I barely yelp when he scoots to the edge of the bed and stands. I put a condom packet between my pouting lips.

"Very on brand," he says gravely. "Did you want me to take a picture?"

And as I double with laughter, he snatches it away with his own lips, winks at me, and carries me into my bathroom, setting me down only when we get to the shower.

We're still laughing while he turns the water on and swings me inside the shower.

"What's this?" I ask, surprised as he turns me around and runs a bar of soap over my belly.

"I thought maybe we could get clean while we tried out those condoms. You realize we're going to have sex with your dad's logo right here on the most personal parts of my body."

"Family is everything," I say with a straight face and when his eyes look like they really will fall out of his head I burst into laughter and he takes that moment to laugh with me but the laughter turns to quiet and his eyes widen as he watches me with hungry eyes before leaning in to steal a soft, slow kiss.

Last night, he laid everything at my feet. This morning, I want to do the same for him. I take the soap and gently run it over his body, caressing every part with my hands until the soap bubbles and foams and makes him so slippery that my hands run easily over him.

His smile is tender as he watches me, letting me do as I please, and my breath is stilted and gasping as I work. I love the feeling of him under my hands, love getting this chance to know all of him and at the same time to do something for him — something personal and intimate.

The thought of that is almost too much. He's precious to me in a way I can't quite communicate. It's something that makes me feel hot and intense inside, that makes me want to do everything I can for him — every little act of service or care that I can think of. It's how I love. And I want to love him more than anyone.

I rinse off his soap and kiss his neck, his chest, his side, before pressing myself full-length against him so I can feel every bit of him in the warm intimacy of this moment. His gasp of surprised delight sends little tingles all through me and so do his gentle fingers holding my waist delicately as if I am a camera lens he just bought.

"Are we good then?" he asks me shyly.

"We are more than good," I say, trying to shine all the warmth I have into him through my eyes and my smile. "We are the very best together."

His kisses start on my brow and move down to my lips and when he meets me there I pour my whole heart into the kiss, pressing myself against him and sliding up his wet skin to meet his mouth better. He moans through the kiss and I'm thrilled. I let my hands wander, sliding over him, feeling, caressing, trying to show him with every ounce of myself that if he keeps trusting me, I will take very good care of him.

And then, while I'm still busy exploring, he breaks our kiss and he bends to press a kiss under my breast. I let myself thread my fingers through his wet hair and enjoy the feeling of his affection.

"How are you so good at this if you've never been with someone else?" I groan.

"I have an amazing imagination. For instance, I very accurately imagined this," he murmurs as his fingers run down my side oh so lightly and then slide very accurately to the exact right spot in my most intimate of places, softly finding his way to caressing me there.

"How often did you *accurately imagine* this?" I gasp, my eyelids fluttering shut, and oh wow that is … amazing.

My eyes drift half shut and I'm watching Jasper through the rain of the shower, watching his heavy-lidded eyes, how the water soaks his hair between my wide-spread fingers and teases it into little soft spikes. It runs down those glorious shoulders — did I say they were wide? Because they're amazing, like drool-worthy all on their own. It sheets down his flat chest and belly and trickles from either side to meet in the middle and flows down the narrow trail of hair that bisects his abdomen and lands directly where his arousal is full and thick and I don't get a chance to let my eyes drift down to his muscled thighs because he's dropping to his knees, palms running down my thighs and then up again and he looks up at me with an enraptured expression lighting those boyish eyes.

"Yes?" he asks and I don't know what he's asking at first, but when he parts his lips and looks at me with hope bright and gorgeous in them I know.

"You get to pick." I sound breathless even to myself. "It's your turn."

He laughs then, like he's the victor here, and his palms

smooth up the backs of my thighs and catch on my ass as he tilts his chin up and forward and opens his lips to receive me. Just watching him like that, wet and so, so sexy with his pink tongue peeking out between his lips and with the scruff of his face scraping roughly against my inner thighs — it's nearly enough to undo me utterly. I have to brace myself on his wide shoulders, savoring the give of his wet flesh under my fingertips and his throaty laugh gusting into my inner parts is my reward.

He's pleased with me.

Jasper Hunt is pleased to have his tongue and lips all over me and he sucks me relentlessly, teasing and taunting and then taking me firmly into his mouth, and I look down and watch his closed eyelids, at the water making the lashes dark and thick, watch the muscles of his jaw tighten and lengthen to aid his clever tongue and I tangle my fingers in his dark hair again, over-whelmed that he would want me enough to give me this, that he would hold me with this kind of tender sweetness without expecting anything in return. And then it's too much.

Pleasure sweeps over me, heavy and hard, making me rock and gasp against him as he murmurs happily in his triumph. I cling to his shoulders for support until the last wave rolls through me and I'm done.

I want him forever. I want him in my bed and my shower and my heart. I want to mend all his broken spots with mine.

And then suddenly he's standing and he's lifting me up on his forearms and wrapping my legs around his waist, fumbling with a BOOM package that I can't quite see and he's so sweet that I can barely breathe, so gloriously, perfectly sweet. His eyes flick to mine, checking to be sure that I want this and I take the moment to seize his face between my palms and kiss him thoroughly, the way he deserves to be kissed, the way I've been dreaming of kissing him for years. He kisses me back with his own fervor, as if he's just as hungry for this as I am — but that can't be possible because nothing in all the world can beat the craving I have for him or the way I want it to last forever. Nothing.

And I don't want to cry, but I think I might if I dwell too much on how tender he is and on how absolutely exquisite.

And then he gasps and I gasp with him, our breath shared for a moment as he sinks into me. He slides his wet torso against mine and tucks me sweetly into his chest as if he's protecting me as he moves, his strong arms holding me up and in place, so that he can whisper my name again and again into my hair until he's shaking as he comes and comes and comes.

It's like he's given me a gift so priceless I didn't know it could even exist.

I wonder if he imagined this, precisely, and just the thought of him alone, imagining this, sends me over the edge a second time and when I come it's for him and I gasp his name into his skin like a prayer.

When we're done and both gasping together, he chuckles into my hair. "One down. Nine hundred and ninety-seven more to go."

I'm laughing with him and it feels so terribly good. And I'm still laughing when he starts to soap my body slowly, reverently, spreading bubbles with a shy, playful smile. I smile with him as I slowly move with his caresses, teasing him with little glances and smiles and enjoying his half-smile of bliss as I rinse off all the bubbles for him.

It's the hot water tank that lets us down. Damn thing wasn't made with enough stamina. But I don't mind. Not even when I have to condition my hair in ice water.

"Everyone is going to know," I tell him, my cheeks red and flaming as he follows me out of the shower, clearly staring at my naked form as I walk, and biting his lip like he wants to bite it instead.

"Know what?" he asks, distracted.

"That we had sex," I say, laughing. I feel … not lonely. I feel like the bliss inside me is going to leak out everywhere.

"They already know we're married," he says, waving a hand dismissively.

"We did not have this afterglow when we announced we were married." This time I try to impress on him that I'm serious, but when his dancing eyes meet mine I almost try to pull him into bed again and it takes all my resolve to cross my arms sternly. All that does is lift my boobs higher and his eyes are glued to them now as he speaks.

"Let's make it a game," he says. "Every time you catch one of them noticing, send me their name and the emoji reaction you think they're having and I'll do the same for you."

"We're not going to get any work done," I chide him.

"I wrecked my truck yesterday," he says with a shrug. "I'm pretty sure I'm out of the competition."

I probably could think of something smart to say back. Probably. But damn, how is him putting *on* his pants as sexy as him taking them off? I think I'm frozen for a full minute before he looks me up and down and says, "If you show up like that, they'll definitely know."

I laugh and grab a pair of underwear and wonder how I could have been missing this for years without ever realizing it. It's crazy wonderful. I want to keep it forever. And something inside me feels almost sad because there's one thing I know about life: happiness doesn't last. This moment, too, will be gone in the blink of an eye. And what will I do then?

JASPER

I'm just pouring the first cup of coffee while Gracie does her hair when I hear the knock at the door. I saunter over, barefoot, happily drinking my coffee. I've never felt quite like this before. I am completely relaxed. Completely happy. I feel like a bubble some kid has blown at a party drifting over the grass and up into the cookout smoke.

I don't want to do anything to disturb it or end this buzz.

I open the door already smiling.

It's Gracie's dad. He's wearing a bright orange T-shirt with the BOOM logo on it. The sleeves have been cut off to show off his guns — as per usual. He shoves a second T-shirt at my chest, forcing me to take it or watch it fall to the ground and I should get an award or something for not laughing right now.

Even this dominance routine of his isn't enough to kill my buzz.

I take a slow sip of coffee, fighting my grin. The sun is warm on my face and a breeze ruffles my wet hair. I'm still scruffy. In my enjoyment of Gracie this morning I completely forgot to shave.

"Nice T-shirt," I say coolly.

"Isn't it?" her dad asks, puffing out his chest so I can see the logo better — as if there was some way I could've missed it. "Isn't the color great?"

"Traffic cone orange," I say, keeping my straight face.

"Exactly!" He's glowing again. If you could bottle Adam Boomhower you could sell his glow to people suffering from depression as a permanent cure. "That one's for you. You can wear it today. You're a medium, right? Or is it a small? I can go grab a different size for you."

"I'll live with the medium," I say, meeting his eye to remind him that he doesn't intimidate me. "I do love wearing your logo. All over my body."

Behind me, in the house, I hear Gracie's shocked snort-laugh.

Fortunately, her dad has no idea that I'm messing with her.

"So. You crashed. Big time," he says, looking very sober. "I'm sending the guys over for the recovery this morning and I need to be there, too. We're going to use the new branded BOOM yank rope."

"Sounds like a great time," I agree. "I'll get my camera."

"Actually," he says, rubbing the back of his neck. "I was hoping you could do something else for me."

"Sure."

"Since you're here."

"You mean living in your daughter's house?"

"Exactly."

"Don't worry," I say. "I'm sure I can find different accommodations."

I need to talk about this with Gracie. Should I look for a separate place? For me? For us? But I don't want to push her right now when this is all still new. What if it freaks her out to think about moving into a new place with me? It's one thing to pretend here at her house but it's more intense if we get a new place.

I feel a little stab of uncertainty as I realize that whether she loves me or not, we're still playing here. No one has said anything about this relationship lasting longer than the time it takes for me to walk out the door. For a man who has spent his entire adult life on the move, the idea of *not* being anchored to her makes me very uncomfortable.

Play it cool, Jas. You don't want to freak her out. Just earn her trust and then cross that bridge when you get there.

"No need," Adam says with a huge grin that I don't fully trust. "This works out perfectly for me. I have an RV at Ron's Wraps and they're finishing up today. I need someone to grab it for me and bring it over to the BOOM shop, and since you don't have a truck to drive today and everyone is busy driving the rest of them out for the recovery ..."

"No problem," I say. I'm relieved, to be honest. My head is in the clouds this morning. Images of Gracie in her bed last night and in the shower this morning keep flooding back to me and I'm pretty sure I'll be less than useful for anything major.

And I also have to think about how to approach her about where we're going to live. Don't I?

Because she can't expect me to be her dad's scut boy forever. Living here in his house. Running his errands. Suddenly I feel cold and a bit ill.

"We're going to go straight from the recovery to the dune racing with the trucks that still work, so when you get the RV to the BOOM shop, you can take the day. Your Jeep is still there, right?"

I'm nodding. Take the day. I glance over my shoulder at Gracie who is gathering her purse up to leave. She doesn't look at me and I know without having to ask, that she isn't planning to take the day off with me.

I've been dismissed like an unwanted dog. Because this is a family business, and married to Gracie or not, I'm not family. My mouth feels dry. I take a sip of coffee but it doesn't help.

How did I not see this coming? But I definitely can imagine it now. Years stretching out ahead where my photography work is stunted because I spend my time on stupid online competitions, useless stunts, or running BOOM errands. I'll be Tanner in five years' time.

"Can we have dinner tonight, Gracie?" her dad asks. "We have a few things to talk about."

"Sure!" she says, bright and happy. "We'd love to, right Jas?"

She turns all the weight of that smile on me and I manage to stay calm and take a sip of coffee before I say, "Sure, Gracie. That's fine."

But it is not fine.

"Try on the shirt, Jasper," Adam says eyeing me up and down. I look back at Gracie and she's eyeing me, too, and suddenly I feel claustrophobic like I can't breathe.

"Later," I say, slipping on my boots.

"I need to know if the size fits you," her dad pushes.

With a grunt of irritation, I shove the shirt over my head on top of my current T-shirt and struggle into it. I feel like I'm in the grip of a python. It's crushing the life out of me.

"I knew you weren't a large," Adam crows. "I'm a double XL," he shout-whispers to Grace and I scowl at him as I rip the shirt off again.

Adam's still laughing when he calls over his shoulder, "Two minutes and we're going."

Gracie looks up at me, worried. "Are you okay, Jasper?"

My voice is tight when I answer, "Sure."

"It's only ..."

"One minute!"

"We can talk later," I say, grabbing my stuff — and yes, my camera, because screw you Adam Boomhower.

But we don't find time to talk. Not in Adam's truck where he talks Gracie's ear off relentlessly.

Not when I'm dropped off at Ron's Wraps and have a fight with the desk lady because someone left a pink silk robe on the driver's seat that's monogrammed "Linda" on the back and there are no Linda's in the BOOM Empire.

Not when I get to work and find that Adam had taken Gracie off with him for the recovery. And they're out of cell range. And all I have on my phone is one text from Gracie that says: "Dad" with the mind-blown emoji.

I'm nearly about to leave in a huff when I find my own dad in the office at the BOOM shop.

"Dad," I say and he jumps like he's guilty. "Everyone's out."

"I came to see you," he says trying to sound casual and not succeeding at all.

"Oh yeah?"

"I thought maybe we could have more of your terrible spaghetti."

"When?"

"Tonight?" He runs his hand through his beard nervously.

"I'm busy tonight," I say apologetically.

"Okay then," he says and he's gone before I can puzzle out why he was so jumpy. Maybe he really wants that dinner? Maybe he misses me? That doesn't sound right.

My afternoon should be relaxing. I go out to the desert and try to photograph. But all I see are memories of Gracie moving up and over me, her beautiful curves under my hands. And all I can think about is being trapped here working like a dog for her dad.

Eventually, I go back to my dad's place and do the one thing I never wanted to do. I open up his garage and I start going through my mom's stuff like he asked me to.

It's not better than thinking about Gracie and the future. It's a lot worse. But when I leave to go back to her place, everything is sorted and boxed for storage, except a few things I'm taking with me. Including a photo of Mom. What would she think if she saw me now?

"Stop worrying, silly boy," is what she'd probably say. She said it an awful lot. "Things always work out."

But they don't do they? Because they didn't work out for her. And I'm nervous that they aren't going to work out for me, either.

Chapter Thirty-Five

GRACIE

OMG, Melissa, I type frantically as I finally get back into cell range.

I'm a dirty, dusty mess and all I had to eat today were peanut butter sandwiches and sodas because Tanner was tasked with "food" and his idea of "nutritious" is that it can be classed as edible. I didn't need to be there today. I couldn't even upload to our socials because we were out of range and I've been *dying* all day. I want to tell Melissa how things have changed for me and Jas, and I want to tell Jas ... I want to tell him that I've been thinking of him constantly.

What? Are you okay? she texts back, and then it's a flurry of texts about how her medical condition is going and how her family won't let her come home because they're all worried about her. I try to be a considerate friend and listen to her complain about her brother — and honestly, it's all super interesting and engrossing — but eventually, I can't help myself. I shove a comment in between her frat boy gifs.

Remember how you told me not to fall for him again? I think I did it anyway.

You did? Tell me everything.

Remember that shipment of pink things my dad got by accident?

Do I ever. Eyeroll emoji.

There aren't a thousand of them anymore.

She sends me a shocked emoji and then a high five emoji and I'm bright red, trying to angle myself so that Pretty Boy in the seat beside me won't see what I'm texting. I glance up at him but he's fast asleep already, his head bobbing all around as the vehicle turns. I sigh and ball up a sweatshirt to jam under his head for him. He's going to hurt his neck like that. And then I'm back to texting.

I don't tell Melissa every detail. But I do imply the gist of it. Mostly through the use of clever emojis.

We're excited about this, she says. But are we? What if he runs again? He looked like he wanted to this morning when my dad sent him on that stupid errand.

What if he's unhappy here with me? I text. *What if I cramp his style?*

So, don't cramp it.

What if he always dreams about traveling and I'm the one who holds him back?

Don't hold him back. Go with him. You know your dad is loaded, right? Money is not an issue for you.

I won't take his money.

Fine then, go budget. Go glamping.

I text her an eye-rolling emoji and a tent emoji.

Tell me all about how great he is at pitching a tent.

MELISSA.

Or don't. Just … don't let it be like last time. Don't let it all dissolve because you're too scared to tell him that you want to keep him. Even if that means both of you fly the coop together this time.

It's good advice, but I'm worried about it. He didn't ask for any of this. He just kind of fell into it all. He was packing to leave when I practically jumped him last night. What if he really wants to go? What if he stays anyway and it sucks the life out of him? And if I traveled with him, what would I do? Would I just be his living carry-on? That feels ... kind of empty to me. I like to be busy. I like to help people.

I don't know.

I'm tired and worried when I finally get home and I just need a shower and something to eat that isn't peanut butter.

I walk in the door, and there he is, sitting on my empty living room floor with pictures and papers spread out around him and a box in front of him. He's so absorbed in what he's reading that he doesn't notice me come in. And he's so beautiful sitting there, the masculine angles of him catch the light and look even sharper than usual - his wide shoulders bunch under that stupid orange shirt my dad made him wear. His shoes and socks are off again and his jeans have slid up, and while he concentrates and the longer hair on top of his head has slipped down over one eye and the combination looks so boyish and vulnerable.

When he finally looks up at me, I'm not prepared for that expression on his face. Even though I've seen it before. It's a kind of sorrow mixed with a lost look.

"Jas," I say gently. "Do you want to stay here and work for my dad?"

He barks a cynical laugh, "Why not? I think in the end everyone works for your dad. Look at these pictures. Do you think our moms were happy doing this?"

Ouch. *I* work for my dad. Is that something he thinks I should be embarrassed about?

But more than the sting of his comment, I feel a sizzle of unease as I see what he's looking at. It's copies of everything I gathered for my book. The one I was writing when they died. The one that killed them.

It's all spread out around him and he's flipping through photos - not the smiling ones I planned to include, but other photos. Candid shots. One of my mom glaring at the camera as she looks up from trying to clean a muddy child — me — with water from a water bottle while my dad laughs in the background. Another one is of a truck, but in the background, his mom is whispering in his dad's ear and his dad looks nervous as they glance at the person taking the picture.

My dad, I realize. He took these photos. If he hadn't, he'd be in them. He's never been shy about photobombing at every opportunity.

There are more. And they are not my laughing, happy memories. How could I not have seen them? I mean, for every unhappy picture there are four more of smiles and poses and great vehicles, or of family all gathered in tight, but it's those random candids that pierce right into me.

"You don't want a life like this," I say and I know it's true as I look at the pictures even though saying it makes me feel hollow inside. I have to swallow hard to push this emotion aside and concentrate on him. "You don't want to be stuck here working for my dad like your dad was."

"They were partners," he tries to say, but I keep talking.

"You can see yourself getting bitter and shriveling up and then fading away, or dying in an accident before you ever really got to live — like your mom did."

His huff of breath might be pain or might be an objection. I don't know which one but I can't look at his eyes to decide which it might be, because I have a terrible feeling in my belly like someone put a brick in there and my body hurts any time I move at the heaviness and sharpness of it.

"Gracie, that's not it," Jasper tries to say.

"Would you be happy living here forever?" I push, and my vision is a bit blurry.

"No, but —"

"Working for my dad?"

"Gracie, I just think you should finish your book. That it could be a tribute to our moms."

It's an excuse that falls flat. I think even he can hear that. That's not what he was thinking at all. He was blaming my dad for their lives before they died. The lives that they wasted living for other people. Kind of like my life here with dad, wasted on all these little things I do for other people instead of doing big meaningful things like writing this book. Or taking pictures of beautiful things all over the world.

"I'm happy with my life," I say, blinking back tears. Because what happened to them was not my dad's fault. He was just doing his best. It was *my* fault.

But also because today I'd started to think about what it would be like to live with Jasper forever. Maybe in a place we got together like he was talking about with my dad. We *are* legally married. Why couldn't we just stay that way and live together and have a ton of mind-blowing sex and sweet sleepy cuddles? Who was to say it ever had to end? Maybe we'd even have little Jaspers and Gracies and they could wear ridiculous big orange shirts to bed.

And wow, I was an idiot. Because he wasn't thinking any of that today, was he?

"I didn't say you shouldn't be," he says in a small voice like he's far away.

I dash my tears away and meet his eyes. He looks horrified like he doesn't know what to do about my crying.

"Well good, because my life says I need to be at my dad's for dinner in ten minutes and I need a shower," I say and I stand, ignoring the hand he reaches out and tries to catch me with, and I'm in the bathroom and stripping down with way too much energy, blinded by these stupid tears that will not stop coming and ignoring the knock on the door and then the "Gracie?" And then the whispered, "I'm so sorry, Gracie," as I let the hot water wash over me and violently scrub myself with soap and shampoo.

He has no right to make me feel like my life is small. No right. My life is what I chose and who cares if people think it's stupid? It's what I wanted. And maybe it's what my mom wanted, too. Maybe she picked to wash off toddlers in the desert and live with a man who always called the shots. Maybe she wanted that and who is he to come here after the fact and ask if she was happy?

But that thought is too much, and I find myself leaning into the corner of the shower, resting my head on it, and sobbing silently because I miss my mom and I didn't like seeing those pictures like that and I don't want to consider what it might mean if she wasn't happy like I thought she was.

Chapter Thirty-Six

JASPER

I've blown it and I know it, I'm just not sure how or what to do about it. That she's locked herself in the bathroom crying is kind of a big clue. I pack up the photos and change into a button shirt and fresh jeans and head over to her dad's place. She'll come when she's ready.

I feel like it shows I'm not hostile to her family if I go over on my own without her, right? Like an olive branch? It shows that I don't need her presence to make it easier for me. It's the grown-up thing to do. Right?

When I make it past the pool to the patio where Adam is waiting for us, I know I've made the wrong decision, but it's too late to change my mind now.

Adam is sitting with someone perched on his lap — a beautiful woman about his age. She's dressed the way rich older women dress when they're trying to look casual but still wearing clothes that cost more than average people make in a month.

My mouth falls open at the same time that I hear a squeak

from behind me and see Gracie emerge and come to stand beside me. Her eyes are still a bit too bright, but otherwise, she looks cheerful and ready for an evening with her dad.

We're both so shocked by the sight of Adam cuddling a woman, that it takes me a moment to register that my dad is there, too.

"What's this?" I ask as the woman gets up from Adam's lap and takes the seat beside him. He opens his mouth to speak but then he starts coughing, that terrible wracking cough, and beside me Gracie tenses and then shoots me a tiny glance and I see it all in that glance.

She still is certain her dad is dying. Still is certain his entire life and fortune rest on her. Still thinks she needs to be with me to make that safe. And she also thinks I don't want any of it. I should have stayed and tried to talk to her when she came out of the shower. She's just ... she has it all wrong. Maybe I don't want to work for Adam long-term. But that doesn't mean I don't think she can or should. And it doesn't mean we can't work together, stay together, be married together. Does it?

Or is working for her dad a dealbreaker I didn't realize existed?

And if it is ... will I still choose her, knowing it means the rest of my life working for BOOM Enterprises? Maybe she has a good reason to be nervous because the thought of that makes me ill. I clench and unclench my fists as her dad finishes coughing and turns to the woman beside him.

"I thought you got rid of the cats?"

"I did," she says, placing a hand on his arm in a very familiar way. "I'm so sorry, Adam. Their hair must still be on my clothing."

"It's not the hair, it's the dander. Triggers my cough-inducing asthma. You know that," he says.

I feel the blood rush out of my face as I realize what he's

saying, and I look at Gracie's face in time to see her turn pale when she realizes it, too. She's white as a ghost. She stumbles forward and I manage to pull a chair out for her and slide it behind her right before she falls into it. She's lovely even when she's had a bad shock — like she's having right now.

"This is Linda," her dad says, beaming. "She's why I've invited you here tonight. I wanted to introduce you."

"Hi!" Linda says brightly.

She's all class as she looks at Gracie and then me, managing to disguise whatever reaction she might have to Gracie's gasping breaths and white face. I force myself to smile. Whatever is happening here, it's not her fault.

"Linda is a tour organizer who is going to run the first ever BOOM worldwide tour. And I've been seeing her for the last few months, haven't I, honey? " Adam says glancing at her and then beaming at us like he's announced that he is the one who invented sunshine. He has no idea what's happening to his daughter right now.

"So you're not retiring," I say, realizing what's happening here and flicking my eyes over to my dad who has a very cagey look in his eye. "This successor thing and trying to rope Gracie further into the business is because you're doing a worldwide tour and you need someone to mind the storefront while you're out."

"See? I knew you were a clever fellow, Jasper!" Adam says, gesturing to his chef to serve up the meal. I'm pretty sure Gracie won't be eating anything. I place a hand on her back to try to comfort her and she subtly shifts so my hand falls away.

Ouch.

"Don't worry, Jas," he says to me, still grinning. "I realized after the crash yesterday that you're not the man to take over the face of the company."

"Mmhm," I agree but I'm watching them, one face after another. "When does this tour start?"

"Next week," Linda says with a brittle smile. "I'm going to tour with your father-in-law. We were just waiting ... to tell Gracie."

Gracie looks up, and now everyone can see her puffy eyes — my fault — and her shocked expression — her dad's fault.

"Gracie, you can't take it this hard," her dad says, stern now like she's a kid still. "You had to know I'd date again and Linda is a wonderful woman."

"You're not dying?" she gasps out.

"What?" He seems genuinely concerned. "You're not upset about Linda?"

She waves her hand like she doesn't care and I think she doesn't. It might actually make her life easier if her dad has someone else to tangle up in his schemes. Despite everything the absolute surprise on Linda's face almost draws a laugh from me.

"I thought you were dying," she chokes out. "The coughing."

Adam looks guilty and my eyes narrow. He knew she thought he was dying. I'm pretty sure of it. He used it to get what he wanted, but what was that?

"What about the competition to marry me off," she says, aghast.

"Well, I hated the idea of leaving you here on your own but Linda said I could wait until you got married someday, and I thought, well, why not speed that up?"

Linda looks like she wants to sink through the floor. I give her a commiserating look. She's the other innocent victim trapped in this Boomhower madness. But what is my dad doing here?

I look over at him suspiciously and he sips his beer all nonchalant like nothing is happening here and that's all it takes for me to know. Somehow, he's part of this. Has been from the beginning.

"So when Mikey mentioned Jasper was between jobs I

posted that opening," Adam says, tucking into his steak as if he's not dropping bombs into his daughter's life. "Because we thought it would be better to keep things in the family. Now, I know you can't be the face of BOOM Enterprises, Jasper, but I think you've shown you can do all the behind-the-scenes work with Gracie and your dad has agreed to come back to be the front man for a while."

I look at my dad and he's straight-faced as a good stand-up comedian, looking like he's chill as ice. I feel a stab of something like betrayal in my belly. All that drinking and sleeping. He's been playing me. He's fine right now. He's not estranged from his best friend. He's been secretly plotting with him all along.

"And that's why you pushed me with this competition?" Gracie asks, her voice going up an octave. "So that I would choose a safer option and marry Jasper?"

Her dad has the grace to look abashed. "Well, I thought it was a safe bet."

"Like the bet you placed on my fake marriage? That it would last? The one where you wagered everything?"

I take a step back. She sounds like she might start smashing things. Gracie. Who doesn't ever talk like that to her dad.

"Don't be like that, Gracie!" he scolds like he thinks she's just going to get over this. "I knew it wasn't fake. Mikey made sure of that."

And that's when I see what my dad is feeling so guilty about and my eyes swivel to him and I lift an eyebrow and his eyes meet mine all bold, like he has no reason to feel guilty that he submitted that paperwork on purpose. That he made sure we were married for real *on purpose*. That maybe he even switched out the original fake paperwork I had brought right before we signed.

"It's best," he says with a shrug. "Keep it all in the family."

Gracie's chair pushes out with a squeal as the metal leg tears into the concrete and then she's running off as her dad says, "Come on, Gracie!" like she's the unreasonable one here.

He rises to go after her, and I catch his arm.

"No," I say and it's a low growl. "No. You don't get to go after her."

He tries to shake me off, but this time I'm not having it, and I hold on to his arm and take a step forward, forcing him back.

"You have guests," I say, nodding to poor Linda, who is bright red and looks like she wants to die, and my dad whose eyes are dancing because he knows damn well there's nothing I can do to him. "You owe them better than this. And you owed your daughter a whole lot better than this. She's given her whole life to you. Every whim you have, she accommodates. You have an ambition? She makes it succeed. You have a need? She fills it. And you manipulated her to get what you wanted instead of just asking."

"It's not like that," he says, stern, glaring down at me from his greater height. "I built something amazing. Something that helps people. And I'm practically giving it to her. She doesn't have to do a thing to build it, it's here ready to go."

"Maybe she doesn't want it," I say, quiet now.

"She doesn't know how lucky she is. I've worked and fought for this and taken huge risks and seen them pay off and she doesn't have to do any of it. It's just handed to her on a silver platter and what? She's going to say no to that?"

"I don't know," I say and I'm so mad I want to shake him, but I keep it all bottled up because angry or not she won't appreciate it if I get into it with her dad. "But I'm pretty sure it's her decision to say yes or no to, not a decision you get to make for her — or worse, push her to make through deception."

He shrinks down and into himself and I release his arm and step back, pointing at my dad.

"You, I will get to later."

He just chuckles like he doesn't care, and he probably

doesn't. I can tell he's entertained with this and he hasn't been entertained or even very sober in years. It's hard not to be madder when I realize that Adam asking him to help mess up my life might be what has saved him from himself.

"Where are you going?" he asks as I spin around and start to stride away.

"To see my wife," I snarl.

"You should be thanking me that you have a wife," Adam calls as I hurry away. "Thanking both of us. You were single before and miserable and now BOOM you have a whole life just handed to you."

I pause, looking at him across his pool with his giant-scale mansion framing him from behind and the blades of his helicopter just visible off to the side. He has everything, and he just threw away the only part of it that counts.

"A life you just blew up," I shoot back. "A life you just trashed along with your daughter's. Add your catchphrase to that, Adam. BOOM!"

"When you calm down, come back and run my company. You'll be a millionaire in a few months," Adam calls like he's certain it's just a matter of patience to get everything he wants. "But don't take too long, Linda and I are dying to hit the open road!"

I shake my head, so furious I can hardly think. "What happens next is up to your daughter. It's not up to me, and it's for fucking sure not up to you."

And then I'm gone and I'm trying to think of what I'm going to say to her. I'm trying to think of how I can save this — save her — keep a little sliver of what we've built together, but before I even reach the door I hear the squeal of her Bronco tires, and I catch only a glimpse of blue vehicle and streaming blonde hair before she's gone.

When I open the door, the house looks like it's been robbed. Her drawers are open, clothing and underthings spilling everywhere. The sleeping bag is missing. And so is the box I carefully packed with all the papers and pictures of our moms, and my heart sinks. Because that's the kind of thing you take when you don't plan to come back.

I know how that is. Because last time, the person running was me.

GRACIE

If you turn around and go home, he'll already be gone, too, I tell myself for the third time this morning. Somehow these talks never work and I end up having to give them to myself over and over again. I'd text Melissa, but I think she's sick of hearing from me.

You're crazy, she told me that first night. *He's probably out of his mind worried.*

He was tricked into marrying me. For real. And tricked into being part of my dad's business which he doesn't want and never wanted, I texted back. *If he ever speaks to me again, I'll be surprised.*

Me, too, seeing as you ran the second he found out and you haven't answered his texts, she said, followed by the eye roll emoji and the shrugging emoji.

And she's right. I haven't answered his texts. The first one was too much.

Gracie, it said. *Gracie, don't run. You don't need to run. No one is trying to make you do anything you don't want to do.*

The second one said, *Okay, fine, your dad is. But not me, okay? I don't care if you want to work with him forever okay, it's your decision.*

He thought I was pathetic. Clearly. So dependent on my dad that I'd keep working for him even after he lied to me to get me to marry - marry! - someone so he wouldn't have to worry about me.

The third text said, *You left a lot of projects for people here. Are you sure you shouldn't finish them first?*

He knows me pretty well, I guess because that one made me pull over to the side of the road for a bit and breathe hard but he undermined himself when he typed.

I'll just go ahead and finish them, then.

There, see? No reason to go home.

I slept that first night at a wayside rest curled up in my Jeep in the sleeping bag, eating chips and drinking pop from a vending machine, and sobbing my eyes out. And I kept thinking of how much I wished I was in his arms — those strong arms that made me feel so safe and treasured. And how he would brush my tears away and kiss me softly. But I couldn't crack. Not now.

If I went back I'd have to face him knowing that he knew that we were tricked into marriage together by our parents. That we hadn't chosen each other at all. Our choice had been made by them. How can you love someone picked out by your dad? It was pathetic. And I'd know he was staying because he felt obligated now and felt bad for me — that he hated his life working for BOOM Enterprises and was only doing it for me.

He'd be my mom scowling at the camera. He'd be his mom sad as she whispered to her husband. And that would all be my fault.

If I didn't go back, then he'd be free to live his life. He could go out there and start making his way freelancing again. Free as a bird.

Now that I was out of his system, maybe he'd find a nice girl. One who didn't have a crazy family. One who wasn't going to go right on back and work for them. Because yeah, I knew I would. I had already accepted my dad's abject apology via text and agreed to meet Linda again sometime under better circumstances. I hadn't told him where I was or what I was going to do. But I answered *his* text.

Why him and not Jasper? I spent most of the next day wondering about that because at first it didn't make sense. But eventually, it came to me. My dad was the way he was. I didn't expect anything else so finding out he was being a narcissist who was utterly certain he was a helpful and goodhearted one wasn't much of a surprise. As much as it had ruined everything for me, I probably should have seen it coming.

But Jasper was different. I thought he understood me. I thought he respected me a bit. And all that had to be gone now because he'd feel tricked and held back and tied to someone who he'd never pursued or chased. He'd been caught like a wild thing in a trap and forced into a harness and how could he help but hate me when he realized it?

I miss you, he'd texted the first night at midnight. *Please come back to me. Let me make it all right. You can have anything you want. A marriage. A divorce. A kiss. Space. Anything, just please come here and tell me what it is.*

And then later at three the next morning. *Or don't come. Just text me and tell me what you want and it's yours. Just please don't leave without a goodbye.*

But he'd left me without a goodbye and maybe he'd been right all along because things had been fine when we were apart and they'd only gotten complicated when we came back together. He'd been happy, accomplished, secure, traveling the world. Now he was offering his freedom to me like it was worth nothing. For his own good, I had to say no — or rather, say nothing. It was the only way he could stay free.

So, I headed for the coast and when I got there, I stayed in the first Air B&B with an ocean view and I took out the box and looked for what he'd seen in it. And then I cried a bunch more.

And when I was done crying, I read my notes for the book, and I began to plan a different kind of book. A real tribute. One that showed the kind of ingenuity and courage it took to be like our moms, but also the subtle sacrifices. The things they gave away before they ever really had them.

Would you rather travel the world with your dad and Linda or only ever use BOOM branded condoms? he texted me that second day.

I didn't answer, but I did laugh. The condoms, obviously. But I would never need them again. Not now.

I tried a new B&B three days later. This one was right on the sand. I spent a lot of time just sitting there looking at the ocean and regretting not wearing sunscreen and then I took everything I owned with a BOOM logo on it and put it in a pile on the beach and tried to burn it with driftwood until a bylaw officer came and screamed at me and gave me a ticket.

Tanner when he realized we had sex, Jasper texted me. The emoji he sent was the angry red devil face. Uh oh. I could only imagine.

I laughed at that, too. And I still didn't answer. But I worked on the book that night. And the next night and the next night.

And on the morning after that, I found a new Air B&B further down the coast with a surf rental place next to it and a little cafe that sold the world's worst coffee and I was drinking that coffee and doing very sleepy beach yoga — yeah, that's what I'm calling lying on the beach with yoga clothes on — when I got a text from him that wasn't funny at all.

Would you rather be married to me or never see me again?

I didn't laugh at that one. And it wasn't until after a long day of writing and beach yoga that I received my next text from him. He was playing our game again — the one where we pretended to be each other.

I think my husband was part of the setup and that's why I'm never speaking to him again.

This time, I texted back.

I'm a class A moron and that's why I don't understand the gift of freedom when it's given to me, but eventually, I'll get the hint and go back to my happy James Bond photographer life with fast cars and really classy enlightened women who use non-branded condoms.

And after I sent it, I blocked his number and turned off the ringer on my phone, and put it in airplane mode.

Which was why I didn't see my dad's frantic texts the next morning.

Or see the news as I packed up my Bronco in the dark of early morning and continued further down the coast.

There's no point going back, I told myself again as I drank gas station coffee. He'll just be gone already.

But even though I told myself that, I was so lost in memories of him in the shower and how his wet eyelashes looked against his cheeks as he shut his eyes to kiss me, that I didn't bother turning on the radio and wasn't too worried when I had to slow down for congested traffic — it just gave me more time to sink into longing memories mixed with self-pity.

I snapped out of it, though, when I realized that traffic had slowed because of a crash. Someone had gone over the steep embankment. Up ahead, the guard rail was completely shattered and first responders were crawling all over the road. Lookie-loos had pulled over to be "helpful."

I flicked on the radio as I slid in behind a huge RV with its blinkers on. It wasn't going anywhere anytime soon, and I couldn't see a thing around its monstrous orange rear end.

"... a blue Ford Bronco. First responders are on scene. Expect traffic delays."

The man on the radio was still talking but I wasn't listening. That poor person. They'd been driving a vehicle just like mine. What were the odds of that?

And oh no. This RV ahead of me that I'd been mentally cursing was maybe a family member. Ooops. I guess they had a right to be there after all. A man had his head leaned against the side of the orange vehicle, his whole body shaking with silent sobs.

My chest squeezed as I watched him and I wished I could help. Was that his wife? Brother? Mother? I thought of that trucker so long ago walking with Jasper to tell me the news and holding onto us until our parents got there, and without realizing it I was putting on my four ways, and putting my vehicle into park, and slipping out.

It was time to pay it forward.

I moved before I could chicken out, striding toward the poor broken man. He was young — barely older than me. His cell phone was shoved into the back pocket of his jeans and his T-shirt hugged him in a way that seemed really familiar, but that was only because I saw Jasper absolutely everywhere. Heartbreak tends to do that to a person.

I was only a few steps away now and I heard him trying to get his breathing under control, and I bit my lip, trying to remember how the old cowboy had been with us.

"Hey," I said trying to be gentle. "Did you lose someone you love?"

His head jerked up and he straightened, looking at me in shock over the barrier of his tensed bicep. His mouth had fallen open and his glassy eyes were black and howling, his unshaven jaw rough, neglected, hair a turbulent mess.

The bottom fell out of my belly.

I wasn't seeing things after all.

His face made this expression of agonized disbelief that melted into something that seemed to stream down and puddle around us. He took a halting step forward and reached for me and I reached back as he hitched me against his chest. It heaved with silent gasps.

"Gracie," Jasper whispered. "Oh God, Gracie."

He was shaking so hard that I had to wind my arms around him to keep him from collapsing. How ... how was he here?

He sank into me, forehead against my shoulder.

"I thought I lost you, just like her. I thought..."

The car just like mine. My phone on airplane mode.

Oh.

"It's okay, Jas," I whispered, barely able to breathe as my chest squeezed in sympathy. "I'm right here."

"Please don't go, Gracie," he whispered, clinging to me. "Not yet. Not until we can talk."

But I wasn't going anywhere. As much as he was clinging to me, I was clinging to him, too, feeling again all those terrible feelings of being abandoned that I'd felt back then. Because someone had been in that Bronco even if it wasn't me. And they had family who would be feeling just like this, too.

And if my breaths were a bit panicked, could anyone blame me? If I held him tighter than I should, was that really so unreasonable?

"I'm here, Jas. Okay? Just breathe. I'm here."

Chapter Thirty-Eight

JASPER

"I'm here," she's saying to me and I can't believe she's in my arms. I cling to her, trying to find my lost breath.

I had been traveling along the coast looking for her, following her digital path. She kept leaving these glowing online reviews of her Air B&Bs and they were attached to her BOOM social accounts. But she only left them after she'd already been there, so it was like following a breadcrumb trail.

And then the news: a vehicle just like hers plummeting over a cliff beside the ocean.

Her dad's frantic calls to me.

My thoughts were fractured and distant when I arrived and looked over the edge. I was right back at Mom's crash all over again, smelling cigarette smoke and hearing that deep voice guiding me.

"Don't look," I heard in my mind but I looked and looked and there was no sign of her, and when I couldn't take another moment of it, I turned my back. It felt like a betrayal to stop looking, like I was giving up on her. So, I went back to that stupid RV and broke down.

And like some kind of miracle, she found me.

I thought her voice was a hallucination. But if it was, then I was fine with that. I was happy to hallucinate her alive and talking to me. She was the best kind of hallucination. So real. So achingly sweet.

There was that line in her forehead she got when she was worried for someone. There was the way her hair was never quite tame as the breeze picked and chose what curls to mess with. There were her huge caramel eyes looking at me.

"Gracie," I whispered.

I couldn't help it. I reached for her — even knowing I'd be disappointed when she faded away.

But my arms came around real flesh. Around a firm, living body. It couldn't be her, and yet here she was.

Hope was painful as it flooded through me. Like when your blood rushes back into a numb limb and lights up every nerve pathway with a painful reminder that you're alive. That's what the feel of her was. Agony and hope and something tumbling loose in my chest.

I'm swept away even minutes later. Swept away with her.

"My sweet Gracie," I whisper again, in awe.

I can't let go. I just lean my forehead on her shoulder and shake with all the emotions tearing through me, and she holds me and shushes them sweetly until I have the strength to lift my head and look in her eyes.

"Why the hell would I ever want to be free of you?" The words tear out of me but I say them gently. Softly. "What is freedom if it isn't loving as hard as you can? What point is there in being able to go anywhere, if you can't go the one place you want to be? I only ever want to be with you, Gracie. That's kinda what love is. Do you remember that I told you I love you?"

She nods and her lower lip is trembling when she curls her

hands around my face like it's precious. While I'm still talking, she draws me in gently, all kindness to my desperation. All softness to my hard edges.

"I thought you would feel caged," she whispers. "And I never want to cage you."

"The only cages I'm worried about are the ones keeping me from you," I whisper. "Unless ... unless you're the one who needs freedom, Gracie? Do you need me to go away?"

She's already shaking her head. I don't wait for more.

I lean in and catch her lips in mine. It's a soft kiss, but it isn't gentle. It's trying to catch her. It's trying to keep her. It's a seeking, hopeful, wanting kind of kiss. And I think the kiss she's giving me back is the same.

We come to our senses enough to realize we shouldn't be here. We're breathless and dazed in the exact same way. We need to drive our vehicles to a safe place out of the way of the people who actually belong here, but tearing myself away from her isn't easy.

"Don't run away before we can talk," I say nervously, my fingers still twined in hers even as we step apart. "Please?"

"I won't."

It's a simple kind of promise but it holds my sanity as we maneuver through the long, slow wait to get back into traffic and wind our way through the chaos to the other side and then down the highway to the next safe stop miles and miles south of where the tragic crash happened. It's still busy here, but no one else has stopped at the little lookout.

When we park, I leap out of the RV almost before it's stopped, but I only make it a step before Gracie crashes into me, almost knocking me over with the force of her embrace.

I close my eyes and I cling to her. No promises have been made. No plans discussed. She might get in her car and drive away again. She might.

And because she might, I need to savor this moment.

I let it sink all through me, memorizing how she feels against my chest and thighs and I can't quite hold in my groan of happiness. Worse, I can't seem to stop my hands. All my passion for her seems to have moved into them and they climb up her back and into her hair and then they keep moving, touching, smoothing, feeling every part of her, as if by memorizing her, they can charm her into staying with me.

"We need to talk. Please," I whisper into her hair.

"Let's go inside," she gasps. She's as swept away as I am.

I can tell, because she barely blinks at what I'm driving — a huge orange BOOM RV — the very one I'd picked up from her dad at Ron's Wraps. It's marked with his logo. And it has his grinning face with its long beard and perpetual ball cap staring at us across the entire back half. It would be creepy as hell, but nothing can dent my buzz in this moment.

"Okay."

I follow her as she rounds the RV and ducks in the door. Follow her, as she inspects the fancy leather captains chairs, the little sofa in front of a huge screen tv, the high-class kitchenette complete with a wine fridge and little stools around the curving island, the plush bathroom and shower, and then into the back where a bright airy bedroom is dominated by a full queen bed and a plush chair draped with her dad and Linda's monogrammed bath robes. Yeah — I'd been wrong about that robe and the girl at Ron's Wraps had been right. I owe her a huge apology. She can get in line.

"Nice digs," Gracie says, and she's so pretty that I can hardly take it. I reach out without thinking about it and I take her hand in mine, drawing it up to my cheek so I can lean against it.

And maybe she's going to leave me again. I don't know. I'm trying not to think about it. I'm in a kind of daze as I angle toward her, exploring the edge of her waist with my fingers.

"Gracie," I start to say, but before I can think of what comes next, she's biting her lip and then speaking.

"I keep springing everything on you," she says. "I'm the one who came and asked you to marry me. I'm the one who kissed you first. I'm the one who seduced you."

I shiver a little at the word seduced. That is the best memory. I turn my face so I can kiss her palm. I'm listening, but also, she's so distracting just by being here. And I don't care. I'm going to be distracted. I'm the worst because I'm going to suck every bit of opportunity out of this moment before she breaks it to me that we're not going to be together anymore.

"I think that maybe I've never given you a choice," she says and I move to kiss her wrist. The skin is so soft, so ridiculously smooth. Would the inside of her elbow be the same? I go to find out.

"I've just kept pushing you," she says, and hmmm yes her inner elbow really is that soft. I tuck her hand against my waist and try her shoulder — her shirt is sleeveless — and it's firm with muscle and I want to nip it gently but she's trying to talk, so I settle for an open-mouthed kiss where I can swipe my tongue lightly over it and move to her collarbone to do the same.

"Pushing you into places where you can't really say n— are you listening to me?"

"Yes, I think," I whisper as I trace my way up her neck, trailing little kisses. "Why are the curves of your neck so kissable? I've never really cared about necks, but I care about this one."

I let my nose trail down her skin so I can edge her neckline aside and kiss her chest right over her heart. It's beating hard under there, faster, lighter than my heart does.

"I'm trying to tell you that I want you to decide this time," she says.

"Decide what?" I whisper as I move up again to kiss the shell of her ear and then gently draw her earlobe between my lips. I'm addicted to her. One taste is not enough. A thousand tastes won't be. My lids are heavy and my breathing has slowed. I'm like the charmed snake relaxing into my own captivity as I sway in the dance of my intoxication with her.

"I can't remember," she whispers.

"Mmm," I agree, moving now to her lips and taking my time, starting with small soft kisses that open so that tongues can mingle and the soft inside parts of our lips can caress and slide and taste and I could keep doing this forever, except that my pulse has split now and half of it is down much lower than my heart. "Then let's do this until you do."

I think her moan is her agreement.

I sweep her up so her feet are off the ground, my arms supporting her weight and I kiss her, long and deep, my mouth showing her what it never seems able to say.

I'm glad this bed is full-sized. Glad I can lay her out across the white coverlet. Glad when I break our kiss and pull back to look at her and she's like the most lovely fruit waiting to be bitten and tasted.

Her lips are swollen from my kisses and it seems impossible not to keep going, but I pull myself back firmly. I must not be a fool about this. Not when I'm not even entirely sure what I did last time.

"Do you want me to stop?" I ask her. "We have so much to talk about. Do we need to do that instead?"

She shakes her head and she looks as drunk on this as I am when she pulls me down over her and inhales into my shoulder before she gasps in pleasure and that's all it takes for me to decide talking is best saved for later.

I've missed her and the relief of having her here — alive and in my arms — is almost too much. I crave her closeness.

I'm gentle and attentive when I draw her shirt up over her head. Much more gentle than she is when she rips mine up and over, pausing only a moment to untangle it from my arms and throw it away. When she runs her hands over my biceps and shoulders with a look of appreciation in her eyes, I shiver.

Two can play at that game. I unclip her bra and spend some time appreciating, catching her soft breasts in between hungry lips and letting my cheek smooth into them as I close my eyes so there's only that sensation filling me up. I could stay here, grazing on her skin for the next few hours. I could.

I'm so busy with it that I hardly notice that she's opened my pants and is taking them down until the back of her hand skims down my hardness and now my eyes are rolling in the back of my head and I have to pause to hold myself together.

A breath gusts out of me and she laughs in delight, as if entirely amused by what she does to me. I can do that, too. I slide her pants from her body.

"Is this okay?" I ask as I do it. Undressing her still feels like a privilege that shouldn't quite be mine.

"Is it okay to give me what I want?" she asks, teasing. "I think so, but I'm kind of biased."

I like her teasing. But I'm not in the mood to tease right now. I'm so full of emotion that it's making my head spin. I just keep thinking that I almost lost her again. That I barely have her back. That I want to keep her here with me forever. It fuels something in me that's rough and a bit painful.

I don't realize that I've spoken out loud until she whispers, "Then, keep me. Show me that you want me to stay."

I close my eyes at that and lean my head down so I can press my forehead against her shoulder to try to deal with the overwhelming desire rushing through me. I want to show her. I want to show her all the ways. But I don't want to screw it up this time. I want to do it right.

I start by kissing her lips, but I don't stay there. I draw her up to sit with me so I can trace my hands down her back and front and follow every touch with reverent kisses. I spin her so she's on her front and I can kiss her from the top of her head and then down her spine and down one leg to the very tip of her toe, smoothing her skin with my hands gently as I go, kneading into it in the meatier places to relax and tease and tempt. And then I gently draw her over again so that I can kiss my way back up the front of her, indulging myself in her taste, in the skim of her over my lips and tongue.

I linger, kissing her inner thigh for a moment before moving higher. I'm not ready to take her silky panties off yet, but they tantalize me with what is underneath.

I move further up her body, trying to show her how badly I want her, how much I need her near, and when I think she's getting the idea, I wrap my arms around her and hold her chest to mine and I bury my face in her long hair.

When her hand wraps around me, I shudder at the feeling of it. And when it starts to move firmly up and down the length of me, I move unconsciously with it. When she hitches her fingers in the waistband of my boxers and slides them down, I match her movement, sliding her tiny silk things down for her, too. I reach for her, gasping at her wet readiness for me.

I can barely take the feeling of that and I have to hide my face in the crook of her neck and take long, gasping breaths as I play with her, softly opening her to pleasure, feeling her respond and follow my touch, even as I am following hers.

I love how I make her breathe, hard and fast and broken. I love her tiny gasps in my ear or against my skin. I want to memorize her every sound and find all the ways to tempt her to make them again.

"I love you so much, Gracie," I whisper into her hair. "You intoxicate me. I can't quite think. I'm unraveled by you."

"Then don't think," she whispers back. "Just be here with me. Just let me wrap myself up in you for a while."

And those words alone are almost too much. I hear her moan of pleasure and mine follows it and then I'm fumbling for the drawer at the side of the bed where I brought her stash of unwanted branded items and I'm readying myself and whispering new things into her ear.

"Do you want me, sweet girl?"

"Yes." Her whisper in my ear, as she clings to me with fingers and lips, is intense.

"This way?" I press myself to her so she can feel all my skin. There's no question what I mean.

"Yes." Her word is a little gust of magic that wraps me up in the smell and taste of Gracie.

"Right now?" And now I'm just teasing her as I draw soft, tempting circles around and through her flesh with one finger and press against her, suggesting what else may be, with my harder more insistent parts.

"Yes, please, yes Jas," her whisper now is almost a moan and it's enough to shake my last shreds of control away.

I press into her slowly, moving back and forth to give her time to adjust to me, time to get me situated as she needs it, and when she is squirming against me, and grabbing my hips as if to move me if I won't move myself, then I lean in and get to work, teasing out from her every gasp and shudder, enjoying how it makes me sweat, makes me put in effort to draw out her pleased moans and tiny cries. And when she seems to be getting closer, I increase the pace, bringing her along with me as my pleasure and delight builds and builds with hers.

It's like we're racing side by side. We're two rivers joining and about to tumble over a ledge of rock and create a waterfall. We're a pair of meteors on a collision course. When our mingling sets one of us loose, the other follows immediately and we're sparking like pepper sprinkled on a candle, fracturing like concrete under a chisel, wheeling away insensibly like the seeds of a dandelion blown in the wind. And when we're done I catch her, like I always will, and I turn and flip onto my back so I can cradle her on my chest and let both my arms fall around her and press her right where she belongs — against my heart.

And my eyes close tight as she whispers to me the two words I want to hear the most.

"My Jas," her lips sliding in half-kisses over my chest as she repeats herself, "My Jasper."

She's damn right. The one thing I am is hers.

Chapter Thirty-Nine

GRACIE

My chest squeezes tight and I can hardly breathe. He's magnificent. A king among men. Seriously, if this was like a movie or a book he'd have basically ridden up on a black charger to save me. Or maybe an orange charger with my dad's face painted on it. Okay, the metaphor is breaking down, but here with my face pressed against the warm firmness of Jasper's chest, with him still inside me and all around me, I don't care. I just want more, more, more and it's hard to think straight.

But eventually, I do. I slide off of him and sit up — very naked here on this bed that I'm pretty sure belongs to my parent because his name is monogrammed on a ridiculous robe nearby. I want to cover myself up, but I definitely don't want to do it with a robe that says "Adam" in cursive writing. I settle for stealing Jasper's shirt and tugging it over my head. It smells so crazy good, just like him. His smirk when he sees me in it nearly makes me lean down to kiss him again, but no. I need to focus. We haven't talked at all and there's so much to be said.

He seems to agree because he awkwardly takes care of tidying himself up and shrugging his jeans back on, but he's doing that barefoot, bare-chested, boyish thing again and his hair is tussled from my hands and his lips swollen with my kisses. I start swimming in a lake of thick desire again and have to shake myself loose to speak to him.

"You found me."

"I was following your online reviews," he says looking abashed.

I could bring up all the obvious things with him — that we both saw something that brings back old trauma and maybe we aren't thinking straight. That I wanted him to be free. That being with me is complicated. But none of that will bring up anything new. Instead, I drive to the heart of the matter. The thing that made me run.

"I don't want my dad choosing our lives," I say, twisting my hands in my shirt and then glancing up at him shyly. Why is it so hard to talk when sex is so easy?

He barks a laugh but his eyelids are still heavy, still not fully out of his bliss. Even the bulge in his jeans is a fierce reminder of that. And that we could easily get back to it if I wasn't spoiling it with talk right now.

"I don't want that either," he agrees.

"So, what then?" I say and my voice sounds as miserable as I feel. "They set us up. They picked this for us. Our whole lives chosen by them instead of us!"

He's quiet for a long moment, but he's looking at me the whole time, and I can tell he's thinking really hard — the thing is, I don't know if he's thinking of a solution or of how to let me down easy and my pulse is hammering in my temples.

When he finally speaks, he sits on the edge of the bed beside me and raises his hands like he's talking to a skittish dog and is trying to calm it down. I draw my knees up under my chin like it can protect me, but it can't because he's already so deep inside me — metaphorically, though, heyo! he was physically inside me, too, just a few minutes ago. But we can't let our desire for each other cloud this. It's important.

"Okay, okay," he says in this slow, convincing way. "Just think this through with me, okay? So we get the divorce."

I didn't expect that.

"Yeah," I say and I'm imagining it. My empty life of beach yoga and social media work and no Jasper ever. None of his beautiful chest to lie on. None of this glorious body I'm seeing. None of his clever fingers or easy way of making me laugh. None of him *getting* me the way no one does. Fuck it. I hate this. I start to shake my head.

"So, we get divorced," he says, pushing forward. "Do you ... still love me?"

I choke on that. I know the answer. I'm going to love him forever.

"Of course," I say.

"Okay, are we still together, then?" he asks, biting his lip and my stomach flips at how ridiculously sexy he is when he bites that lower lip.

"Don't you dare leave me," I gasp and that seems to be the right answer because his eyes smolder and his chest heaves with his breath.

His hand twitches and I'm sure he's about to reach for me all over again, and I'm getting spooled up just thinking about it, when he breaks into that daydream. He's holding himself back. I can, too.

Maybe.

Most likely.

"Okay," he says, blowing out slowly like I'm not the only one trying to dismiss distracting daydreams. "So, I hate to tell you this, but I'm kind of a spontaneous person and I tend to go for what I want. So, in maybe a month I'll probably go down on one knee."

And to my shock, he slides off the bed and gets around to my side and he's on one knee on the faux wood floor of the fancy RV. He reaches into a pocket and at first, I think he's miming a proposal but a real ring box comes out. And he opens it. And there's a real ring inside.

And I know this ring.

I'm not sure I can breathe.

I'm pretty damn sure I can't see a thing through these tears.

"And I'll be offering you my mom's ring," he says, and his voice is wavering with emotion, too. HE blushes when he passes it to me. "I found it when I was cleaning out the garage with her things. I like the one I gave you before but this ..." He shakes his head like it's too much to try to explain, "I'll offer you this."

"You will?" My voice is small and vulnerable.

"And why would we wait?" he says gently, like he's trying not to scare me.

"We wouldn't," I say, sure of myself as I dash aside my tears of happiness.

"So, we'll be getting married," he says, smiling shyly and I don't know anymore if we're still pretending or if he means this, but either way, I'm in. "How would you want that to look?"

I smile back, delighted by the gleam in his eye and wanting to share in the fun. "Something really small. At a church. No cut flowers. Your dad can come, but my dad isn't invited because I'm mad at him."

Jasper smirks and I swear he batts his eyelashes jokingly. "I have this really good friend Scotty who I'd like to see perform the ceremony."

I put a hand over my mouth to hold in my laugh.

"And I'll be too nervous to tell you that you look beautiful," he says with a half-smile that brings out his dimple in one cheek.

I decide to tease him back. "I'll be too nervous to tell you that I've been in love with you for five years and I'm hoping you'll come inside me when the wedding is over."

This time he's the one who chokes on a surprised laugh, but then his expression sobers.

"There's just one problem."

"What?" There have already been too many problems. I want more sex and fewer problems.

He makes his voice sad and it's a full beat before I realize he's teasing me. "We'll have to wait to get married until our divorce papers come through."

I can't help my laugh even though I'm still blinking back tears.

"Are you saying it would be more convenient to just stay married?" I ask him tenderly.

He smiles, and it makes his whole face light up. "I'm saying why don't you take this pretty ring and instead of spending thousands on a divorce, we'll spend it on a road trip starting right now. You've already had the exact wedding you want. And I have the exact bride I want. And I'm sick to death of jumping through hoops for it."

"I love how you think," I say with a laugh. "And I love you."

But now he looks sheepish as he says, "But also, we could go on vacation — well, sort of vacation — for free. I told your dad that his tour idea was not sound business-wise. That no one wants to watch an old man and his girlfriend tour the country when they could watch a pair of newlyweds. And that I'm sick of his stupid games."

"And what did he say?" I ask him. I can only imagine that my dad must have hated that.

"He muttered, 'Play stupid games, win stupid prizes.'"

"And you said?"

"I said, 'Great. I'm taking all the prizes.' And then I drove off in the world's tackiest RV to go find you. But only after I filled it with branded products."

"You did not," I say, laughing with a hand over my mouth. But when I slide open the drawer by the bed, he's telling me the truth. He brought all nine hundred and ninety eight … wait maybe nine hundred and ninety seven? of the branded products I had in my drawer.

"You didn't answer my question about whether you'd rather use these or travel the world with your dad. I went ahead and made a guess."

"It's a good guess," I say, holding in a laugh.

"I didn't get you a branded ring, though," he says, looking meaningfully at the ring he's still offering me.

"Thank God for that," I say as I take the ring, switch it with the one I was wearing — it was nice but this one, this one means something. I look down at it for a moment and I think of my mom and Alisha, best friends. And I wonder what they would have thought of this. Likely, they would have been right there with our dads planning this whole thing.

He must be thinking that same thing because his expression is wistful.

"Is that a yes, then? You'll stay my bride?"

"Yes," I say with a wicked gleam in my eye, "but we still have one last problem."

"What?" he asks me, looking worried.

"What will I do with the Bronco if I'm riding with you from now on?"

He laughs and gently slides his shirt up and over my head, leaving me naked before him and as his eyes grow heavy as he says, "I like you wearing only my ring. Let's save all the other problems until later."

"All the other problems?" I say, laughing. "What problem do we have right now?"

In answer, he kicks off his pants, looks down, and then meets my eyes with a pout on his lips. "A very big one. I was hoping you could help me with it."

And I'm still laughing when I roll on top of him and take his very big problem as my own.

Epilogue

JASPER

She's so excited that I'm feeling excited, too. I pack up the last of the gifts she's bought everyone into the fourth suitcase full of them as she fixes her curls one last time.

"Do you think Tanner will like the scuba gear I got him?" she asks.

"I have no idea," I say, smirking at the thought of stoic, desert-bound Tanner receiving a case of expensive scuba gear Gracie got him because he once told her he wished he could expand his horizons.

"What about the alpaca wool for Melissa?"

"You're sure she said she wanted to take up crochet?" I ask, and not for the first time.

"She did! She's just allergic to sheep's wool."

I nod, and I'm smiling, and it's all so ridiculous and I don't care.

We're on our way to her dad's engagement party. He has finally convinced that poor woman Linda to marry him. Don't ask me if manipulation and blackmail were involved, but if I were a betting man, I'd bet yes, after how he treated us. Not that I can complain. I've been married to Gracie for a year now and we've spent most of it on the road, touring in a bus with her dad's face on it, filming amazing off-road races and stunts and selling his gear and as much as I want to resent him, I have never been happier and I can't help but realize that's partly thanks to him.

Doesn't mean he doesn't deserve what's coming next, though.

"Do you think he'll be surprised?" Gracie asks with huge eyes.

I love when she plays innocent like that, so I lean in and steal a kiss and she drops her hair things and wraps her arms around me to kiss me back, totally uncaring that it's messing up the hair she was trying to tame and the makeup she just spent so much time on.

But that's my girl. She loves one hundred percent. She gives more than anyone should. And she badly needs me to guard her heart against all the people who might take advantage of her.

Including the bearded man whose face is on our ride.

"I'm sure he will be," I whisper to her as I steal one more kiss for the road. "Just remember, whatever happens, I've got your back."

"And I've got yours," she agrees.

I'm glad I promised her that, because an hour after getting to Big Daddy Boom's house, I have to throw Pretty Boy into the pool for knocking Gracie into the punch bowl, I have to remind Tanner of his manners when it turns out giving him scuba gear is a deadly insult, and I have to tell Linda twice that no, Gracie does not agree to renew her vows on the same day her dad gets married because that would just be weird.

And I'm so happy that I'm here to do it. I'm so happy because I know I almost lost all this. I almost had a free, easy life totally devoid of nonsense and hilarity and my bright, big-hearted girl.

I'm watching her proudly when my dad saunters up. He's wearing dress camouflage. If you don't know what that is, you shouldn't ask because you're one of the lucky ones.

"How are things?" he asks.

"Fine," I say, looking sideways at the pop he's drinking instead of a beer.

"Figured I'd get sober. In case you have grandkids for me to babysit." He says it so casually, like it's not a huge deal.

"That's great," I say, trying to be casual, too. And then, when he looks at me expectantly, I clear my throat. "Umm, no grandkids yet."

"But you'll let me know."

"Sure." I think my own eyes must be huge. Gracie catches my gaze from across the room and gives me a questioning look but I wave her concern aside. We're not planning on having kids yet. Although last night we finally ran out of those hot pink condoms. It was bittersweet. Turns out a thousand don't last nearly as long as you might think.

"Ladies and those who call yourselves gentlemen," Gracie announces, tapping her glass and getting our attention. "I have an announcement to honor my father, one of the two people we're celebrating. Are you getting this live, Jas?"

I hold up my camera. I'm not filming it. Not live, at least. I do want to get this preserved forever, though. It will be something to show those kids my dad wants us to have.

"Dad," she says, smiling and waving him over. He's proud and smiling, puffing out his chest the way he always does, but today he's wearing a tuxedo jacket over his jeans and BOOM shirt. "Family is the most important thing."

"That's right Gracie," he says enthusiastically. "Which is why —"

"Which is why," she says, rolling right over him — which is

something I've never seen anyone do ever. It's amazing. "It's important that family be involved in all the big decisions in life. A year ago, you hosted a competition for my hand in marriage. It ended up being just a fun time for a group of guys to build some rigs and go racing. There turned out not to be a winner because I sabotaged it all by choosing my own groom."

"Who, technically, I chose," her dad interrupts, "which is a great story our subscribers should hear —"

"Later!" Gracie says, cutting him off a second time and I'm grinning so proudly my face might split in two. "Because tonight we are announcing that as part of the launch of my new book, "Off-Road Girls" and the new BOOM PINK line of products, we're going to run the competition a second time. And this time, no one gets to sabotage it, right Dad?"

"Ummm?" her dad says, and I've never seen Adam speechless before. And it's amazing. And it's all because of his glorious daughter who I get to call my wife.

"Because this time, my Dad is going to marry the winner. Whether it's Linda or someone else, right Dad? Because we keep business in the family."

"I ... wait ..." he's looking pale and I'm catching it all on camera and Gracie winks at me and turns to tell him she's joking, when suddenly Linda is *right there* with her face in my camera and before I can shut my gaping mouth she's screaming a war cry into the camera, ripping off her fancy silk scarf, and then tying it around her head.

"Come at me, bitches," she calls to the camera. "I'll take you apart piece by piece."

And I'm so shocked I drop the camera and then I'm so busy trying to see if I can save my poor beloved camera with the newly cracked lens, that I miss Gracie trying to tell them all it's a joke, and having to apologize to Linda, and to her dad, and to Tanner who choked on a chicken bone when he heard the news and realized he couldn't compete in this round of the competition either, and by the time I realize that my lens is toast, she has them all calmed down, and to my surprise it's my dad who is talking.

"Now, you shouldn't give heart attacks, Gracie. And you should probably give Adam back his RV, Jasper because he hasn't reported it stolen even though it's been a year and I've been telling him every day that he should." Thanks, Dad. "And you should take the scarf off your head, Linda, because you don't do a very good Rambo impression. And then we can all go back to this party and have a good time, what do you say?"

"And?" Adam prompts him.

My dad rolls his eyes but when he looks at me he's smirking.

"And then you'll have to find a new lens, Jasper, because we do expect you to go live when we fly from here — streaming out to everyone — to take you and Gracie by helicopter to the house we built you while you were gone."

And I think I'm pale again.

I rub a hand nervously over the back of my neck and meet Gracie's eyes right before she spins to confront her dad. "You chose everything for us *again?* Don't we ever get a say?"

"Well, you can hardly complain, Gracie, honey," her dad says as if he doesn't see what the big deal is. Again. "After all, we did such a great job of it the first time."

And I want to tell him that he's wrong and he needs to butt out of our lives. And I want to tell him that we'll make our own way in life. But Gracie is looking at me hopefully and biting her bottom lip and there's nothing I wouldn't do to make her happy, so instead I clear my throat and I deadpan as much as I can.

"We'll look at this house, Adam, but we won't live there unless my Gracie wants to." She's beaming at me like I put the sun up in the sky. "And there's no way I'm letting you do dramatically in an orange helicopter with your logo all over it. We'll go in something less obvious — this RV with your ten-foot face on the back half of it."

And when they all laugh, I know I've done my job. I had her back. And I get to stay by her side through all the drama and madness of her life and I couldn't be happier.

We could have done this the normal way. But instead, we did it the only way that ever would have worked for us. On the steps of a tiny church with neither of us realizing it was real until it was all over.

And when she comes to my side and puts her arm around me, I'm beaming so hard that I almost look as happy as Adam. And no one has ever looked that happy.

THE END

Bonus Scene

Haven't had enough of Jasper and Gracie? Join Alice's Mailing List and get a bonus scene featuring them!
www.alicedukeauthor.com

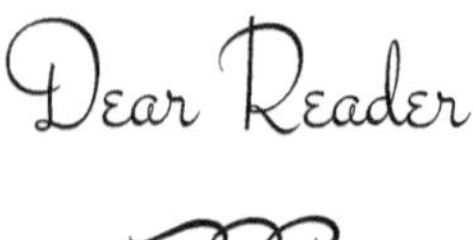

Dear Reader

You don't need to be an adrenaline junkie or obsessed with swoonable romance, but it will help!

Join us in cheering on these adorable couples. We're smitten with them and we're certain you'll love their spark and sizzle just like we do!

Each of Alice Duke's books is a stand-alone romantic comedy ready for you to savor, but they all share one thing in common: unforgettable characters, falling in love like only they can.

So, come join us to thrill at the sizzle and swoon at the heat!

TWO RIVALS. ONE PROJECT. THREE DAYS TO BLOW UP THEIR LIVES.

When Ada's tiny vlogger channel, "Pin Up Stichin" finally takes off, she hopes it will mean success for her hotrod upholstery company. What she doesn't expect is that enigmatic billionaire Big Daddy Boom will hire both her and her professional nemesis to work on a super-secret project.

But Ada can't pass up this opportunity when it means finally "making it" and finally being able to pay down her Pop's ongoing debts. Not even when she realizes the person she'll be working with is her most vocal critic.

Nicola has been in the business of vehicle restoration for a long time and between his obsession with perfecting his craft and his family issues, he hasn't had much time for anything else. When he's offered the chance to get ahead in business and also work with a woman whose work he admires -- even if he expresses that through online critique -- he's in.

Until one huge mix-up leaves them stranded in the woods together with the project on the line and two huge personalities in the way. Ada sparks all kinds of emotions in Nicola -- including some he's never felt before.

Suddenly, this project -- and maybe even the state of California -- don't seem big enough for the both of them, and what seemed like explosive online content might just be explosive. Period.

Alice Duke

SWOON & SIZZLE

Alice Duke is someone who is always falling in love: with fresh ideas, with mouthwatering foods, with beguiling books — and now with vivid characters and their romances on the page. Come fall in love along with her, again and again.

www.alicedukeauthor.com

www.ingramcontent.com/pod-product-compliance
Lightning Source LLC
Chambersburg PA
CBHW021752190726
48290CB00008B/2589